Advocate
Of
Honor

by
Linda J. Cutcliff

Writers Club Press

ISBN: 1-893652-16-5

Library of Congress Catalog Card Number: 99-62669

This book was published using the on-line/on-demand publishing services of Writers Club Press.

405 N. Washington St.
Suite #104
Falls Church, VA 22046

URL: http://www.writersclub.com

For my children; Keith, Brian, Ashley, and Chris
You are the reason I look forward to each new day.

Acknowledgments

A true friend is a rare and precious gift. My life is richer because I have been blessed with many friends who have been there for me through tragedy and triumph. I cherish each of you.

About eight years ago, I took a leap of faith and asked my friend, Deb Hipple, to read the manuscript of my first full length novel. She accepted the invitation. Since then, she has read, reread, and read again. She has edited and critiqued my writing with honesty and fairness. Deb's support and encouragement have carried me through all of my writing ups and downs. Deb, a golden key to the iron gates awaits you.

I would also like to extend my gratitude to Jim Shepard who generously shared his extensive knowledge of computer systems with me. His creative ideas and technical advice helped me create an exciting premise for ADVOCATE OF HONOR.

Cynthia Collins owns the Ironwood Bookstore in Zionsville, Indiana. I had never met Cynthia until a friend of mine had mentioned to her that I had written three novels. Cynthia offered to read my manuscripts. It was the start of a budding friendship. Cynthia, you have energized and motivated me. I thrive on your enthusiasm.

Finally, to the people at the FBI and CIA. You answered the questions of an unknown author with unexpected openness. Thank you. You have taught me that there are ordinary, decent people behind those usually formidable initials.

1

It was a sweltering August afternoon when I entered the emergency department behind the paramedics. Their patient, Latisha Jones, was yet another victim of the domestic violence that seems to escalate proportionately with the rise in the heat index, that abstract concept which attempts to quantify a person's comfort level. Normally, what we refer to as the "knife and gun club" becomes active later in the day and on into the night after enough beer and whiskey have been consumed to alter peoples' grip on reality. That day, with the index temperature exceeding one hundred ten degrees, beer had become the breakfast of champions, and the knife and gun clubbers and wife beaters started their activities earlier in the day.

Though the paramedics' arrival with a domestic violence victim wasn't particularly surprising, Latisha herself was a bewildering sight. A twelve inch butcher knife—we measured it later to be sure—was buried in bone, like Excalibur, behind her right ear while the blade protruded from her mouth. The paramedics had wrapped the blade with wads of gauze at the scene to prevent Latisha from shredding her tongue. In all, we counted eleven stab wounds in Latisha's body, including one that had severed her spinal cord, leaving her paralyzed from the waist down.

"Dr. Hunter, thank God you're here," Michelle Johnson called out. She was the R.N. who had been unlucky enough to draw charge duty that day. "We're already running three trauma resuscitations. Can you pick this one up?"

There was no time to change into my scrubs, so I handed my purse to the secretary behind the admissions desk and jumped into the middle of insanity.

"What the hell happened here?" I asked one of the paramedics.

"This is one for the books," he replied. "Apparently her husband didn't like what she made for breakfast, so he took the butcher knife to her. When her mother tried to stop him, he stabbed the old woman in the chest. She's down the hall in trauma one. Hubby caught up with Latisha on her way into the bedroom to get a gun. I'm not sure exactly what the scenario was after that, except she managed to shoot him in the chest some time between the first stabbing and when he buried the knife in her skull."

"Jesus," I whispered.

Forty minutes later, Latisha was on her way to surgery with Excalibur still protruding from her skull, a new tracheostomy tube in her neck, a urine bag taped to her leg, and her veins attached to enough wide open I.V.'s to drown an elephant. Her mother and husband were on their way to the county morgue.

After changing out of my bloody clothes and into a scrub suit, I settled down onto a sofa in the staff lounge and sipped from my cup of Plantation Mint tea. I allowed myself a momentary respite from thinking while I savored a mouthful of the warm, minty liquid. It turned out to be the briefest moment in my history.

With a rush of air, the door swung wide to reveal Michelle's smiling face. I knew that smile, and it wasn't a happy one. "We've got another one," she announced through clenched teeth.

"How much time do we have?" I asked, unable to hide my disappointment and gazing longingly at my teacup. I don't mind working trauma cases, in fact, I thrive on them. They are the stuff of emergency medicine, the adrenalin rush, when doctors and nurses are called upon to use all the facets of their training and apply their skills with the greatest of efficacy under intense time pressures. Lives truly hang in the balance.

"If you want that tea," Michelle said, "you'd better gulp it. The paramedics are in the driveway."

"What! Why didn't they notify us?"

"Hell if I know."

I got up and hurried down the corridor along side Michelle.

"You picked a helluva weekend to work," she said.

I rolled my eyes. "You've got it backwards. It's a helluva weekend *because* I'm working."

"Yeah, well, I was expecting the shit to hit the fan. When I saw your name on the schedule, I popped an extra ginseng and laced up my Nikes."

"As we arrived at the entrance to the trauma suite, the paramedics were already rolling through the door with their patient whose face and body were covered with blood. He had an IV in each arm, running wide open."

"Talk to me," I said to the paramedic in charge as I followed the entourage into the trauma suite.

"We've got sa street knight the cops found in an alley just a couple of blocks from here. He's been beaten and stabbed. Pulse is a thready 160, and the B.P.'s at 50 palp. This guy's Alpo."

"I can see that," I said. "Has he got a name?"

"Yeah," another paramedic replied, "John Doe."

John Doe was bleeding to death from a half dozen stab wounds to the chest. From the looks of his face, these came after someone had used him for batting practice.

"Why the hell didn't you call ahead?" I asked reproachfully as I followed them into the trauma suite.

"Sorry," replied the paramedic in charge, "we're having a major SNAFU day. Our goddam communication system has gone schizo on us. We've had to fall back on radio traffic alone. Since we only had a couple of blocks, we just booked."

"What system's down, nine-one-one?" I asked.

"The whole fuckin' mess, and that's just what it's created. Hard lines are cutting in and out. Christ, we've been chasin' ghosts the whole afternoon. People call in, but their addresses don't seem to jive with anything. In fact, the computer spits out the same address for anyone who calls in from this sector. Even the on board computers aren't transmitting correctly—ours or the cops'. Have you checked your phones lately?"

I took up my position at the head of the trauma table. "I've been hiding in the doctor's lounge."

"Yeah, well, I sure wish I could go hide somewhere," the paramedic said.

"Technology, you gotta love it," I replied.

The paramedics rolled their transport stretcher next to the trauma table, and five of us gripped the hand holds in the back board. "Are we ready?" I asked as I watched for the affirmative nod from my four co-workers. "On my count, one-two-three." Together, we lifted the backboard and set it on top of the trauma table. The transfer went smoothly, but Murphy's laws were working in over drive, and John Doe went into ventricular fibrillation, a fatal heart rhythm, in the midst of the transfer.

You know you are working with a top notch emergency staff when you can run a major trauma resuscitation with few words spoken. Michelle was immediately at my side presenting me with a laryngoscope and an endotracheal tube, before my mouth had opened to request them. A paramedic pumped John Doe's chest while two other nurses were cutting his pants off.

I tried to intubate Mr. Doe, but his lower jaw had been fractured in so many places it felt like I was holding a slimy bean bag instead of a mandible. His cheek had been split through, and blood was pouring into his mouth making it impossible to expose his airway and insert the endotracheal tube.

Michelle grabbed a handful of gauze sponges and pressed them against his ravaged cheek, giving me a chance to suction out enough blood to see the airway. I had inserted the laryngoscope and was guiding the endotracheal tube along it's blade when my patient decided to have a grand mal seizure. His thrashing knocked the metal blade against what few teeth he had left in his head, taking out two of his molars.

"Dammit!" I complained as I tossed the teeth onto the instrument tray. "Hold him!" I shouted as I made another futile attempt to intubate him. I finally gave up and tossed the endotrach tube onto the instrument tray along side the man's teeth.

"I need a trach tray," I called out. It was opened and ready before the sound of my words faded. "Hold his head," I said to Michelle, who was trying her best to hold the gauze against his cheek. It was too late. The seizing stopped as abruptly as it had begun. I glanced up at the monitor, and saw the erratic waves of a dying heart. I checked John Doe's pupils. They were fixed and dilated. The man with no name was dead.

After I called time, I had an opportunity to study the lifeless form that moments earlier had been a living human being. The corpse lay naked on top of the bloody backboard. With I.V. tubing dangling from arms that lay pointlessly outstretched on either side of the table, the body was already turning mottled and blue. I reflected for a moment, wondering if anyone would miss this man, or had he already been dead to his family?

The longer I stared at the body, though, the more its appearance bothered me. This was supposed to be a homeless guy they had scraped off of the streets, yet he was clean shaven, and well muscled. While his arms were dirty and his body was covered with clotted blood, his fingernails were relatively clean and with the exception of a few chips which may have occurred during the attack, well manicured, not ragged and caked with dirt as I would expect to see in someone who hadn't bathed regularly. The most conspicuous clue, however, was the absence of the characteristic odor of the streets; a potpourri of sweat, alcohol, old urine, and feces. This man smelled only of death.

Tony Jackson, our department aid, was already bagging the man's clothing. "Just a minute," I said as I sniffed the bag. I would have expected to be bowled over by the odor of clothing that hadn't been laundered, possibly for years. Again, I was hit only by the metallic smell of drying blood.

"Where are his shoes?" I asked Tony.

"He only had one," Tony said as he dug through the bag and pulled out a fairly new, black, leather, wing tip.

I took the shoe in my hand.

"Is everything OK, Doctor?" Michelle asked.

"Hm?"

"Is everything all right? Can we bag him?"

"Not yet," I replied. "I want to talk to the police first."

I found a couple of uniforms outside the trauma suite. Their faces were new. "I thought I knew all the cops in the district," I said.

They both accommodated me with ingratiating smiles. "They're running a little short today, so they borrowed us from downtown." The cop who replied, Eberhardt was the name engraved into his nameplate, was at once tall and strikingly handsome with the rich golden brown skin and hazel eyes often seen in someone of mixed race. The other cop, Krandall, was the antithesis of the first with ruddy jowls and a gut that had been home to too many beers.

"Are you here to take Mr. Doe to the county morgue?" I asked.

"I take it that means he's dead," Eberhardt said.

"I don't believe this guy was homeless," I replied, ignoring his statement of the obvious. "His body's too clean and healthy looking to belong to someone who's been living on the street."

"Maybe." Eberhardt shrugged. "Maybe he's new to the street."

"I suppose that's possible," I said, "but you might want to dig a little deeper. This guy might have a family that's expecting him home for dinner."

"Sure," Eberhardt replied with a chilling nonchalance.

I had no time to concern myself with the officer's cavalier attitude or John Doe's identity. The "in" tray was spilling over with patient charts. I knew I had better get to them before we had more trauma cases roll in.

Hours later, when my shift had ended and I was changing into fresh scrubs to wear home, since my street clothes were caked with dried blood, Tony came looking for me. He was holding a clear zip lock bag. "Dr. Hunter," he said. "Sorry to bother you, but we've got a slight problem."

"What, are the phone lines down again?" They had only been working for the last hour.

"No, they're O.K." He held up the zip lock bag for my inspection. "These're John Doe's teeth. Y'know, the guy whose chest was turned into Swiss cheese. These're his teeth. The cops hauled him off before we had a chance to inventory his stuff. They didn't wait for any of it. Don't they always want clothing and things for evidence?"

Tired, hungry, and disinterested in what was clearly an administrative rather than a medical problem, I said, "Why are you coming to me with this? I made out and incident report about his teeth, so I'm done with it. Toss them into the bag with the rest of his things and call the county morgue. They'll send someone by as soon as they can."

"We tried that, but the morgue can't seem to find the body. They don't even have a record of the cops dropping off a John Doe from our ER."

"So?" I shrugged. "They didn't lose the body, just the paper work. The body'll turn up sooner or later. Trust me." I grabbed my purse and shut my locker door. "Label the tooth bag and toss it in the big yellow one with his other belongings, then call the precinct and tell them the stuff's here. They'll come for it when they need it."

As soon as I stepped through the automatic doors into the night, I was hit with a tidal wave of humid air. I said good night to the security guard who had walked through the doors with me and would watch me walk to my car. He always offered to walk with me, but I felt silly accepting, since we both knew that I am a TaeKwonDo instructor.

My husband, Sam, finally convinced me to train in Taekwondo when our daughter, Shelby, was five. Shelby had been going to the dojang with Sam since she was barely able to walk. To her, TaeKwonDo was as natural a part of life as walking or eating. I, on the other hand, didn't look at it that way. Somehow breaking boards and chunks of concrete with my bare feet and hands hardly seemed natural, and it surely didn't appeal to me.

By himself, Sam was never able to break my resistance, but

then he enlisted little Miss innocent, angel-faced Shelby to go to work on me.

What can I say? I got hooked. Eleven years later, I was a third degree black belt working enthusiastically toward my fourth. I had done it all; the wood, the concrete. . . It's hard to explain what an exhilarating feeling it is to drive your bare hands through concrete blocks. With three gold stripes on my black belt, I had become the macho queen whose ego could no longer accept protection from a man who was at least twenty years my senior and probably less capable of defending me than I was myself. He *did* have a gun, but who knows if he knew how to use it.

I was always cautious walking to my car, following the usual rules of safety; always looking around, checking under the car as I approached, checking the back seat before climbing in, but I was never frightened. That night, though, I experienced an uneasiness that I hadn't felt before. It was as if I were being watched. "This is silly," I said to myself. "You *are* being watched." I turned back toward the guard and waved. He smiled and waved back. But the feeling did not dissipate as I had expected. Someone else was watching me, I was sure of it. I picked up my pace and got into my car quickly, locking the doors immediately. I looked up toward the ER entry one last time as I started the engine and turned on the headlights. The guard waved and disappeared into the building.

The drive home seemed endless. I couldn't shake that damn feeling of being watched. I must have checked the rearview mirror a thousand times more than I usually do. Though the ride home remained uneventful, I breathed a sigh of relief when the garage door lowered behind me.

Waiting for me in the kitchen, was a place setting laid out on the table. A note on the plate read, *Dinner is in the microwave. Just push start and it will be ready. Wake me up when you get in. I will sit with you while you eat your dinner. Love, Sam.*

You would think after nearly seventeen years of marriage, the fire of romance would have dimmed like the flame of a long burning candle whose wick is drowning in its own liquified wax. That was not, however, the case with Sam Hunter. He was an incurable romantic who believed in sending his wife love notes and flowers just because.

I tip-toed into the bedroom where I was comforted by the rhythmic vibrato of Sam's snoring. I slipped quietly passed him and into the bathroom where I stripped and climbed into a much needed shower. I would have preferred a Jacuzzi filled with muscle soothing mineral salts, but I knew I would fall asleep while the tub was filling and flood the house.

While rolling my head under the hot shower spray, I allowed my mind to drift along its own course without conscious guidance. This was my pattern after every shift. It seemed if I gave my mind the license to relive stressful events, it would then let them go. If some memory was particularly horrifying, I would write about it in my journal or talk it out with Sam. It was easy to share my experiences with Sam. An agent on the FBI's Critical Incident Response Group, he had seen it all and understood what I might be going through. After receiving his degree in Criminology at the University of Utah—he really went there to ski— Sam returned to Chicago and became a cop. A couple of years later, he joined the FBI.

Sam's dad and sister were cops, and his mom was an emergency room nurse. That's how I met Sam. He was barely out of the academy, and I was a first year medical student using my own nursing degree to work weekends in the emergency department where Marilyn, Sam's mom, was head nurse. Marilyn and I hit it off immediately, and she decided to fix me up with Sam. Of course, she neglected to mention her decision to me or Sam. Though she didn't tell me that it was a party celebrating Sam's birthday when she invited me to dinner, I should have guessed what she was up to, since she talked about him all the time. Sam and I knew, the minute I walked through the door, what Marilyn was up to. It was a contest to see whose face turned the deepest shade of crimson. The way my cheeks burned, I'm sure I won. Sam quickly apologized for his mother's Cupid syndrome. Little did he know, the arrows had already struck their targets.

A year later, on Sam's birthday, under the painted ceilings of the cathedral-like Catholic church where I had been Baptized, we exchanged vows.

Two years after that, Shelby became part of our lives, and I watched Sam immediately coil himself around her little finger. Though it was a struggle raising a child while I finished medical school and residency, Sam never complained. In fact, he relished the opportunity to take his turns with Shelby as much as she cherished the time with her dad.

My life seemed so wonderful that it scared me. I spent my days surrounded by human tragedy, and I knew I would only escape for so long. Then that fanciful bubble I was living in would burst, and my worst fears would be realized. Little did I know that a nightmare was imminent.

I was rinsing the shampoo from my hair when I heard the shower door open and felt a momentary rush of cool air.

"Hi, babe." Sam's lips followed his words to my ear. He kissed me sweetly on my ear and my neck and my shoulder while his arms encircled me.

It is amazing how much energy a tired body can find given the right motivation. I grabbed Sam and yanked him under the shower spray, then pushed his back against the wall and began to kiss him all over.

"Wow! I thought you'd be tired," he exclaimed through heavy breath. "I was just going to wash your back."

"You can," I said as I dragged my tongue along his torso from his neck to his pelvis.

"Oh God," he sighed. Then he took hold of my shoulders and lifted me until our mouths met. "I love you," he admitted when we came up for air.

"I love you, too."

We made love until the shower turned cold. Afterward, we raced each other to the kitchen where we ate ravenously. It was past two when we finally curled up in each other's arms and fell asleep.

2

The next day the sun rose crimson behind hazy skies. "Red in the morning, sailor take warning." A sailor heeding the warning can't stop the storm, but he might be able to change the outcome with the proper preparations. I wonder if I could have changed the outcome of my personal storm had I seen warning signs.

I have known many people who, when tragedy strikes such as divorce, a heart attack, suicide, say they never saw it coming. Retrospectively, though, they see the danger signals flashing at them like Las Vegas neon: the teenager who withdrew from his friends and family and became enamored of death; the man who ignored that nagging ache in his jaw or down his left arm and the tightness in his chest; the woman whose husband seemed to be spending a lot more time at the office.

I look back and see nothing. There was no red sun in my horizon.

The instant the radio kicked on, my well-trained fingers pounced on the snooze button like a pack of wolves on a felled antelope. I hate mornings. Well, not exactly. I like mornings. I just hate dragging my tired ass out of bed before noon, especially when my sleep has been rudely interrupted by some overly zealous radio personality who's been up since four in the morning drowning himself in caffeine.

Still basking in the afterglow of great loving-making, I didn't mind the alarm that particular morning. It was for Sam, not me. I wasn't getting up for anyone or anything. Without opening my eyes, I snuggled closer to Sam, buried my nose in his chest, and inhaled. His aroma was warm and masculine laced with a hint of my Goldleaf and Hydrangea bath gel. My skin had been covered in the lather when he had joined me in the shower. I hoped, in a way, he wouldn't shower that morning. It would wash my scent off of his skin. I liked having it there. It was as if part of me would be with him throughout his day. He might lean his head in a certain way, or the breeze would change and carry Goldleaf and Hydrangea to his nostrils, reminding him of me. I rubbed my skin against his, hoping some of his aura would cling to me also.

Sam groaned sensuously. "Again? You? This early in the morning?" He enveloped me in his arms and drew me closer, if that were possible.

"Why not? I can go back to sleep afterward. You're the one who's gotta get up," I said.

"I do? Why? It's Saturday." Sam's muffled words rose from between my breasts.

"Yes, but you promised to spend the day with Shelby."

Sam rolled onto his back and slapped his forehead. "That's right." He righted himself on one elbow and faced me. "What's on the agenda?" He asked as his index finger began circumscribing one of my nipples.

"Let's see, you begin with her—" Sam's face dove for my neck where he tickled my skin with his lips and nibbled my ear. I gasped. I didn't want him to stop. . .ever. God, it was wonderful. "—You begin with. . .a. . .with her volleyball serv-a-thon from eight to ten." Seventeen years of marriage, and it still felt that good.

"Eight?" Sam's lips abruptly pulled away from my neck. It was the sexual equivalent to having a chair yanked out from under you as you sit. In the same instant, the radio kicked on. Sam gave the clock a cursory glance. "It's nearly seven-thirty," he complained. "We don't have time even for a quicky."

I was hoping he wouldn't notice. My skin was on fire. I voted for the quicky. "It's OK," I said hungrily, pulling him toward me. "You can shower fast."

"You're right," he breathed, and his lips fell upon mine.

I don't know which interrupted us first; Shelby's knock at our door or the intrusive ringing of the phone. "Jesus," Sam moaned as he rolled off of me and picked up the phone. My skin flushed from passion, I threw on my robe, straightened my hair, and opened the door to our daughter.

Dressed in her team uniform complete with kneepads hanging around her ankles, Shelby's azure eyes regarded me with a twinkle that told me my baby was no longer a totally naive little girl. "Is daddy ready?" She bubbled as she stepped past me into our bedroom. Her deep auburn hair, which usually flowed to the small of her back, was gathered into a ponytail and tied with a blue and gold ribbon to match her school's colors. Shelby's complexion was flawless. I swear I never saw a pimple or blackhead on that child's face, not even the kind that crop up on a young girl's nose or chin at the most inopportune times. While I, auburn haired as well, never suffered from acne, I also never went to a formal dance without the company of an isolated zit the size of Mount Everest enhancing some already prominent facial feature.

Sam, who had been sitting on the side of the bed with his back turned to us and his ear glued to the phone, hung up and turned around. His eyes immediately connected with mine. His hovered in a dark sea, that immediately filled me with trepidation. Sam frowned apologetically and his lips parted as if to speak, but the moment he caught sight of Shelby, the darkness faded.

"Ah, miss teenage jock. Ready to go already?" he asked with a broad smile, leaving me wondering if I had misinterpreted what I saw in his eyes.

"Good morning, daddy," Shelby replied. "I don't know if you noticed, but it's time to leave."

"Uh," Sam uttered penitently.

Shelby's face fell and her shoulders slumped, as did mine. We both knew what that "Uh" meant: Shelby and I would be spending the day together. Don't get me wrong, the sun rises and sets on my only child, but any woman who's been blessed with a teenage daughter knows that the spice in "Sugar and spice and everything nice..." is cayenne pepper.

Friends who had already weathered the tumultuous teenage years, warned me to be prepared as Shelby approached thirteen, though their warnings were unnecessary. I had seen this particular storm on the horizon. Shelby had been perfecting stair stomping, door slamming, and that oh so defiant look—you know, the one where her lower lip protrudes from a stone-like jaw and her arms are folded across her chest— since she was two. By fourteen, she had added her favorite whine song, "But mo-o-o-o-om-m-m-m!" If they handed out black belts for driving parents crazy, Shelby would have attained the level of Grand Master by the time her fifteenth birthday rolled around.

"There's a situation," Sam said.

"But you're not on call," I complained. I usually didn't question Sam about his call outs, and rarely complained. I'm a doctor, so I know about crazy hours. Besides, I learned early on that Sam wasn't allowed to talk about it, and I knew I would eventually learn about it on the evening news. Sam never got called out like that that it didn't end up on the evening news.

"I know, and I'm sorry," Sam said, "but I have to go."

I caught another glimpse of the unsettling dark expression in his eyes. "Sam, what is it?" I asked.

Sam glanced at Shelby, and he shrugged his shoulders. "It's nothing," he said. I knew it was a lie, but I didn't press. Whatever it was, he didn't want to talk about it in front of Shelby. I trusted that he would tell me when he could.

Shelby regarded me with disappointed eyes. "I can't be late, Mom," she announced before she spun on her heels and headed down the hall toward her bedroom. I closed my eyes and waited for the expected banging of her door. She didn't disappoint me.

I lingered in the bed listening to the morning news on the radio while Sam showered. The newscaster was discussing the previous day's chaos with the phone lines, especially the nine-one-one system. Not particularly interested in reliving the events, I reached over to shut it off when I heard the words "terrorist act." My interest was definitely piqued. The newscaster went on to say the nine-one-one systems breakdown had not been unique to our district or even to Chicago. Similar malfunctions had occurred in New York and Los Angeles. The authorities had called in several experts who were looking into the problem.

Sam soon emerged from the shower with a towel wrapped around his hips and beads of water glistening on his back and shoulders. I lay in bed watching him dry off and dress in his fatigues. I enjoyed watching his muscles move beneath his skin. Even the simple act of pulling on a pair of pants caused them to contract, revealing their shapes. It was for me a sensuous experience.

Sam was about to pull his tee shirt over his head when he stopped and glanced at me with his lopsided smile. "What?"

"What do you mean 'What?'"?

"You're staring at me," he said.

"No, I'm ogling at you."

"Well, O.K. then," Sam said. He performed a couple of muscleman poses before putting his shirt on.

"Were the Bureau's phones messed up yesterday?" I asked, making small talk to cool my smoldering libido.

"For awhile," Sam said as he laced up his boots.

I raised up on one elbow and combed my hair with my fingers. "The news said they suspect terrorists caused the problem."

Without looking up from his task, Sam replied, "Yeah, well, the news says a lot of things."

"I suppose you're going after the telephone terrorists." I don't know why I said that. It was more for levity than anything, but Sam's head popped up and he shot me the strangest look. He seemed startled, even a little guilty, like a cat caught with a feather hanging from its mouth. Again, the look faded quickly.

"Stop that," Sam said.

"Stop what?"

"Doing that thing with your hair. It drives me crazy." Sam smiled, leaned over me, and grabbed a handful of my hair. He pulled my head back, covered my mouth with his, and kissed me long and hard. Then he pulled back and asked, "Why do you do this to me?"

"Because I want you to look forward to coming home," I replied flirtatiously.

With a deep, sexy groan, Sam got up. "It worked," he said. Then he grabbed his SWAT bag and called out to Shelby, announcing his departure. Shelby joined us at the front door. Sam hugged and kissed her, then turned to me. Holding me in his arms he kissed each of my eyes then he whispered into my ear, "Look under your pillow." In a moment, he was gone, leaving Shelby to nag at me to hurry up or she would be late.

I suppose I could have worried whenever he left for the job, but Sam had always been a cop. Chicago, FBI, it didn't matter. A cop's a cop. There are inherent dangers in the job, but there are inherent dangers in driving to work. I had stopped worrying a long time ago. I had faith in Sam. He was intelligent and level-headed. The way I figured it, he was probably safer going to his job than I was going to mine at an inner city teaching hospital. That morning felt different, however. For the first time I felt a sense of dread nagging at me. Maybe there had been a red sun in my horizon after all.

Weighed down by an uncharacteristic worry, I returned to my bedroom and was getting undressed for my shower when I heard an insistent rapping at my bedroom door.

"Mom? Mom? Are you almost ready? It's after eight."

"I just have to take a quick shower, and I'll be ready."

"A shower! But Mo-o-o-o-m-m-m-m, I'm already late."

I took a couple of deep breaths and replied, "The serve-a-thon goes on all day. You don't have to be there exactly at eight. I'm sure it will begin just fine without you." I ignored the next "But mom" whine and climbed into the shower.

As expected, no one but Shelby cared that she arrived at eight-thirty. In fact, several of her team mates didn't arrive until nine. I wanted to make some kind of "I told you so" comment, but I thought better of it. Fifteen-year-olds have well developed passive aggressive skills, and I would have been punished the rest of the day.

After her serv-a-thon— she dropped a hundred twenty over the net—Shelby and I went shopping. Rather, Shelby shopped while I avoided critiquing her clothing choices or making any recommendations. As long as she stayed within a set budget and confined herself to outfits that didn't stretch my conservative nature beyond its limits, I found it prudent to say nothing.

The cosmetics counters were a little more dicey. Shelby wanted to wear all the "in" colors; dark purple, burgundy, navy blue. I would not allow her more than brown mascara and a light lipstick. I couldn't warm up to the idea of my daughter walking around looking like an escapee from THE NIGHT OF THE LIVING DEAD.

Having survived shopping, we ate lunch, and took in a "chick flick." By the time I headed to work, I was ready for a nap, but I sucked down a giant cup of coffee instead. I hated leaving Shelby home alone, but she was, after all, fifteen.

When I pulled into the driveway along side the emergency department entrance, I saw two ambulances lined up outside the door. It was going to be another busy night. Not surprising. The temperature was hovering near ninety-seven, and in Chicago, that meant we were also drowning in wet air. It felt like lake Michigan had lifted itself up and dropped on top of us.

I was stopped inside the entrance by our admissions clerk, Tamara Thompson. We called her "T". Somehow the nickname, Tammy, didn't seem suitable to her three hundred pound frame. Tamara was our town crier. As soon as you walked in, she would bring you up-to-date with the headlines of the day. Later, if time permitted, she would fill you in on all the gory details. Of course, her headlines were all tabloid, and her beat was University Hospital. She didn't bother herself with such trivia as world politics. Saddam who?

"Oh, Dr. Hunter? Dr. Hunter," Tamara called to me from behind her desk. How could I resist? I thrived on hospital gossip as much as anyone else.

"What is it?" I asked feigning indifference.

"There were some heavy duty suit types in here tonight."

"Oh really?" I asked.

"Yes, and they was lookin' for you," Tamara said with a broad smile.

"Who were they, the Publisher's Clearinghouse prize patrol?"

"Mm! Mm! That would be nice wouldn't it? No, they said they was from the fed'ral gove'nment, and they asked for you specifically."

Tamara's words took my breath away. "Did they say what they were here for?" I asked with growing trepidation.

"Not exactly."

"Did they tell you their names?"

"No." Tamara shrugged indifferently.

"You didn't check their ID's?"

Now Tamara was becoming irritated with me. Her stubby fingers folded into a fist and buried themselves into the generous mound of adipose covering her hip. "I didn't check no I.D.'s. All I know is they said they was from the gove'nment. That was all th'I.D. I needed. Anyway, you weren't here, so it didn't matter much."

"Thanks, T," I said, and I continued my journey to the interior corridor, wondering, fearing why someone from the federal government would be looking for me. The most obvious and frightening reason would be that something happened to Sam. I maneuvered my way through the corridor, with the perfunctory hello's to the staff. When I arrived at the doctor's lounge, I dropped my purse on the sofa and immediately called Ben Scolnik, the Special Agent in Charge (SAC) of Sam's field office. Unsuccessful at reaching him directly, I left a message with his answering service. Then the interminable waiting began.

3

Patients poured into the waiting room like ants into a California kitchen. I know this first hand, having spent part of my childhood in California's Pomona Valley, drowning ants with the water from my inflatable pool. The relentless pace was a blessing in disguise. There was no time for me to dwell on my fears, and the unavoidable humor of the human condition crept slowly into our evening. People who work in the stressful environments of emergency rooms cultivate bizarre senses of humor. We find reasons to laugh when others might cry, not to be callous or cruel, but to survive with our human sensibilities intact.

"What's next," I asked Michelle when I had finished the admission papers on a man who had suffered a mild, though dangerous, myocardial infarction, better known as a heart attack. Michelle's face was blotched red and she was trying to hold back a snicker when she stuffed a chart into my hand and pointed toward one of the ambulatory examining rooms.

"What's so funny?" I asked, wanting to enjoy the same joke.

"Just"….giggle, giggle… "read the name on the chart"… .Snicker….And ask her mother how she came up with that name."

I glanced down at the chart and smiled. "This is a mistake," I said.

"No it's not," Michelle giggled.

"Come on. Really?"

Michelle nodded her reply, desperately trying to suppress her laughter.

"So how does she pronounce it?"

"Fimali," Michelle squeaked out.

"Fimali?" I asked. "Are you sure you've got this right?"

"Oh, it's right all right," Michelle said.

"You can't be serious," I insisted. Then it dawned on me. "This is some kind of joke, right? What am I going to find when I walk into that room?"

"Deb, as God is my judge, this is no joke," Michelle said with as much sobriety as she could muster.

I looked again at the chart. The patient, an eleven-year-old girl, was complaining of an ear ache and a sore throat. Her temperature upon admission was one hundred two. If I did find a legitimate patient when I opened the door, this was no joking matter. The child probably had strep with a serious otitis media, ear infection, and she was surely miserable.

When I entered the room, I found my young patient accompanied by a woman who couldn't be much older than twenty-three.

"Fimali?" I asked the child, hoping my pronunciation of her name was at least close to correct.

She nodded tearfully.

"Are you her mother?" I asked the young woman.

"Yes," she replied.

I showed her the chart and asked, "Is your child's name spelled correctly, f-e-m-a-l-e?

"Yes."

"I am curious. How did you come up with that name?"

"The hospital gave it to her."

"The hospital?"

"Yes, it was on her birth certificate."

I looked at the mother a moment longer, understanding the confusion of a twelve-year-old child giving birth. I wondered if it had dawned on her since then that she had named her daughter after a sex designation.

"So, Fimali, you have a bad ear ache?" I asked while taking the otoscope out of its bracket on the wall and attaching a disposable earpiece to it.

An hour into my shift, Ben Scolnik finally returned my phone call. Though he assured me that Sam was just fine as far as he knew, his answer did little to allay my fears.

"Why are you worried?" he asked.

"A couple of agents came to see me," I replied.

"Really?" Scolnik sounded surprised.

"You didn't send them?"

"No, why would I send agents to speak to you?" Scolnik asked. "Are you sure they were from the FBI?"

"The secretary said they told her they were from the federal government," I replied.

"I don't know who they were, but I will look into it for you," Scolnik offered. Then he asked the strangest question. "Where is Sam? Maybe you should ask him if he knows anything about those men."

"Ben, I don't know where Sam is. Don't you?"

"Should I?" Ben asked.

For a moment, surprised and confused, I said nothing. How could Ben forget that he had sent Sam out on an assignment just that morning, an assignment that required Sam to take along his SWAT ordnance bag?

"You don't remember calling our house and sending him out this morning?"

There was a long silence, then Ben said, "Uh, yes. Was that this morning? It seems like a million years ago."

"More like twelve hours, Ben," I replied, letting him hear the irritation in my voice."

"I am sorry. I've had a lot on my mind lately."

"Fine," I said incredulously. "See what you can find out about those agents who were looking for me?"

"I will call you if I find out anything."

As I hung up the phone, Tamara came waddling toward me. "Doctor Hunter, I remember why the suits were here."

"And?"

"They was asking about that John Doe character that was in here last night. They said they wanted his clothes."

I rolled my eyes toward the ceiling. "This is timely," I whispered to myself. I'd been sweating bullets worried that my husband might have been hurt or killed, and all the men were after was John Doe's personal effects. "Did you give them the clothes?"

"No," Tamara said as she drew in her chin and cocked her head. "I thought Tony got rid of them."

"No, T, he didn't. They're in the storage room," I said. "Are you sure the men said they were federal? Might they have been CPD?"

"They was federal," Tamara replied adamantly.

"Do me a favor, T. Next time people like that come in, get their names, a phone number, and take a message. And make sure you write it down."

"Yes, ma'am," she replied in a spicy tone. Then she turned and waddled toward the admissions desk with her fist firmly planted in a mound of adipose and her hips swaying deliberately from side-to-side.

The onslaught of ambulatory patients mingled with the usual trauma cases, mostly stab and gunshot wounds, didn't let up until after one a.m. It took me until three to finish my paperwork and drag my tired buns out the door.

The security system was armed when I got home, and Shelby was fast asleep. Like her father, Shelby left enough lights on to welcome me home. A place setting awaited me, and a bowl of spaghetti sat in the microwave ready to nuke. Shelby left a note on my plate with microwaving instructions. I am a competent physician who saves lives all the time, but at home my family seems to think I'm incompetent. Shelby's note ended with the usual, Love you, mom. XOXOXOXOXO. I was a surprised and after my somewhat unsettling conversation with Ben Scolnik, worried that there was no message that dad had called.

Though I was starving and appreciated the effort, I couldn't bear to do anything but fall into bed. It took what little energy I had left to take the bowl out of the microwave, cover it, and place it in the fridge. I probably stank and should have showered, but I didn't bother with that either.

I rearmed the security system, shut off the lights, stripped to my underwear, and fell into my bed. As I tucked my hands under my pillow to smush it around my head, my fingers found what felt like an envelope. I sat upright and switched on the lamp. The word, *surprise*, was written in Sam's handwriting. Suddenly, I remembered what Sam had whispered in my ear before he left. I tore the envelope open and found a packet describing an Ambassadair family vacation package to Curacao along with an itinerary that included two dives each day. Sam had planned the vacation on his own. The note that he had tucked inside of the envelope said that he had even cleared the week off with my partners. I placed the papers into the envelope and hugged it to my chest. My body ached for Sam.

In spite of the thrill of finding Sam's surprise, weariness regained its dominance. I set the envelope on my nightstand, propped up against the lamp so I could see it the moment I woke up, then I lay back onto my pillow. I drifted off in the middle of a fantasy about long walks with Sam along picturesque beaches.

I had been asleep less than an hour when the phone rang. At first, my fingers did their usual dance over the snooze button on the clock radio, but as my brain rose to a higher, though not complete, level of consciousness, I realized the snooze button wasn't going to quiet that incessant ringing.

"Yes," I said barely above a whisper as I lay the phone against my ear.

"Deb?" It was Sam.

Though the hour he chose to call was odd, I was happy to hear from him. I rolled from my belly to my back and switched the phone to my other ear. "Hi, honey. What time is it?"

"You don't want to know," Sam said.

"I found your surprise under my pillow," I said sleepily. What a wonderful thing for you to do."

"I'm glad you like it," Sam said. I couldn't exactly put my finger on it, but his voice didn't sound right somehow.

"Sam, is something wrong?"

Though brief, there was a moment's hesitation before he answered. It was enough to bring me fully awake. Something *was* wrong.

"No. Nothing's wrong," Sam answered with that same odd quality in his voice. He was lying to me. Sam never lied to me, but he was lying now. I looked at the clock. It was four forty-five. My heart was racing.

What was I going to say to him? I didn't want to accuse him of lying. I had no proof, just that intuitive feeling peculiar to women. How was I going to sound casual at nearly five in the morning?

"I miss you," I said as calmly as possible.

"I miss you, too," Sam said.

"When are you coming home?"

Another hesitation. "I don't know," was all he said. He was never so brief. The last time he was on one of his away assignments, he had been sent to Montana where a bunch of freedom fighters had holed up until—What was it he said? "Until the Second Coming."

"The ER was insane tonight, so I never caught the news. Where are you?" I asked.

"I. . .I can't tell you that right now."

"Are you sure you're all right?"

"Have you had anything unusual happen at work lately?" What an odd question for Sam to ask.

"Unusual? Like what?"

"Have you had any unidentified patients?"

"That would hardly qualify as unusual, Sam. You know that."

"I mean recently, like last night."

My thoughts went immediately to the John Doe with the bean bag jaw whose teeth I knocked out. "We had one. Why, Sam?"

"What did he look like?"

"His face was messed up. He was white."

"How old?"

I thought for a moment, and my mind recalled the heinous

image of a man whose face had been all but obliterated. "I don't know, Sam. I'd have to guess. Maybe about your age."

"Where's the body now?"

I thought about the two cops whom I hadn't seen before, and about Tony telling me that the county morgue had no record of the body. I never thought to ask Tony if he had found the body, or if he'd been able to get the man's personal effects picked up. It suddenly dawned on me that Tony hadn't been at work. He worked every Saturday. I can't remember him missing one in years.

"I'm not sure," I replied.

"You're not sure? How can you not be sure?" Sam's voice was edgy, impatient.

"Two cops from outside the precinct collected the body and left his stuff behind. Now the morgue can't find the body."

"What belongings did he have? Anything special? Did he say anything? Who were these cops?"

"Slow down, Sam. You're scaring me." Sam was unshakable. He was always confident and in control. Trepidation knotted my stomach. I didn't like not knowing where he was, or if he was safe. I wanted him home with me, in our bed with my arms wrapped around him.

"I'm sorry," Sam said.

"I don't know who the cops were. I've never seen them before. John Doe was unconscious when he arrived. He died without regaining consciousness."

Sam said nothing. His silence was more frightening than his words.

"Sam, do you know who he was? They said he was just a bum from the streets, but he didn't look like a bum to me."

"How did he die?" Sam. He sounded like a relative who'd just been told his loved one has died, rather than a cop looking for answers.

I hesitated, unsure of how much detail I should reveal.

Sam, sensing my reluctance, said, "It's all right. I can handle it."

"He was pretty messed up, Sam. His jaw was broken, and he'd been stabbed many times."

There was a profound and painful silence on the other end of the line. "Sam? Who was he?"

"I'll tell you when I get home." Sam's voice had thickened. He was crying. Where are his things?"

"I'm not sure. Tony stuck them in a storage room until the cops could come get them. They might be gone."

"Was there anything special?"

"I'm not sure what your looking for, Sam. He just had the clothes he was wearing. Tony stuck his two teeth in with them and put them away."

"His teeth?"

I cringed. Why did I say that? If Sam knew the guy, he didn't need to hear all of the gory details. "Yes. His teeth were loose from the beating. He had a seizure when I was trying to intubate him, and I knocked a couple out with the laryngoscope."

I could hear Sam inhale sharply. "Deb, I need you to do something for me."

"What is it?"

"I need you to go to the ER, find his stuff, and bring it home."

"I don't see why—?"

"Just do it," Sam interrupted. "And, Deb, don't talk to anyone."

"What if the stuff is gone?"

"Then it's gone."

"Should I call you when I get home?"

"I'm not anywhere you can call. I'll call you later."

My hand gripped the phone tightly. I was afraid to let Sam off the line. If I did, my gut told me I might never hear from him again. "I love you, Sam. I want you to come home."

"I love you, too, babe. I'll be home as soon as I can."

I held the phone against my ear long after I heard the disconnecting click. I was gripped by an overwhelming nausea, and my whole body shivered. After several seconds, I finally gave up my futile death grip on the phone. After dressing and jotting off a quick lie to Shelby, saying I got called back into work, I headed out the door.

4

The emergency department waiting room was all but deserted when I walked in. The knife and gun club had called it a night, and people with minor to imaginary ailments, who usually frequented our department for lack of anything better to do, were home gearing themselves up for a new day's complaints. A lone man lay on a bench against the wall, snoring. His body odor, a product of long term hygiene deprivation combined with eau de alcohol and ratty clothing were as familiar as my old shoes. Henry Jackson was one of our regulars. You name it, he took it or drank it, including Listerine, an all time favorite.

I glanced at his chart when I entered the interior triage area beyond the automatic doors. Henry was here for an abscess drainage. He must have run out of disposable needles or hustled himself a bag of heroine cut with corn starch or flour or some other kind of crap. It's easy to fool addicts like Henry, whose brains have turned into a gelatinous ooze.

"Well, well. Doctor Hunter. Slumming?" Marcia Hanson, the night nurse, teased when she caught sight of me reading Henry's chart. "Want to drain it?"

"No thanks," I replied, dropping the chart into the in-patient tray.

"I thought you went home," Marcia said.

"I did, but I forgot something."

"Well, you'd better get your little hiney in and out fast before we put you to work."

Looking around at the empty exam rooms, I said, "Not much chance of that." I took off down the corridor toward the doctor's lounge. When I reached the door, I turned to see that Marcia had disappeared into one of the exam rooms. Feeling like a criminal, I dashed into the back corridor and found the yellow trash bag with John Doe's clothing. It was tucked away at the rear of the storage closet. I grabbed the bag and ducked out the service entrance. It was a long walk from there to the parking lot, but I didn't want anyone to see me with the contraband. Not that anyone would give a damn if they did see me.

Again, on my way home, I had the uncanny sensation that I was followed. When I looked in my rearview mirror, I saw a police cruiser behind me and my heart leapt as if they knew I had stolen police evidence, evidence that was so important that they had forgotten to take it with them and hadn't bothered to pick it up since. I almost choked on my heart when their blue strobes kicked on. *My God, they are after me*, I thought until they did a one-eighty and took off.

My relief was short lived, though, because that feeling of being followed quickly returned. "You're a paranoid idiot," I said trying to calm my fears. When the self recriminations didn't work, I blasted the radio on one of Shelby's rock stations. The pounding of the drum beats inside my skull didn't completely alleviate my anxiety, but it kept me from losing my cool altogether until I got home and inside the safety of my garage.

Before entering the house, I peeked outside from behind the blinds covering the garage windows. A dark blue Blazer had slowed to a stop directly across the street, waited a moment, then rolled slowly away. I had been followed!

Leaving the bag inside the trunk of my car, I raced inside, disarmed, and immediately rearmed the security system. My trembling fingers had to run the code twice. Once the system was reset, I looked in on Shelby. Watching the rhythmic rise and fall of her chest, I envied her innocence, and prayed God would bring her father home to us.

Wearily, I crawled into bed. Two hours later I was yanked out of a dreamless sleep by the ringing of the phone. Hoping it was Sam, I was instantly awake and sat bolt upright in my bed. I had forgotten for a moment that there was a teenager in the house. I waited and listened. If it was for me, Shelby would be yelling, "Mom!" any second.

When I didn't hear her call out to me, I fell back onto my pillow and stared at the ceiling. The worry demons immediately began play their songs inside my head. Where's Sam? Is he all right? Why hasn't he called? What if he's hurt, and nobody knows?

It was pointless driving myself crazy with unanswerable questions, so I got up, made myself a cup of coffee, and started preparing breakfast. Busying myself with familiar chores, calmed my raw nerves.

"Are you hungry?" I called out to Shelby as I plugged in the Belgian waffle iron. When she didn't answer, I placed an ear against her closed door. She was still on the phone engaged in non-stop chatter. I knocked. "Shelby, are you hungry?"

"Just a minute. My mom's banging at my door." I heard the receiver plunk on the floor followed by a "dammit." then a "Sorry." A second later her door opened. "I'm on the phone, mom," she announced with exaggerated impatience.

"I'm aware of that, but answering me supersedes your phone conversation," I replied in a motherly tone, and I don't mean the affectionate kind. "I asked you if you are hungry. I'm making Belgian waffles."

"Sure." Shelby started to close the door, but I stopped her. I am expecting an important phone call from your dad. Please don't ignore the call waiting beep."

"Yes, Mom," Shelby said, rolling her eyes and placing excess emphasis on "Mom," making it sound like an epithet. Then she closed the door and returned to her conversation, keeping her voice low. I'm sure she didn't want me to hear her complain to her friend about what a pain in the ass her mom is.

"Teenagers," I said, comforted by the normality of the moment. I returned to the kitchen and mixed up the batter for the waffles. When breakfast was almost ready, Shelby, as if with a psychic's certainty, appeared in the kitchen.

"Mom," she said in her most ingratiating voice, "Jenny's invited me up to the lake today with her family. They're going to be there all week. Can I go, pleeeeease?"

"What about volleyball?" I asked. "Won't the coach be mad?"

"She'll get over it."

"Is that your idea of commitment?" I said as I ladled batter onto the waffle iron.

"Mom, school's starting in less than two weeks," Shelby complained.

Normally, I am a stickler for honoring commitments, but at that moment Shelby's request was like a blessing. After seeing that Blazer in front of the house and worrying about Sam, I thought it would be best for Shelby to be out of the house. What if the people in the Blazer were dangerous? Would they hurt Shelby? I didn't know what was happening, and it worried me. "O.K.," I said without hesitation.

Shelby stared at me in total shock. "That's all? Yes? No questions? No, 'I'll have to think about it?' Just yes?" She lay her hand against my forehead. "Are you sure you're all right? Maybe you need to see a doctor."

"I'll look in the mirror. Now eat your waffle before it gets cold and before I change my mind about the trip."

Shelby's bottom dropped into the chair faster than I've seen for a long time.

The Coopers arrived in their customized van before ten to collect Shelby. She and their daughter, Jennifer, had been classmates since kindergarten, and we had a social relationship with Tom and Barbara. I felt quite comfortable letting Shelby spend the week with them. Jennifer hopped out and helped Shelby with her bag while I said, "hello," to Tom, Barbara, and their son, Michael. As they backed out of the driveway and I was waving good-bye, I noticed the dark blue Blazer parked near the end of our street. My blood turned to ice, but I stood my ground until the Coopers' van had turned the corner and was out of sight. Then I glared at the Blazer's windshield, hoping its occupants would know that I was not about to become anyone's victim.

After a moment of defiant posturing, I marched toward the Blazer, keeping my eyes locked on the driver's side. Before I closed half the distance to the vehicle, its engine revved and it backed to the end of the street, spun around the corner, and took off. My heart pounding, I hurried into the house, locked myself inside, and armed the security system. That done, I cried and prayed that Sam would call back soon.

5

The hours passed at an evolutionary pace. Five of them had crawled by when the walls began closing in around me. I had not heard from Sam, and I was not sure when I was supposed to hear from him. If he had given me a specific time, I could have done something useful, gotten out of the house, done anything to kill the time. Instead, I waited. I scrubbed and laundered everything I could get my hands on. After that, I tried reading. A stack of medical journals had been collecting dust and spider webs in the corner of the closet, so I thought I might catch up on my reading, but all I did was mindlessly sift through them. Next I tried a Dean Koontz novel. I was attempting to immerse myself in the story when the phone startled me.

"Sam? Why didn't you call me sooner," I said breathlessly. But Sam did not respond. Instead, all I heard was raspy breathing. "Who is this?" I demanded. I wasn't in the mood for pranks. The breather didn't answer, so I hung the phone up with a loud thud.

Though I tried to stay cool about the incident and blow it off as a child's prank, I couldn't help but wonder if it had anything to do with Sam's strange phone call or the Blazer that had followed me home and had taken up a vigil at the end of my street. When the phone rang again a short time later, I was ready to pounce on whoever was on the other end of the line. "Yes," I said harshly.

"Mom? Are you OK?"

"Hi, Shelby. I'm fine. I thought you were an obscene phone caller."

"Really? You had an obscene phone call? Tell me, what did

he say?"

"Don't get too excited, kiddo. It could have been a she for all I know. It was just a breather."

"Oh." Shelby sounded genuinely disappointed.

"Are you having fun?" I asked, trying to sound lighthearted.

"Jen got a new Skidoo. We've been out buzzing around on it. It's like really too much."

"Sounds like fun.'"

"Well, Mom, gotta go. I'll call you tomorrow. Bye."

Click.

"Bye, dear," I said to the silent phone line. Then I smiled. Another injection of normalcy.

Between the breather and Shelby, I resorted to pacing and listening to the sound of my blood pulsing in my ears with each bounding heartbeat.

After an eternity in hell, the phone finally rang.

"Deb?"

Tears welled up in my eyes the moment I heard my name.

"Sam!" I cried.

"I don't have much time," Sam said, his voice subdued, hollow. "Did you get Cal's things?"

"Cal?" I asked, clutching the phone as if it helped me hold on to Sam.

"John Doe."

"You *do* know him."

"Did you get his things?" Sam repeated with a subtle urgency a stranger might not have detected. But I heard it. Whatever Sam's situation was, it had not improved.

"Yes."

"Did you find anything?"

"No, Sam. I didn't look through the bag."

"You didn't!" He snapped, as if I should have known what to do.

"Sam, I—"

"Where is it?" he demanded.

"In the trunk of my car." My whole body was trembling. The voice on the other end of the line was Sam's, but it wasn't. Sam was always calm and even-tempered, but this man, this Sam, was desperate, frightened. And he frightened me.

"Get it fast!"

I dropped the phone and raced out to the garage where I grabbed the bag and ran back into the house. "I have it," I said breathlessly, my growing panic sucking the air from my lungs. I ripped open the bag and was immediately struck by a miasma of old blood mixed with urine and feces. Major trauma victims quite often lose bowel and bladder control. "Jesus," I whispered trying not to breath too deeply.

"O.K., I've dumped the stuff onto the floor," I said. "What am I looking for?"

There was a moment's hesitation before Sam answered. "I'm not sure exactly. A note, a computer disk, film. Anything that might have a message on it."

I ran to the kitchen and grabbed a pair of rubber gloves from beneath the sink, then sorted through the dead man's clothing. I checked every pocket as well as inside his only shoe. At Sam's request, I even tore out the shoe's lining. I found nothing. Someone had cleaned him out before he had landed on my trauma table. "There's nothing here, Sam," I said, and wondered, if luck would have it, that what I was looking for would be in the missing shoe.

"He's missing a shoe, Sam. He didn't have it when they brought him in."

"Sonuvabitch."

"Sam?"

Silence.

"Sam?" I repeated.

"That's it then."

"What do you mean? What's it?"

"I'm out of time here. I'll call you tomorrow."

"Sam, you can't leave me hanging like this."

"Listen, Deb. You might hear things. . .about me. . .uh. . ." The urgency was gone from his voice like a balloon that had suddenly lost all of its air.

"What things?" I asked, not sure I wanted an answer.

"Do you trust me, Deb?"

"You know I do."

"I need you to hold onto that trust and know that I would never do anything to hurt you or Shelby."

"What's happened, Sam?" I asked. My knuckles had gone white from the death grip I had on the phone. If I could have climbed through the wires to be with him, I would have.

"I can't talk now. I want you to know, there will always be a special place for you in my heart."

"Sam, I don't like how this sounds. You're scaring me."

"I'll be home."

"When, Sam? When will you be home?"

Sam's only response was a wretched sigh. *Please, Dear God,* I thought, *don't let him hang up.*

"Sam?"

Click.

I stayed in the chair for a long time, holding the receiver and staring at the pile of filthy, torn rags that had been John Doe's clothing. But he wasn't a John Doe, not really. Sam gave him a name, "Cal." He called him "Cal." I racked my brain trying to recall a Cal in Sam's past. Was he a friend of Sam's, a co-worker? Jesus, I had to go to work. But I couldn't work, not at a time like this. I couldn't sit there, either. I'd go stir crazy.

Sam said he would be home soon. But when? What if he called again? What if he needed me?

The telephone receiver suddenly emitted its high pitched complaint that my phone was off the hook. It was enough to draw me out of my unproductive reverie. Sam knew I was scheduled to work that night. If he needed me, he would call me there. Besides, I couldn't sit at home alone with my thoughts. I would surely go crazy. At work I would be busy, maybe too busy to worry, at least for awhile.

I gathered up the clothing, stuffed it in the trash bag and tied it tightly. Then it dawned on me. The man's teeth were not in the bag. It was a trivial detail. I had no idea why I remembered it. I made a mental note to ask Tony about the teeth.

I showered and dressed for work, then gathered up the trash bag, armed the security system, and exited to the garage.

I thought of the mysterious blue Blazer as I backed down the driveway, so I stopped at the end and looked up and down the street. It wasn't there. Feeling a guarded relief, I pulled out of the driveway and started for work.

I'm not sure how I missed it or how long it had been tailing me, but I caught sight of the Blazer within a mile of the hospital. It stayed three cars back, but there was no doubt it was on my tail. I made three unscheduled turns just to check it out. I lost it after the second turn, but it found me again after the third. That made me feel even more uncomfortable. How did the driver know where to look?

The Blazer turned into the visitor's parking lot as I pulled into the adjacent lot reserved for the Emergency Department staff. It stopped with its headlights pointed in my direction. I pulled my cell phone from my purse and switched it on. With my hands shaking so violently they could barely respond to my commands, I punched in nine-one-one. It took me three tries.

My thumb hovering over the send button, I climbed out of my car and held the cell phone aloft, so the Blazer's occupants could see what I was doing. Hoping my jellied legs would hold out, I marched boldly, albeit stupidly, toward the Blazer. As I crossed the street from the staff lot toward the visitor's parking, the Blazer quickly reversed its direction and exited. As it retreated, I tried to read its mud smeared license plate, but it was no use. Funny, the Blazer was immaculately clean.

For an eternal moment, I stood in the middle of the street unable to move my lead filled feet until a car came along and honked at me, startling me into action. Resolved to report the incident to hospital security and the police, I returned to my car, and collected the clothing bag. I felt compelled to look over my shoulder repeatedly as I carried my contraband into the hospital.

6

The emergency department was hopping when I arrived. My presence was acknowledged only in passing, and no one noticed the oversized yellow trash bag I carried. I dumped the bag in the storage room, then headed straight for the staff lounge and my locker where I bumped into one of my partners. Joel Freedlove greeted me with his gentle brown eyes and an engaging smile. Though only five feet nine inches tall, Joel was larger than life. A deeply Christian man, he always exuded warmth and compassion. "Hey, Deb. Welcome to the land of the pit bulls."

"Busy?" I said flatly, unable to muster even minimal enthusiasm.

"That's an understatement. Looks like we'll be doubling up tonight."

"That bad?"

"That bad." Joel started for the door then stopped. "Are you O.K.?" he asked.

"Why, don't I look O.K.?" I replied defensively.

Joel smiled and shook his head. "You look just fine. You just seem a little tired, that's all."

"I guess I'm not used to sleeping in an empty house." The word "empty" seemed to land like a boulder in the pit of my stomach, because that is exactly how I felt.

"I know how you feel," Joel said. "All you can think about is peace and quiet, and then when you get it, it drives you crazy."

I forced myself to smile my agreement, as I stuffed my purse into the locker.

"Where's the rest of the family," Joel asked, "gone camping

without you?"

I kicked my shoes off and tossed them into the locker with my purse. "Sam's on a call out, and Shelby's gone for the week with a friend."

"Then you'll be alone for awhile. I'll call Karen and see when we can have you to dinner."

"That sounds good," I said vacantly.

"Gotta go. See you in the pits," Joel chirped as he flew out the door, leaving me to change into my scrubs, a job I normally completed in under a minute. This time it seemed like an insurmountable task. It was as if someone had sucked every ATP molecule (the basic source of energy) out of my body. I stopped several times during the process, wondering if I should give it up and go home. How could I be of any use to anyone when I felt so shitty? I knew going home was not an option, so I forced myself to finish dressing. Then I grabbed my stethoscope, a pen, notepad, and a pencil out of my locker, shut the door with a bang, squared my shoulders, and dove into the "land of the pit bulls."

"Where's Tony?" I asked Ellen, a staff RN, as she shoved a patient chart into my hands.

"That's what we'd like to know," she replied. Then she pointed me to an exam room and said simply, "The Red Baron."

As I approached the room, I could hear the familiar verbal "rat-tat-tat" of another of our regulars, a lunger named Elijah Walker. Lunger is the term we give to people who suffer from chronic lung diseases usually associated with smoking. With emphysema, chronic heart failure, and a rock hard alcoholic liver the size of New York, Eli was a walking example of what medical science can do to keep dog food alive. God knows, Eli had dedicated his life to killing himself one drink and smoke at a time, but the medical community was determined to beat God at his own game. Of course, doctors don't save lives. We may have an effect on the time and means, but in the end, God always wins.

His brain cells having floated away decades ago, Eli spent his life living out a perpetual fantasy in which he believed he was the

Red Baron. He usually arrived on a stretcher, wheezing and choking on fluid-filled lungs, yet "rat-a-tat-tatting" with his index finger machine guns pointed toward the invisible enemy in the sky.

"Hello, Eli," I said loudly as I entered the exam room with Ellen who had the IV's and bronchodilators ready to go. The Red Baron sounded juicier than usual. His "rat-tat-tats" were raspy and barely audible, and his normally dusky color had turned a deep purple. God was finally winning. "Looks like you're in a bit of trouble," I said calmly as I tightened a tourniquet around his clammy arm.

Ellen walked around the other side of the stretcher and checked his pulse. "Thready, one hundred and sixty," she said as she placed an oxygen cannula in his nostrils and set the gauge at only two liters per minute. She didn't want to give him too much oxygen and depress the only automatic breathing response he had left.

We breathe because the level of carbon dioxide (CO_2) in our blood gets too high or the oxygen level gets too low. Lungers' CO_2 levels are chronically high, so the body learns to ignore that signal. All they have left is their low O_2 levels to stimulate breathing.

"I don't doubt it," said. I was slapping and massaging the skin beyond the tourniquet, trying to stimulate a vein to bulge enough to get a line into him when the exam room curtain flew open. "You're needed in Trauma one," Joel said in a voice filled with quiet urgency.

I didn't understand why he wanted me to take a trauma case when he was obviously free to do it himself. "Can't you see this guy's in deep trouble here?" I said. "Where's Art?"

Art Hamilton was the other emergency physician who had been scheduled to sign off when I arrived, but never got out the door.

"I'll take over here. You get your ass into Trauma one," Joel ordered. He took hold of my shoulders and forced me out of the exam room. Pissed as hell, I hurried to the Trauma suite. Joel and

I would have a serious talk when I returned.

I stormed through the double doors into the trauma suite and found a flurry of activity surrounding a man who was covered with blood. At first I wondered if it were yet another street knight that had fallen victim to the same kind of attack as Sam's friend, Cal. Art was at the patient's head, intubating him and directing traffic.

"So what's so urgent that I had to be in here, Art?" I asked impatiently. Suddenly, all eyes were on me as if I had taken center stage at the Oscars. "What is it? What's going on?" I asked uneasily, knowing by their reactions that something was terribly wrong.

Art slipped an endotracheal tube down the patient's throat then placed a stethoscope against his chest to make sure he was pumping oxygen into the lungs rather than the stomach. Once he was sure that the intubation was successful, Art turned a sympathetic gaze on me. Though my conscious self had not admitted it, deep in my gut I knew who was on the table. As I moved in closer, I studied the patient's bloody face, praying that my instincts were wrong.

"Now stay calm," Art was saying, stepping toward me with his arms extended. "He's stable."

Art's words echoed to me down a long tunnel. I no longer saw him or anyone else, and I never felt my feet move across the floor toward the table where my worst nightmare was awaiting me. I tried to call Sam's name, but it caught in my throat. I couldn't breathe. Suddenly, I felt like I was floating in a place separate from reality, as if the scene being played out before me was on a movie screen, and I simply a detached observer.

A pair of arms wrapped about me, sending shards of reality into my brain and galvanizing me. "Sam!" I yelled. "My God! Sam!" I spun around to Art. "What happened? Why are you just standing there?"

I grabbed a handful of gauze sponges and wiped at the blood pulsing from Sam's cheek. My actions revealed a gaping hole in the side of his jaw. "Oh, God," I cried as I immediately held pressure against the wound. "Sam, talk to me. Please, Sam," I begged.

Art had busied himself at Sam's side, inserting a chest tube to drain blood from his chest cavity, allowing his lung to re-expand. I plugged a stethoscope into my ears and listened to his chest. My ears were greeted with a sickening sound of a racing heartbeat barely audible beneath the gurgling of his blood filled lungs.

"What's his pressure?" the doctor inside of me called out.

"It's up to ninety over fifty," Michelle answered.

"Forget it, Deb," Art said as he finished suturing the chest tube in place. "You're his wife, not his doctor. We're taking good care of him. The OR's standing by."

"But—"

"No buts, Deb," Art said. Then to the nurses he said, "Let's roll." He stepped on a pedal and released the brakes and the team rolled Sam out of the trauma suite and down the corridor to the operating room. I raced along side the stretcher, holding my unconscious husband's hand. As they rolled the stretcher through the automatic doors leading to the operating suites, Art stopped me.

"Deb," he said sympathetically, " I think it's best that you wait here. I'll turn him over to the surgeons, then we'll talk." He squeezed my hand and followed the stretcher into the OR. As I watched the automatic doors close behind them, I felt a painful tugging at my chest as if someone had reached in and yanked my heart out. My feet grew roots into the floor, and I didn't move from the spot until the doors swung open a million lifetimes later, and Art reappeared.

"Is he—?" I couldn't finish the question, because I didn't want to hear the answer.

"He's alive," Art said flatly, wrapping his arm around my shoulders and guiding me down the hall toward our lounge. "He took three in the chest. Luckily none of them hit his heart or aorta."

I suppose I should have felt a sense of relief at his words, but—there was a but, and I knew what it was.

"The three bullets in his chest did their share of damage, but the one that pierced his jaw is lodged in his brain. We don't know how much damage, but his left pupil is blown and. . . Well . . ."

"I know," I whispered. My words stung as if I had pronounced Sam's death sentence. Though I willingly clung to that one in a million thread of hope, I knew the moment I laid eyes on Sam's bloody face that he was never going to wake up. After you've resuscitated a few hundred critically injured people, you develop a sixth sense about them and can, with reasonable accuracy, identify the winners and the losers before the battle begins. Sam wasn't going to win the battle. Still, I prayed for a miracle.

I stared blankly at Art. While my brain was grasping the reality, my heart and soul could not. It was as if someone had pulled a plug and drained me of all emotion. All that remained inside the shell that had been my body was a dead calm vacuum.

Art opened his mouth to say something when Michelle stuck her head inside the doorway. "I'm really sorry," she said, "but we have a triple coming in. MVA. Two of them are kids."

"I'll be right there," Art told her. "Deb, I've got to go," he said apologetically.

"It's all right," I said. My life had come to a screeching halt, but the world hadn't stopped spinning.

7

An hour after Sam was taken to the OR, I had not yet seen a single cop. No one from the FBI had shown up to inquire about his condition or to talk to me. I had left a half dozen messages with Ben's service. Ben Scolnik had been the local bureau SAC, since God created the earth, or so everyone said. He had been a friendly and flamboyant man until he lost his wife in an auto accident in the late eighties. Rumor had it that her death was a homicide, that she had been run off the road, but it had never been proven. Ben sent his daughter away to live with relatives shortly after the accident, and he had become introspective and reclusive. Though he had been a guest at our dinner table many times before and since his wife's death, I can't say that I knew the man Ben Scolnik had become. I'm not sure anyone really knew him anymore. Sam liked him, though, and trusted him. It had been good enough for me until my phone conversation with him the previous night. That, followed by the lack of Bureau response to Sam's critical injuries, left me feeling more than a little cold.

Not knowing who was responsible for investigating the crime against my husband, the FBI or the Chicago police, and unable to sit and do nothing, I tried calling the CPD local district office. After a major runaround, I was directed to Detective Kim Hawthorne.

"Detective Hawthorne." The voice on the other end of the phone sounded as young as my daughter's.

"My husband was admitted with multiple gunshot wounds more than an hour ago," I barked angrily. "Why haven't I seen any detectives working on the case?"

"And your name is. . .?" Detective Hawthorne inquired in an even, condescending tone.

"Doctor Diane Elizabeth Hunter," I replied sharply. Few people know me by my legal name, Diane Elizabeth. I was born Diane Elizabeth Black. A friend in the third grade began calling me "Deb" when she saw my initials, D.E.B., on a bracelet my grandmother had given me. By the end of the school year, everyone was calling me Deb, and my legal name had been banished to distant memory, only to be resurrected by my mother whenever I got into trouble. Then "DIANE ELIZABETH!" would roll off her tongue like a river of lava from Mt. Kilauea. The nickname stuck even when I traded my maiden name, Black, for my married name, Hunter—though now I'm legally a "D.E.H." instead of a "D.E.B." I sometimes look at the address on my personal checks and wonder who Diane Elizabeth is.

"Your husband was shot?" Hawthorne asked.

"Yes, dammit! Don't you have a record of it?"

Detective Hawthorne didn't answer immediately. I could hear the faint but familiar clicking of fingers racing across a computer keyboard. She was searching the department database for any record of the incident.

"What is your husband's name?"

"Sam Hunter."

"And your address?"

"Do you have a report of the shooting or not?" I demanded. This was absurd, I thought, the cops deposit a victim with multiple gunshot wounds at the local hospital, and there's no record of it?

"Mrs. Hunter, I assure you the matter is being taken care of."

"It is? And how is that?"

"I have a reported shooting of a John Doe late this afternoon, but I need to confirm some information before I am sure this is the right record."

"Where did they take the John Doe?" I asked.

"University Hospital."

"Then you have it," I said. "My husband, Sam Hunter, was

the only gunshot victim brought in today."

"Your address please." Hawthorne's even, non-committal tone was beginning to really piss me off. I knew, however, I wouldn't get anything out of her until I supplied her with the information she wanted, so I gave her my address, phone number, and current location. Afterward, Detective Hawthorne agreed to meet me at the hospital. I felt only minimal satisfaction, but minimal was about as much as I was going to get. An FBI agent was gunned down, and the best I could hope for was a detective who didn't seem to give a rat's ass about it. I comforted myself with the thought that things would be different when Scolnik got my messages.

Waiting was the worst. I don't normally do waiting very well, and this was intolerable. At least a half dozen times, I wandered out of the staff lounge and found myself standing in front of the O.R.'s automatic doors. A couple of times, I nearly gave in to the urge to boldly march through those doors and demand that they tell me what was happening, but I chickened out both times. I didn't want to see my husband splayed out on top of the operating table with his life soaking into the surgical drapes and spilling onto the floor. Unlike the controlled environment of elective surgery, where blood vessels are tied off or cauterized as soon they are cut, trauma surgery is bloody. When a patient is hemorrhaging from multiple sources, the surgeon or surgeons aim for the biggest vessels first and work down from there. The plan is to pump enough fluids into the patient to compensate for blood loss until all the bleeders are caught. Each time, frustrated with the endless waiting and angry at my own cowardice, I wandered back to the staff lounge and kicked a locker or a garbage can. Finally, I gave up and stared out the window at nothing in particular.

Every once-in-awhile, someone from the E.R. staff would stop in the lounge to offer me support. Either Joel or Art would periodically check on the progress in the operating room and report back to me that things were moving along as well a could be expected. How many families have I said that to? Now I was on the receiving end of the bull shit words and phrases. They weren't comforting, not in the least.

I don't know how long it took Detective Hawthorne to show up. Since time had stopped the moment I caught sight of Sam's bloody face, I had no point of reference to judge from. I was standing watch at the window, my head filled with so many conflicting thoughts and images that I couldn't focus on a single rational idea, until I heard the whoosh as the door to the staff lounge swung open behind me. Then only one image filled my head, that of the figure of a surgeon standing in the doorway—his scrubs spattered with blood, and his silent, pain filled eyes staring at me from above a surgical mask, telling me that Sam was lying dead on the operating room table.

I didn't turn around. I couldn't. Each time the door opened, the image became clearer, more vivid. Maybe, just maybe, if I never turned around. . .

"Doctor Hunter?" The voice was young, feminine. I breathed a silent sigh of relief, and yet I felt the skin twitch under my left eye. It often did that when something really irritated me. I recognized that voice.

"Yes" I replied without turning around.

"I'm Detective Kim Hawthorne." This time the voice was next to me. I hadn't heard her cross the floor.

"It's about time," I snapped as I turned to find Farrah Faucet dressed like Lolita standing next to me. What the hell kind of cop was this? She offered her hand for me to shake, but I kept my arms folded across my chest. My face must have betrayed my shock at her appearance.

"Uh, sorry about the get up," she said, "I was headed out to my corner when I got your call."

I felt my eyebrows disappear into my hair line. "Your corner?"

"Yeah, I was gonna help Vice out with John patrol tonight. This is my hooker costume."

Suddenly she cocked her head and giggled. She actually giggled. This person who looked like a hooker and giggled like a kid was going to investigate my husband's shooting? It was definitely time for some reflection. God had to be pissed at me for some past transgression.

Hawthorn suddenly had this surprised look on her face. "You didn't really think a detective would dress like this normally, did you?"

"Of course not," I lied. "Can you tell me," I asked, "how an FBI agent can be shot down in the line of duty, and no one seems to know or care?"

"You're a straight to the point lady, aren't you, Dr. Hunter?" Hawthorne said, then she wrinkled her nose and leaned toward me, lowering her voice as if we were sharing a bit of gossip. "We're not so sure about the line of duty part now, are we?"

I drew back sharply. "What do you mean?" I demanded, feeling the tiny hairs on the back of my neck rise to attention.

Hawthorn's face darkened. Her giggly facade all but washed away. "We both know your husband wasn't on duty when he was shot."

I could feel the sting of my face flushing with the anger growing inside me. "Excuse me?"

Detective Hawthorne sat down on the sofa and removed the bright red faux leather purse from her shoulder. She rummaged around inside the purse for a few seconds and brought out a small steno-style, spiral notebook. She flipped over several pages, forward then backward, until she found the one she was looking for. "Here it is. According to the report, Sam Hunter was shot during a drug deal."

"What?" I was dumbfounded. Sam's job didn't include drug busts. "I don't get it," I said. "Why would he be arresting a drug dealer?"

The little bitch looked up from her notes and smirked at me. "Do I really look that stupid, doctor?"

Actually, she did look pretty stupid dressed like a cheap whore. I handed out a lot of penicillin to women dressed just like she was.

"He wasn't arresting anyone," Hawthorne continued, "He was selling the drugs."

Her statement took my breath away and paralyzed my vocal cords. I felt like I had just been kicked in the chest. Did she just accuse my husband, my Sam, of dealing drugs? Was she as stupid as she looked, or just insane? After a minute of choking on my own spit, I found a hoarse remnant of my voice. "Are you nuts!" I croaked.

"Listen, honey, I didn't investigate the shooting, and I didn't write the report. I'm just telling you what's on it."

She called me "honey." God, I wondered, would this nightmare keep getting worse or was there an end in sight?

"Dear," I said in my most condescending tone, "you've obviously been misinformed.

Hawthorne's eyes narrowed. "I doubt that very much."

"If I recall correctly, the only report you had was about a John Doe. And you doubt that you're misinformed? How often do you use the name John Doe on your reports?"

Hawthorne breathed deeply and set her jaw. "We have a lot more than a name to go on. You, yourself, said your husband was the only John Doe carted into this emergency room today. It's the same man."

"Then the cops who wrote the report made a huge mistake. Sam Hunter is an FBI agent with an impeccable record. If he was in the company of drug dealers, then he was on the job. Besides, why aren't the original investigating detectives following the case?"

Hawthorne looked doubtful for a moment. "I don't know," she said. "It's done from time-to-time when certain detective's case loads get too big."

"So Sam was a dump," I said more to myself than to Hawthorne. "They dumped his case on a rookie."

"I'm not rookie," Hawthorne snapped defensively. "I've worn my gold shield for a long time."

"Really? Then tell me, Detective, what are those experienced instincts telling you right now? Are they telling you that an FBI agent with an outstanding record is nothing but a sleaze ball drug dealer? Do I look like someone who would be married to a drug dealer? I'm a doctor for Christ's sake."

"Listen, I—"

"I suggest you get that narrow, little ass of yours off the couch and do some real police work before you dare accuse my husband of dealing drugs, or suggest that I might somehow be involved. My husband was a victim of a crime, not a participant in one. If I find your investigation lacking because of false assumptions, I'll turn the legal tables around and sue your ass and the City of Chicago. You got that!"

"I understand your being upset—"

"UPSET! UPSET! Outraged is more like it." I could feel what little fingernails I had digging into my palms. "How dare you come in here and accuse my husband of dealing when he's down the hall fighting for his life.

"I'm sorry, but it's all in the report."

"The report is wrong," I said. "The police must have made assumptions at the scene. Sam was unconscious, so he couldn't tell them that he was with the FBI." Hearing my own words explaining the situation, I felt relieved. This would all be cleared up as soon as Scolnik got back to me. "You need to talk to Benjamin Scolnik, the head of the local FBI field office. He'll straighten all of this out for you," I said. "In the mean time, you should be out looking for the shooters."

Hawthorne's eyes narrowed until the irises were barely visible beneath a heavy canopy of faux eyelashes, then she cocked her head and frowned. "There's no mistake, Doctor. The report was clear. The cops didn't just happen to show up after a shoot out. They've had your husband under surveillance for months. They were about to step in and arrest him and his drug dealing buddies when a battle broke out between your husband and a buyer. It made our job easier, because Sam Hunter is the only one who survived, and he's probably not going to make it."

This wasn't real. It couldn't be happening. She couldn't be

talking about Sam. She was wrong. Why couldn't she see that?

"My husband—"

"Your husband was a common criminal. No, he was worse than a common criminal. He was a dirty cop." Hawthorne spat the words out. "Face it, you didn't know the man as well as you thought."

In that instant, I understood what it meant to feel black rage. How easy it would have been to unleash that rage on that pompous little blond-haired bitch. I'll never know if I would have actually gone through with it, because Art walked through the door just as I was posturing and about to pounce on her.

"Deb, are you all right?" Art asked nervously.

My fiery glare jumped from Hawthorne to Art. "No," I hissed.

Art stepped inside the room, and Ben Scolnik entered behind him. My whole body was trembling from the rush of adrenalin that accompanied my rage. "Ben," I said breathlessly. "Tell this. . .this woman that Sam is an FBI agent and not a drug dealer."

To my surprise, Ben did not talk to Hawthorne. Instead, he approached me with a look of sympathy in his eyes. Reaching for my shoulders, he spoke in a calm, soothing voice. "Deb, why don't you sit down, so we can talk."

If anything, his approach fueled my rage. Backing away from his hands, I yelled, "Tell her! Tell her about Sam!"

Ben turned to Detective Hawthorne and Art. "Would you excuse us please?"

As soon as they left the room, Ben turned to me. "Please, Deb, sit down."

"No. I can't sit. Why didn't you tell her the truth?"

A heavy sigh escaped Ben's lips. "Because I don't know what the truth is, exactly."

The nightmare was taking on a life of its own, a beast that was devouring my life. "I don't believe I'm hearing this. What do you mean, you don't know what the truth is? Sam works for you. You're the one who assigned him."

Ben shook his head. "I didn't know how to tell you last night.

I thought you knew all along, but last night it became evident that Sam never told you."

"Told me what?"

"Sam has been on disciplinary leave for the last six months."

8

Scolnik tried to explain what had happened to Sam and why he had been placed on disciplinary leave, but his words were garbled and inaudible above the buzzing already filling my brain. It was as if my head was encased in a vat of honey, and bees were swarming in anticipation of a feast. ". . . racketeering. I couldn't believe it myself when I read. . .," Ben was saying. "I had no choice. . . pending a review and possible indictment."

This wasn't real. It couldn't be. For the first time in my life, I wished an alarm would yank me from my dreams. I wanted out of this nightmare. In spite of my wishes, the nightmare persisted. Six months? How could I have missed the signs? I tried to recall a half year's experiences, searching for some hint that Sam had been troubled. I couldn't point to a single incident or change in behavior that would retrospectively jump out at me with that "Ah Ha!" feeling that comes with hindsight's twenty-twenty vision. Life with Sam had been as normal as it had been for seventeen years.

"He could be facing a prison sentence, if he lives," Scolnik continued.

Though I previously felt sympathetic toward Ben after his wife died, I now hated him for his disloyalty to Sam. "So that's it," I said as I stood up and glared down at the object of my hatred who was still seated on the sofa, "my husband, your friend, is tried, convicted, and sentenced," I said icily.

"No, he's not," Ben said as he stood up to face me. "I am his friend, but I am also his boss. The rules are clear. There are affidavits from agents who had Sam under surveillance as part of an internal investigation. The order to suspend Sam came down from

Washington. I had no choice, but that doesn't mean I believe a word of it."

No longer interested in hearing whatever bullshit Ben had to say, I turned to walk away. When I felt his hand on my shoulder, I stepped out of his reach and spun toward him. "Don't touch me, you sonuvabitch!"

"Deb," he said softly, "I don't know why all of this is happening to Sam. I have my theories, but none of them lead me to his guilt. I know him too well. He is innocent, but my opinion doesn't count. They have hard evidence. I can provide nothing more than a character reference and an impeccable record."

"That should be enough to cast doubt on the accusations," I said.

"It does for me, but good cops have gone bad before."

"Not without a reason," I insisted. "Sam had no reason to become a dirty cop and every reason to be a good one."

"I know, Deb. I know. This all stinks of a—," Ben halted his sentence abruptly. His mouth remained open as if he intended to finish the sentence.

"Of what?" I asked impatiently. "Stinks of what?"

Ben's eyes fell toward his shoes. He shuffled his feet then looked at me from beneath deeply furrowed brows. "This isn't the time to bring it up. It wouldn't be fair to you. Besides, I don't have enough information, not yet at least."

"Are saying you think Sam was framed?"

Ben walked over to the window and stuffed his hands into his pockets. He stared out at something, or nothing at all. Without turning around, he cleared his throat and said, "I think your biggest and only concern right now should be Sam's survival. Let me worry about his job."

I had my answer, and I was nonplussed. Why would anyone want to frame Sam? He was well-liked and respected, not by criminals, of course. But the criminals he dealt with were not in a position to frame him. Then who? Why?

I was about to demand that Ben get his ass out into the field and find a way to clear Sam, when Art entered the room. "Sam's out of surgery. Tom wants to talk to you." Tom Holter was the trauma surgeon who had been operating on Sam. He was one of the best in the business. If there was a thread of hope, he would find it.

I inhaled deeply, steeling myself for what I was about to hear. Art's somber face told me it wasn't going to be news of a miraculous recovery. I looked at Ben who told me to go ahead. We would finish our discussion later. Art rested his arm across my shoulders and walked with me to the recovery room were Sam lay in stillness surrounded by a team of doctors and nurses, their anonymous faces covered by blue fibrous paper masks. S a m ' s bruised and swollen face was barely recognizable. His eyes were taped shut, a common procedure used on anesthetized or comatose patients whose eyes never completely close. It prevents the corneas from drying out. Sam's head was wrapped in a gauze turban, and his chest, likewise, was wrapped with layers of gauze. A recovery room nurse was connecting one of Sam's two chest tubes to a wall suction unit. Another nurse had disconnected him from an ambu bag, a football shaped manual respirator, and attached his endotracheal tube to an MA-1 respirator. The MA-1's corrugated bellows hissed and popped as it moved up and down inside its clear cylindrical housing—an external lung breathing for Sam. Everyone had a job and performed it efficiently. Tom, a tall, attractive man with distinguished looking silver hair peeking out beneath a surgical cap and his mask hanging around his neck, was quietly directing traffic. He was the stereotypical surgeon, pompous and arrogant, but he was damn good. In fact, he was one of the ten best in the world. I guess, in a way, his arrogance was earned.

When Tom's eyes met mine, he handed the job of directing traffic to his assistant and walked toward me. Taking me by the arm, he directed me to the corridor outside the recovery area and out of earshot. "Are you OK?" He asked. "Do you need to sit down?"

"No. I just need you to tell me how Sam is."

Tom rubbed his chin and gazed at me with sad, compassionate eyes. All traces of his supercilious attitude were gone. "I'm not going to pretend with you, Deb. It doesn't look good."

I swallowed hard in an attempt to hold onto my composure. "Art told me he was shot with a hollow point bullet."

"It looked like it at first, with the amount of damage it did to his jaw, and his neuro exam suggested extensive brain damage. As it turns out, the bullet was a standard nine millimeter. It did its share of damage, but nothing we couldn't fix given time."

For a split second I felt hopeful, but Tom's voice betrayed another "but". "That's good news," I said, trying to convince myself that I had misread his voice.

Tom frowned and tilted his head quizzically. "Deb," he said, "there's no easy way to ask this." He hesitated for a moment, then dropped yet another bomb on my already devastated brain. "Was Sam using drugs?"

I must have moved beyond shock to a dissociative state where emotions no longer existed. On an intellectual level, my flat emotional response surprised me. "He never touched anything stronger than Motrin or Tylenol. Why are you asking me that?"

"The anesthesiologist found traces of a white crystalline powder in his nostrils. It could be cocaine or heroine. We think that's why his initial neuro exams were so bad. To complicate matters further, he arrested several times during surgery. If the drugs hadn't factored into the situation, he might have had a chance."

"Did you run a tox screen?" I asked with clinical detachment as if I were talking about a total stranger.

"Yes. The results aren't back yet, but I have no doubt he has controlled substances on board."

"You could be wrong," I argued, but without the fuel that normally energized my debates.

Normally, Tom would have some biting counter attack when I questioned his judgement about anything. This time, however, his response was soft spoken and kind. "How often are *you* wrong about that kind of thing?"

"Rarely," I replied.

Tom returned to his patient, promising to notify me of any changes in Sam's condition, and to tell me when they were transferring him to the Trauma Critical Care Unit(TCCU), an eleven bed unit designated for the care of massive trauma cases. Left with a sense of total helplessness, I wandered back toward the familiarity of the emergency department and the safety of the staff lounge.

9

Back at the staff lounge, I paced back and forth, sat down, got up, walked to the window, and stared at the walls. I was lost. My mind was a jumbled mess, and I was incapable of completing a single rational thought. So much had happened. Not only had I to deal with Sam's critical injuries, but also the accusations against him. And I had to tell Shelby. How could I tell Shelby what had happened? What would I tell her? She would surely hear about it sooner or later. An FBI agent caught dealing drugs? It would be all over the news. I wouldn't allow Shelby to hear it that way. What was I going to do? She was so far away. I couldn't tell her over the phone. I had to get her home somehow.

I called the Coopers' cottage. There was no answer, and the answering machine didn't kick in. That was fine with me. I didn't know what kind of message I would have left on the machine had it been working. I hung up the phone and returned to my post in front of the window where I watched the deepening crimson of the sunset reflected in the windows across the courtyard. It still hadn't registered that it was August and the sky didn't turn that dark until late. Not until a light swallowed the sun's fading reflection on one of the windows and illuminated the patient's room directly behind it, did I think to look at my watch. It was nearly nine o'clock. In my mind, time had slowed down to a crawl when all the while it was speeding past me like a video tape in fast forward. Had five hours really elapsed since Sam had been admitted?

I tried Cooper's again. Still no answer. And again, I was relieved. On one hand, I was anxious to tell Shelby and get it over with, but on the other hand, I felt no urgent need to become the purveyor of the bad news that would steal my daughter's happiness away from her.

As I lay the receiver in its cradle, my pager vibrated on my hip. The LED showed the extension for the TCCU. I knew the page was to inform me that Sam had been transferred to the unit, so I headed straight for there without bothering to answer the page.

It may sound strange to say it, but I loved the TCCU. I found myself most alive in that place where people were closest to death. Working with patients under such adverse circumstances requires total focus, total use of every skill, talent, and brain cell I have. Losing such patients is inevitable and tragic, but winning. . . My dream had been to become a trauma surgeon, but it's a profession that owns your life. I knew I wanted to be a mother to my child and a wife to Sam, so I opted to become an emergency room physician. It's a great profession for a man or woman who wants to participate in family life and still provide valuable service to people during some of the most frightening and tragic moments of their lives.

The first cubicle I saw, when the automatic doors leading to the TCCU swooshed open, was Latisha's. I didn't recognize the person mummied in gauze, but Paula, the nurse who was suctioning Latisha's tracheostomy tube, saw me and pointed at her patient. "She looks pretty good considering, wouldn't you say?"

Paula must have seen the confusion on my face as she left Latisha's cubicle and walked toward me. "It's Latisha Jones. You know, the butcher knife lady?" Paula said as she acted out the shower scene from psycho complete with a shrill "Ee. . .Ee. . .Ee
. . .Ee. . ." Under normal circumstances I would have laughed at her sick humor, but my ability to laugh at life had flowed down the drain in the floor of the emergency trauma suite along with Sam's blood. In a way, I wish I had been able to muster a laugh. I think it would have helped.

"Are you OK?" Paula asked.

"I'm looking for a patient."

"The one they just brought in?" she asked. "Is he yours?"

"Yes, he's my husband."

Paula gasped and her hand flew to her gaping mouth. "You're kidding? she said. "I heard rumors, but. . . He's in bed eleven."

"I'm really sorry." I heard her say as I walked briskly toward cubicle eleven. Tom greeted me at the doorway to Sam's cubicle. "How is he?" I asked looking past him to the still figure that lay in the bed in front of me.

"About the same," Tom replied.

"What's that for? Have his kidneys failed?" I asked when I noticed a technician setting up a portable dialysis machine next to Sam's bed.

"No, but the results of the tox screen came back."

"And?"

"Deb, he has enough heroine on board to kill an elephant. Frankly, I don't know how he can be alive. We flushed his nose and mouth as soon as we saw the crystals, and we dosed him with Naloxone. It's probably too late, but we're going to dialyze him, and try to clear it out of his tissues."

"I don't believe it."

"I don't know what to tell you," Tom said as he shrugged and shook his head. "There's no mistake. The lab report confirmed our findings."

I could feel a fullness in my eyes as if they were trying to expel tears, but nothing came. Instead, I hurt all over. It was an ache that surrounded and crushed my body. How could I miss heavy drug use in my own husband? I'm a doctor who works in an inner city emergency department. I see drug abuse all the time. There are signs and symptoms, especially in the heavy users. But there were no signs in Sam; no runny, red nose, no weight loss, no personality changes, no signs at all. None of this made any sense.

"May I be with him now?" I asked.

"Deb, you look exhausted," Tom said. "Spend a couple of minutes with him then go home and rest. He's stable right now, and I'll be right here with him for the next several hours."

"I can't go home. What if—?"

"You know he couldn't be in better hands. The nurses in this unit are some of the best in the country and like I said, I won't be leaving for awhile. I'll page you the instant we see any change, any change at all, good or bad."

He was right. I was exhausted. I hadn't eaten in hours, and I had barely slept, but I wasn't about to leave the hospital, not with Sam hanging on by a thread. "I'll be fine," I said. Then I stepped past him into the cubicle and next to Sam's side. I found it difficult at first to touch or even relate to the figure in the bed. It was as if this was not a real person, but a mannequin who merely looked like my Sam. I reached for his hand, then hesitated. Though I was a doctor and knew better, I was afraid that it would be cold and clay-like attached to a seemingly lifeless body. I didn't want to feel Sam's hand if I couldn't feel the life in it. That wasn't the memory I wanted to carry with me for the rest of my life.

Finally, I found the courage to brush my fingers lightly along the back of his hand. It felt warm. It felt like Sam's hand. I took it into mine and caressed it. Then I dragged it along my cheek and kissed it. I studied the little bit of Sam's bruised and swollen face that was showing beneath bandages and tape and behind the endotracheal tube.

"Sam," I said, "it's Deb. I don't know if you can hear me, but I'm here. I will always be here for you. I love you, Sam." I kissed my fingertips and touched them to Sam's cheek. Then I pressed his hand against my cheek. "I need you, Sam. Shelby needs you, too. Try to find your way back to me, please, baby, please."

It's an inexplicable feeling, only those who have experienced it can understand, to touch a loved one whom you don't know is alive or dead. Before technology, recognition was clear, a person was either alive or dead. But now, we can keep bodies going long past the moment when their brains have died. Being a devout Catholic, I believe in the human soul. I wondered, as I held Sam's hand, whether his soul was still with him or if it had already moved on to another place, leaving me holding its empty shell.

As that thought ran through my head, I begged God to give Sam back to me. If that weren't possible, I wanted Him to let me know beyond all doubt that Sam was gone. It would never be Sam's wish to have his body hover in perpetual limbo. If it came to a decision, and looking at Sam, I knew it might, I wanted to be relieved of all doubt before I had to sign the appropriate papers.

I continued to linger at Sam's bedside until I felt the weight of Tom's hand on my shoulder. "Deb, it's going to be a long night. Go lie down before you fall down."

Reluctantly, I let go of Sam's hand and stepped outside of the cubicle, so Tom and the staff could get their work done. I continued to stand in corridor and watch over Sam until I felt my legs turning to rubber beneath me. Tom was right, I needed to eat and sleep if I was going to be of any use to my husband and daughter. Again, I glanced at my watch. It was after ten. Shelby and the Coopers would have surely returned to the cottage by now.

As I passed by the desk on my way out of the unit, I impressed upon the unit secretary that she was to page me immediately if there was any change in Sam's condition no matter how slight. Then I headed toward the cafeteria where I planned to force myself to eat or at least drink a large glass of juice. On the way, I stopped in the staff lounge to call Shelby. Michelle was sitting in the lounge with her shoeless feet lying across the coffee table, a cigarette in one hand and a Diet Coke in the other.

"How's Sam?" she asked.

I shrugged and shook my head. "I don't know," I replied as I mindlessly fanned the smoke away, a habit born out of years of experience growing up with and then working with smokers.

Michelle looked at the cigarette then at me. "I know. I should quit," she apologized, "but they do calm me down after a night like we just had."

I responded with a minimal half-smile and dropped into the chair across from Michelle and next to the phone. As I dialed, I tried to pump myself up so my voice wouldn't betray the gravity of my current situation. The last thing I wanted was to have the Cooper's racing Shelby home in a panic with her sobbing in the back seat. A series of ideas about what I might say were bandying about inside my mind when the phone began ringing.

After fifteen rings went unanswered, I began to feel a spark of uneasiness. Something was wrong at the Coopers'. I didn't want to think terrible thoughts, but I worked in an emergency department, and my husband was in critical condition from multiple gunshot wounds. My mind had no place else to go but to the frightening possibilities.

"What's wrong?" Michelle asked.

"Huh?" I replied only vaguely aware that she had spoken.

"You look worried?"

Still a little confused, I looked at Michelle then at the phone, and it dawned on me what she was asking. "Oh," I said. "It's just . . .well. . . Shelby's staying with some friends, and I can't seem to get ahold of her. They haven't been home all evening."

"Shelby doesn't know yet?"

"No."

"Oh, Deb, I wish there was something I could do?"

"Pray, I guess."

"Have you eaten?"

"No."

"I'm off duty. I'll go with you to the cafeteria."

"That's all right. You don't have to."

"I want to. My stomach's empty, and this Coke's doing shit for it."

I acquiesced easily, because I didn't want to be alone. As I got up, Michelle said, "You're probably going to spend the night here, aren't you?"

"I can't go home," I said.

"You're going to need a shower and change of clothes. Why don't I run to your house and pack a small bag for you?"

"Michelle, that's very nice, but you have to be exhausted."

"I'm young. I can take it." She said as she slipped her arm

through mine and walked with me out of the lounge and down to the cafeteria." I was reminded why I dearly loved Michelle. She truly had a heart of gold.

10

While Michelle and I were eating— I use the term loosely, since I had a plate full of food in front of me that I had been stirring with my fork, but none of it had reached my lips—Kim Hawthorne showed up and plunked herself down at the table. "So, what are you ladies talking about?" she asked effervescently.

I didn't like Detective Hawthorne very much. In fact, I didn't like her at all. She was a space cadet, and I never liked women who acted stupidly.

Growing up, I had always been irritated by the girls who practiced and perfected their ditzy routines for the sole purpose of getting dates. And the boys flocked to them. Even then, the boys were easily dragged around by their dicks. Any girl who was willing to apply war paint to her face and act like a helpless bimbo was on a different date every night of the weekend, while the rest of us earned a lot of money babysitting.

Kim Hawthorne acted like she had not yet outgrown bimboism. I did notice, however, that her choice of attire had become more conservative; a tailored white blouse, navy slacks, and black pumps. I wondered if the business look was for my benefit. Since I was under her scrutiny, she might try to dupe me into trusting her more if she played the conservative role. I didn't buy it for a minute.

"What can we do for you, Detective?" I asked coolly. "I thought my husband's was and open and shut case."

"Well, actually," Hawthorne said, "I'm not here about your husband, doctor."

"Really?" I responded, my curiosity piqued.

"Do you believe in coincidences?" Hawthorne asked, continuing before I could answer her. "I don't. I guess I used to, but I've learned that there's no such thing as a coincidence. It only appears that way." She took a bite out of the greasy hotdog she had on her food tray. Instantly, her face twisted in disgust, and she tossed the hotdog onto the tray. "You eat this crap?" Then her eyes fell to my plate where my food had been sculpted into a grotesque mountain. "I guess not," she said, again answering her own question. For a moment, I wondered if I were to become an active participant in this conversation.

All this time, Michelle was eyeing the bimbo-like creature and recoiling in her chair. "Uh, if this conversation is private, I can leave," she said, sporting a sarcastic smile.

I glared at her with an "if you leave me now, I'll kill you" look.

"Please don't leave, Ms. Johnson. It is Ms. Johnson?" Hawthorne said, leaning over to see Michelle's name badge, thus perpetuating her autonomous conversation. "This involves you, too."

Michelle's face sobered. "Me? What do you want with me?"

Before answering Michelle, Hawthorne whipped out a small spiral notebook and a pen. She flipped past the first few pages, then asked. "You both work with a man named Tony Jackson. Am I right?"

Michelle's and my jaws dropped simultaneously. "Tony!" I snapped.

"What did Tony do?" Michelle asked.

"He didn't do anything." Hawthorne shrugged. "At least I don't know that he did anything," she said.

"What do you want with him?" I asked.

"When's the last time either of you saw him?"

"A couple of night's ago," I said, and Michelle nodded her agreement. I pushed my food tray aside and rested my elbows on the table, a move that brought me into closer eye contact with Hawthorne. "Something's happened to Tony, hasn't it?"

"You haven't heard? I'm surprised. I thought surely you people would have been told by now. You worked with him."

"Worked?" Michelle's eyebrows shot skyward. "What do you mean worked? We *work* with Tony."

"Not anymore, honey. Mr. Jackson is dead." Hawthorne's words shot through me like a razor sharp dagger. I immediately looked at Michelle whose face had paled to a grayish clay.

"Dead?" I asked in a hoarse whisper. "When? How?"

His body was found a few hours ago. He's been dead for about two days, give or take. We're trying to establish approximate time of death."

"I thought the forensic entomologist could do that?" I said, having recovered from the initial shock.

"Familiar with crime investigations, are you?" Hawthorne said, her voice laced with sarcasm. I guess she took to me about as well as I had taken to her. We were oil and water.

"Somewhat, I replied. "My husband was a Chicago cop before he joined the FBI. I took an interest in his work and did some reading on my own."

"Nice for you," Hawthorne said.

"How did Tony die?" I asked.

"I don't think you really want to know."

Hawthorne's answer turned my blood to ice. Her reluctance hinted at the possibility that the details were especially gruesome. Detectives become desensitized to crime scenes fairly quickly. It's necessary to their survival. If Hawthorne thought Tony's death was too horrible to talk about, it had to be unusually bad.

"You forget, Detective, that we work in an inner city emergency department," I said. "I don't think you could shock us."

"Well, I'll tell you this much. Mr. Jackson did not die quickly."

"I don't understand," Michelle said.

But I understood from the look on Hawthorne's face and the sound of her voice. "He was tortured?" I asked barely above a whisper not wanting to hear the words I had just spoken.

Hawthorne nodded, and Michelle paled even more. "Michelle? Are you all right?" I asked.

"I. . ." Her eyes glazed over.

I jumped up, snatched her food tray and tossed it onto a neighboring table. "Put your head down," I ordered. Obediently, Michelle folded her arms on the table and lay her head down. I scooped an ice cube out of my water glass and rubbed her neck with it.

"Is she going to be OK?" Hawthorne asked. This time her voice was filled with genuine compassion.

"Michelle and Tony are very close friends. They attended school together since the second grade."

"I'm sorry. This was a dreadful way for her to find out about him."

"Yes it was," I said.

After a minute or so, Michelle sat up. Her color had returned, and tears filled her eyes. I envied her her tears. I had not been able to shed any.

"I've got to get out of here," she announced. "I'll answer all your questions, Detective, but I need to. . . I don't know. . . I just need. . ."

"Go ahead," Hawthorne said. "But I want to talk to you soon. I can come to your apartment, if it's more comfortable."

"No," Michelle said. Then she looked at me. "Give me your keys. I'll pack you a bag. That'll give me time to clear my head."

"Are you sure?" I asked.

"Yes," she replied. Then she turned to Hawthorne. "I should be back in less than an hour. I'll meet you in our staff lounge. Will that be OK?"

"Yes," Hawthorne replied.

I gave Michelle's hand a squeeze as she started to rise out of her seat. "I'll be fine," she said, returning my squeeze. "You've enough on your mind without worrying about me." Then she departed, leaving me to stare at Hawthorne.

After a few moments of strained silence, Hawthorne spoke. "You remember what I said about coincidences?"

"You don't believe in them?"

"I meant that."

"What does that have to do with this?"

"I've been doing a little checking," Hawthorne said while flipping through her notebook. "Let's see, you got a John Doe in here Friday night, and the body seems to be missing. At least the morgue hasn't got it." All traces of the ditz I had previously seen had vanished. Hawthorne's demeanor had become serious and professional.

How did she know about the missing John Doe? I wondered. Why was it important to her? Hawthorne definitely had my attention.

"The next night, you're seen removing John Doe's belongings and later returning them," she said.

I stared at Hawthorne in total shock and disbelief, but said nothing. How did she find out about that? Who would have told her, and how did she know to ask the questions in the first place? Then I wondered; had *she* been driving the Blazer?

"Your face has confirmed what I already knew, Doctor, and all I've got to say is this: You may be skilled in medicine, but stealth isn't one of your strong suits," Hawthorne said with an impudent smile.

Should I admit to taking the bag, or should I act like I just had a frontal lobotomy? Why was the bag that the other cops thought insignificant suddenly so important to Sam and now to the CPD? There wasn't anything worthwhile in it.

"Why d'ya take the bag, Doctor?"

I sat stone faced while my brain raced through a million possible excuses. I wasn't about to tell her that Sam asked for the bag. She had already convicted him in her mind, and I wasn't about to serve him to her on a silver platter. I had no idea what Sam's connection was with this "Cal" person, and I wasn't going to say anything until I knew what that connection was.

"Well, Doctor? I'm waiting."

Keeping my facial expression as blank as possible, I lied through my teeth. "I was wearing a very special locket when I came to work that night, and I didn't realize until the next day that it was missing."

"Wait a minute. Let me get this straight. You had a locket that was so special to you that you forgot you had been wearing it. Then, in the middle of the night, you decide to drive all the way into work and take home a bag of smelly, bloody clothing so you can look for the locket?" Hawthorne sat back and folded her arms across her chest. "And you expect me to buy that?" she said incredulously.

"Yes." My glare challenged her to prove otherwise.

Hawthorne smiled and sat forward in her chair. "Did you find your locket?" she asked sarcastically.

"No."

"It's too bad, really. Tony might be alive today, had you found your locket."

"What!" My voice erupted in a near screech. "Are you saying I had something to do with Tony's death?"

"Lighten up, doctor," Hawthorne said. "I'm not accusing you of anything, yet. I'll tell you this: I don't like being lied to. We'll get along a helluva lot better if you remember that about me." She leaned back in her chair. "The fact of the matter is, your orderly, Mr. Tony Jackson, called the county medical examiner's office and our district office several times each, trying to get someone to pick up a bag of clothing and. . ." She glanced at her notepad. ". . . Some teeth(?) that belonged to John Doe."

"Yes, I told him to make those calls."

"Don't you see it? We have a John Doe who's been beaten and stabbed to death. His body disappears on the way to the morgue. Then we have the orderly who contacted us about John Doe's belongings. He's been tortured to death." Hawthorne looked at me squarely, her eyes cold, and deadly serious. "And you sneak John Doe's clothes out of the hospital the day before your husband gets shot up in a drug bust. Now you're lying your ass off as to the reason you took the bag of clothing home. "D'ya see it now, Doctor? I don't like coincidences."

11

Detective Hawthorne had surprised me, bowled me over was more like it, and I was beginning to question my initial impression of her. If she was as astute as she now appeared to be, then she might be someone who would track down the necessary evidence to clear Sam. I thought of telling her the truth about Sam's phone calls and his connection with "Cal," but unsure of her response and worried that I might say something that would incriminate him further, I held my tongue.

Hawthorne leaned toward me and her eyes narrowed. "What I'd like to know is: What's your husband got to do with all of this?"

"Why do you think Sam has anything to do with the others?" I asked innocently, trying not to allude to the fact that there was, indeed, a connection.

"Let's just say it's a hunch," she replied, her voice cryptic. She knew something she wasn't telling me. Not only did I hear it in her voice, I could see it in the glint in her eyes.

"This situation is a little too serious for you to be acting on hunches, isn't it?"

Hawthorne smiled. "We couldn't solve a single crime without them, Doctor. Hunches or gut feelings, whatever you want to call them, don't just crop up on their own. We take in information through all of our senses. We don't usually see one big thing that leads us to solve a crime. Y'know, the ol' smoking gun theory. Instead there're a lot of little things that don't seem so important by themselves, but together. . . well. . . they become a hunch."

She studied my face for a moment. She was sizing me up,

reading my body language, possibly even my thoughts for all I knew, forming a 'hunch' about me, maybe. I wasn't sure, but suddenly I felt uncomfortable, like I was under the lens of a microscope.

"I'll bet it happens to you sometimes," Hawthorn continued, "a patient comes in with some vague complaint, yet you know right here," she pointed to her belly, "that there's something serious going on inside, so you perform more tests than your patient's complaint might call for." She tilted her head quizzically. "You know what I mean, doc? If your gut didn't warn you, you might miss finding a serious illness."

I nodded my agreement. I knew exactly what she meant. I also knew her cop's gut had steered her onto the right path, and that path led to my husband and the so called charges against him. I wondered if that over active gut of hers also told her that the charges against Sam couldn't possibly be true. They didn't even make sense.

"I can't imagine what I can do for you, Detective," I said.

"You can start by telling me who this John Doe was? Was he one of Sam's buddies? A customer perhaps?"

"So now you're accusing Sam of killing John Doe?"

"It's a definite possibility."

"This is insane. Sam had nothing to do with it, and he doesn't have any customers!"

"Then why were you tampering with evidence?"

"Wait. You think I'm part of this?"

"The thought had crossed my mind."

I was wrong. She wasn't astute, she was certifiable, and a real idiot. "I can't believe it!"

"Listen, Doc. In the courts, everyone's innocent until proven guilty. In order for me to do my job, everyone is guilty until proven innocent. It has to be that way. If I assume you're innocent, I might stop looking for the important clues. A suspicious mind is always open to the details and never leaves a stone unturned."

"So I'm under the microscope along with Sam."

"That's about the size of it."

"Should I be interviewing defense attorneys?"

"Not unless you know something I don't. All I have on you right now is your marital relationship with an accused drug dealer, and the fact that you took a bag filled with potential evidence away from the hospital."

"Great. Now what am I suppose to do?"

"Well, I'll tell you. Your full and honest cooperation will be greatly appreciated and might convince me of your innocence. In spite of all I've said, I'd prefer to believe that you're innocent."

"That's comforting," I snarled. Hawthorne shrugged away my comment, demonstrating her lack of concern for my discomfort. She was really pissing me off. I fantasized hanging her from the ceiling, like one of the heavy bags we use in Taekwondo, and using her for kicking practice. Instead, I decided that it might be to all of our benefits to be cordial to this woman who, I believed, had the power to help or destroy both Sam and me. An antagonistic relationship with her wouldn't be productive. "So where do we go from here?" I asked with forced affability.

Again the scrutiny before the words. "When's the last time you saw or spoke with Tony Jackson?"

I thought for a moment. I couldn't remember what day or time I was currently existing in, so I had difficulty remembering when it was that I last spoke to Tony. I knew it had been in the locker room about John Doe's teeth. John Does teeth. What had happened to them? I had told Tony to put them into the bag with the guy's clothes, but they weren't there when I took the bag home. I guessed it wasn't important, since the body was nowhere to be found. The man wasn't going to miss his teeth.

"Can you remember when you last saw Tony Jackson alive?" Hawthorne's re-stated question resurrected me from my musing.

"It was Friday night, I believe. I was getting ready to go home. Tony stopped by the locker room to ask about the disposition of John Doe's body."

"Why'd he want to know?" Hawthorne asked.

Not seeing what Tony's and my conversation had to do with anything, I shrugged and replied. "We had the bag of clothes and a couple of the man's teeth. The cops who hauled him to the morgue forgot to take them."

"Which cops?"

I shrugged again. "I don't know. I never saw them before. They said they were from downtown."

Hawthorne frowned deeply. "D'ya remember their names?"

I could barely remember what day it was. How was I to remember the names of two total strangers? "Now you're asking a lot," I said.

"I know, but it's important if I'm going to get to the bottom of this."

I closed my eyes and tried to recall the two cops. I immediately remembered that I hadn't liked their attitudes. "One was tall and the other short and fat, not grossly obese but round. He had a big gut, a beer belly." I opened my eyes and glanced at her in search of affirmation that my information was useful.

"That's a start," Hawthorne said without looking at me. She was writing furiously in her notebook. I guessed that meant I should continue, so I closed my eyes again. At first, I could see the two uniformed men, but their faces had no detail. With a little more effort, though, they came into focus. "The tall one," I tried to see his name badge in my mind's eye, but it wasn't coming to me. "was attractive. He had light brown skin, curly hair and hazel eyes."

"Light brown skin? Was he white, black?"

"Mixed, I think."

"Mulatto?"

"I think so."

"You said he was tall. How tall?"

"Over six feet," I said.

"Good. Good. Can you remember his name? Do you have a copy of the forms he signed when you released the body to them?"

"I don't know who signed the forms, but one of them must have before they took the body."

"Good," Hawthorne repeated. "That'll help us *if* he didn't falsify the signature."

That took me by surprise. "Why would he falsify his signature?" I asked.

"There're a lot of possible reasons," Hawthorne said, "but we don't need to bother with them now. How about the short one?"

"Like I said, he had a beer gut. He was light complected, but his hair and eyes were dark." I pictured him again. "Actually, his complexion was ruddy. He had spider angiomas on his nose and cheeks."

Hawthorne's left eyebrow shot up. "Spider angiomas?"

"Little bluish-red veins on the nose and cheeks. They're often a sign of chronic heavy drinking."

"A boozer cop, eh?" Hawthorne said.

"That surprises you?" I asked.

"Not at all. My dad was one. It finally killed him."

"I'm sorry."

"Don't be. I'm not. If the booze hadn't killed him, I might have."

Hm. Another peek behind the eyes of the young woman detective, I thought. The more we spoke, the more enigmatic Kim Hawthorne became. Was my original impression of her something manufactured inside my own mind, or did she exploit her demure, child-like appearance by acting like a bimbo? I thought about the TV series, COLUMBO, in which Peter Faulk played a detective in a raggy looking overcoat who stalked the guilty by acting absentminded and pestering them until they either tripped themselves up or confessed out of sheer frustration. Maybe Hawthorne used her bimbo act so people wouldn't feel threatened. One thing was for certain; Kim Hawthorne wasn't grilling me like an airhead.

"Other than not knowing them, did anything bother you about them, their behavior, their uniforms, anything?" Hawthorne asked.

"They were cold-hearted bastards. I remember that much." I

thought some more. "Their uniforms were fine. They were wearing name plates. The tall's guy's name began with an E, I believe." I struggled to pull a name out of my memory. "Erikson? No. Evan? No. Heart, something heart."

Hawthorne watched me struggle and listened intently, but she offered no help. A good detective knows better than to lead a witness, and it was becoming unmistakably clear that Kim Hawthorne was a good detective.

"Ern...?" Then suddenly it came to me. "Eberhardt! That's it. Eberhardt."

"Which one was Eberhardt?" Hawthorne's eyes were twinkling with excitement. My giving her a name clearly meant something to her.

"The tall blond one," I replied. I was pleased with myself for having remembered what, at the time, had seemed incidental. Since I hadn't liked the cops, and they didn't work in my district, I had not tried to remember their names.

"How about the short one? Do you remember his name?"

That one escaped me. I guess I must have been taken with the tall one's good looks more than I realized. "I'm sorry, but it's not there," I said regretfully.

"What you've given me is good. This'll help. We'll check the release forms. Maybe the other one signed them. It's a start. It's definitely a start," Hawthorne said.

"Why do you think Tony was killed?" I asked.

"I suspect that whoever killed John Doe was looking for the same thing you were looking for."

"What?"

"John Doe must've had something that belonged to the killer or killers. They must've assumed Tony had it or knew where it was."

"I was looking for my necklace," I insisted, "and I can tell you there wasn't anything in the bag besides his clothing."

"If you're being honest with me and you're not involved, then you and your co-workers might be in danger," Hawthorne said soberly.

"So you believe me now?"

"About your quest for the missing locket? No. But I've got to be open to all possibilities, including the fact that you could be telling the truth, in which case, you could be the next target."

"In danger?" I whispered, suddenly recalling the blue Blazer that had followed me home, and fearing for Shelby's safety.

"It might be a good idea for me to have the list of names of all the staff that was on duty that night. Any one of you could be targeted."

Jesus, I thought. The blue Blazer left almost immediately after Shelby and the Coopers. Could it have followed them? "What about our families?" I asked.

"What about them?" Hawthorne returned.

"My daughter, Shelby, is she also in danger?"

"Not directly, but there's always the potential risk. Where is she now?"

"Staying with some friends in their cottage in Wisconsin. I've been trying to reach them to bring Shelby home."

"If you want my advice," Hawthorne said, "don't call them."

"But Shelby has to be told about her father."

"I realize that, but hold off until I find out more about the situation. At least, she's safe where she is? Right?"

I was ambivalent about calling Shelby, but I understood Hawthorne's point. I relieved my guilt over not calling her with the idea that there might be better news a few hours from now. "I'll wait, but only until late morning."

12

Hawthorne finally concluded her interrogation, though she insisted that it wasn't. We were leaving the cafeteria when my pager went off. The display showed my home number. It was Michelle. She probably couldn't find everything she was looking for. I stopped at one of the in-house phones hanging on the wall at the exit and had the hospital operator dial my number. Michelle answered before I heard it ring. "Deb? Is that you?" She sounded distraught.

"Yes, Michelle. Is there a problem?"

"I think you'd better come home quickly."

"Why? What happened?"

"Just come home," Michelle said despondently, and the line went dead. I re-dialed, but there was no answer.

Jesus! I thought. Now what?

I started out the door when Hawthorne appeared. At first, I wasn't going to say anything, then I thought better of it. "Detective," I said, "I just talked to Michelle. She's at my house and wants me to go home immediately. Something isn't right."

"I'll drive," Hawthorne said without hesitation.

Parked in the visitors' lot, her car was considerably farther away from the hospital than mine. When I pointed this out and offered to drive, she declined saying I didn't have a souped up engine, siren, and flashing red light.

No, I thought, but I drive like I do.

We covered the distance from the hospital to my street in about half the time it normally takes me. Granted, Hawthorne didn't have to stop for any lights, but still . . .

"And they call me 'Lead Foot Lizzy'," I said as we turned onto my street.

"Why do you think I became a cop?" Hawthorne joked.

"There, that's my house."

"Gotcha." She parked and killed the lights and engine in almost the exact spot where the Blazer had been parked a couple of days ago. I knew immediately why she chose that spot. It wasn't visible from any windows in my house.

Hawthorne took a serious looking stainless steel Smith & Wesson automatic pistol from her shoulder holster and, directing me to cup my hand over the interior light, opened the car door. "You wait here," she said. "I'll check it out."

"Why do you need a gun?" I asked. "Michelle didn't say there was a prowler or anything like that."

"Maybe, but the hairs on the back of my neck are standing at attention. Considering what's happened to all the others, I would rather be safe than sorry."

I didn't argue. She was the cop, and I had to accept that she knew what she was doing.

I watched nervously as she darted from tree to tree. The occasional street lights guided her way, but also afforded her the cover of shadows. It was when she moved around to the front of my garage that I saw it. It seemed like a phantom at first, a trick of the eyes, but a second movement and a glint of metal told me my eyes were working just fine. Someone had come out from the rear of my house and was now stalking Detective Hawthorne.

I felt a sudden deep churning inside my gut, and my heart pounded in my chest. What the hell was I going to do? Should I try Hawthorne's radio and call it in? But what if the police got here too late? I had to do something and fast. I reached up and popped the covering to the dome light and unscrewed the bulb, then I opened my car door as quietly as possible and slid to the ground. I didn't bother closing the door for fear the sound would attract the phantom's eye. Moving in closer, I got a glimpse of the metallic object that had flashed in the light. It was an impressive blade, military issue, double-edged and serrated. Its owner, dressed in black, moved swiftly and silently like a great panther stalking its prey. He was closing in on Hawthorne. I circled around to the side of the garage and behind the man. As I closed in on him, my foot crushed a twig and my heart sank. The man, his face smeared with black paste, spun around toward me, but I must have been better hidden by the shadows than I thought, because his eyes scanned the darkness around me without seeing me. I held my breath, hoping he would assume that an animal had made the noise and give up his search. My hopes were dashed when he started in my direction, though his eyes were, as yet, not on me. Panic was threatening to overwhelm and disable me as he closed the distance between us. Clearly, in spite of my training, this man would overpower me. Not only was he twice my size but staring at the serious blade in his hand, it was easy to assume that he was better trained in hand-to-hand combat. Besides, I had never used Taekwondo on anyone other than in class or at tournaments. In neither instance had my life been at risk. It was now, and I could only hope that I'd have the courage to do what was necessary. I *did* have enough adrenalin coursing through my veins. Another step closer and I was faced with the "now or never" decision.

My first thought was to aim for the knife, so I flung my foot toward it with a crescent kick. While I didn't knock the knife from his hand as I had hoped, I did manage to move his hand to his inside across his chest, exposing his rib cage. Seizing the split-second window of opportunity, I spun around with a backside kick and slammed my heel into his ribs. I know I cracked at least one. I heard it snap and felt the rib give under my heel.

With a groan, the man recoiled from my kick. Convinced I had not done enough damage to stop there, I slammed into him with a side kick followed by a roundhouse to the head. Each time, he stepped backward, but he never fell. Damn, I thought, I can plow through four boards like they're butter with these kicks. What's this guy made of?

The man was staggering, looking as if . . . One more kick, I thought. One more kick has to do it, but that one more kick brought the unexpected. As my foot flew toward his head, the man caught it with his massive left hand and tossed me backward, pouncing on top of me before my body hit the ground.

A malign smile spread across his lips, and he held his knife against my throat. I could feel the sting of the razor sharp edge sink into my skin and the man's hot breath on my face. "So, you're a fighter, bitch," the man whispered. "This'll be more fun than I thought." He positioned himself over me, sitting his full weight on my belly and pinning my arms with his knees. Using his teeth, he removed the glove from his free hand and let it drop to the ground next to me. "First you, then your friend," he whispered as he reached under my blouse and pulled my bra upward and off of my breasts.

So this is it, I thought, feeling his rough, sweaty hands exploring my nipples, this is how my life will end. I closed my eyes and braced myself for the inevitable, but it never came. Instead, I heard the report of Hawthorne's Smith & Wesson and felt the man's body arch then fall on top of me.

"Oh, God, Jesus, I cried out while I struggled to toss his limp body off of me. Hawthorne grabbed one of his arms, and together we were finally successful.

"For Christ's sake," Hawthorne said. "What the hell were you doing?"

"What does it look like? I was lonely. He looked like a fun date," I retorted. I readjusted my bra and straightened my shirt as best I could.

"You're damn lucky the arrogant sonuvabitch tried to cop a feel." She nodded toward the knife lying on the ground next to the man. "He could've just used the saw right away to separate you from your head."

"Well, thank my lucky stars."

"So you do have a sense of humor after all," Hawthorne said as she offered her hand to help me up.

Accepting her offer, I got up and dusted myself off. My blouse felt wet, and I had a momentary panic attack, thinking it might be my own blood. I felt my throat. The knife had left nothing more than a shallow cut that wasn't worth losing sleep over. The blood on my blouse had come from my would-be assailant.

"Is he dead?" Hawthorne asked, looking around toward the house.

"Probably," I answered.

"You'd better check him to be sure. I don't want to find him breathing down my neck later."

I squatted next to him and laid my fingers against his neck. "Hurry," Hawthorne said. "There might be others." My eyes opened wide when I felt a pulse that was stronger than I had anticipated, since I had expected it to be absent. "Damn! He's alive," I said just as his hand appeared out of nowhere, latched onto a handful of my hair, and hurled me forward in a somersault. As my back hit hard against the ground, knocking the wind out of me, I heard Hawthorne scream out, followed by the multiple sharp reports of three rounds being squeezed off in rapid succession. I rolled over and saw the backlit silhouette of Hawthorne standing over our attacker in a wide-legged stance, her arms locked straight, holding her gun pointed at him.

"You OK?" she asked as I got up.

"Yeah. How about you? I heard you scream."

"He took a chunk out of my ankle, the sonuvabitch."

"How badly are you hurt?"

"I'll live."

"Is he dead?" I walked toward them.

"He is now." Hawthorne relaxed her stance and allowed her gun to fall to her side. She reached in her pocket and produced a penlight and pointed it at the man's face or what had been his face. Normally seeing someone who had died like that would have made me feel sad that the victim had to have his life end in such a horrible fashion, and sad that I couldn't have done something for him. This was no victim. We were his. I felt only contempt for the person who had owned that face and lost it.

"Do you know how to use a gun?" Hawthorne asked.

"Uh, yes," I replied. I didn't lie. I know how to fire guns, all kinds of them. I also know out to strip and clean them, and how to make my own ammunition. It was a side effect of living with a Chicago cop turned FBI agent. Though I wasn't happy about it, Sam also taught Shelby all he knew about guns. He said it was no different than teaching her martial arts. A martial artist uses his hands and feet as weapons, and they can be lethal. A gun is just another weapon. It is the user who is responsible for the result. Sam contended that if Shelby understood and respected their power, she would resist using them, but she would know how to use them if it ever became necessary.

"Good. Take his," Hawthorne said.

"But I'm not a cop," I argued. "Besides, I'm a suspect, aren't I? Are you sure you want to risk it?"

"Shut up and take the gun. If there are others around here like him, you might need it."

"So I'm not a suspect anymore?"

"Jesus! Dispense with the suspect crap already. You've convinced me. If you were guilty, you'd have let the asshole take me out." She offered her hand for me to shake.

"What's this for? I asked.

"Hi, my name's Kim. What's yours?"

Convinced that Hawthorne was just a little crazy, I decided to humor her. I shook her hand and replied, "My name is Diane, but everyone calls me Deb."

"Good," Kim said. "We're best friends. Now pick up the goddam gun."

"Why don't you call for backup?" I asked.

"I will, but if a fleet of squads rolls up with lights flashing and someone's got Michelle inside, he won't hesitate to kill her. I'd rather check things out myself . . . Quietly."

My neck and back both aching from the last time I squatted next to the guy, I nervously I dropped down on one knee, filled with the unrealistic fear that he might rise from the dead and grab me again. I felt behind his back and slipped my fingers around the grip of his gun. It felt heavier than Sam's Smith & Wesson. Hawthorne shined her penlight on it. "Colt Double Eagle," she said. "Nice one. Think you can handle it?"

"Yes," I replied without hesitation, thinking suddenly, how strange it was for me to be in a position to possibly kill someone. Here I was, a doctor whose entire life was dedicated to saving lives and yet, without a moment's hesitation, I took a gun into my hand ready to do the opposite. "What do you want me to do?" I asked.

Hawthorne took a cellular phone from her pocket and called for back up, requesting they give her time to check out the house first. Then looking at me, "You go around back. I'll take the front," she ordered.

"You want me to break in?" I asked anxiously.

"No," she said. "Stay there. If anyone comes out, shoot him. Otherwise, I'll call to you if I need you." She took off around the front of the garage while I obediently headed around to the back of my own house. On my way, I whispered to myself. "What are you doing, you idiot! You're a doctor, not a cop. Damn! All you had to do was blink the headlights and honk the horn. The man might have run away on his own. But nooooo, you had to be stupid and play hero."

When I finally arrived at the rear of my house, I peered in through darkened windows. Though the sky was clear, the moon seemed to be nowhere in sight. I peered into the darkness inside, hoping to see something. It was quiet in there. The eerie silhouettes created by the somber wash of light from the street seemed out of place.

Suddenly, there appeared a shadowy figure inside the house moving toward me. I tried to breath quietly, but I seemed to be hungering for air. Beads of sweat were trickling down my face into my eyes and mouth. I rubbed them away with the back of my hand, but for each droplet I swiped, ten more took its place.

I lay my ear against the outside wall of the house, trying to discriminate between the footsteps in the house, and the thumping of my heart inside my chest. The insect cacophony in my wooded backyard didn't help matters much.

A thousand years later, I heard the "thunk" of the deadbolt as it was turned. The lump in my throat had grown so large, I thought I was choking on my own heart. I felt the gun in my hand. I would use it if I had to. Then I wondered: What if this guy knows something that might clear Sam? I readied myself to kick the asshole harder than I had ever kicked anything in my life, but when the door opened slowly, I heard Hawthorne say, "Deb, it's me, Kim. I'm coming out. Don't shoot."

It took a minute for her words to find their way through my adrenalin rush and sink in. "Kim?" I called out to confirm that it was her.

"Yes," she replied. Then her face appeared in the doorway. "It's all clear."

I took a deep cleansing breath and consciously relaxed my body which had been cocked and ready like a gun with the hammer pulled back.

"Where's Michelle?" I asked.

Kim opened the door, allowing me to walk through. "I don't know," she said. "There's blood spattered. . . I don't know," she repeated.

When will it stop? I asked myself as I heard the cry of sirens in the distance.

13

As I walked through the door into the ruins that had been my home, I felt as though I stepped through a doorway into another world, a frightening, joyless world where violence reigned. Whoever had torn through my home had gone beyond searching for something. They wanted to leave me a rage-filled message that would scare the life out of me. It worked. I don't think I have ever been so frightened. I thought I had understood that the world was a violent place, but my perceptions were those of an observer rather than a participant, a member of the audience watching the movie go by. Now I was living inside the movie.

"You're bleeding," Kim said, looking at my shirt.

"It's mostly his," I replied. I noticed her torn, bloody pant leg.

"Let me take a look at that. You might need stitches."

"Later," Kim answered. "We're not finished here."

I started to pick up a family photo that had been tossed onto the floor, it's frame smashed. "Don't!" Kim commanded. "Don't touch anything until the crime scene unit has gone over the place."

Startled by the harshness of her voice, I yanked my hand away from the photo and glared at her. "Sorry," she said. "But I had to stop you. If we're going to find the perps, we've got to have uncontaminated evidence. You understand, don't you?"

I nodded then looked beyond the family room, where we were standing, toward the front of the house. "May I turn on a light?"

"Not yet," Kim said. "I don't want to give up our location if anyone else is nearby." Her eyes roamed the room and beyond into the adjacent entry hall and kitchen.

"Michelle might be upstairs," Kim said.

"Or downstairs," I added.

Kim glanced at me then navigated her way through the obstacle course that had been my family room to the stairs. "Do you want me to look downstairs while you look upstairs?" I asked.

"No. You wait for me here."

Her reply was both welcomed and unwanted. I did not savor the idea of being left alone, nor did I want to go searching through the house. The scream of the sirens, however, had grown loud enough that I was sure they would be pulling up in front of my house any second, so I felt somewhat relieved as Kim left me behind and disappeared into the blackness of the upstairs.

As I had predicted, the blare of sirens became deafening then died abruptly at the same time I saw the flashing blue strobes and the headlight beams shining in through my windows. I breathed a long sigh of relief at the sight of them, but my relief was short lived. With the headlights shining into my home, I was better able to see the devastation, and the blood. It was spattered on the walls near the front door. A puddle of blood had soaked into the champagne colored carpet on my living room floor, while a smeared trail of the congealing liquid led from the carpet across the wood entry and out the front door. I prayed that Michelle had died quickly.

Within seconds, the house was surrounded by police, and Kim reappeared from the upstairs. "Anything?" I asked.

"It's trashed, but—" Kim stopped when she caught sight of the blood trail. "I guess that answers our question better than anything."

She walked to the front door, but didn't immediately open it. Instead, she called out to the cops on the other side of the door and informed them of her identity. "I'm coming out," she shouted. Then she opened the door and allowed only the watch commander inside.

The sun was warming the horizon by the time Kim and I climbed into the back of the ambulance that would take us to the hospital. The paramedics had bandaged Kim's leg and cleansed my neck.

I needed nothing more, but Kim's wound definitely required suturing.

"What's next?" I asked as we bounced along inside the ambulance.

"Do you have steady hands?" Kim replied. Her voice sounded as tired as I felt.

I flared my fingers out in front of me. The shaking had all but ceased. "Pretty steady. Why?"

"Then I guess 'what's next' is you stitch me up," she said.

"I'm not sure. After last night—"

"It'll be good for you to do something familiar, something you're used to. It'll help you get over last night."

I smiled thinly and shook my head. "I don't think I'll ever get over last night."

"Maybe." Kim shrugged. "But it won't hurt to try. Besides, you've got a lot on your dance card right now. You'll need some kind of focus to keep your sanity."

Sanity, I thought as I lay my head against the sidewall of the ambulance and allowed it to rock freely from side-to-side with the movement of the vehicle, what's that?

I must have dozed off, since the next thing I remember was Kim telling me we had arrived. I was disoriented at first and wondered if I had been dreaming the whole thing. One look at Kim's leg lying across the stretcher covered by her torn, bloody pants, and I knew it had been all too real.

The paramedics insisted upon rolling Kim into the emergency room on their stretcher, and I walked along side. Our entourage of paramedics and uniformed cops drew stares from both patients and staff alike. The morning shift was just arriving, and the night shift had not yet gone off duty. Judging from Kim's appearance, they had reason to stare. Tamara, her generous breasts bulging over the deeply scooped neckline of a neon green sun dress, greeted us with the smile of a gossip columnist who's about to spread the juiciest story of her career. "Rough night, ladies?" she asked.

"About average," Kim replied as we passed Tamara's desk and entered through the automatic doors where we were greeted by even more stares. We declined to answer any questions beyond the fact that, with the exception of the obvious non-fatal wounds, we were both fine.

I left Kim to fill out the required medical forms, and looked in on Sam. Again, my wildly dishevelled, bloody clothing drew the stairs of the TCCU staff. I barely glanced sideways, avoiding all eye contact, but I felt their eyes follow me into Sam's cubicle.

Once inside his cubicle, hidden from the inquiring stares, I worked to calm my nerves and focus on my husband. It felt strange to stand at the bedside of that lifeless form, touching a hand that could not touch me back, and trying to convince myself that Sam lived somewhere inside of that shell. Though I am a doctor, and considered a woman of the nineties—whatever that means—deep down, I had always believed that Sam was the stronger of the two of us. Somehow, if anything went wrong, Sam would make it all better. Now, I inherited the job. I didn't want it, and I knew that no matter how hard I tried, I couldn't make it all better. I took Sam's hand in mine and rubbed it against my cheek, then kissed it. "Oh, Sam, what am I going to do?" I felt like crying, but my uncooperative eyes remained as barren as the desert.

After my visit with Sam, I showered quickly, washing away blood and dirt, and trying vainly to wash the pain away. I changed into a clean pair of scrubs and returned to the ER in search of Kim.

By the time I entered the suture room, Kim was lying on the table, and the nurses had the suture tray set up and ready to go.

"How long have you been a doctor?" Kim asked through flinches and grunts while I injected the wound with lidocaine.

"Longer than I care to think," I said. I finished injecting the anesthetic and sponged away the oozing blood. "How about you?"

"Six years in a radio car and one month with Investigative Services."

"You handle yourself well," I said as I cleansed the area with an anti-bacterial cleansing solution.

"You did OK, yourself," she said. "I hope you're as good at sewing people up as you are at fighting."

"You hope I'm better," I said.

We continued the small talk throughout the procedure. I learned that Kim had become a cop against her parents' wishes. They believed her father's alcohol problem was job related, and they didn't want their children to suffer a similar fate. Her parents had wanted her to become a lawyer, but Kim had been enamored by the action on the streets and enrolled in the academy against their wishes.

I found out that, in spite of her youthful appearance, Kim was only four years my junior. She had three brothers—two were cops and one was a lawyer—and she was already divorced. She had married in Vegas three weeks after she met another rookie cop. The marriage ended six months later, no kids.

A bond of trust was building between us, so I let down my guard, and I told her about my life with Sam, and about our daughter, Shelby. It took a leap of faith, but I also told her about Sam's phone calls before he was shot, and about him knowing John Doe and calling him Cal. I admitted that my search through Cal's belongings had not been for a missing locket, but rather at Sam's request.

14

After I finished suturing Kim's leg, she left the hospital and returned to the crime scene that had once been a safe haven for my family, or at least that's what I had always believed. Now I wondered if there was such a thing as a safe haven.

My partners, Joel Freedlove and Art Hamilton, found me as I was walking toward my on-call room where I hoped to lie down and catch up on sleep that was way overdue.

"We heard about Michelle and the attack at your house," Joel said. "Have you heard anything more? Have they found Michelle's . . . Have they found Michelle?"

"No," I replied flatly. Joel's eyes fell to the floor and he shook his head. "I don't understand any of this."

Art wrapped his arm around my shoulder. "If there's anything we can do—"

"We'll cover for you, of course," Joel interrupted. "Take as long as you need."

"I might need to work," I said.

"With all of the stress you're under, I don't think the patients need you right now," Art said.

"So what you are really saying is, you don't want me to work," I shot back angrily, too stressed and fatigued to perceive their good intentions. They were right. I was in no condition, emotionally, to be responsible for people's lives. I just couldn't see it at that moment.

"It's only for a few days." Joel tried to keep an encouraging tone in his voice. "Let's see what happens to Sam and the rest of this trouble before we worry about work. OK?"

"The rest of the trouble must be having some impact on your emotions, too," I insisted. "Both of you were close to Michelle and Tony."

"Michelle and Tony, yes," Art said. "But the other…Well—"

"The other?" I interrupted. "What do you mean, the other?"

"This drug thing," Art replied, his eyes failing to connect with mine.

"What drug thing!" I snapped.

"You know," Joel said. "The charges against Sam, and the concerns about your involvement."

Who the hell told them? Had Kim said something? It didn't sound like something she'd do, unless I continued to be fooled by her behavior. "Where are you getting your information?" I asked angrily.

"There were a couple of FBI agents in here asking questions," Art said.

"About Sam and me?"

"Yes." Both men nodded.

I let my body slump against the wall. I wondered how everything in my life could go so wrong all at once. I closed my eyes and breathed deeply, calming my frayed nerves. Then I looked at my partners, making sure I made direct eye contact with each of them. "You've known Sam and me for a long time."

Joel and Art again nodded their agreement.

"Then you've got to look beyond what's happening right now and trust your instincts about us, especially about me. Have you ever known me to commit an illegal act of any kind? Well, maybe I drive too fast."

Both Art and Joel smiled.

"The charges on Sam are trumped up, and I mean to find out who did it and why. If you can hang onto your trust in me a while longer, I'll provide you with enough evidence to alleviate all of your suspicions."

Both partners promised their continued support and offered to let Shelby and me stay with them until my house was put back in order. I had always known my partners were decent men, but I don't think I had appreciated the extent of their kindness and generosity until that moment. When our conversation concluded, I thanked them both with hugs and told them I would keep them informed and call upon them if needed.

They finally returned to the E.R., leaving me to find my way to the on-call room where I locked myself inside, wishing I could keep my present life at bay so my past could find room to return. I thought about the promise I had made to my partners, and wondered what possessed me to make it. I had no idea how to prove Sam innocent. I knew how to investigate the cause of illness, but this, this was Sam's territory. He'd know exactly what to do, and where to look. Oh, Sam, I thought, how can I help you? How can I make this better for you, and for me? Tears tried to force their way to the surface, but my eyes stung only from dryness, as I undressed. I began to panic, thinking I had lost the ability to cry. It was like having insomnia when all you can think about is sleep.

Though as a physician I had become accustomed to long sleepless nights, I had never known fatigue like I felt at that moment. The physical stress alone would have worn me out, but the mental and emotional stress carried me over the edge. Feeling shaky and weak, I collapsed onto the bed and once again, I cursed God for abandoning me. Then for the first time in my life I came to believe that God didn't exist at all. How could He? The God I had believed in when I was growing up wouldn't sit by and let people suffer like this. I remembered what my Grandmother used to say: "God never gives us more than we can handle." She was wrong! I couldn't handle this. It wasn't fair. What had I done to deserve it? Though I truly believe I could never commit such and act, I understood more clearly then, than any other time in my life, the kind of desperation that drives a person to suicide. Eventually sleep crept over me and carried me away from my life, if only for a short time.

***

With sudden urgency, the overhead speakers crackled with words I never wanted to hear, "Code Blue TCCU. Code Blue TCCU." The instant I heard the announcement I shot up from a sound sleep, dressed, and raced toward the unit.

My heart stopped as soon as I stepped through the automatic doors leading to the TCCU. My worst nightmares were realized. The crash team was in Sam's room. "God, no!" I heard myself cry out. Tom Holter, Sam's surgeon, spun around toward me. Then he glared at the nurses and yelled, "Jesus Christ! Get her out of here."

One of the nurses took my arm, but I yanked it away. "I'm staying here, dammit!" I yelled.

"You don't belong here, Deb, not now," Tom said.

I refused to leave, but the nurse managed to convince me to have a seat in the nurses' station. It was enclosed behind glass, so sounds were not as easily transmitted, and I could watch the resuscitation through a closed circuit TV. Tom was right. I had no business being there. Watching the resuscitative efforts was pure torture, but misguided by the irrational thought that Sam's survival depended upon my physical presence, I couldn't leave.

In the midst of watching them pump on Sam's chest, shock him repeatedly, and ram six inch needles into his heart, my pager went off. I ignored it at first, thinking there could not be anything more important than what was happening to Sam, then I remembered Shelby. I checked the display. It was my home phone number and realized it must be Kim. I grabbed the phone and dialed. Kim answered.

"Hello," she said.

"Kim?"

"Deb, we need to talk. Where are you now?"

"Sam's in cardiac arrest. I'm in the unit. What's wrong?"

"I'm on my way over. We'll talk when I get there." She hung up before I could say anything. I glanced at the television screen and saw that the activity surrounding Sam had all but ceased. Everyone's eyes were on his monitor. My first thought was that

Sam had died. A quick glance at his monitoring screen inset into the nurses' console proved me wrong. He was in a normal sinus rhythm. Disbelieving, I tapped the monitor, but it continued to show a normal heartbeat. For the briefest moment, I allowed myself the luxury of believing everything was going to be all right and thanked the very God whom, a short time before, I had accused of deserting me or worse, not existing at all.

When a solemn looking Tom left the cubicle and walked toward the nurses' station, I rose from the console and met him halfway, still clinging to the fanciful notion that Sam would wake up and my life would return to its previous state of naive bliss.

Tom stopped and gazed at me sadly when he saw me emerge from the nurses' station. Then rubbing his chin contemplatively, he walked up to me. Our eyes met, and my hopes dissolved.

"He's gone," Tom said softly.

"But the monitor?"

"I hate to bring this up, but we need to work swiftly if there's going to be a chance. . ." He inhaled sharply and pressed his lips tightly together, then he continued with what I already knew was coming. "I won't know, until I go in, what his organs—"

"You're asking me for his organs?" I snapped. "This is a goddam critical care unit. How can you give up so easily?"

"Let's go somewhere and talk," Tom said, taking me by my upper arm and nudging me gently toward the exit doors.

"No! Dammit! We'll talk here."

Tom looked around the unit. "I think we need to go somewhere private," he insisted.

I followed his eyes and saw that everyone was looking at us. Suddenly feeling self-conscious, I acquiesced to Tom's request and left the unit with him following me. A private conference room adjacent to the unit's waiting area had been designated for situations such as mine. Tom followed me into the room and closed the door, separating us from the world.

The sound insulated room was decorated in pale grays and soft pastels with comfortable, upholstered furniture. It was self contained with its own rest room and a wet bar stocked with a variety of juices and sodas, providing grieving family members a place to linger in solitude.

"Why don't we sit down over here," Tom said, pointing toward two chairs in the corner of the room set at right angles to one another. A large brass bowl filled with a luxuriously rich bouquet of freshly cut flowers sat on the table between the chairs.

"I don't want to sit," I replied angrily. "And I don't want you to patronize me."

"Patronize you? I have no intention of patronizing you," Tom said. "You're in a lousy situation here. I don't know what I would do if my wife, Carol, were lying in that bed.

"I'll ask you again, Tom, and I want a straight answer this time: Why are you giving up so soon? You've saved people a lot worse off than Sam."

"Worse in some ways, but not in the important one. Deb, Sam's brain has died. I don't know where Sam is, but I do know he's no longer living inside that body in there." Tom tilted his head in the direction of the trauma unit. "We can drag this out, but I don't see the point. Why torture yourself?"

I melted into one of the chairs. Tom was right. It was silly to pretend. Sam was gone. The flip of a single switch would confirm that as reality, but I couldn't let him go, not like this, not with accusations of criminal activities staining his reputation. Sam had to be allowed to die like he had lived; with dignity. He was a courageous, decent, and honest man who deserved no less than to be honored in that way.

Tom sat in the chair next to mine, his face tense with anticipation. "Tom," I said, looking him squarely, "I can't let you do it. I can't let you turn off the machines, not yet."

"But, Deb—"

"I know what you're saying," I interrupted, "but I still can't do it. I can't let Sam die this way." I got up and started for the door, then turned to Tom who now stood dumbfounded in front of his chair. "Do whatever it takes to keep him alive," I ordered.

Filled with a sense of purpose, I turned on my heels and dashed out of the room before he could argue.

15

I marched purposefully away from the quiet room, leaving Tom to ponder my request. I was on a crusade to save Sam's reputation, yet I had no clue where I was going or what I was going to do. I didn't even notice Kim approach until she took hold of my arm and said, "We have to talk."

"I don't have time to talk," I replied.

Not letting go of my arm, she asked, "What's your hurry?"

"I have to do something for Sam," I announced with bravado.

"Whatever it is can wait," Kim said, "We have to talk *now!*"

"So talk," I demanded.

Kim looked from side-to-side. "Not here," she said, "somewhere private."

I showed her the room where Tom and I had spoken just moments before. She followed me inside, closed the door, and started in before I had a chance to ask why she was being so secretive. "Something's going on here, and I don't like what it is."

"Tell me about it," I chimed in sarcastically. "I've just been informed that my husband is brain dead, and I should pull the plug. He's been accused of dealing drugs which, by-the-way, isn't true no matter what anyone says. My co-workers are being murdered, my colleagues think I may be involved with dealing illegal drugs, my house is in shambles, and I have yet to inform my fourteen-year-old daughter that her daddy is, for all practical purposes, dead."

Kim sighed deeply. "I'm really sorry," she said with sincerity, "but the problems go way beyond the obvious."

Now she had lost me. "What do you mean?"

"You know the guy I killed last night? I checked out his prints locally. I got back a big fat nothing, so I faxed them to the FBI, and you know what I found? The guy's a cop."

"What!"

"He's a goddam cop from New York City."

"You mean he was a cop at one time, don't you?"

"No, I mean he's currently on the NYPD payroll. In fact, he has a spotless record, ten years on the force."

"You've lost me. What was a New York cop doing here? Wasn't he a little out of his jurisdiction?"

Kim's eyes sparkled with the excitement of a cop who found herself in the middle of a case that was way beyond the usual knifings and shootings, and with frustration, because I didn't see things as clearly as she. "This had nothing to do with jurisdiction," she complained. "He was here to eliminate someone, and that someone was you."

"You mean like a hit man?"

"That's exactly what I mean."

"How can you be so sure? Did you call his precinct?"

"Yes. They said he was on sick leave. Sick leave my ass."

My mouth suddenly felt dry as sandpaper. I found a styrofoam cup in the cabinet above the sink and filled it with water. The action gave me time to organize my thoughts and try to grasp what Kim was saying. "Why would a cop from New York City be hired to kill me?" I asked after wetting my mouth with the cool liquid.

"That's what I'd like to know."

"Maybe he was after the person who killed Tony and Michelle."

"If Michelle's dead," Kim said.

"I have to believe she is. I don't want to think of her going through what Tony went through." I took another sip of water. "How do you know that the cop wasn't on some kind of special assignment?" I asked.

Kim rummaged around in the refrigerator and pulled out a Doctor Pepper, popped the cap, and tossed back a sizeable gulp.

"Because a good cop doesn't sneak up on people ready to gut them with a foot long serrated blade." She took another gulp, dropped into a chair, crossed her legs on top of the coffee table, and allowed her head to roll onto the back of the chair. "Jesus, I'm tired," she moaned. "I haven't slept in over thirty hours." She peeked at me from beneath half-open lids. "You look even worse than I feel."

"Thanks," I said as I sat in the other chair. "I glanced at my watch for the first time since I had been yanked out of my sleep by the Code Blue call. "I think I slept about an hour." I didn't dare lay my head back. If I did, I would have fallen asleep instantly. With Sam hanging on by less than a thread and Shelby in possible danger, I couldn't afford the luxury anymore. "I can't put it off any longer. I have to call Shelby and bring her home. Sam's only alive because the machines are keeping him that way, and I'm not sure how much longer that will last. Then I have to go back to the house and search Sam's office. I have to find something that will clear him."

"OK," Kim agreed. "We'll bring Shelby home, but forget about Sam's office."

"What?"

Kim sat on the edge of the chair. "I want you to stay away from your house altogether."

"Why? I... don't understand. I won't trample the crime scene. All I want to do is look through Sam's papers in his office."

"There are no 'Sam's papers'," Kim said.

"What do you mean?" I asked.

"There's a lot more going on there than the dead cop and Michelle's disappearance."

"Like what?"

"I've been tossed off the case. In fact, CPD has been excused from the whole thing. The FBI's crawling all over the place and tearing your house apart."

"Is Ben Scolnik one of them?"

"No. None of them are local."

"What are they looking for?" I asked. "Drugs?"

"They wouldn't say, but after they tossed all of us locals out, I dug out my binoculars." Kim flashed a Cheshire cat smile. "Your neighbors weren't home. I didn't think they'd mind if I sat in that big old oak tree in their back yard."

"And?" I pressed.

"The feds ignored the obvious crime scene, walked all over the blood as if they didn't give a shit that someone had been either badly hurt or murdered. They focused their search in a room next to the living room that looks out over your backyard."

"Sam's office," I said.

"Yeah. That's what I figured. They hauled out a bunch of files."

"Do they think they'll find evidence to incriminate Sam in that bogus drug dealing thing they suspended him for?"

"Maybe." Kim shrugged. "Who knows?"

"I doubt they would find anything even if he were involved in something illegal, which he wasn't. Sam's not that stupid. He wouldn't keep records of illegal drug dealing in his home office."

"What did you think you'd find there?" Kim asked.

"Sam kept notes on open cases in his office. Maybe one of the people or groups he was investigating set him up."

"What were you going to do with the information, chase down the people he was investigating and expect them to tell you if they framed your husband?"

"I don't know what I was going to do." I shrugged stupidly. "I guess I was hoping I would find something that would naturally lead me to the next step."

"I wish it were that easy," Kim said. "Anyway, it's kind of a waste worrying about it now. The feds have his files."

"It seems that everywhere I turn another road block gets set in my path," I said, my disappointment showing.

"Don't let it bother you," Kim said. "I'm always banging my head against concrete, but I usually find another way to solve the puzzle. You will, too. Oh, here, Kim said, rummaging around in her purse. I almost forgot." She handed me a stack of mail. "I commandeered this from the mail carrier before she got to your house."

"Are you allowed to do that? Isn't that breaking some kind of rule or something?"

"Yeah, well, the rule book's not the goddam Bible or anything. So, I may have broken a teansy weansy little rule." Kim held out her thumb and index finger millimeters from each other. "It's not like I broke one of the Ten Commandments."

Smiling, I said, "thanks" and took the mail. I sorted through it, tossing away anything marked "bulk rate". There were a couple of bills and what looked like a greeting card with no return address, but the handwriting was unmistakable. My blood turned cold when I saw it. The card was from Sam.

I stared at the sealed envelope for a long moment. I knew I had to open it but having no idea what he might have written, I was afraid. In the past, when Sam was away on long assignments, he would send me a love note or card every few days as his schedule allowed. If this was one of those love notes, I didn't feel I had the strength to read it, not then. On the other hand, after his two strange phone calls, Sam might have sent me something that would help his case. I knew I had to open it.

I raised my eyes to meet Kim's. She looked puzzled. "What is it?" she asked.

"It's from Sam," I said.

"That's heavy."

"Yeah." I stared at the card, glanced at the post mark, and ran my fingers over the address that Sam had written the day he was shot.

"Are you going to open it?" Kim asked impatiently.

I nodded silently and peeled the envelope open. Inside was a plain piece of stationary folded in half. As I lifted it out of the envelope, two metallic objects dropped out and hit the floor with a ping and a clank. I saw that the one object that landed against my toe was a key. The other rolled under the toe kick at the base of the cabinets. Kim retrieved the round object while I picked up the key.

"What's it to?" Kim asked of the key.

"I don't know." I shrugged. "What was the other thing?" I asked, trying to see the object that she held captive inside her fist. Kim hesitated opening her hand, and she had an apologetic look in her eyes.

"More bad news?" I asked flippantly, trying to suppress the dread growing inside of me. Without a word, Kim opened her hand to expose a simple gold ring—Sam's ring. Stunned by the sight of it and struck by the irrational fear that touching it would make it and all that it represented disappear as if that part of my life never existed, my fingers hovered over the ring for several seconds. Sam had never taken his ring off since the day I slipped it onto his finger while professing to him my promise of eternal love. I remembered how Sam's fingers trembled as I took them into mine, and his eyes filled with tears.

Now tears stung my eyes as I took the ring into my hand. "He must have known he was going to die," I cried, "or he wouldn't have taken it off."

"But why would he take it off at all?" Kim asked. "What was he trying to tell you?"

"That he loved me . . . until . . . until death do us part." I broke down and cried.

Kim held me in her arms like a mother comforting her disconsolate child, and held me to her while I cried.

"Why didn't he tell me something was wrong? Why didn't he warn me this was going to happen?" I was searching for answers that would never be forthcoming. "He could have warned me, helped me to prepare."

"You can't prepare yourself for something like this," Kim said quietly, "not in a million years. We all know we're going to die someday, but when someday comes, it's always too soon. Sam's a cop. You're a cop's wife. You always knew this could happen, but it still didn't prepare you."

Kim was right. I always knew I might face this day. As a

specialist in emergency medicine, I had patched up and pronounced more cops than I care to remember. Yet, I had convinced myself, if not on an intellectual level then on an emotional one, that it would never happen to my Sam.

"May I take a look at the key?" Kim asked.

I raised my eyes from my hands where they had been buried, then held my left hand open to her. Kim took the key, and I stared at its impression in the center of my palm while I slipped Sam's ring onto my finger next to my own wedding band.

Kim studied the key for a moment. "I wonder what it opens," she said. "Do you have any idea?"

I shook my head. "None."

Kim leaned over and glanced at the note. "What does the note say?"

I had avoided reading the note that I had been clutching in my right hand. The sight of Sam's ring had been painful enough, and I doubted the note that had accompanied it would cheer me up. When I finally unfolded it, I found an object inside that looked like a clear piece of rice. It was fastened to the paper with Scotch tape, and Sam had written a simple note.

Remember what we taught Shelby about strangers, and never forget my last words to you on the phone. I meant every one.

I love you, Deb.

Sam

I handed the paper to Kim. "What this?" she asked, her lips curling with curiosity while she unfastened the object from the paper and rolled it in her palm. "What does the note mean?" she asked without taking her eyes from the piece of rice.

"I don't know. I can't imagine what it has to do with this key."

"Why would he send you a key and not tell you what it unlocked?" Kim asked. "Could he have assumed you already knew?"

"Sam was very thorough. He never made assumptions. I think that's why he was so good at his job. He never let the details escape him."

"Then the note must have the answer. What's this about strangers?" Kim asked, pointing to that particular sentence.

"I don't know why he wrote that. Maybe it is a warning."

"A warning against who?"

"I don't know. I don't know," I repeated out of sheer frustration.

Kim got to her feet. "We're not going to get very far standing here. I'm starving. How about you? My brain can't function when it's low on fuel."

"You can eat at a time like this?" I asked, surprised by Kim's flight from one subject to another.

"Hell, yes," she replied, "especially when I haven't had any sleep. I've got to re-energize somehow. We'll eat while we puzzle this thing out. Now c'mon. I'm parked in the driveway outside of the ER."

Reluctantly, I followed her. We stopped by my on-call room where I changed out of my scrubs and into street clothes. Then we made our way through the emergency department where I was approached by the staff. They had a thousand questions about Sam and about my well-being, but Kim ran interference saying I had to leave with her on urgent police business.

When we got to the exit doors, the electronic eye sensed our presence and the doors swung wide, but I didn't walk through. Instead, I grabbed Kim and held her fast. "Stop," I said quietly, trying not to attract any unnecessary attention.

"What?" Kim said, stepping away from the doors and allowing them to close.

"It's the Blazer," I whispered.

"The Blazer?" A puzzled frown crossed Kim's face.

"The one that followed me home."

"Are you sure it's the same one?"

"Aren't you the one who doesn't believe in coincidences?"

106

Kim smiled wryly and peered through the glass doors at the Blazer. She dipped her head and tilted it from side-to-side. "It looks empty," she said as she turned toward me. Then her eyes moved away from my face and locked onto something behind me.

I turned to see what she was looking at and found two well muscled and formidable looking men in suits standing directly behind me. "Doctor Hunter?" One of the men asked.

"And who are you?" Kim chimed in before I could reply, and she immediately insinuated herself protectively between the men and me.

The man's face darkened. "Our business is with Doctor Hunter," he said icily.

"I am Detective Kim Hawthorne of the Chicago Police Department. I'd like to see some identification, gentlemen." Kim's voice had become authoritative, cop-like. Standing firm with her open palm extended, Kim waited for the men to produce the requested ID's. They glared at her and postured intimidatingly, but Kim did not flinch. She simply raised her eyebrows and tilted her head slightly as if to say, "Well, let's have it."

When it became painfully clear to the two behemoths, that the feisty little lady detective was not going to cave, they looked at each other then reached inside their coat pockets. With lightning quick movement, Kim's fingers unfastened the strap to her automatic and grasped the handle. Now her demur posture matched theirs.

Both men immediately held open palms toward Kim. "Take it easy, Detective. We're just doing what you asked. See?" the one man said, holding open the lapel of his suitcoat with two fingers so Kim could see that he was reaching for his ID case. He held the case out toward her and let it fall open. Kim took it and studied it carefully, then handed it back to the man.

"And yours," she said holding out her hand to the other man who then handed his ID to her. She studied it also and returned it to its owner. "So, agents Boyle and Wood, what do you want with the good doctor here?" Kim nodded toward me.

"This is federal business, detective, and none of yours," Boyle, the one who seemed to be doing all of the talking, said.

"I am afraid it *is* my business, gentlemen, because Doctor Hunter is a material witness in an ongoing murder investigation, and she's under my protective custody. I've got reason to believe an attempt will be made on her life."

"We'll keep her safe," Boyle said as he reached for my arm. Kim immediately sidestepped and blocked his advance. Boyle's face turned a deep crimson. "You are interfering with a federal investigation. I can have you brought up on charges," he growled through clenched teeth.

Seeing where the confrontation was leading, I stepped around Kim. "I'll be happy to talk with you two gentlemen."

Kim's face fell so hard her jaw almost hit the floor. I turned to her with my hand in my pocket. "Wait for me," I said then I slipped the note and its contents to her as I turned toward the men and gestured to them to start walking toward a conference room halfway down the hall. "Gentlemen," I said graciously. I felt Kim take the note, but I didn't look back.

When we arrived at the conference room, Boyle, the one who had been doing all of the talking, opened the door and let me pass. Wood followed me into the room.

The conference room was basic hospital decor; safe, muted colors, no imagination. The walls were papered in vinyl; mauve and gray striped on top and solid gray on the bottom, separated by a horizontal strip of gray vinyl that acted as a chair rail. The carpet was a speckled mix of mauve and gray, while the table and chairs were gray laminate with the chair seats upholstered in a gray and mauve geometric print. An abstract, generic painting hung on one wall, its colors coordinating with the dichromatic room.

"Have a seat, Doctor," Boyle ordered, pulling a chair away from the table and gesturing toward it with his hand. His gentlemanly behavior seemed artificial, and noticeably insincere. I took my seat. Boyle took his across from me. Wood stood with his back against the door, his arms folded ominously across his chest. I wasn't going to get out of there until they were ready to let me out.

"O.K., you have me here. What do you want?" I asked in a tone that was designed to let them know I was not going to be intimidated. I'm not sure if it had any impact on them. It didn't convince me. I was already quite intimidated.

Boyle leaned on his elbows and regarded me for a time. "What do you know about the recent break down in our telephone systems?"

His question took me by surprise. I thought he had come to talk about Sam, and he was asking about telephones? "I don't understand," I replied stupidly.

"Oh, c'mon, Doctor, you know exactly what I'm talking about."

"Do you mean the day the nine-one-one system went down?"

"Among other things."

"I don't know anything about it other than it happened. Why are you asking me about it?"

"Your husband's kind of a computer whiz, isn't he?"

"Yes," I answered skeptically, wondering where this was leading.

"He knows a lot about hardware as well as software, right?"

I let out an exasperated sigh. "Where are we going with this?"

"Just answer the question, doc."

I rolled my eyes. "Yes, he knows about software and hardware. So what?"

Boyle leaned closer to my face, and his eyes narrowed. "Do you know how information is transmitted across telephone lines?"

"I haven't got a clue," I said. Then it dawned on me. My God! Were they trying to say that Sam had something to do with. . .? "What are you saying?" I asked, the narrowing of my eyes matching Boyle's. "Wait a minute. They called it an act of terrorism on the news. You're not saying—?"

"That's exactly what we're saying, Doctor. We believe that

Agent Hunter is very much involved with the communication systems break down."

My mind was reeling. First, they told me that Sam had been dealing drugs, then he was been suspended and under surveillance for six months, now he's a telephone terrorist. "When are you people going to make up your minds? I argued. "Is Sam supposed to be a drug dealer or a terrorist?"

While Wood remained at his post and stone-faced like a cigar store indian, Boyle's reaction, though subtle, was a bit more pronounced. I don't think he knew about the illicit drugs accusations. His eyebrows twitched almost imperceptibly upon hearing my rhetorical question, and he hesitated for a moment. Then he laughed awkwardly. It was as artificial as his politeness. "I guess we're saying your husband's been a busy boy."

I'd had enough of this bull shit, so I rose from my chair. The cigar store indian immediately dropped his arms and took a step toward me. I glared at him, daring him to come closer. My bravado was pure facade. Inside, I was shitting my pants. "You seem to know more about it than I do, so I think I'll be on my way," I announced as if we had been having a casual chit chat.

"Sit your ass back in that chair, Doctor," Boyle ordered as he rose to his feet, and leaned over the table on both hands.

My eyes were locked in a staring contest with Boyle's, but my peripheral vision caught a glimpse of Wood's hand reaching inside of his suitcoat for his gun. I remained motionless for a long moment, forcing myself not to look in Wood's direction. Knowing I had no choice, I finally acquiesced and settled into the chair. "Am I a suspect?"

"After the fact, primarily," Boyle answered as he also sat down. Wood returned to his previous inanimate posture.

"We think you know exactly what your husband's been up to, and we think you may have important information for us," Boyle continued.

Air was slowly escaping from that fanciful balloon I had been living in. This was the second time I had been accused of knowing about and possibly participating in criminal activity. What had Sam been up to for the last six months? Had Scolnik been telling me the truth? Had Sam been on suspension for the last six months? Could it be possible that I didn't really know him? Would Sam—? Suddenly the voice of reason inside of my head spoke up. "Never!" it said. "Trust Sam. He's a good man." But the seeds of doubt had been planted, and I couldn't let them grow. I had to find out the truth for Sam and for me.

"Well, now that we're nice and comfy again, Doc, what can you tell us about your husband's criminal activities?" Boyle asked.

"Sam was not involved in any criminal activities. Besides, you supposedly had him under surveillance. You would obviously know more than I."

Boyle cocked his head and furrowed his brow. "Surveillance?" Then suddenly he caught himself. "Uh, yes, surveillance. Well, we've had him under surveillance, but there's still a lot more to learn."

"You're not going to learn it from me," I announced.

"Are you telling us you're not willing to cooperate with the FBI?"

"That, too. What I'm mostly telling you is that I don't know anything, and even if I did. . ." I cocked my head to meet Boyle's gaze. "Have you ever heard the term 'frontal lobotomy?'"

"Frontal what?" Boyle asked, righting his head.

"You can ask me questions until your balls turn blue, but I'll never be able to answer any of them because I've suddenly developed a spontaneous lobotomy. It's like someone just drilled a hole in my head, and my brains leaked out. Oops! Memory's gone!" I rocked backward in my chair, folded my arms across my chest, and smiled smugly.

More than an hour later, I emerged from the room feeling like I had been squeezed through an old wringer washer, but the two agents looked much worse than I felt. And they were hopping mad. I left the two of them stewing in the conference room while I met Kim and we strolled out of the hospital.

"You're looking full of yourself," Kim said.

"Yes. I always wondered how I'd hold up if I were under interrogation. I don't have to wonder anymore. I'm pretty damn good at it, even if I do say so myself."

Kim laughed, but I did not. We were walking past the blue Blazer. "It's still here," I said, pausing to stare at it.

Kim took hold of my arm and urged me onward. "So, what did they ask you?" she asked, her curiosity nearing explosive proportions.

"I'll tell you everything, but let's get out of here. That car gives me the creeps."

"You took a big chance talking to them, you know," Kim said as she unlocked the passenger door to her cruiser. Why'd you do it? I could've prevented it."

"I didn't want to get you into trouble. They *are* the FBI. You could lose your badge for interfering with their investigation, couldn't you?" I climbed into the passenger side, and Kim slid behind the wheel.

"It's no big deal. There's no love lost between the CPD and the FBI," Kim said. "They like to muscle their way in all the time. I might've gotten a reprimand, maybe a two-day suspension at the most. It would've all been for show to keep 'Big Brother' off our backs." She stuck the key in the ignition and started the engine.

Kim started to pull away from the curb, then stopped and dug her notepad and pen out of her bag. She leaned toward me, stretching her neck to look through my window. Sitting upright, she jotted down the Blazer's license plate number. "It's a local non-commercial plate. It should be easy to trace," she said as she dropped the notebook on the center console and pulled away from the curb.

Kim drove to the end of the driveway, turned into the visitor's lot, and found a parking space that was not visible from the parking area in front of the ER. She killed the engine and turned to me. "Wait here. I'll be right back."

"Where're you going?" I asked.

"I want to check something out."

"Not this again," I said.

Kim let go a single chuckle. "No stealth attacks this time. I just want to see if the two suits get into your favorite car." She climbed out and darted between parked cars, then waited behind a customized van. I couldn't see the Blazer from my vantage point and I wasn't about to get out and follow Kim again, so I waited. A few minutes later, Kim returned to the car and climbed in. She buckled her shoulder harness and started the engine.

"Well?" I asked.

"Yep."

"So, what does that mean? Am I under FBI surveillance?"

"I don't know. Something's not right here."

"What do you mean?"

"Just one of my hunches. Don't worry about it for now. I'll tell you if it turns out to be more than a hunch."

"Oh, just what I need, more suspense," I complained.

"What we both need is food. Let's go somewhere, get something to eat, and re-read Sam's note. There's got to be something to it."

As we headed down the road to a destination guided by Kim's stomach, I glanced at my watch. Shelby could call home at any time to say hello. She'd go nuts if the FBI answered. I had to call her and soon.

16

Known for its incredible cinnamon rolls, Baker's Square was busy with the late morning breakfast crowd. By the time we were seated and my senses had been stimulated by the sights and aroma of food, I was feeling hungry. I decided to indulge and order myself a giant cinnamon roll—half usually filled me up—along with a large orange juice and a life-saving cup of caffeine. Kim, about a size four, whose head barely met my chin, ordered two cinnamon rolls, a large milk, a large orange juice, and a cup of coffee.

My mouth must have been in the fly catching mode, because Kim looked at me and said, "So? I'm hungry."

I just shook my head and smiled. I am always amazed when I see tiny people pack away enormous quantities of food. It just isn't fair.

While we waited for our breakfast, Kim handed me Sam's note to study while she played with the key and the rice object. I read the note, but nothing was jumping out at me. Focusing on Sam's sentence about Shelby and the strangers, I remembered that we told her that strangers weren't necessarily people she didn't know. They may be people who have nice faces and act friendly at first. They may even be people she knows casually. We hadn't been trying to make her paranoid, but we wanted her to understand that child molesters and kidnappers are quite often people in trusted positions, and we wanted Shelby to be aware of the danger signs. It had always been a narrow line to walk along trying, on one hand, to protect our daughter with knowledge, and on the other, trying not to make her afraid of everybody she knows. Shelby seemed to be doing pretty well so far, so we must have found the right balance between the two positions.

"I think this reference to strangers is a warning," I finally said. "I can't come up with anything that would have to do with a key."

"How about the other part?" Kim asked.

"You mean his last words to me?"

"Yes."

I thought hard. What had he said to me? I had been so caught up in my fear over his bizarre behavior, had I bothered to listen? He meant every word, I repeated in my mind, paraphrasing his note. It must have had something to do with his feelings for me or for Shelby.

My pager vibrating on my belt, broke my concentration. The number on my LED was unfamiliar. When I dialed and the other party picked up, I heard a sound that took my breath away. It was that same raspy breathing I had heard on the other end of my home phone before Sam had called about John Doe's clothing. "Who is this?" I demanded angrily.

The breather inhaled deeply. It sounded like his breath was being dragged across sandpaper. "You have something we want."

"Who are you!" I barked. My eyes met Kim's and she understood that something was very wrong.

"That's not important," the disembodied harsh voice replied. "That you do exactly as you are told, is."

"And if I don't?"

"There is a certain young lady staying with some friends at their lake house in Wisconsin. You wouldn't want her to have an accident, would you?"

The breather's last sentence burned into my brain like a branding iron into a cow's hide. "You harm a single hair on my daughter's head, and I will not sleep until I have destroyed you," I threatened, surprised at the sound of my own words. I looked across the table at Kim who was now hanging on my every word, while she was dialing her cellular phone.

"If you give us what we want, your daughter will be unharmed," the breather continued. "Oh, by-the-way, tell your little detective friend to hang up her phone immediately or your daughter's dead."

My God! They were watching us. I looked around me, trying to see someone looking in my direction. Everyone seemed to be staring back at me. Paranoia clutched at my throat.

"How do I know you haven't hurt her already?" I asked as I gestured to Kim to hang up. She complied reluctantly.

"Call the lake house. Oh, but they may not answer. They're all down at the dock, enjoying the warm water and sunshine."

"Jesus," I whispered. I closed my eyes and drew in a deep breath. Blood was surging inside my ears, my heart was threatening to jump out of my chest, and my skin felt cold and clammy. I shivered and spoke as calmly as possible. "What is it you think I have?"

Another dry, wheezing breath preceded the man's reply. "Your detective friend is holding it in her hand right now."

Stunned by his last sentence, my eyes opened wide and I scanned the room frantically, searching for a clue to the man's identity.

"What does he want?" Kim mouthed.

I pointed to the key. Then I gestured that he could see us. Kim, too, searched the room, but neither of us was able to pinpoint anyone who might be the speaker.

"Are you talking on a cellular phone?" I asked. I kept glancing around, hoping to catch a glimpse of someone with a cell phone pressed against his ear.

"Now, now, Doctor Hunter. Stick to what you know; medicine. Don't try to play detective. You'll only get burned." Another drag of sandpaper air sent a chill down my spine. "Are you ready to follow your instructions?"

"Yes," I said with certain desperation in my voice.

"Good." The man directed me to a phone booth on the city's southwest side approximately five miles from the Baker's Square. I was to leave the key on top of the phone along with Sam's note and the bullet lens.

"Bullet lens?" I asked.

"That odd little object that the detective's holding in her other hand." The voice continued with the directions. If I made any stops along the way, or if I tried to give them the wrong key, they would know, and Shelby would die slowly. As I listened, I picked up the key. How did they know whether or not I was leaving the right key? It was an innocuous brass key that didn't look terribly different from my own house key. There was a logo stamped into the key, but I had always assumed that such a logo represented the key's manufacturer and wouldn't lead anyone to the lock it opened. My current state of paranoia caused me to doubt my previous assumption. I found myself wondering if it represented something more. Would the key lead them to what they wanted? If so, what exactly was it that was more important than human life?

Feeling in no position to argue further, I agreed to his terms. Kim and I left the restaurant just as the waitress arrived with our rolls. Kim handed her a twenty and grabbed the rolls and our two napkins. "We'll eat in the car," she said.

On the way to the designated phone booth, I began to have second thoughts about leaving them the key. It was, for me, the only link to helping Sam and possibly the only protection against them killing Shelby. "Once I give them the key, what's to stop them from killing Shelby?" I asked.

"I'll get her some protection." Next thing I knew, Kim was talking with the Wisconsin State Police. I supplied her with address and phone number of the Cooper's lake house which she passed on to the police. Kim then explained that Shelby was not aware of the situation and asked them to use discretion. When the conversation ended, she shut off her cell phone and laid it on the seat next to her. "Now we have some assurances."

While Kim was talking to the Wisconsin State Police, I was on my own phone trying the Cooper's number. As the man with the raspy voice had said, there was no answer. If only I could have heard Shelby's voice.

Kim made another call, this time on her radio. She was patched through to her boss, gave him the drop address, and arranged for the booth to be placed under surveillance. When Kim was about to sign off, the dispatcher informed her that the plates she had been running were stolen.

That piqued my interest. "You mean the men who interrogated me weren't FBI?"

"I doubt the FBI is in the habit of stealing license plates." Kim was thoughtful for a moment. "Goddam ID's had me fooled."

"Who are these people," I asked, "who have the balls to walk around in broad daylight impersonating federal agents? Don't they worry about getting caught?"

"Those two American Gladiator rejects didn't seem too concerned to me," Kim replied. "Damn," she said more to herself than to me. "A New York cop, FBI agents—or facsimiles of—driving around in a stolen car, a John Doe stiff hauled off by two as yet to be found Chicago cops, the same two cops who generated the report of the shooting involving your husband. We're circling a vat of dog shit and if we're not careful, we'll be finding ourselves drowning at the bottom of the vat."

"Do you think someone in the FBI is involved?" I asked. I could feel my stomach coiling itself into a tight knot.

Kim shrugged. "Whoever these people are, they have to be getting help from somewhere. The other question I have is: What's this all about?

"Drugs?"

"I haven't seen a single tangible piece of evidence pointing to drugs."

"What about the report on Sam?"

"Yeah, but where're the drugs?"

"The surgeon said that Sam O.D.'d on drugs; coke or heroine," I said. "I know he wasn't a drug user, so someone had to pump them into him."

"Probably for show," Kim remarked.

I opened my hand and stared at the key and the other object. I hadn't realized I had been squeezing the key so hard that it had made a deep impression in my palm. Droplets of blood showed in several places where the points of the key had broken my skin. "That man, the one who called me, referred to this as a bullet lens." I rolled the tiny object between my thumb and index finger and held it up to the light. It was clear, not opaque like rice. We had made assumptions about it without really looking closely at it. Our assumptions clouded our perception, so we only saw a piece of rice.

"Bullet lens? What the hell's a bullet lens?" Kim asked.

I rolled the so-called bullet lens along Sam's note paper. Tiny dust particles and paper fibers seemed to jump out at me from behind the lens. "Holy shit!" I exclaimed.

"What? What?"

"It magnifies things."

"What d'ya mean?" Kim asked.

"It's like a little magnifying glass," I replied. I held the note closer to my face. "It's really powerful, almost like a tiny microscope."

"What's it supposed to magnify? Why do they want it?"

"Don't ask me. I don't have the answers." I was becoming increasingly frustrated and angry with Sam. Why had he sent this to me? He knew I didn't know anything about his work. Would I send him an MRI and ask him to interpret it? Would I expect him to know how to do a differential diagnosis on a patient who presents with abdominal pain? No, dammit! He should have sent these things to Ben Scolnik. Ben would know what to do.

I stuffed the bullet lens into the envelope along with Sam's note and the key and tossed the envelope on the seat next to me. "What'd you do that for?" Kim asked.

"I don't want to look at it anymore," I snapped. "We'll be at the phone booth soon. I can't do anything about it anyway."

"Getting a little testy, are we?"

I flashed Kim a cursory glare then stared out my window.

"I think we can do something about it," Kim said.

I gave a disgusted sigh. "What?" I asked unenthusiastically.

Kim was thoughtful for a moment, then she eased her foot off the accelerator and the car slowed from ten miles an hour over the limit to ten miles an hour below it. The car behind us immediately rode up on our tail. At first, I thought it might be someone who was following us, but I knew I was wrong when the car horn blared, and I turned to find the driver flailing his hands about in exasperation and flashing us the "bird".

Undaunted by the man's outrage, Kim directed me to her back seat where she had a case filled with detective toys including a camera, tape recorder, fingerprint supplies, evidence bags and a tub of putty. As she instructed, I made an impression of both sides of the key in the putty, and snapped photos of the bullet lens, key, and the note. Then Kim directed me to her cosmetic case in the glove compartment. Inside the case, I found a diamond nail file. I used the file to wear down several points on the key in hopes that it would prevent it from turning in whatever lock it was designed to open.

"How is any of this going to help?" They're going to find whatever this opens before we do. They seem to know what they're looking for.

"Maybe." Kim shrugged. "But they won't be able to get in. If there're any witnesses around, they won't want to break in forcibly until much later."

"So how is that going to help us?"

"It'll just buy us time to figure out where the lock is. Sam believed you'd be able to puzzle it out, or he wouldn't have given you the job."

"Are you sure it'll work?" I asked, studying my filing job.

"It's all we've got, so we might as well give it a try."

"How do you know the Wisconsin State Police can protect Shelby?"

"Because these guys won't try to kill her, not yet at least."

"Why not?"

"You're their only link to Sam and whatever it is they think he has. They'll keep Shelby alive and dangle you at the end of their string until they don't need either of you anymore, and—"

"I know the 'and'," I said.

"That's it." Kim gestured with a nod toward a phone booth on the street corner.

I started to open the door then turned to her. "You're sure this is the right thing to do?" I asked.

"There aren't a whole lot of other options here. Besides, there's a dozen cops watching the phone booth as we speak. They'll latch onto the pawn who'll be sent to pick up the key and follow him.

I smiled and thanked her for being so damn good at her job. Then I climbed out of the car. Afraid that someone might choose that moment to shoot me down, I nervously looked around before proceeding to the phone booth. I didn't see anything out of the ordinary. If the cops were there, as Kim had said, they were so well hidden that I began to doubt they existed. My confidence waned.

I placed the envelope containing the key, note, and bullet lens in the phone booth as instructed and returned to Kim's car without incident. Buckling my seatbelt, I asked her if she was sure the cops were watching. "They're watching," she said with a reassuring smile.

I stared back at the phone booth and prayed for Shelby's safety as we drove slowly away.

17

"What's the game plan from here?" I asked when we had driven out of sight of the phone booth.

Kim craned her neck while her eyes darted from one rearview mirror to the other. "First, we get rid of our tail," she said. "Face front!" she scolded when I started to turn around to see the car she was talking about. "I don't want them to know I know they're back there. Not yet anyway."

"Them?" I leaned toward my window to get a peek through my rearview mirror. I could only see the driver in the car directly behind us. The shock of blue curls barely showing above the steering wheel convinced me that she wasn't our tail.

Kim gave me a cursory glance as she grabbed her phone. "There're two cars. One's three back and the other's hanging on in fifth place. They're taking turns." She punched in a number and stuck the phone to her ear.

Looking in my mirror, I could see the passenger sides of the two cars. One looked like a white Taurus, and the other was a green sedan of some kind.

Kim finished her conversation and turned to me with an impish glint in her eye. "Seatbelt fastened?"

I gave my shoulder harness a tug to confirm that I was, indeed, buckled in safely. Kim didn't wait for a reply. Ramming her foot practically through the floor boards, she announced, "Let's see if we can't ditch these bastards."

I felt a sudden surge of power beneath me as we raced forward like a jet barrelling down the runway. The roar of the souped up 5.7 liter engine, customized for police use, was deafening.

Though I held on to my shoulder harness for dear life, and my teeth were cutting a hole in my cheek, I found myself exhilarated by the experience. Hyde Park streets are narrow and congested, but that didn't seem to bother Kim, who darted in between and around cars with the proficiency of an Indy race driver. She'd slow only slightly as we approached intersections, while she flipped the toggle on her siren, sending out a trio of short blasts to alert the cross traffic she was coming through.

When I had the presence of mind, I checked my rearview mirror. The two cars were still on our tail. We circled the Museum of Science and Industry. "It won't be long now," Kim said

as we entered Lake Shore Drive and headed toward downtown, and were met by no less than four radio cars. The blue strobes flashing on their roof tops was a welcomed sight. The squad cars had taken up positions across all the lanes, causing what is referred to as a traffic break. It is a strategy used to control traffic approaching an accident. This time it was going to help a sister cop and her passenger escape trouble.

Kim maneuvered skillfully through the slowing traffic with our tail following close behind. We moved in behind one of the radio cars, and Kim greeted her fellow officers on her radio. "Hi boys and girls," she chirped. "We have a white late model Taurus directly behind us followed by a green Caprice. Maybe you could say hello to our friends and invite them to the next policemen's ball." She hung up her handset, and the radio car we were following sped up, leading us out of the building traffic jam. The other three squads spun sideways, bringing the flow of traffic to a dead stop. Brakes squealed, and horns blared.

When we were near McCormick Place, Kim slowed to a normal speed and gave her siren a short burst. The cop in the radio car responded in kind. Then he turned off at the next exit.

"Now we can get something useful accomplished," Kim said in a calm, businesslike tone. I was beginning to understand why Sam loved his work so much.

"What's next?" I asked reluctantly, afraid of what the answer might be.

"We pay a visit to a locksmith," Kim said. Her foot eased off the gas pedal and moved to the break. We were approaching the traffic nightmare around the Field Museum and Shedd Aquarium created by a massive road construction project that promised to re-route and improve traffic patterns in the future. Most Chicagoans who travelled downtown wondered if that "future" would come in their lifetimes. Even Kim's skilled driving couldn't get us quickly through that mess.

"Do you know a locksmith?" I don't know why I bothered to ask. I was beginning to think Kim had the entire city wrapped around her little finger.

"I've got someone in mind. We're very close—"

"Why am I not surprised," I interrupted.

Kim smiled.

"Where is this locksmith with whom you're very close?"

Kim's smile turned apologetic. "Hyde Park," she said. "Hand me a cinnamon roll, will you? I might as well eat now. It doesn't look like we'll get anywhere very fast."

"I opened the napkin that had been wrapped around one of Kim's rolls and picked away the bits of fuzzy paper that were clinging to the sticky frosting. Kim took the roll and bit into it, letting a hedonistic moan escape her lips. When I think back to that time, I have little doubt that it was Kim's antics and her upbeat personality that saved my sanity during the darkest hours of my life. "Hab fum," Kim offered, her cheeks looking like a chipmunk's filled with nuts gathered for winter storage.

I was considering her offer, trying to determine whether or not a roll would settle my stomach or make me puke, when my pager beckoned. This time I recognized the number. It was Ben Scolnik's.

"Ben," I said when he picked up.

"Deb, where are you?"

"In the car," I replied.

"We need to talk. How soon can we meet?"

"Is it about Sam?"

"Yes."

"What've you found out?"

"I can't talk over the cellular phone. Can you meet me somewhere?"

"Yes, but not right now. I have a lot of questions for you, Ben. Can I call you?"

"Yes."

"At work?"

"No." To my surprise, Ben alluded to the fact that people in his office could not be trusted. He gave me what he referred to as a secured number and told me to call him from a hard line. I wondered if Sam's note about strangers was referring to people in his own office. It certainly sounded to me like Ben had the same worries.

I shut off my phone, laid it in my lap and stared out my window at the chaos surrounding the construction zone. I noticed the faces of the other drivers trapped with us in what promised to be a perpetual traffic snarl. Some were taut with frustration while others showed no emotion at all. A few of them glanced my way, and I wondered if they could see on my face the hell I was living in.

After a moment, I turned to Kim who was busy licking her fingers while working her way through the traffic. She looked at me then quickly at the cars in front of us. "So what was that all about?" she asked.

"Ben Scolnik wants to talk to me."

"About what?"

"I don't know. He wouldn't tell me. He said it wasn't safe to talk on cellular phones."

"Is he the paranoid type?" Kim stepped on the gas and the car moved forward, then her foot shot to the break and we screeched to a halt once again. "Asshole!" Kim hissed at the car in front of us. "He couldn't even tell you what it was about?"

"He said it had something to do with Sam."

"How informative of him," Kim said.

Kim's radio crackled to life and she grabbed the handset. The dispatcher directed her to switch to a private channel. When a man's voice crackled "Hey, woman!" over the speaker, Kim responded with, "Hey, Ebola, what's up?"

"Ebola?" I whispered.

Kim let go of the speaker button and said, "His name's Ebolansky. We couldn't let that one slide."

"Wasting our time, that's what's up. And it's your fault," the disembodied voice answered.

"Aw, Ebola. They got you babysitting the phone booth?" Kim asked.

"Yeah. My ass's growing blisters sitting on this goddam rubber roof."

"Any action?"

"There's action all right. The feds just kicked our asses off the case."

"What d'ya mean, they kicked you off the case? How could they kick you off the case? How'd they even know you were on the case? Who the hell called them in?" Kim asked.

"Nobody called them, sweetheart. They called us."

Kim's eyes met mine, and she frowned deeply. "They called you?" she asked into her mic. "How'd they find out?"

"You tell me?" the voice called Ebola said.

"What about the guy who picked up the package in the phone booth?" Kim asked.

"The booth hasn't seen any traffic."

"How long ago did you leave?" Kim asked.

"Leave! I'm still up on the friggin' roof."

"Is there any way you can stick around and keep an eye on things?"

"I'm already farther into overtime than I want to be," Ebola said. "I'm off duty, and I'm going home as soon as I get my gear packed up."

"There's a coffee shop in sight of the phone booth." Kim's

voice had become deliberately ingratiating.

"Aw Jesus, Hawthorne. I'm dog tired. I don't want to do this," Ebola complained.

"Y'know, Ebolansky, I have this marker in my wallet. You remember it from our last poker game, don't you?"

"That's extortion, Hawthorne!"

"Technically speaking." Kim's face was alight with a playful smile. It was clear she liked having control. "That marker could disappear."

"OK. OK. You win. I'll stay one hour. Not a minute more."

"Try the chocolate latté. It's delicious."

"Yeah, Hawthorne? Try kissing my—"

"Uh, uh, Ebola," Kim interrupted. "I'm sure you don't want to make any anatomically explicit comments over the open air waves. Do you?"

"We're on a private channel," Pete reminded her.

"That's right. Talk to you later." Kim signed off, squelching Pete's chance at a comeback, and found a break in the traffic. "So, your buddy, Scolnik, calls and wants to talk to you and at the same time, the feds take over the watch at the phone booth. Funny little coincidence, wouldn't you say?"

"I think this time it is just a coincidence."

"How well do you know this Scolnik character?"

"Well enough. We can trust him," I assured her.

"If you say so." Kim didn't sound convinced, but then I remembered her statement that everyone was guilty in her eyes until proven innocent. I decided Kim would probably make the Pope prove his innocence to her.

"If I can't trust the people I know, who can I trust?" I said in an attempt to ease her suspicious mind and convince her that Ben was one of the good guys.

"Me," Kim said.

18

Kim's locksmith friend greeted us at the front door. He turned out to be her brother, Richard, a Chicago cop who was hobbling around on crutches.

"This is the gimp," Kim said to me as she breezed past her brother. "Say hello, Gimp," She chirped at him.

"Hello." With a warm smile, Richard placed both crutches in his left hand and offered his right hand for me to shake.

"What happened?" I asked, looking at Richard's casted leg. I thought it appropriate to ask, since Kim had made an issue of Richard's physical state.

"I tore my Achilles tendon."

"Ow, that's smarts," I said sympathetically. "Did you hurt it on the job?"

"No. I tore it during a pick up basketball game." Though four years Kim's senior and nearly a foot taller, Richard looked like her fraternal twin, and he was every bit as lively. Like his sister, Richard was divorced and living in the family home with Kim and their mother, Margaret, a tiny woman who measured five-feet-tall, if she raised her heels off the floor. Margaret welcomed us with open arms and offered us her own home baked coffee cake along with steaming cups of freshly brewed coffee. Her maiden name was McGill, and her voice sparkled with remnants of the Irish brogue she had carried with her from the Emerald Isle at age fifteen.

We sat around the Hawthorne's kitchen table listening to Margaret's stories of Kim and Richard's childhood antics, for a time, avoiding discussions of the present. The warmth of the

Hawthorne's bungalow, the delicious food, and the delightful company carried me, although temporarily, away from my problems.

Life has a way of sneaking into our fantasies, however, and that time was no exception. I was yanked back to the cruel reality of my own life, when my pager came to life yet again. This time it was the number at the Cooper's cottage.

"May I use your telephone?" I asked. "It's Shelby." Three pairs of eyes immediately fell upon me.

"What're you going to do?" Kim asked.

"Call her."

"How much are you going to tell her over the phone?" Kim continued.

"Damned if I know," I stated, as I pushed myself away from the table and stood up.

"You can use the one in my room," Kim offered. Then she led me down a hallway lined on either side with a photographic genealogy of the Hawthorn and McGill families.

Kim apologized in advance for her bedroom decor. "Mom's kind of sentimental. She didn't want to change it. She says it keeps me close even when I am away. Besides, I'm only here temporarily, since my divorce."

"That was quite a while ago, wasn't it?"

Kim's lips twisted. "Yeah. O.K. So it's a long temporary." She opened the door, and I found myself surrounded by childhood memorabilia. It gave me an opportunity to step back in time and meet the child that had grown into the tough little cop with whom I had become friends. A pair of twin beds separated by a night table occupied one wall. The bed spreads were white, covered in a print of tiny lilac bouquets while waterfalls of sheer ruffles spilled over the sides. The night table was classic little girl's bedroom, white with gold trim. Against the wall opposite the beds stood a matching five drawer dresser, covered with trophies from volleyball and softball, and in the corner, sat a desk, complete with pencil cup and dictionary. From the myriad touched-up nicks in the wood, I surmised that Kim was a lot rougher on her things than I had been on mine. The wall paper, a perfect match with the bedspreads, had faded and yellowed with time, and curled edges where they had pulled away from the seams. School and sports pictures of Kim hung on the walls along with graduation ribbons, pendants, and a pom-pom, its bright blue and gold clashing with the delicate lilacs. A mountain of stuffed animals kept each other company in the corner. The only modern looking object in the room was the white trim line phone on top of the night table. There was no sign of the adult who now inhabited the room. I half expected a twelve-year-old Kim to bounce into the bedroom, golden hair braided tomboy style and hidden under a baseball cap, and plop her school books on the desk. Then my thoughts wandered to another little girl's room. Shelby was a lot like Kim; a tomboy with all of Kim's energy and athleticism. That's probably why I had grown to like Kim so fast, once I got past the bimbo concept.

My heart ached when I thought about Shelby. Her life had been idyllic until now. She was a happy, well adjusted teenager with two parents who were devoted to her, and each other. I pictured my daughter's smiling, bubbly face the last time she saw her father. Her eyes had been so bright, so full of innocence. I felt an overwhelming grief, because I knew, once I made the phone call, the light of innocence would be gone from Shelby's eyes forever.

I sat down heavily on one of the beds and reached for the phone, steeling myself for the conversation that I was about to have with my only child. I tried to organize my thoughts as I picked up the receiver and punched in the Cooper's number. I knew I had to tell Shelby about her dad, but should I say exactly how grave his condition was? Should I tell my child that her own life was in danger? Three rings later, Barbara Cooper was saying, "Hello."

"Hi, Barbara."

"Deb, the police are here. They say they're here to protect us, but they won't say from what. They just said it had to do with

Shelby." Barbara's voice trembled anxiously as mine would have had I been in her shoes. What a shock it must have been for her to open her door to a state cop and then be told that she and her family were in danger. "What's going on, Deb? Why do I have squad cars parked in my driveway and troopers invading my home?"

"It's a long story, Barbara. I can't go into all of it right now, but Sam's in . . . " I took a deep breath and fought back tears. "Sam's in the hospital. He's been shot."

I heard a loud gasp on the other end of the line. "Oh my God! Will he be all right?"

"No." Now it was my voice that trembled. "He's in a coma," I said thickly. Another gasp. "But please don't let on to Shelby how bad it is. I'll tell her that in person."

"I'm so sorry, Deb. If there's anything—"

"Just be there for Shelby. It's going to be hard enough for her even without knowing everything."

"I'll take care of her," Barbara promised.

"I need to talk to her now. Where is she?"

"She's coming up from the dock. She'll be here in a minute."

"Thanks."

"Deb, what about the police? Why are we in danger?"

"The people who shot Sam seem to think I have something they want or I know where to find it. They've threatened Shelby's life if I don't give it to them."

"What is it they're after? Why don't you give it to them?"

"They asked for a key that Sam sent me. I gave it to them, but I'm not sure it's everything they want."

"Why can't the police take Shelby into protective custody?"

"They could, I guess, but I'm not sure if you, too, are at risk since Shelby's been staying with you."

"You mean my family might be hurt because of something you and Sam have done?" Her voice was suddenly sharp and tinged with anger.

"You make it sound like Sam and I are in some kind of conspiracy. I'm sorry you're caught up in the middle of this, but I'm as much a victim as you. As for Sam, he was just doing his job. I'm sure he didn't invite any of this."

"Did you know about the danger before you let Shelby come with us?" Barbara asked coolly as if she had suddenly become a stranger.

"If I had, d'ya think I would've let Shelby out of my sight for even a minute? You know me, Barbara, well enough to know I would never knowingly put you or anyone in your family at risk." My words were met by silence.

"Here's Shelby," was the next thing Barbara said.

"Hi, Mom," Shelby bubbled. "Something's going on. The cops are here, and Barbara looks really mad. Is she mad at you?"

"I think so. A little," I answered quietly.

"What'd you do? She's never gotten mad at you before."

"It's only temporary. I think Barbara's more upset than mad."

"Mom, your voice sounds kinda funny. What's wrong?"

"Just a minute." I grabbed a tissue and wiped my eyes and blew my nose. "Shelby, honey, Daddy's . . ." The word's caught in my throat.

"Mom?" I could hear a subtle trembling in Shelby's voice. "Is something wrong with Daddy?"

The room suddenly felt like a vacuum. I groped for air. Telling Shelby finally made it real. "Daddy's in the hospital. He's been shot."

"Daddy? Is he—?"

"He's sleeping right now," I interrupted, not wanting her to ask me a direct question like: Is he going to be all right? or Is he going to die? I didn't want to lie to her. "He sends his love. You can see him as soon as you come home." That wasn't exactly a lie, because I did know that if Sam could, he would send her his love.

"Is that why the police are here?"

"Yes, partly. It's just something they do for the families when an agent is shot," I lied.

"I want to come home, Mom," Shelby cried. "I want to see Daddy."

"I know, Sweetheart. I'm coming up to get you."

"When will you get here?"

"It might be a few hours, but I'll be there as soon as I can." Hearing my grief stricken daughter sobbing on the other end of the line, made my heart crumble. "It'll be all right, baby," I consoled. "God will take care of us."

"I don't want Daddy to die," Shelby wailed.

He's already gone, baby, I thought. He's already gone. Our conversation continued for a few more minutes. Little new was said. Instead, I spent the time trying to find the right words to comfort both Shelby and myself. There were none.

After I hung up the phone, I remained seated until I was able to compose myself. On my way back to the kitchen, I found the bathroom, and washed my face in cold water. When I examined myself in the mirror, I was shocked to see the blotched, haggard looking face of a stranger staring back at me. I looked like I had aged a hundred years.

Upon my return to the kitchen, I found Kim, Richard, and Margaret still seated around the table.

"Do you have the key mold?" Richard asked Kim. Kim produced it from her handbag and gave it to him.

"How'd it go?" Kim asked when she saw me enter the kitchen.

I just shook my head and shrugged my shoulders.

"I'm so sorry, my dear," Margaret said to me, her eyes expressing motherly compassion. I needed a mother about then.

"I explained the situation to them while you were talking to Shelby," Kim said.

I was glad she told her mother and Richard the story while I was out of the room. It was bad enough living it and telling Shelby about it without having to relive it from Kim's perspective.

Kim tossed the stack of Polaroids that I had taken of the key, bullet lens, and Sam's letter onto the table in front of Richard, who was examining the key's impression in the putty.

"I don't know if these'll help," she said.

That's when Margaret got up to leave the kitchen, saying, "I'll leave you children alone to discuss your police business." Then she headed down the hall to her bedroom.

"Gonna finger the ol' beads, ma?" Richard teased.

"I'll be throwin' in an extra Novena for you," she retorted.

Kim chuckled. "Mom never warmed up to police work. It always made her nervous. She'll be in her rocking chair saying the Rosary all night."

Richard picked up the photos of the key. "This is definitely a locksmith's custom key logo. I can find the locksmith easily enough, but he probably won't know exactly who this particular key was made for."

"He'll have a list of people and businesses he makes custom keys for, won't he?" Kim quizzed.

"Probably," Richard answered, "but that could be a mighty long list. This *is* Chicago, you know." Richard looked at the photo of Sam's note. "It would help to know what your husband said to you on the phone."

"What?"

"Well, if it was me writin' this note. I wouldn't give up the location in the note itself. It's clear he wants you to remember what he said to you."

"That was a million years ago," I expressed, spiritlessly.

Kim rested her hand on top of mine. "I know you've been through a lot and you're exhausted, but you and I both know Richard's right. It's what Sam didn't put in the note that's important. That's why he referred to it."

No matter how hard I tried, the last words Sam had spoken to me were lost. "I'm sorry. I can't remember."

"That's O.K.," Richard said. "I'll duplicate the key and look up the locksmith. Maybe when you're looking at his customer list, something familiar will jump out at you."

"D'ya know anything about this?" Kim handed Richard the snapshot of the bullet lens.

"We're really getting into the heavy duty spy shit here," Richard told her.

"Spy shit? What do you mean, spy shit?" Kim asked.

"You never paid attention in the museums, did you?" Richard goaded. "All you ever did was zip past the exhibits and aim for the gift shop."

"All you did was eat," Kim retorted.

"Yeah, but I was chomping' while I was lookin' at the exhibits and learning something."

"So you're saying you saw this in a museum?" I asked.

"Yeah," Richard replied. "At the Smithsonian. This technology's about forty years old. I think the CIA still uses it, but not too often. With all the new computer technology nowadays, they don't need to bother with this. Now they just surf the net with encrypted messages. The encryptions are so complex, they can't be broken without the proper codes to unlock them." Richard stared at the picture of the tiny lens. "This is still a handy little toy when it's used unexpectedly."

"That's all wonderful, Richard, but what the hell's it used for?" Kim asked.

Richard let out an exasperated sigh at his sister and rolled his eyes. "Have you ever heard of microfilm or microdots?"

"You're shittin' me! You mean like real live spy stuff?" Kim said as she snatched the picture of the bullet lens from Richard's hand. "So where's the microdot buried?"

"It could be in the note," Richard said. "Sam could have used it to dot on one of his I's."

"This is just too cool!" Kim could hardly contain herself.

"Can we read it in the photo?" I asked.

"No," Richard said, "the camera wouldn't have recorded the detail. It doesn't matter anyway. I have no idea how to find a bullet lens. The only one I've ever seen was at the Smithsonian."

"How about a microscope?" Kim asked. "You have one in the toy palace, don't you?"

"Toy palace?" I asked.

Kim turned to me with a wry smile. "It's in the basement. You're looking at the world's biggest geek," she said, pointing her thumb at Richard.

I tried to picture Richard as a geek wearing glasses taped at the nosepiece and belted trousers pulled up to his armpits. No, Richard definitely didn't fit the geek role, action hero maybe, but not a geek.

"It's not going to work," Richard said.

"It won't hurt to try," Kim insisted. "You're going to be down there anyway, making the key."

Richard frowned then snatched up the stack of photos and got up from his chair. "C'mon with me," he said as he pulled my chair out for me, then started toward the basement door.

"How 'bout me?" Kim asked, hinting that he should also pull her chair out for her.

"Oh, you can come too," he replied impishly. Then he flipped up the light switch and headed downstairs with Kim and me following.

Kim was not kidding. Her brother was the ultimate toy freak. Along one entire basement wall sat a bench loaded with computer equipment. The four CPU's, two flat and two high rise mega computers, were Apple Macintosh. One color monitor was a basic fifteen inch Sony, while another was an oversized model used by engineers. There were Hewlitt Packard color scanners, a variety of laser printers, ink jets, and CD rom drives. You name it, it was on that bench. Along the adjacent wall, was a workbench littered with a variety of electronic toys, including the microscope, a couple of radios, and three very old Lionel model train engines. "Where's the railroad?" I asked facetiously, not expecting the answer I got.

"In the other room," Richard said, nodding toward a darkened room on the other side of the basement stairs. "Would you like to see them?"

"Don't get him started on that now," Kim warned. "He'll have you here for a decade."

"I'd love to see your trains when this's all over," I said.

Richard smiled almost flirtatiously. "I'll be happy to show them to you."

"Remember, we're down here to look under the microscope and make a key?" Kim reminded us.

Richard frowned his disappointed at Kim's interference with his fun, then he dropped the photos on the workbench next to the microscope. He selected the picture of Sam's note, reached under the workbench and brought out what looked like a clothing steamer, and explained to us that he would use the steamer to lift the photographic film, which contained the actual image, away from the backing. If it worked, he would have a transparency that could be examined like a slide under the microscope.

"This'll take some time," he said, "and it's a waste of time. Anything to please my baby sister."

Kim swatted him on the back. He glanced at the third bench along the wall opposite the computers. This was his locksmith's shop. A mind-boggling collection of uncut keys dangled from pegboard hooks on the wall above the bench. The cutting machine sat at one end while a box filled with an assortment of tools sat at the opposite end of the work table. Beyond the table was a wall safe large enough for an adult to walk through. "After I finish with the picture, I have to make a cast from the key impression. That will be the template from which I'll cut the key. It'll take a while."

"Great." Kim said. "We'll leave you alone so you can concentrate." She took me by my arm and led me toward the stairs.

"What's in there? I asked, pointing toward the safe.

"That's my weapons collection," Richard said, apparently delighted that he had a new audience interested in all of his toys.

"Richard loved museums so much, he decided to start one in his own home," Kim said.

"I'll be happy to show those to you also," Richard offered as Kim pushed me up the stairs.

"That would be fun," I barely had time to answer before Kim closed the door behind us.

We found Margaret in the kitchen, the Rosary's Crucifix dangling outside her apron pocket. She was busy slicing tomatoes and washing lettuce. "Is Richard coming up?" she asked.

"He's doing a couple of jobs for us," Kim answered.

"You two look a fright," Margaret said. "Why don't you lie down and take a nap?"

"I don't dare," I argued.

"Oh, but you must," Margaret insisted. "How can you be strong for your little girl, if you haven't had any sleep?"

I looked at Kim and she at me. The thought of sleeping, if only for a few minutes, was too inviting to turn down.

"It's settled then," Margaret said before we had a chance to reply. "You two run along to Kimberly's room while I start dinner."

I was sitting on the far twin bed, slipping my shoes off when I decided that I shouldn't sleep. It wasn't right. How could I sleep while some homicidal maniacs were threatening my daughter's life? "I can't do this," I announced as I stuck my feet into my shoes.

Kim was already under the sheets. She leaned up on one elbow and looked at me, shaking her head. "Mom's right. We won't be of any value to anyone if we don't buy ourselves a few minutes rest. There's not much we can do until Richard finishes, so we might as well make good use of the time."

"What about Shelby? Maybe I should forget about the key, and go get her."

"Listen, Deb, Shelby's safe with the police watching her. Like I said, as long as these people don't have what they want, they probably won't do anything to her or you. It'll be a different story if they get their hands on whatever it is they're after. I think you'll help yourself and your daughter a lot more if you get to it first."

I stared at her skeptically. "If we can figure out what we're looking for."

"I've got a feeling we'll know what it is when we find it."

Kim won the argument, not necessarily because she said anything that calmed my fears, but because my body was crying out for rest. I gave in and let my head sink into the downy soft pillow beneath me and closed my eyes.

Some time later, I was awakened from a dreamless deathlike sleep by Margaret's gentle, yet persistent, nudging. When I first opened my eyes, I thought I saw my own grandmother's face smiling at me. It was as if I had leapt into the past and was again a tiny child waking in my grandma's home.

"So you're alive," I heard Kim say from the other bed.

Not fully awake, I turned toward her voice in confusion. Gradually, my conscious brain kicked in and I remembered where I was and what I was doing there. I sat up sleepily and swung my feet over the side of the bed toward Kim, who was rubbing her neck and rolling her head around. "How long have we been asleep?" I asked.

"A couple of hours," Margaret replied. "Richard's waitin' for you in the kitchen. I've placed some towels and face cloths in the bath, so you girls can freshen up a bit." Margaret left the room, closing the door behind her.

"You first," Kim offered.

My body complained fiercely when I got up from the bed and wandered around to the other side where I had dropped my. I wished I'd had a little more sleep, like about twelve hours. After a short but delicious shower, I felt as though I'd had a full night's sleep. Years of medical training had taught my body to re-energize itself with minimal rest and a hot shower.

I left Kim to shower and joined Margaret and Richard in the kitchen where Margaret had laid out a banquet of sandwiches, salad, fresh fruit, and apple pie. Though I had eaten my fill of coffee cake a couple of hours earlier, my stomach started growling at the sight of food.

"Sit down and eat, dear," Margaret encouraged. "You'll need your strength."

Richard was already seated at the table, making himself a sandwich of ham and cheese on homemade bread. "Come, join me," he said as he jumped up, nearly knocking his chair over with his clumsy, casted leg, and pulled out a chair for me.

I accepted his kind offer and sat. "Thank you for everything. You've been very kind."

Richard patted my shoulder awkwardly. "You're having a rough time. I wish I could be more help." Once I was seated, Richard sat down and slid his chair next to mine.

"Did you find anything in the photo?" I asked.

"I'm sorry. I didn't think it would work. I usually like winning arguments with Kim, but I wish I would've lost this one."

"That's O.K. You tried. I can't ask any more than that. How about the key?"

"That part worked out fine," Richard announced as he proudly produced the key and slapped it onto the table. I picked up the key. Except for its new shine, it looked exactly like the key Sam had sent me.

"Thanks," I said.

"I hope it works."

"Me, too."

"Enough about keys and business," Margaret interjected. It's time for some nourishment."

Obediently, I filled my plate with fruit and salad, and made myself a turkey sandwich.

"Did you know that I knew Sam?" Richard asked.

I looked at him, surprised. "You did?"

"We went through the police training program together. I even met Sam's mom and dad a few times. They seemed like a real nice family."

"They are."

"Sam and I were assigned to different districts after training. We hung out a little after that. Then he fell in love, and gave up the bachelor scene. I guess that was with you." Richard flashed me an endearing smile.

"Yes, that was me."

"Sam's dad died last year, didn't he?"

"Heart attack," I responded vacantly, because a vision of a

lifeless Sam lying in his hospital bed with tubes protruding from every orifice and places where there weren't any, filled my head and tugged at my heart. I knew Sam would be joining his dad soon, if he wasn't with him already.

"How about his mom?" Richard asked, drawing me out of my musing. "She must be in pretty bad shape, losing her husband and now having this happen to her son."

Suddenly my tongue felt too large for my mouth, and I fought back tears. I hadn't called Sam's mom, Marilyn, or his sister, Annie, to tell them about Sam. In fact, I hadn't thought of them at all until that moment. Maybe it was better this way. What would I say to them if I did call? "Your son's brain dead and by the way, he's being investigated for trafficking illegal drugs?" No, I would wait. A call to tell them Sam died a hero would, at least, give them something positive to hold on to in light of the tragedy. "Marilyn is living in Seattle with Annie."

"That's right, Sam's sister," Richard said. "Is she still a cop?"

"She works weekends as a reserve deputy. She'll do that until her kids are older."

"And Sam. Is there any chance—?"

"No, none," I replied, my voice barely audible.

"Great! More food. I'm starving!" Kim chirped as she bounced into the room and plopped herself into the chair across from me. "Eat, girlfriend," she commanded.

Kim made herself a sandwich and devoured it while she and Richard discussed her loosely planned strategy which consisted mostly of winging it. Richard cautioned her to be careful and offered any help he could provide.

A call from Kim's friend, Ebolansky, ended the planning session. "They have the key," she said to me after she had hung up, her coldly focused cop's face replacing the playful visage that had been there minutes earlier. "They're on the move. We book." Kim jumped up from her chair, and I followed.

"Just a minute," Richard said, his chair vibrating loudly against the linoleum floor as he got up. "You'll need some help."

"That's OK," Kim said. "Jean Claude Van Damm here and I will manage just fine without gimp baggage, thank you."

"Chuck Norris," I corrected facetiously. "He has his black belt in Taekwondo, even though he lets people think it's in Karate."

"I stand corrected," Kim said, smiling.

"Hands and feet are fine, but sometimes you need to make a stronger impression," Richard stated.

"I don't think Deb will need a gun, Richard," Kim said.

"She needed one last night, didn't she?"

"Well, not really," Kim replied. "She never used it. Besides, we still have it if she needs it."

"Do you need ammo?" Richard asked. I could tell he really wanted to show me his gun collection.

"We're fine," Kim insisted.

"How about a machine pistol?" Richard did not give up easily. I have an Uzi."

Kim patted him on the cheek. "Thank you, dear, but save it for Rambo.

Soon we were on our way, armed with a new key, a locksmith's address, and our old guns. Kim had parked her squad car in Richard's garage, and we were riding in his dark blue Dodge pickup. Richard had insisted, saying, "It might keep away a few unwanted tails." On the floor between my legs, sat a cooler filled with sandwiches, fruit, and soda. Maggie worried that we might get hungry.

19

Pachkow's Locksmiths was located near Midway airport. The owner, a young macho type in his mid-twenties with a mustache and five o'clock shadow, was reticent to show us his customer lists. "Why can't you people get together on this stuff?"

"What do you mean?" Kim inquired.

"The FBI was in here less than an hour ago looking for the same thing."

"They were here? They were here?" My heart began pounding. "We're too late?"

Ignoring me, Kim continued to quiz the locksmith. "How many of them were there?"

"Three who came in, but I saw more outside."

"More? How many more?" Kim was jotting in her notebook.

The man shrugged indifferently. "I didn't count. A bunch."

Kim continued her interrogation. "What'd they look like?"

I couldn't tell if the man's response was due to the fact that he was a complete idiot, or he was just being a jerk. "All of them?"

Kim glared at him, and her answer was seethingly deliberate. "No, the three who came in."

The locksmith leaned across the counter bringing his face close to Kim's. He smiled salaciously. Bits of chewing tobacco clung to his teeth. Kim did not flinch. "Two had that concrete block look, and one was tall with silver hair." He stuck a toothpick in his mouth and lewdly rolled it around on his tongue.

"Eyes?" Kim continued, showing no response to the jerk's behavior.

"Yes."

Kim twisted her lips, and her shoulders sagged in disgust. "What color were their eyes?"

Upon seeing that he was getting nowhere with Kim, the man stood up, turned his back to us, and began sorting keys, hanging them on hooks on the wall behind the counter. "I don't remember what color the tanks' eyes were," he said without turning around, "but the tall, silver-haired guy had a pair of ice cubes in his head. He was a mean looking bastard that one. His voice didn't help none neither."

"His voice?" I chimed in.

The man finally turned around and rested his palms on the counter. "Yeah, rough, sand-papery."

"It was him," I said. "What are we going to do?" My voice squeaked from growing terror.

Kim looked at me squarely. "We're going to get the lists of clients and find the location. That's what we're going to do." She stuck her lips near my ear and whispered. "How much money do you have on you?"

I opened my wallet and pulled out fifty dollars in fives and tens. Kim took the cash and turned to the locksmith. She laid the money on the counter, five dollars-at-a-time. "We'd like to see those lists now."

At first, the man acted insulted that she would think he could be bought, but forty bucks did the trick. As he handed her the lists, she waved the last ten in front of his face. "You could have had fifty." She pocketed the money ceremoniously and brought the lists to me saying, "You'll get it back later."

Then it was up to me to search the lists for the location of the lock. The clients who used that particular type of lock ranged from offices to shops to self-storage facilities.

Kim studied the list. "Sam rented a place to keep something hidden away from our felonious friends. Wouldn't you agree?"

"Yes. That something would have to be awfully large, or he would have leased a safety deposit box," I responded.

"I think we can eliminate all the obvious unlikelies such as

Hallmark cards," Kim said.

We scanned the list of companies and private clients who had purchased locks for their offices. Most were doctors or lawyers, a couple of accountants, and a State Farm Insurance agent. "None of these names jump out at me," I admitted.

"That leaves self-storage facilities."

There were thirteen storage complexes on the list with anywhere from twenty-five individual units to over two hundred. I couldn't fathom how long it would take us to drive to each one and try each lock. If we were unsuccessful opening any of the doors, we couldn't be sure we hadn't had the key in the right lock. Richard's key was cut from a template made from an impression I had taken of the original key. What if I had jiggled the key in some way, making the impression inaccurate? How many times in the past had I taken a key in to be duplicated only to return it, because it didn't work in the lock?

I suddenly felt defeated. "We'll never find it."

"Yes we will," Kim replied optimistically. "It's a simple process of elimination."

"There's nothing simple about it," I complained. "We don't have time to check every lock, and if THEY get to whatever it is first, Shelby could die."

"Don't start decompensating on me now," Kim scolded. "You've worked under time constraints when lives were at stake. This isn't any different. We're both detectives, you know. We just work on different puzzles."

"Some puzzles can't be solved in a reasonable length of time," I said. "This is like the jigsaws that come with five thousands pieces, all green peas."

Kim laughed out loud. "I finished one of those once, except it was cherries, goddam Bing cherries. It took me nearly a year."

"We don't have a year, Kim."

"No we don't," she replied soberly, "and this isn't a monochromatic puzzle either. One piece, the most important piece will stand out, and Sam gave it to you. Now look at the list and read each name, out loud if you have to."

With determined skepticism—I just knew Kim was wrong. There wouldn't be anything on any of these lists that would speak to me—I read the names of the self-storage companies. Kim was right! One name leaped right off the page and slapped me in the face, and I laughed in spite of myself.

"What's so funny?" Kim asked.

"You were right. You were right. This is it. It has to be. Then, as if hit by a revelation, I remembered Sam's words and the puzzle suddenly snapped together. "I didn't think anything of it at the time other than worrying that something was terribly wrong, but now I see. He's an FBI agent. He loved the movie." I'm sure I was rambling, but I felt elated. "It all fits. The anagrams were showing. Even in the middle of all of this, Sam never lost his sense of humor."

Kim was staring at me, incredulous. "What the hell are you talking about?"

"THE SILENCE OF THE LAMBS."

"What?"

"Don't you go to the movies?"

"Movies? What does that have to do with anything?"

"Everything. It has everything to do with everything."

"Are you telling me you found a name that's familiar?"

"It's from the movie," I continued, forgetting that a simple "yes" would have satisfied Kim.

Kim leaned one elbow on the desk and ran her fingers through her hair. "I'm kind of a bottom line type, Deb. Can you get to the point? Give me the Reader's Digest version."

"You'll love this," I said. "One of Sam's favorite movies is THE SILENCE OF THE LAMBS. He said it was the first one he had seen in a long time that didn't make the FBI look like a bunch of boobs or criminals."

"Wow," Kim said sarcastically, "that's really insightful. So what lock does our key open?"

"Did you see THE SILENCE OF THE LAMBS?"

"O.K. I'll play along. Yes, I saw it."

"Do you remember when Hannibal the Cannibal told Jodi Foster something about "places in the heart" or something like that?"

"Not really."

"Remember? Later she figured out that Doctor Lector never said anything without a reason, and that led her to the self-storage garage. The name of the facility was Heart Storage, if I remember it right. That's where Lector had stashed the first victim's head sealed in a jar of formalin."

Kim sat up and listened with a renewed interest. "So you think Sam rented a place at—?"

"Hart Storage," I interrupted, pointing at the name on the list.

Kim jotted down the address. "Let's go."

We thanked the locksmith, who tried to get Kim's phone number before we left, and hopped into Richard's truck. Sure our destination was the right one and forgetting that we had no idea which door the key would open when we got there, my spirits were soaring higher than they had been in days.

20

Surrounded by an eight-foot chain link security fence, Hart Storage Systems was more vast than I had anticipated.

"Here we are," Kim said. "I hope your instincts about your husband are right."

"I hope so, too," I said, my confidence deflating. "It'll take us forever to find Sam's garage. If it is here." A sinking feeling was tugging at my stomach as we drove toward the entrance.

"I don't think it'll take that long," Kim replied confidently. "First, I figure we can eliminate all the oversized garages used to store boats and Rv's. Sam surely wouldn't need something that big."

"Do you think the others got here first?"

"We'll soon find out, but I doubt it. They'd have to be awfully lucky to end up here so fast. Remember, they don't know what Sam said."

"You're assuming I'm right."

"Nothing else to assume. Besides, I'm going with my gut, and my gut says you're right." She drove through the gate and parked outside the office. "How long did Scolnik say Sam had been on suspension?"

"About six months."

"Why don't we concentrate on units leased within the past eight months. If we come up empty-handed, we'll widen our search."

"But what if the key isn't cut right?"

"Are you always so cynical?"

"I don't remember who I was before." I tried to recapture a

glimpse of the person who had been blissfully married to Sam Hunter and the mother of an intelligent and beautiful teenage daughter, but that Deb Hunter no longer existed. What had taken her place was an angry, frightened woman standing at the precipice of a complete breakdown.

"Try not to focus on failing," Kim encouraged. "It's always a risk, but it's a sure-fire guarantee we won't succeed if we give up."

· We entered the office on a cloud of humid air that condensed when it contacted the unusually frigid air inside. My whole body shivered at the dramatic drop in temperature.

"Christ! I feel like I'm walking into the damn morgue, it's so cold in here," Kim complained.

Then we saw the reason for the interior arctic atmosphere. I have rendered medical care to some obese people throughout my career, but I have never—at least not in person—seen a human being that large. The man, looking more like the Homo sapiens version of a beached whale, easily tipped the scales at more than six or seven hundred pounds and reeked of stale body odor arising from crevices that surely hadn't seen soap or a wash cloth in decades. In spite of temperatures that would keep meat fresh for days, the man, dressed in a fiery red polo shirt with a white heart on the pocket, was sweating profusely. I prayed he wouldn't have a myocardial infarction while I was present. The thought of trying to resuscitate him was incomprehensible.

Though his appearance was grotesque, the man was quite pleasant and helpful when we explained our dilemma to him, or as much of our dilemma as he needed to know. He even apologized for the ambient temperature when he saw us shivering. Kim questioned him about the silver-haired man with the harsh voice and his two thug friends. He told us that we were the first to show up since early afternoon.

"Do you have a picture of Sam in your wallet?" Kim asked me.

I dug one out. It was a snapshot of Sam taken in front of his

DoJang the day he opened it. Kim showed it to the man, and any doubts we had that we were in the right place dissolved when the man's face lighted up and he nodded. "Do you know which unit is his?"

"Not off hand," the man said. We have so many. Once they rent a unit, people come and go as they please. I have seen him drive down either C or D section."

"May we look at the renter's list for those sections?" Kim asked.

The man seemed more than happy to show us to the inner office and his computer system. With surprisingly nimble fingered keyboarding skills, he brought up the renter's list for our examination, and he offered to print out anything we needed.

I scanned the list. None of the names jumped out at me until I came across one. "Hopefully your coincidence theory will continue to hold true, Kim," I said.

"Really?" Kim leaned over my shoulder and read the name I was pointing to. "Dan Masters?" she asked with a puzzled frown. "You don't know anything about Taekwondo, do you?"

"I know police self defense and seizure tactics, but no, I haven't had any training in one specific martial art," she admitted.

"In Taekwondo, an adult black belt is referred to as a 'Dan'. I am a Third Dan or third degree black belt. I have three gold stripes on my belt. Sam has six. He is a Master Instructor."

"A light bulb flashed brightly behind Kim's eyes. More SILENCE OF THE LAMBS anagrams?" Kim smiled facetiously.

"Anagrams, yes, but not from the movie."

"What are we waiting for?" she said. "What's the unit number?"

My roller coaster emotions were once again on an upswing, and I suddenly felt exhilarated like a hound who's just picked up the scent of the fox. "Section D, unit six."

We thanked the man in the office, and Kim gave him her business card, requesting that he page her with the code 666 if anyone else came looking for the same storage unit. The man agreed

and pointed our way to what we hoped would be Sam's garage.
"Why six-six-six?" I asked as we hurried toward the garage.
"That's supposed to be the devil's signature number. I think
it's appropriate."

We finally came upon a garage identified by a large, tarnished
brass numeral six. I dug the key out of my pocket and, taking a
deep breath, slipped it into the lock. It fit. I looked at Kim and she
at me, then I turned the key. It started to turned then stopped, and
my heart sank. We're so close, I thought. Dear God, let it be the
right lock. Let the key work, I prayed. I wiggled the key and
returned it to the neutral position. With another deep breath I
turned the key again, and again it stopped. "Damn it!" I complained.

"Give it to me," Kim said. When I handed it to her, she rubbed
it against the concrete on the wall of the garage. "It's a trick I
learned from a realtor friend of mine. Sometimes the locksmith's
polishing brushes don't smooth all of the rough edges. Here, try it
now," she said, returning the key to me. Determined to have it
work this time, I wiggled the key hard, and it completed it's turn.
We had found the right storage unit.

Kim exhaled sharply as if she had been holding her breath.
"We're in," she said, grabbing the handle on the overhead door
and lifting.

Inside, we found that the garage had been converted into an
office complete with desk, file cabinet, sophisticated computer
and cellular phone equipment, and the Braun coffee maker I gave
Sam last year for his birthday.

A sleeping cot sat against one wall. The sheet and blanket
were tossed into a pile on top of the cot. That didn't surprise me.
Sam never made the bed. He couldn't see the point of making it
every morning just to mess it up again every night. I walked over
to the cot and sat down. There was still an impression in the pillow where his head had been. I ran my fingers lightly over the
pillow then over the sheet, and I tried to imagine Sam lying there
alone, missing me. I lifted the rumpled sheet and blanket and

pressed them to my face. Sam lingered there.

Next to the cot, I noticed a large cardboard wardrobe, the kind movers use. I got up and tilted the fold-down flap along the front of the box. A half dozen shirts and four pairs of slacks hung from the metal rod that straddled either side of the box. A pile of clothing lay at the bottom of the wardrobe. Overwhelmed by my emotions, I turned away from the box and surveyed the rest of the room.

Kim was standing at the room's center with her hands planted firmly on her hips. "Who's Sam's decorator, Alcatraz Interiors?" Kim joked as she surveyed the spartan furnishings.

"That's not funny, " I reproached, though I needed her humor at that moment.

"Sorry," Kim said. Her eyes opened wide as they moved from the monastic living accoutrements to Sam's computer system. "Whoa! High tech! Richard would have a drool fest over this."

"Maybe," I said, "but you'd better wipe your chin."

Kim glanced at me with smiling eyes. "I think I detected a touch of mirth in you, Doctor. Very good. Now, how about you work the computer while I search the files."

"I'm not familiar with this system," I confessed.

"That's OK." You use a lot of fancy computers at work don't you?"

"Not in the ER. Most of the toys are in the Radiology Department and the cath. labs." I was already booting up the computer as we spoke. Luckily, in spite of high tech appearances, Sam was no more knowledgeable about the workings of computers than I. He had installed a desktop program that was relatively user friendly and employed point and click icons as guides.

Kim and I worked in silence for a long time. Like everything else, police work has its tedious side. While I opened and read through obscure and often painfully dull files that had no meaning, and puzzled through potential passwords for protected files, I occasionally heard Kim sigh or groan softly. They were sounds of concentration. I presumed she wasn't even aware that she was making them.

My eyes were drying out from lack of moisture—people often forget to blink when they are working at their computers—and my neck was getting stiff when I heard Kim say, "Bingo!"

"What is it?" I asked as she got up and walked over to the computer desk, a manilla file folder opened in her hands. "Have you found any references to California in there?"

"Not yet? What have you found?"

Kim half sat against the desk. "Sam refers to a computer expert from California."

"Cal," I said softly.

"All I've found here are pieces of note paper and a few napkins with messages scribbled on them."

"Like what?"

"Pay phone numbers. Names of cities. Most of them are in the US, but some are in other countries."

"Do you know what they're for?" I asked.

"No, but they must have something to do with what we're looking for. Sam has dates and times on all of them, and they're all within the last six months."

I continued typing while Kim was talking. I maneuvered my way through cryptic messages and opened files that were buried in files hidden inside more files. I was pleased with myself successfully breaking passcodes once I discovered Sam's system. He used words and events from our private lives. Things that only he and I would know.

I had just come to a file entitled, "California Dreamin'" when I heard an all-too-familiar buzzing sound. "Is that you?" I asked nervously.

Kim depressed the readout button on her pager. "Jesus, they're here," she said, grabbing a handful of the scribbled notes and stuffing them into her pocket.

My eyes flew around the room searching for an alternate escape route. To my horror, the only way out was the way we had come in. "We've got to go now!" I cried.

"Is there a blank disk around?" Kim asked.

I searched through the desk drawers and found what I hoped was a blank disk and stuffed it into the slot. The icon was "untitled". I dragged the file called "California Dreamin'" over to the disk icon and dropped it. Within less than five seconds, the transfer was complete. I ejected the disk and shut down the computer then stood near the exit. "Kim," I urged in a loud whisper. We've got to go!"

"I'm coming." Kim stuffed the file folder into its drawer. When she was about to turn off the lamp, a memo pad on Sam's desk caught her eye.

I heard the sound of a key in the lock, and every muscle in my body tensed. "Kim, there's no time to be looking at things now. We have to hide."

"We have time," she whispered. "You filed the key. Remember?" She tore the top sheet from the memo pad and stuffed it into her pocket along with the other notes, then she hit the light switch and we were thrown into pitch darkness. Kim pulled her penlight from her other pocket and switched it on.

Suddenly, something crashed against the door with such force I thought door was going to collapse inward. Then someone cried out, "PLEASE stop." It was the man from the office. He cried out again, no words this time, just an agonized whine.

An instant later, the door reverberated with the sound of a thousand boulders slamming against it. "Sonuvabitch!" Kim said. "They're shooting out the lock." Her eyes darted wildly around the room then came to rest on the wardrobe. "Get in there!" she ordered, grabbing me by my arm and pushing me toward the box.

"I don't think I'll fit," I said, resisting her tugs.

"You'll fit," she insisted as she scooped an armful of clothing from the bottom of the box. I climbed in and she piled the clothing on top of me, and I found myself enveloped by the aroma of Goldleaf and Hydrangea mixed with Sam's unique scent. He had carried me with him.

"Shut up and don't move!" I heard Kim say as she pulled some boxes out from under the sleeping cot and dove underneath. I repositioned myself, so I could see out through the box's handle hole. I saw the beam of Kim's penlight disappear as she dragged the boxes under the cot with her. She had just finished sliding the last box into place when the gunfire stopped and the door rolled open.

Peering through the handle hole, I was surprised to see that the sky had grown dark. A mound, silhouetted by the lights in the parking lot, lay on the ground beyond the doorway. A pathetic moan erupted from the mound, and it moved. It was the obese man from the office. His body was what I must have heard crashing against the door.

"What do we do with this pile of trash?" The words came from outside the garage. I saw no one, but the voice was vaguely familiar.

"Kill it and put it out of its misery," came the reply in a low raspy voice I knew only too well. As soon as I heard that voice, I took out the Colt Double Eagle I had lifted from the dead man outside my home and released the safety, hoping I would have the skill necessary to fire a gun successfully in a real life and death situation. I no longer entertained any doubts that I would shoot someone if I had to.

A shadowy figure appeared in the doorway. I could see by its shape and size that the gun in his hands was a small caliber pistol equipped with a silencer, an assassin's weapon. The obese man whimpered, and the shadowy figure pressed the end of the silencer against the man's head. A split second later, there was a muffled pop. The man mound trembled for a few seconds then lay still. Held rapt by sheer terror, I was unaware that the Double Eagle was now in front of my face. My sites trained on the killer's head, I was convincing myself that I should shoot him, if only my hand would hold still.

After kicking the mound to confirm the kill, the shooter stepped inside the garage and switched on the overhead lights. I suddenly felt naked and exposed to all the world as the bright light filtered through the hole in the box and washed over me. I drew my head away from the hole. The man, I recognized him as Boyle, one of the Neanderthals who had represented himself as an FBI agent at the hospital, did not react as his eyes roamed the room. "It's clear," he said to the others who were waiting outside.

He was immediately joined by four other men. I had seen three of them before; Eberhardt and Krandall, the two Chicago cops who had taken John Doe's body out of the ER, and the other bogus FBI agent, Wood. The last man to enter was tall and fit with angular features and an aquiline nose. His hair was streaked silver and his eyes were stainless steel blue. "Search the files and grab the computer," he ordered in a raspy voice. The other men immediately went to work unplugging computer equipment and tearing through the files.

"Do you think it's all here?" Wood asked.

"We'll have to wait and see," the raspy throated man answered.

"What about Hunter's wife?"

"We'll hold on the lady doctor until we know we have what we want."

"And the daughter, should we—?"

"Leave that tasty little morsel to me."

My heart filled with white hot rage at the man's words, a rage that galvanized every muscle fiber in my body. I was posturing for an attack when Eberhardt walked toward me.

"What are you doing?" Boyle asked Eberhardt.

"Maybe something's in here," Eberhardt replied, peeling back the box's front flap.

I held my breath and had the Double Eagle, covered by one of Sam's shirts, pointed toward the top of the box where Eberhardt was using the tip of his Uzi to poke at the clothes on the hangars. I saw his eyes peering into the box. I was sure he could see me, but his actions said otherwise. After a thousand year second, he turned away from the box, and I exhaled slowly and quietly, my body trembling and my intestines cramping.

"There're some boxes under the bed," I heard Eberhardt say, and I leaned toward the handle hole and saw him kicking the boxes. I started to panic. What the hell was I going to do? I couldn't let him find Kim. He'd shoot her on the spot, but if I shot him, the other three would drill me for sure.

"I have something here," Boyle said. Eberhardt suddenly lost interest in the boxes under the cot and walked over to Boyle, who was holding the same manilla folder Kim had had in her hands just minutes before. He handed the folder to Scolnik.

"This is it," Scolnik said.

When the men were satisfied they had found what they were looking for, at least in part, they dumped the files out onto the floor. Then they backed out of the garage, taking the computer with them.

I coiled myself like a cat, prepared to jump up and follow them as soon as the door was closed. Instead, the raspy throated man gave an order that sent an ice pick up my spine. "Burn it," he ordered. An instant later, Eberhardt and Krandall stepped inside and doused the files with gasoline. Then Krandall struck a match and tossed it onto the gasoline soaked heap while Eberhardt rolled the door closed.

The world exploded into flames, trapping us inside and filling the small windowless concrete box with smoke. The wardrobe box fell over as I untangled myself from Sam's clothing and scrambled out of it. Kim shot straight up, lifting the lightweight cot with her and dumping it on top of the flames.

My lungs burned as I gasped for what little oxygen was left. I could not see through the smoke filled blackness, so I dropped to the ground and crawled along the concrete wall, hoping I had chosen the right direction. I tried calling out to Kim, but I had no voice. Soon, the world closed in around me then disappeared.

21

I had no idea who or where I was. A relentless clanging in the blackness was all I knew, and it had to stop or my skull would surely explode. My chest felt like an elephant had taken up residence on top of it. It took all my strength just to draw in a breath, and when that breath finally came, a thousand tiny knives sliced through my lungs, and I was sorry I had bothered breathing at all.

Somewhere between now and forever—I cannot say for I was in a place or non-place where time did not exist—the blackness lifted and my life returned to me. "Where am I?" I tried to say, but the words escaped as a cough that ripped clear through to the bottoms of my feet.

"She's coming around," I heard someone say from a thousand miles away. Who's coming around? I wondered. Coming around from where? I felt something clamped over my mouth and nose. I clawed at it frantically until, finally, I managed to tear it away. "Whoa! Whoa! Careful there," the voice said. "It's just an oxygen mask."

A face took shape above me. "Who are you?" I whispered.

The face, that of a young, dark-hair man, leaned an ear close to my lips, and I repeated my question.

"Joe D'Amico, ma'am," he said with a broad smile. There was a logo stamped on his navy blue T-shirt. It was familiar looking, but I couldn't quite get my mind to focus well enough to remember what CFD meant. All around me, lights were flashing, and I heard myriad voices chattering nearby but not making any sense. "We thought you were a goner." Joe D'Amico said. Then he turned away from me and called out to someone, "Hey,

Ebolansky, this one's awake."

Ebolanski, repeated itself inside my mind over and over as a loud gong. Gradually, my memory returned, and I sat up. "Kim?" I barely whispered when another young, handsome face came into focus. This one had eyes the color of a summer sky set in a richly tanned face framed by sandy hair.

"Kim's fine," he said.

"Who are you?" crackled out of my throat.

"Officer Peter Ebolansky of the Chicago Police Department, Doctor Hunter." The man answered through an engaging smile.

"Do I know you?"

"I don't think we've ever met."

I heard coughing and choking nearby. It was Kim. She was covered in soot and fighting her oxygen mask as I had been moments ago. Joe D'Amico, whom I now recognized as a fire department paramedic, was trying to calm her.

I struggled against weakness and dizziness to get to my feet. "Are you sure you want to do this?" Ebolansky asked.

"I have to," I replied, and he threw his arm around me and helped me to my feet. My head was spinning, and breathing continued to be an exercise in sheer torture, but I wanted to be upright. I guess I believed if I were standing, I would live. Kim sat up as I approached. She, too, spoke in little more than a hoarse whisper. Her hair was singed and her face, behind the soot, looking like she had spent too many hours lying on a Caribbean beach without sunscreen. I assumed that I was but a mirror image of her. The generalized stinging on my face confirmed my suspicions.

I sat on the ground next to Kim, and Ebolansky squatted on her other side. She and I checked each other, assuring ourselves and each other that we were, indeed, alive and this wasn't hell. It just seemed like it. Then Kim turned to Ebolansky. "Christ! I kissed my ass good bye in there," she croaked. "How the hell did you get here so fast, Pete?"

"I followed the guy who took the key from the phone booth. He went inside an abandoned warehouse. A few seconds after he went inside the building, these guys came out, so I followed them here.

"You saw them pop the cap on the fat guy?" Kim asked.

Ebolansky pinched his lips together and nodded his head. "Yeah. I saw that." His voice was apologetic.

"Why the hell didn't you call for backup?" Kim tried to yell at him, but her voice came out as a mere squeak.

"I think the big yellow letters on their back that said 'FBI' might have had something to do with it," Ebolansky snapped back. "Hell, I didn't know what to do. I'm outta my goddam jurisdiction. What am I going to do, call for backup against the FBI? Someone'd have my ass for breakfast for sure."

"How did you know we were inside the garage?" I asked.

"I didn't. But when I saw 'em torch it and take off, I ran over to see if the fat guy was alive. That's when I heard a crash inside and you two coughing and crying." Ebolansky's forehead wrinkled quizzically. "You don't remember me racing into the flames, risking my own life and limb to rescue you?"

"Sorry, Pete, but, no," Kim said.

Ebolansky frowned his disappointment. Then he looked into Kim's eyes for a long moment. "I'm glad you're all right," he said tenderly, and it dawned on me: These two have a thing.

With Ebolansky's help, Kim struggled to her feet. Our young paramedic friend, Joe D'Amico, approached us. "It might be good for the two of you to go to the hospital."

"We're fine," Kim answered through a loud croupy cough, and the paramedic's eyebrows rose.

"You ladies really should consider going to the hospital."

"I'm a doctor," I said firmly. "I'll take care of things from here." Joe D'Amico smiled and wished us luck, then packed his gear and departed. The other firefighters were winding hoses and packing their gear, while a couple of cops from the local district were cordoning off the garage area where an innocent man had been executed like an animal, and Kim and I had almost been prematurely cremated.

"We have to get Shelby, now!" I barked.

"You're right. Let me take care of these guys and we'll go right away," Kim promised. She walked over to the yellow tape and stepped under it as she approached the two detectives. They all shook hands and talked for a few minutes. I couldn't hear what she said, but one of the detectives rubbed his chin and listened intently as Kim talked. A couple of times during the conversation, he looked at me then back toward Kim. More handshakes, and Kim was walking toward Pete and me. "Let's roll," she said as she bent over and stepped under the yellow perimeter tape. Then she stopped and stared at Richard's truck, then at Pete's cruiser.

"Oh no you don't," Pete insisted, stepping between Kim and his car.

Kim dug in her pocket and pulled out the keys to Richard's truck, and the computer disk. She handed both to Pete, then held out her palm, wiggling her fingers. "Hand 'em over."

Pete's head bobbed from side-to-side like a kid who'd been told to give up his pack of chewing gum at school. "Aw c'mon, Hawthorne. What am I supposed to do? What if I get a call?"

"First place, Ebola, you're off duty. Second place, you can take Richard's truck to him and borrow my car until I get back."

"Fine," Pete snarled. He took hold of her hand and pressed the keys into her palm. Not letting go, he pulled her close to him and lowered his voice. "You owe me, woman."

Kim raised one eyebrow and one corner of her mouth turned up in a half smile. "Oo! That's one debt I might enjoy paying." Kim closed her fingers around the keys and shoved Pete away playfully.

"What do you want me to do with this?" Pete asked of the disk.

"Give it to Richard. Tell him I want him to use his geek expertise and break into the files." Kim and I started for Pete's car.

"Watch your backs," he called after us. Kim held up her hand in an OK sign without turning around. A few minutes later, we were on interstate fifty-five headed toward two-ninety-four and

Wisconsin.

22

The trip to the Cooper's cottage, normally a three hour drive, took a little over two hours the way Kim drove. I tried the Cooper's number at least a dozen times while en route. I never got an answer. It was with growing trepidation that we turned onto their mile long gravel driveway. The final leg of our journey seemed to take forever.

The Cooper's van, usually parked in the attached carport, was nowhere in sight. There were no signs of Wisconsin state troopers, nor of anyone else for that matter. Kim pulled to a stop in the parking area near the front porch and killed the engine. For a time, we stared silently at the rustic log cabin that had been in Barbara's family since the early nineteen hundreds. Normally, when people arrived at the cabin with its huge covered porch, furnished with weathered rocking chairs and an old fashioned porch swing, the screen door would squeak open and Barbara would welcome them with open arms and big hugs. Today, however, no one welcomed us. Instead, the cabin stood silent and alone. Kim finally looked at me then withdrew her gun from its holster. "Wait here," she ordered as she opened her car door slowly and quietly.

"Not on your life," I announced, and I got out and followed Kim up the steps to the front door. Kim peeked into the windows and shook her head. I gestured with my index finger, questioning whether or not I should ring the doorbell. Again, Kim shook her head, then started down the steps. I followed, and we made our way around the entire perimeter of the cottage, finding no one.

Finally, we returned to the porch, and I rang the bell. When, as we had anticipated, no one answered, Kim tried the knob. The door was locked. Kim hurried to her cruiser and dug something out of her purse. "What do you have?" I asked when she returned.

"My Ronco breaking and entering kit," Kim replied, holding up a credit card. "It's a sophisticated little device used by cops and criminals alike," she continued while she shimmied the card between the door and jam. It took her all of ten seconds to pop the knob lock, and we were inside.

"Why do we bother with locks at all?" I commented.

Kim shrugged. "To keep the wind from blowing the door open?"

"Cute."

Unlike my house, the Cooper's cottage was left completely undisturbed. It looked like they simply packed up and went home. "This isn't right," I said. "Why would the troopers let them leave?"

Kim was already dialing the phone. "That's what I'd like to know," she said to me, then her focus returned to the phone. My nerves frayed and overloaded, I couldn't stand still and listen to Kim maneuvering her way through the local government bureaucracy, so I wandered out to the kitchen and opened the refrigerator. Except for an open box of baking soda, it was empty. The Coopers had cleaned it out. I walked over to the large picture window that looked out over the lake from their breakfast nook. My eyes roamed over the lake, the pier, and their boat dock. The boat was in its shelter and covered with the fitted canvass tarp. The Coopers had packed up and gone . . . home?

Kim entered the kitchen looking worried, and my mind immediately began to chant; Oh God, Oh God, Please, God. "They said they tried to reach me," Kim said. "It must have been when we were in the fire."

"Reach you, about what?" My mind continued its chanting; Please God. Please let Shelby be safe. Please, God.

"The Coopers were gone when they got here."

"That can't be! Barbara said the trooper was standing there

while she was talking to me."

Kim shook her head. "It must have been them."

"Them! Them! Now they can steal uniforms, badges, patrol cars? What the hell? Who are these people? How are we going to know the good guys from the bad guys?" Then it hit me. "Sam knew they could do this."

"What?" Kim gave me a puzzled look.

"Sam knew about this. It was in his note. We always taught Shelby that strangers could even be people we know or people who pretend to be something they're not. He was warning me that I couldn't trust even the cops." In a moment of irrational, paranoia, I regarded Kim suspiciously. What if she was part of the plan, to endear herself to me and get me to lead her to, what? Hadn't I already lead her everywhere that I knew? Wouldn't she know that I had no clue what they were after? My God, I'm going insane!

Kim's eyes narrowed. "Hey! What the hell's going on? You slept in my bedroom and you ate at my mother's table. Don't you look at me that way."

Feeling totally isolated and defeated once again, I slumped into a chair. "I'm sorry, but what am I supposed to do?"

"Deb, they're doing a number on you. Don't let 'em. I'm not the enemy. You've got to know that. Let your good sense and gut instincts tell you what you know to be true."

I looked directly into Kim's eyes. She returned my gaze without even flinching. How could I have doubted her. She had laid her life on the line for me. I buried my face in my hands. "I'm sorry, so sorry. I don't know what to believe. I feel like I'm caught in the vortex of a tornado. My whole life's just spinning around me. Everything was so stable, so normal. Now, my husband's brain dead and my daughter's missing. People are trying to kill me, and for what? Even Sam hasn't been telling me the truth. You saw the garage. It's like he had a whole other life I wasn't part of or even privy to. What am I supposed to do. Who am I supposed to trust."

Kim took my hands away from my face and held them in hers. "Sam wasn't living another life. He was doing his job. You're not supposed to be part of that."

"But he made me part of it. He dragged Shelby and me right into the middle of it when he sent me that note. What was he thinking?"

"I don't know," Kim admitted with a subtle shrug. "I really don't know."

"Whom are we supposed to trust now; Kim, other cops, the state police? These people, whoever they are, seem to have their fingers in everything. How did they know you requested troopers be sent out to protect Shelby, and how did they get the supplies they needed to represent themselves as cops? How do we know that the real cops didn't take her? The guy at the house was a real cop. You said so yourself. Who are we supposed to trust?" I was pleading, but I was angry and getting angrier by the second. My world had ended, and I didn't like the new one unfolding in its place. It was a world where trust was dead and paranoia reigned.

"I have no idea," Kim said quietly. She sat in a chair across the table from me. "With the right equipment, they could be listening to our cellular phone conversations, but I don't know how they're getting the other things. I don't think the Wisconsin State Police are involved. Cops are just people like everyone else. We're doin' a job, bringing home a paycheck. I'd stake my life on the people I work with."

"All of them?"

"Pretty much, but because cops are people, there're going to be bad apples in the barrel. I think we've just run into a few bad apples who know how to get inside information."

"And I.D.'s, and badges, and uniforms?"

"There are catalogues that sell that shit to cops. It's easy enough to create a package complete with fake I.D.'s that will fool the average citizen."

"But you're not an average citizen. Your trained to spot that stuff, and those FBI agents fooled you."

Kim combed her hair with her fingers. "I know. That bothers me, but I wonder if those I.D.'s were that good or was I that easily duped?"

"I don't think it matters now," I said. Then I thought out loud, "Can you order squad cars through the catalog?"

Kim frowned. "What do you mean?"

"Barbara complained about the squad cars parked in front of the cabin and cops inside her house. She was hopping mad. Can anyone buy a squad car?"

"I—"

Don't you see? How are we suppose to know who to trust?"

Kim took in a deep breath then let the air leak from her lungs while her eyes fell toward the table. She pursed her lips and shook her head thoughtfully. Then her eyes reconnected with mine. "I guess we won't know, so we'll just have to rely on each other, and Richard."

Kim got up and started out of the kitchen. "We'll use hard wire telephones for any important communication. Pay phones, mostly." Now she was talking more to herself than to me. "And we'll have to choose our words carefully." I became aware that Kim's world was crumbling around her as well, and her confidence in her fellow man had been damaged.

"Where're you going?" I asked after her.

"To request an APB on the Cooper's van. You want to give me a description?"

I was about to answer, then a thought struck me. "What if they don't have Shelby and the Coopers?" I asked. "What if they're looking for them? Won't an APB just help them find my daughter?"

"Deb, they already have your daughter. Besides, I don't think we'll be giving away any secrets by describing the van. They already knew that."

Kim was right. These people, whoever they were, already knew everything they needed to know about Shelby, and me. They seemed to have everything, but the one thing they wanted most. God, I would have given whatever it was to them, if only I had a clue.

After Kim ended her phone conversation with the state police, she called Richard and updated him on our current situation. She also asked him to try to find out if any squad cars, police uniforms, and ordnance had recently been stolen in Illinois, or Wisconsin.

Afterward, we left the house and searched the grounds until Kim was satisfied that there was nothing there that would be of any help to us. Finally, we climbed back into Pete's cruiser and sped away from the Cooper's cottage. I listened to the gravel pelt the bottom of Kim's car as she raced down the driveway toward the paved road, and I wondered where Shelby was. Was she alive? Was she safe with the Coopers or in the hands of what I now knew to be vicious criminals who had no regard for human life. Would I ever see Shelby alive again?

"Hopefully the state police will find the Coopers. If not, we'll head back to my house and see if Richard has broken the codes on the disk."

"What about Shelby?" I snapped. "Do we just forget about my daughter?"

"No, we don't forget about her. If they already have her, we're not going to find her by driving up and down streets. We need leverage. The only reason they'll have her is to get to you and whatever they're after. I presume the information on the disk will help us understand what we're all looking for."

Kim's speedometer glued itself to the ninety-miles-per-hour mark and stayed there until her pager sounded. I read the LED number to her. "It's the state police," she said. She turned off the next exit and pulled into a Shell station. We parked in front of a pump and Kim climbed out. Then she leaned her head inside. "Can you fill it while I make the call? Eighty-nine octane." She handed me her charge card then walked into the building, leaving me to play gas pump jockey. It gave me something to do rather than wait in the car tearing at my cuticles.

A few minutes later, Kim hurried out of the building toward me. "You about finished?" she called out.

"I don't know."

"Round it off to the nearest dollar, and let's get out of here," Kim said as she climbed inside.

I stopped the pump at sixteen dollars, collected the receipt, and capped the tank. Kim had already started the engine. "What's going on?" I asked, climbing into the passenger seat. The car started to roll forward before I had my door closed.

"They found the Cooper's van on two-ninety-four, just north of the Illinois State Line." Kim flipped the switch to her strobes and the other to her siren. We flew onto the interstate at a rate of speed that made ninety-miles-an-hour seems like a Sunday afternoon drive.

23

The world was a mere blur speeding past my window, and yet I felt we weren't going fast enough. "Can't you get this thing to go any faster?" I complained.

"Not without wings," Kim shot back.

"You said they found the Cooper's van. What about the Coopers and Shelby?"

Kim gave me a cursory glance. "They started to tell me, but I cut them off."

"Why the hell did you do that?" What was she thinking? How could she not ask about Shelby when she knew I was on the verge of insanity worrying about my daughter?

"I was patched through to the radio car. I don't know why the Coopers took off like they did, and I didn't want unwanted ears hearing who the cops found."

"Yes, but those ears would have already heard that the trooper found the Cooper's van," I argued.

"No, we never mentioned anyone's name. All anyone might have heard was the fact that a vehicle had been found on the interstate."

My skepticism was growing. "Then how do you know it's the Cooper's van? We didn't have a license plate number."

"It's easy enough to get one from the Bureau of Motor Vehicles."

"But you didn't, did you? You don't know whom you can trust any more than I do."

Another fleeting side long glance from Kim affirmed my statement. "The van fits the description."

"That's comforting. We could be on a wild goose chase."

"I doubt it. Remember my coincidence theory? Besides, it's on our way home."

We road the rest of the way in silence, Kim concentrating on working her way through increasingly congested traffic, and I immersed in pleading and bargaining with God for my daughter's safety.

"There it is," Kim said, drawing me out of my meditative cocoon. Three squad cars, lights flashing had lined up, one in front and two behind, with the Cooper's van. I knew it was their van the moment I saw Bugs Bunny and Sylvester Cat suction cupped to the rear window. Troopers were standing outside the van, but I didn't see anyone from the Cooper family or Shelby. "Where are they?" I asked frantically.

"They're probably keeping them inside for protection," Kim answered calmly as she slowed and pulled to stop in front of the first radio car.

"Or they didn't find anyone," I added.

"Let's talk to the troopers before you make too many assumptions."

We climbed out and started toward the van. As we approached, a sizeable trooper, his Smokey the Bear hat tipped forward in a macho, intimidating fashion, blocked our path. "Look at this idiot. What does he think, I'm going to drive up like a screaming Christmas tree and not be a cop?" Kim said to me as she produced her gold badge and picture I.D. The trooper responded with a slight tip of his hat and let her pass.

The driver's and front passenger seat were empty, and I was beginning to think that all the troopers had found was an empty van when the sliding door on the side of the van flew open and Tom hopped out. "What in God's name is going on, Deb? Why did these people pull us over?" His voice was both confused and angry.

"Where's Shelby? Is she inside?" I stepped toward the door, hoping my daughter would jump into my arms, but all I saw was three Cooper faces staring at me from inside the van.

"Why are you asking where Shelby is?" Tom asked. "You should know where she is. You're the one who sent the state police after her. She went with them."

I suddenly felt like I had been locked in a room with no oxygen. I looked at Kim. "They have her," I tried to say, but the words caught in my throat.

"Why did you leave your cottage?" Kim asked Tom.

"What would you do? The state police took Shelby into to custody, and we figured we weren't waiting around for the people who were threatening her life to come for her and kill us."

Kim turned to one of the troopers and confirmed that no Wisconsin state police officer had taken Shelby into protective custody. "Can you describe the officer who took Shelby?" Kim asked Tom.

My blood solidified in my veins as I listened to Tom describe the tall silver-haired man with the raspy voice. This man, whose name I did not know, and whose purpose was yet to be discovered, held my soul in the palm of his hand and could crush it at any moment. Quite possibly, he already had. Didn't he know I would give him my life if he asked for it? Whatever he wanted, I didn't care, he could have it as long as he spared Shelby's life.

I stared at Kim speechlessly. She took me by my shoulders and shook me. "She isn't dead. Killing her before he has what he wants would be counter productive."

"I have my phone, my pager. Why hasn't he called to tell me he has her?"

"Maybe he wanted you to discover it for yourself. I think that's why he let the Coopers go, so you'd find them and know beyond a reasonable doubt that he had your daughter. The mental torture might push you far enough, so you'll do anything for him without hesitation."

"He's succeeded," was all I could say in a barely audible whisper.

"No!" Kim barked. "Don't let him win. That's what he wants,

and if he gets what he wants, Shelby and you are dead.

"If Shelby dies, I have no reason to live."

Kim arranged for the Coopers to have a police escort to their home, and round-the-clock protection once there. They had seen the face of a ruthless killer, and Kim figured now that the Coopers had served his purpose, he would eliminate them. As they drove away surrounded by flashing lights, I wondered if Barbara and I would ever find a time when we could sit as close friends and chat about our husbands and our children, about school and work, and our lives in general. Would Barbara ever speak to me again? Then I wondered if any of us would be alive to worry about it.

24

I slid into the passenger seat of Kim's commandeered cruiser and stared vacantly through the windshield while Kim finalized business with the state police.

"They'll be on the lookout for a rogue radio car, but I doubt they'll find anything," Kim said as she sat behind the wheel. "He's probably ditched the car already."

"So you're saying we're not going to find my daughter?"

"We won't have to. Her kidnapper will find us." Kim started the engine and headed south two-ninety-four toward Chicago.

"So he runs the show, and we sit idly by hoping for a miracle," I complained.

Dialing her cellular phone, Kim said to me, "At the moment, that's about the size of it, but only for the moment." She stuck the phone to her ear and, in a few seconds, began speaking to someone whose name she did not mention. "Have you made any headway?" she said into the phone. "Keep trying. We're on our way." She shut the phone off and flipped the mouthpiece closed.

"I thought we were going to use only hard lines, no cellular."

"It was a generic conversation."

"Where are we going now?" I asked.

"Home. Richard's trying to break the passcode to what he thinks is the primary document. Maybe the scales will begin tipping in our direction, and he'll have it solved before we get there."

Forty-five minutes later we pulled into Kim's driveway. The only lights on in the house came from the basement where we found Richard busy at the computer. "Where's Ebola?" Kim asked as we came down the steps.

"Behind you." Richard nodded toward the room on the other side of the stairs. The lights were on and Pete, White Sox baseball cap turned backwards on his head, was standing at the controls of an immense model train display that nearly filled the entire half of the basement. There were five complete trains in all. Two were passenger trains; one a circa late eighteen hundreds, and the other a scale model of Japan's mag-lev. Three freight trains also spanned the centuries. There were mountains and old western towns at one end and modern cities at the other.

Kim stuck her head in the doorway. "Having fun?" she quipped.

Pete looked up and smiled like a kid on Christmas morning. "Isn't this the greatest?"

"Yeah, right," Kim responded, in a 'seen that, been there, done that,' disinterested voice. "Why are you still here?"

"You have my car, remember?" Pete replied. "Besides, I thought I might hang around and collect on the debt." Pete shut off the trains and walked up to Kim. He stood only inches from her, but she seemed perfectly comfortable with him inside her space. "Debt? What debt?" Kim asked in feigned naivete, her voice changing its texture, becoming soft and teasingly sensuous.

"So when do I collect?" Pete asked in a voice that emitted the same subliminal message as Kim's.

Kim smiled impishly and her eyes twinkled. She patted Pete's cheek and said, "Don't hold your breath." Then she turned on her heel and walked, rather strutted, over to the computer table where Richard was still furiously clicking away on the keyboard.

Pete shuddered. "Bitch," he called playfully after her. "Besides, your face is dirty and you smell like an old fireplace."

Kim turned to him, kissed her fingertips and slapped them against her butt. Pete shook his head and whispered under his breath. "I should be so lucky."

"Are you two always this affectionate toward each other?" I asked Pete.

"We're just having fun," he replied. Then he stepped out of my path and gestured for me to lead the way to the computer desk.

Suddenly, Richard stopped typing and turned to find three of us staring at him. "You know, computing isn't what you'd call a spectator sport. In fact, we 'geeks' usually like working alone." While he made the statement to all of us, his eyes seemed to connect with mine.

Feeling a little awkward, I asked, "Have you found anything useful yet?"

"I'm into the California Dreamin' file. Except for the overview document that you read, the file's protected by a very complicated code."

"Can I help? I figured Sam's system out right away."

"This isn't Sam's personal code. The document was sent to Sam via the internet. It's protected by a very sophisticated encryption. The guy who designed it has to be a flaming genius."

"Then it will take a genius to break it." I was beginning to wonder if Richard had the capacity to do the job.

"We're in luck," Kim jumped in. "If anyone can do it, Mr. Computer can." Richard rolled his eyes and shook his head.

"Listen, I work better without an audience, and you two look like a pair of overdone spareribs," he said to Kim and me. "Why don't you go get cleaned up or something, and I'll send Casey Jones here," he tipped his head toward Pete, "to get you as soon as I have anything."

I sighed heavily, discouraged that everything had to be so damn complicated. "Richard's right," Kim said to me, "you do look pretty crappy."

"Thanks," I retorted.

"You might want to take a gander at yourself in the mirror, also, Ms. Hawthorne," Richard said.

"OK, fine. *We* look pretty crappy. C'mon." Kim took hold of my arm. "We know when we're not wanted." We climbed the stairs to the kitchen where Kim switched on the light, and I felt as though I were having a deja vu. "Go ahead, Deb, take a shower. I'll go next."

I looked at my filthy clothes. "I don't think there's much point if I have to put these on again."

"You can borrow some of mine," Kim offered.

I laughed. With the disparity in our heights, her slacks would fit me like shorts. "I don't think that's a viable choice."

Kim held her hands up as if comparing our heights. "No, I don't suppose it will." Snapping her fingers, she said, "I have it! You can borrow Richard's clothes. You go ahead and get into the shower. Toss your things outside onto the floor. I'll leave you a pair of Richard's jeans and one of his shirts. Then I'll toss your things into the washer."

Grateful for the opportunity to get out of my filthy clothes and wash the acrid smell of stale smoke from my hair and skin, I tip toed past Margaret's bedroom. "Will we wake her with all of this commotion?" I whispered.

"Naw," Kim replied out loud. "Nothing wakes mom up. A tornado could come through and suck up the house, and she'd still be sleeping."

After my shower, I dressed in Richard's clothes and headed for the basement. "You look better," Richard said when he saw me coming down the stairs. Then he tilted his head and smiled. "Those look familiar."

I suddenly felt self-conscious. Maybe I should have asked Richard's permission before wearing his clothes. "I'm sorry. I hope you don't mind, but I'm a little too tall to wear Kim's clothes."

Richard smiled. "Somehow they look better on you than me."

I returned his smile and continued my decent. I heard an authentic sounding train whistle as I passed the doorway at the bottom of the stairs. Pete was back at the controls of the massive train set. Boys and toys, I thought as I turned and walked over to Richard. "I wonder if he'll ever leave," Richard said, glancing past me into the train room.

"Are you getting anywhere?"

"Yeah, about as far as my trains. Just when I think have the code figured out, it bombs on me. This is going to take some time."

"How much time?"

Richard looked down at his knees. "This is the kind of code that takes teams of experts weeks even months to break." His voice was apologetic. "It's not going to happen tonight. I'll have to confer with a few people I know at the University of Chicago first thing in the morning."

Surprising even to me, I no longer had the sympathetic nervous system reaction to what Richard said. In fact, I felt detached from the whole situation. I think I must have unconsciously resigned myself to what I now believed to be the inevitable.

"I suspect," Richard continued, "that the passcode was the thing Sam had wanted you to read with that bullet lens."

"A lot of good that does us now," I said. "They have Sam's computer, the bullet lens, and his note. They've probably opened the file already. That's why they haven't called me to bargain for Shelby's life. My daughter's already dead," I said flatly. An emotional void seemed to be all that remained inside of me.

"Not necessarily." Kim stepped off the last step onto the concrete basement floor. She was holding my pager.

I took the pager from her and read the number. Again, it was one I had never seen. Kim was right. It was probably them. I dialed the number and was almost relieved to hear the familiar sandpapery breath.

25

"Hello, Doctor Hunter," the voice said, and I nodded to Kim to let her know it was him. She immediately used her phone to contact the phone company and find out the location of the number I was calling.

"I know who you are," I replied coldly. I don't know why I said that. I had no clue who he was except that he was a cold blooded killer and seemed to have power over other men who were equally cold blooded. I also knew he had at his disposal whatever he needed for his men or him to pass themselves off as law enforcement. Beyond that, I knew only what he looked like.

"Ah. You recognize my voice."

"No. I said I know who you are." This time I was more emphatic. Kim frowned at me quizzically.

There was a silence on the other end of the line that I assumed meant he was either surprised or unhappy with my statement. "How do you know?"

I was about to blurt out that I had been hiding in the storage unit when he torched it and I saw him order Boyle to murder the behemoth desk jockey who had been so kind to Kim and me, but instead the question "Do the words 'California Dreaming' sound familiar?" seemed to come out of my mouth without forethought. It was as if part of my brain was leading the rest of my brain toward some unknown destination.

Again, a moment of silence. "So, you've broken the code."

"Yes, and now I know everything."

"That is most unfortunate."

"Actually, it's most unfortunate for you." I had no idea where my courage, or more accurately, foolishness was coming from. Nor did I know where I would end up with this charade. I knew only that I had to finish what I had begun.

"You forget that I have your daughter tucked safely away. A simple flick of a switch and . . . Puff. But then, she is such a pretty little thing. It would be a shame to waste that tender virgin body. I may choose to take my time." His words quickened my emotions, and the void was filled with rage. If he had been standing in front of me at that moment, I would have torn him apart with the viciousness of a grizzly who's protecting her cubs.

Kim shook her head and hung up her phone. "They have no record of the number. He's probably on a cellular phone."

"Your life is over," I promised the man on the phone, and Kim looked at me with the big "O" sign like I had gone insane. Maybe I had.

"Oh come now," the man said, "You would throw away your daughter's life over a simple little computer chip?"

Computer chip? I had the disk, but he had Sam's computer. What was he talking about? What had I gotten myself into? I didn't have any computer chip and knew nothing about one. I was standing in a hole that was quickly filling with manure, and I had dug it myself. What an idiot I was to think I could outwit these people. How was I going to respond without letting on that I had nothing more than a summarized statement about a computer whiz from California and a document protected by a code that couldn't be broken? If my response was incorrect, he would know I was bluffing, and control would be his once again. Then I thought; if a computer chip was what he was after all along, then it surely had serious intrinsic value. Was its value sufficient to give me the bargaining power necessary to save my daughter's life? What did the chip do that made it so important? More to the point, what harm could this man do with the chip in his possession? "Simple is hardly the word I would use," I retorted.

"It's of no use to you."

"Your not having it would be of use to me."

"I suppose, but then what's more important to you; preventing me from having the chip or saving your daughter's life?"

"I see your point," I conceded. "Where and when would you like to make the exchange?"

"Is the chip in your possession now?"

"Yes." I had always considered myself a poor liar, yet I was deceiving this man with the cool cunning of one who had honed the skill over many years.

"Good. Get in your car and drive toward downtown. I will contact you while you are en route. Oh, and do come alone."

"How soon will you contact me?" I asked, but my question was met by a dead phone line. "Hello? Hello?" I turned to Kim, "I'm sorry. There was no warning. He just hung up. Did you get anything?"

"Only as close as downtown," Kim said. "What does he want?"

"He thinks I have a computer chip."

"I heard you mention it," Richard said. "What chip?"

"I don't know," I replied. "But he's willing to exchange Shelby for it."

"So all of this is about a computer chip?" Kim asked. "What in the world could be so important about a computer chip?"

"The possibilities are endless," Richard said.

"I don't care why the chip is so important," I complained. "This guy wants me to meet him and hand over a chip that I don't have. Shelby's life is hanging on by my stupid bluff."

"I can supply you with a chip but as you said, it could be a very dangerous ploy. There are so many sizes and varieties of chips, he might know immediately that you're giving him the wrong one. If he does, he'll kill you on the spot."

"Richard's right," Kim said. "You're walking into a deathtrap. You know that, don't you? It won't matter if he recognizes the bogus chip or not. If he thinks it's the right chip, he'll kill you because he doesn't need you anymore. If he knows it's the wrong one, you'll piss him off and he'll kill you. Either way, you're dead and so is your daughter. I can't let that happen."

"You don't have a choice."

"Yes I do. I'm coming with you."

"He ordered me to come alone. If he sees you—"

"He won't see me."

"What, are you going to hide in the back seat and jump up out at just the right time, and save the day? I don't think so," I said angrily. The rage inside of me was spilling out onto Kim. I knew she didn't deserve it, but it was pouring out of me in an involuntary torrent of misplaced fury.

"Lighten up, girlfriend," Kim said. "Remember me? I'm one of the good guys."

I let out a steamy sigh, trying to regain control of my emotions, and Kim continued. "I'll follow you in my car. I'll have Richard wire you for sound, so you can give me your location at all times. I'll be close enough to step in if necessary, but he'll never know I'm there."

"Won't he be expecting that? He knows I'm working with you."

"He'll never find out."

"What if he searches me?"

"He's not going to find the wire, Deb." By the set of her jaw and her hard stare, I could see that she was not about to take no for an answer. Even if I were to refuse the wire, Kim would tail me. Without the wire, she would be forced to maintain visual contact which might draw suspicion.

"O.K." I acquiesced reluctantly. "But you'd better make damn sure that you're not seen."

When it came time to turn me into a walking stereo system, Richard asked me for my bra. Kim dashed into the train room past Pete who was in railroad Never-Never Land, and dug it out of the dryer. "It's still a little damp," she said when she returned. "Will that cause a problem?"

"No," Richard replied. "The system's fully insulated.

I, who had only seen "wires" attached to people in the movies, stared at them totally lost. "I thought you were going to tape a microphone to my chest and a tape recorder around my waist?"

Richard took my bra from Kim, saying, "A little cumbersome, don't you think?" He turned toward his workbench and picked up a narrow tortoise shell barrette. "This receiver will conduct the sound of Kim's voice through your mastoid bone," he said as he tucked my hair behind my ear and clipped the barrette in place. Then he picked up an object that looked like an exceptionally thin tie pin connected to a thread-like strand of wires. The apparatus was connected to a small black disc formed out of a rubberized plastic.

"Is that the transmitter?" I asked in amazement.

"The whole thing will fit inside your bra. Even if they frisk you, they won't find it." He stuck the pin in the stitching along the top of the left bra cup. "This is the microphone. It's so sensitive it can almost hear what you're thinking." He handed my bra to me. "Slip this on carefully, and I'll tuck the rest of it in place."

I turned my back to him, took off the shirt I was wearing and put my bra on. I turned around, and Richard finished the job of hiding the wires and button battery by tacking them into place with needle and thread. When he had finished, I couldn't feel anything. "The only way they'll find this is if they strip search you and examine the inside of your bra," he said.

"And I'm never going to let them get that close," Kim added.

"What d'ya mean you?" Richard piped up. "Pete and I are going, too."

"You forget you're a gimp," Kim said eyeing his casted leg. "Besides, we need you here to work on finding the passcode. The sooner we've got the information in that document, the better off we'll be. Pete and I will go."

"Wait a minute," I chimed in, buttoning my shirt. "The guy tells me to come alone. I finally agree to let Kim follow. How do you think he'll react when I bring my own party with me?"

"Trust me," Kim said. "He won't know any of us are around."

"This whole thing's making me nervous. This may be the only

chance I have of saving my daughter's life. I just don't want to fuck it up."

"You won't," Richard said quietly, "and neither will we."

I nodded my agreement, saying, "Let's do it."

"Great." Richard hopped off of his stool and hobbled to the wall safe. "You'll need a few things, just in case." He spun the dial right, left, and right, then depressed the heavy stainless steel lever and swung the door wide. My mouth fell open at what I saw. The room was large enough for a bedroom, and it was filled with an incredible display of weapons. Three walls were covered with a variety of handguns, rifles, full size machine guns, and machine pistols all hanging from pegboard hooks. On either side of the entry door stood large drawers and shelf cases filled with holsters, and boxes of ammunition.

I glanced at Richard. "You're not one of those wacko survivalist types are you?"

Richard laughed out loud. "No, I'm a collector. If you start at the left side of the room and move to the right side, you'll see a history of U.S. guns and small weapons." He lifted an ancient looking rifle from one of the hooks nearest us and handed it to me. It was quite heavy. "This is a .72 caliber flintlock dating back to the revolutionary war. It weighs over ten pounds. Can you imagine carrying that thing around all day along with all of your other gear?"

"No." I handed the rifle to him. "This is all very interesting." I wasn't lying. "But I have to get rolling."

"You're right. You're right." Richard carefully returned the rifle to its hook and turned to the storage shelves on our right. "You'll need something to back you up, just in case."

"A gun! Not on your life. You can't hide a gun like you did the wire. He'll probably find it and shoot me with it."

"Not this gun." Richard smiled as he opened one of the drawers and pulled out an ordinary looking ball point pen. "I got this off a suspected gun dealer."

"A pen?" What's the point of all of this? I wondered.

Richard handed the pen to me, and I started to depress the lever but it didn't budge. "Careful," Richard said. "It could fire." I frowned at him skeptically. "I'm not lying. It's a real gun," he insisted. "Follow me."

I followed him into the infamous train room where Peter had taken up permanent residence. On the wall beyond the train table was a target, the classic human silhouette. It was pinned to an old mattress that was suspended from the ceiling by a couple of meat hooks attached to a steel I-beam.

Richard took the pen from me, and twisted the cap. He moved closer to the mattress and extended his arm so the pen's tip was no more than a foot from the target. Then he depressed the lever. Damned if the thing didn't actually shoot a small bullet.

Richard took the pen gun back to the safe and reloaded it. "It's a one shot deal and obviously a small caliber, but up close against an eyeball or the neck, it can do enough damage." Richard handed the pen to me, then turned to Kim. "Need anything?" Kim declined, saying she was sufficiently equipped. "Now you're ready," he said.

My angst showed in my trembling fingertips when I clipped the pen gun inside my pocket, but Richard assured me the safety would not come undone without a deliberate twist of the cap.

A few minutes later, I was on my way in Richard's truck. On the seat next to me was a small plastic case the size of an engagement ring gift box. Inside, encased in foam packing, was a computer chip small enough to fit on the end of my smallest finger. Nervously, I checked my communication equipment. "Does anybody hear me?"

"We hear you loud and clear," Kim said. "Pete and I will be only a few minutes behind you, that's if I can drag him away from the toy trains."

Kim signed off and I drove off into the night, feeling more isolated than I had ever felt before and wondering what was in store for me.

184

26

As I entered Lake Shore Drive, my pager vibrated with yet another unfamiliar number. What did this guy do, change phones every time he called, or did he have some kind of device that made it seem that way? With the rampant changes in technology, I figured anything was possible.

"You have the chip with you?" Even dryer and more grating, his voice was getting on my nerves.

"Yes, I have it," I lied, picking up the case that held the bogus chip. I didn't know how long it would fool him, if at all, so I prayed it would serve its purpose.

"You *are* alone?" It sounded more like a threat than a question.

"Yes."

"Drive directly to Buckingham Fountain. You'll find a tape recorder. Pick it up and return to your car immediately. Follow the instructions on the tape."

Click.

Shit! How long was this game going to go on? "Buckingham fountain," I said, wondering if that miniature microphone attached to my bra was still working.

"We read you loud an clear." Kim's voice was sweet music piercing the loneliness I was feeling.

Though it was well past midnight, the fountain was still flowing amid rainbow colored flood lights. I found a nearby parking space and gazed at the streams of water shooting toward the sky and spilling over circular tiers of concrete. The night had become gusty. The wind caught the airborne streams of water and sent a thousand brightly colored prisms dancing toward the sky. I was temporarily gripped by a nostalgic melancholy. I remembered coming to the fountain with my dad and brothers when I was very young. My dad worked for the Chicago Park District, and he had been assigned the job of lighting the fountain. I am sure he thought of the job as grunt work, but I saw him as having the power to control rainbows. Now that power had been given to computers and electronic switches and the magic was gone, but not forgotten. I suddenly missed those days when my dad possessed god-like powers. He was and still remains my hero.

I thought about Sam, whom I realized was a lot like my dad. Maybe that's why I loved him so much. Sam was always a bigger than life, go for the gusto kind of guy, yet he had the heart of a lamb. He proposed to me by the fountain. He said he chose that spot because he knew it held fond memories for me, and he wanted to give me even more memories to hold onto. Realizing that that would be all I would soon have of Sam, my eyes filled with tears. If there was ever a moment I needed a hug. . .

The hug not forthcoming, I climbed out of Richard's truck without bothering with the precautionary survey of the street and sidewalk. I hadn't taken more than ten steps when I felt a hand grab my shoulder and the point of a blade press into the small of my back. I stepped forward away from the blade as I spun toward my attacker. Grabbing his knife hand, I dipped under his arm and dropped him before he knew what hit him. I didn't even realize he was an ordinary street mugger until I had my foot resting against his throat.

Under normal circumstances, I would have exercised more caution, but caught up with real evil, I forgot about the pathetic schmoes who wandered the downtown streets at night mugging people for their loose pocket change. Had I seen him coming, I could have tossed him a couple of bucks and warned him not to fuck with a woman on a mission. "Jesus, lady," he croaked, his eyes wide with startled panic. I raised my foot from his neck and tossed a five-dollar-bill onto his chest. "I ought to call the cops

Linda J. Cutcliff

and have your ass thrown in jail, you little prick, but I don't have the time. So take the fin and consider yourself a lucky sonuvabitch."

The man, who could have dispatched me successfully by breathing his foul breath in my face, grabbed his throat with one hand and the five dollar bill with the other, then scurried away leaving me to face the challenge of my life.

"What was that all about?" Kim asked, her voice coming through with such clarity I thought she was standing next to me.

"You saw that, did you?" I walked briskly as I talked. "We got here just as he put the knife in your back, but your reflexes were quicker than my mouth."

A self-conscious laugh escaped my lips, and my body still trembled from the adrenalin. "Can you believe it? The little weasel tried to rob me."

The rest of my journey to the fountain was uneventful. I walked its circumference until I found the microcassette recorder. I had just wrapped my fingers around it when I heard Kim call out, "There's someone behind you!" Startled, I dropped the recorder and spun around to find myself face-to-face with Ben Scolnik.

27

"Christ! Ben, you scared the shit out of me." What's he doing here? I wondered. Had Kim called him? Had he been following me? I was suddenly filled with a sense of dread. His presence at the fountain was wrong, all wrong.

"I need to talk to you," Ben said, his eyes furtively roaming the landscape as if he were expecting trouble. He grabbed my arm hard and directed me toward one of the park benches near the fountain.

"What the hell's going on?" I demanded as I peeled his fingers off of my arm and sat on the bench.

Ben sat next to me and faced me squarely. His intense expression frightened me. "I have a lot to say and not much time, so please don't interrupt me." He dug into his pocket, and my hand immediately found the pen gun Richard had given me. Only when Ben's hand resurfaced holding a small envelope, did I relax. "You'll need this," he said, handing me the envelope.

"What's in it?"

"A bullet lens. You'll need it to read the microdot Sam sent you."

"What microdot? Where is it? The people who took Shelby have everything Sam sent me along with the bullet lens."

"No, we don't."

Did I hear him correctly? Did he say "we"? Jesus! I tried to ask him to repeat what he had just said, but the question caught in my throat.

Ben must have sensed my quandary and answered. "Yes. I said 'we'."

Though the words flowed from Ben's own lips, I didn't want to believe them. How could he betray Sam, who loved and trusted him and had always been there for him?

Without preamble, Ben began talking. "We all knew each other at Berkeley. I was in pre-law, and my room mate was majoring in sciences; chemistry, quantum physics, and shit like that. Malcom was a real genius. I thought he was a little nuts when he rattled on about overthrowing our government, but he did it with a sense of humor. He had the most active imagination, too. He had dozens of plans to bring the government to its knees. They were all plausible, but I thought he was all talk.

"There were eight of us who hung out with Malcom. Three were in pre-law with me and the other five were chasing electrons on Mars with Malcom. We spent most of our nights smoking dope and laughing at Malcom's big plans.

"With his brains, Malcom had a bright future. He could write his own ticket, and he did. The fledgling computer industry needed people like him and several other brainiacs in our group, and companies were courting Malcom, making all kinds of incredible offers, not unlike today's star athletes. Though the pay wasn't exactly comparable. He was the Michael Jordan of computers."

Scolnik bent forward and shook his head. "I never took him seriously. We all hated what our government was doing, Vietnam, Kent State, the whole thing. I attended a few sit-ins and talked anarchy with the rest of them, but it was all talk. At least it was for me, and I thought it was the same for everybody.

"After graduation, I went on to law school and my two pre-law classmates became cops. Malcom and the other egg heads headed out to Silicon Valley. I lost touch with them until I got a phone call from Malcom shortly before. . . before Angela"

My God! I thought. I didn't know exactly where he was going with this, but I suddenly knew in my gut, that the rumors about Angela had been true. I wanted to say something, but I thought it best to let Ben rattle on without interruption. I needed answers about Sam. I knew he would get to those eventually, and more quickly if I just let him talk.

Ben sighed deeply and stared slump shouldered at his shoes. "Malcom's plan was the craziest I had ever heard, and he wanted my help. He said there were others, but he also needed me on the inside. I was still stupid enough to think he was joking, so I laughed at him. It didn't take him long to convince me that he was deadly serious."

Ben leaned back and stared up at the star-filled sky, and I thought of Kim and Pete. I was glad they were taking this all in along with me. "How could I have been so stupid? I didn't take him seriously even when he threatened me. It wasn't until he made good on his threats that I finally realized what kind of animal I was dealing with."

Ben turned to me with an intense gaze. "They were going to kill Eliza, too. What could I do? I sent her away, but Malcom said he could find her easily. I wasn't sure I could protect her. I had no choice but to cooperate with them."

"What exactly does cooperate mean?" I asked.

Ben slouched back on the seat. "When you're in a position like mine, you have access to information as well as valuable connections." Ben pulled a pack of cigarettes from his pocket and tapped the bottom, causing one cigarette to pop out far enough for him to grasp it. He stuck it between his lips, then he noticed me glaring at him.

"Do you mind?" he asked as he flicked the lighter that had been stuffed in the pocket between the outer cellophane and inner paper wrap on the cigarette package.

"Yes," I replied coldly. "I do mind."

Ben looked at me oddly then took the cigarette out of his mouth and crumpled it between his fingers. He proceeded to peel the paper off of the filter material.

"And?" I pressed.

"And I was in the position to make sure that certain stumbling blocks are removed."

Jesus, I thought. "Was Sam a 'stumbling block?'"

Ben nodded.

I saw Sam in my minds eye, lying helplessly attached to machines that were laboring to hold onto life where there was no life. "You set Sam up? You arranged to have him killed, and then you framed him?"

Ben looked at me through glistening eyes and nodded. "They found Eliza. They had my little girl."

I was suddenly engulfed by a deep sadness. I wanted to hate the pathetic human being sitting next to me, but I couldn't. He had arranged the ambush on my husband, but I couldn't hate him. They had killed his wife and were threatening his child.

"Why, Ben, why Sam?" I heard my trembling voice say, as tears spilled from my eyes.

Ben's eyes glazed over, and his voice became distant. "It's funny how small the world can seem at times. In a million years, who'd ever think Sam would have a friend who knew Malcom?"

He pulled a wrinkled handkerchief from his pocket, wiped his eyes with it and blew his nose into it, then he balled it up and stuffed it back into his pocket.

"Sam came to me six months ago with information he had obtained from some guy who grew up next door to him. The guy was a computer expert who was working in Silicon Valley."

"Cal?" I asked.

"Yes," Ben replied quietly. "You had that poor man beaten and stabbed?"

Ben shook his head. "That was all Malcom's doing. I just covered it up."

"How about Tony and Michelle?"

Again, a silent nod. "Cal told Sam that he had information about a conspiracy to defraud the United States of billions of dollars and possibly kill a lot of people in the process. He refused to talk to anyone but Sam, and insisted that his identification be known only to Sam until it was time to bring everything out into to open. Cal had warned Sam that there might be people in the Bureau who were involved, so I had Sam follow through outside of the office. I was his only contact within the Bureau. He never knew I was involved."

"All that time, you let Sam trust you while you were planning to get rid of him?"

"No, no," Ben shook his head, "I really wanted Sam to find evidence that would put Malcom away. No one knew what Sam was doing. I thought I had found a way out. I thought my daughter would finally be safe. I also planned to testify myself at Malcom's trial.

"Everything was going great until Malcom intercepted a communication between Cal and Sam, and well, you know the rest."

The two of us sat in total silence. I found it hard to breathe. It felt as though I were drowning in the night air. "Why are you telling me all of this, Ben? Won't they kill Eliza if they find out you spoke to me?"

Tears flowed freely down Ben's cheeks. "They already have," he whispered as he rolled the naked filter material between his thumb and index finger, spreading the fibers and letting them drop to the ground.

After another silence, Ben said, "I know where they're keeping Shelby."

"What? You do? Where is she? Is she O.K.?"

"For the moment, but—." Suddenly, Ben sat up erect and his eyes darted around behind him.

"What is it?"

"I thought I heard something."

I studied the bushes behind Ben. They were rustling, but their movement kept time with the wind's mild gusts. "It's nothing," I assured him. "Tell me. Tell me where I can find Shelby," I urged feeling frantic.

Ben turned to me, but his expression remained skeptical. "She's in a—." His body suddenly stiffened, and he stared wide-eyed, terrified. Then his eyes became vacant, and he toppled to the ground.

"Ben? Ben?" I dropped to the ground next to him. I took hold of his shoulders and shook him. "Ben! Ben!" That's when I saw the wires trailing from his back. My eyes followed the wires to their source, a Tazer in the hands of an all-to-familiar figure, Boyle, the phony FBI agent. Or was he phony?

"Kim! Pete!" I cried out, but my receiver remained silent. I saw another figure appear from the shadows. It was the silver-haired bastard, his lips spread in a malign smile, another Tazer in his hand. I knew in an instant it was Malcom. I jumped up and turned to run, but I didn't move fast enough. I was hit with what felt like the fangs of a rattle snake. In less than the blink of an eye, a current passed through me like a million snakes wriggling through my veins. I hit the ground hard, and the world became a confused nightmare. Faces appeared overhead. I knew them, but I couldn't remember why. Hands tore my blouse open and ripped my bra away from my chest. I struggled with all that was in me, but my limbs ignored me. I was helpless and frightened, and at the mercy of madmen who possessed no such virtue. A sharp pain shot through my scalp as they yanked the barrette from my hair. My confusion soon cleared, but my muscles remained paralyzed, as the men lifted me from the ground and carried me to the street where a car was waiting, it's trunk open. They dumped me into the trunk, and slammed the lid leaving me entombed in darkness.

28

Shortly after the car had begun to move, I regained the use of my limbs. I tried to button my blouse, but found only one button still attached. It was better than nothing.

Jostled around in the pitch dark sauna, my stomach soured and churned. My body trembled beneath sweat soaked clothing, and I heaved the contents of my stomach which amounted to little more than gastric juice. Left with a sour burning in my mouth and throat, I scooted away from the puddle seeping into the trunk's carpeting, and I rolled onto my back.

I felt behind my ear where the barrette had been, half expecting to find a bald spot. Tears flooded my eyes as I envisioned Kim and Pete lying dead in the park near the fountain. I thought about Michelle. Her body still hadn't turned up. Where had they taken her, and what had they done to her?

I wondered why I hadn't been killed, and I remembered what Kim had said about Tony Jackson. He had been tortured before he died. Is that what I was facing? Tony had no answers for them, and neither did I. What could I possibly tell them? They knew more than I, yet they continued to search. Not only were they after the computer chip, but Ben said they couldn't find the microdot that had accompanied the bullet lens. He was sure I had it, but on what? Steeped in thought, my fingers absentmindedly found their way to Sam's wedding ring and began turning it around and around on my finger. After awhile I became aware of my actions and realized Sam's ring was the only thing they didn't have. Could it be? Could the microdot be on the ring?

Wanting desperately to save Shelby and myself, I considered

giving them the ring as soon as they opened the trunk. But would that be like signing my own death warrant? What about the computer chip? Had they found the bogus chip I left behind in Richard's truck? Would they keep Shelby and me alive until they had both the microdot and the correct computer chip in their possession? And then what? How did the chip figure into the conspiracy to defraud the U.S.? Would people really die? Should I play the heroine and go to my grave without revealing to them where the microdot could be found? Hell no! All I cared about was saving my daughter, clearing my husband, and hopefully saving my own ass in the process. After that, well, I figured the government could fend for itself. I'd pass along whatever information I had, and then Shelby and I would find a nice safe place to ride out the storm. It was a nice fantasy, but I knew in my gut that Kim was right. As soon as the bad guys had what they wanted, Shelby and I would have no future.

I felt the car slow and stop with a jerk. A moment later, the engine died and I heard a car door creak open. My heart was racing as I tried to formulate a plan of attack when the trunk opened. Plan? What plan? I found a shoe lying behind me. It's sole was cleated like a golf shoe. It wasn't much, but I figured I would toss the shoe at the first face I saw when the trunk opened. Then I would start kicking. My plan never made it to fruition. As the trunk opened, I tossed the shoe, but I was hit once again with the Tazer the instant the shoe left my hand. This time, a cloth bag or pillow case was thrown over my head and tied a little too tightly around my neck. I could breath, but barely. The combination of neurological disruption from the Tazer and the mild hypoxia from the cinch around my neck drove me to unconsciousness.

I don't know how long I was out, but when I came to, I found myself lying on my back on a cold, hard, concrete floor in a dimly lit room. I was gasping for air. My hands shot to my throat reflexively. Though the rope was gone, the sensation of it squeezing my neck lingered.

Once I calmed my anxiety and stopped groping for air, I lay

staring up at rusted cable wound around pulleys dangling from steel I-beams. I knew I had been unconscious for a long time, because a grayish pre-dawn light filtered through twenty-foot high broken windows. The metal window framing, pulleys, and strands of cable cast eerie shadows against the ceiling, like giant spiders waiting for prey to happen upon their webs.

Starlings were already awake, chirping and darting in and out through the openings in the windows. I suppose I should have been thankful for the rest, but I felt only weariness, and a painful awareness of every joint in my body. I closed my eyes, trying to gather my wits as well as my strength. I wondered: Would I find Shelby here? Oh God, let it be. Let me see my daughter.

As if in answer to my prayer, I heard the voice of an angel. "Mom?" At first, I thought the voice had come from inside my own head, a product of wishful thinking. "Mom, are you awake?" This time I knew the question was coming from somewhere other than my head, and I thought my heart would explode inside my chest.

I rolled my eyes toward the sound of the voice and saw Shelby. Her clothes were torn. Her hair looked like she had just crawled out of bed, and her face was soiled, but she otherwise appeared to be unharmed. "My God!" I jumped up, and nearly collapsed on rubber legs.

"Mom! Mom! What's wrong?" Shelby cried out in panic.

"Nothing, Baby. I'm just a little dizzy. It'll pass." As soon as I was able to balance myself, I hurried toward her, but she let out a blood curdling scream that stopped me dead in my tracks. "What is it?" I asked. Then I saw the reason for her scream and my heart stopped as suddenly as my footsteps.

"You can't come any closer," Shelby warned tearfully. "If you do, I'll blow up." She was sitting on the floor, her back leaning against an outside wall, her knees drawn into her chest. She was wearing a vest laden with grayish putty-like sticks of what I presumed to be some kind of plastic explosive. An array of brightly colored wires arose from the sticks and was connected to a portable telephone. The telephone was connected to a digital timer with large red numerals set at the number thirty. A cord ran from the digital timer to a phone jack in the wall. On an empty oil drum next to Shelby sat a lap top computer. It was connected to an adjacent phone jack. The computer's screen was filled with a list of seven-digit numbers. The top number on the list flashed, and I could hear the melodic beep of a telephone number being dialed followed by a woman answering. The connection was broken with a loud click and the next number began flashing on the computer's screen. Additional wires extended outward from the computer to the floor where they were taped in a semi-circular arc around Shelby. A red dot of light shown on the center of each of the anchoring tapes. I looked up toward the ceiling and found the source of each of the lights, an infra red light beam. My daughter was trapped in an electronic prison.

"So, you're finally awake."

I spun toward the hideous, harsh voice and found the silver haired creep standing just inside the exit, dressed in black and carrying an Uzi machine pistol. "You sonuvabitch!" I growled.

"Now, now. There's no need for rudeness. "As you can see, we haven't hurt your daughter. She's just been, shall we say, detained."

"Let her go. You can have me."

The man let go a sinister laugh. "For what? I don't want either of you. I merely want what you have. Hand it over, and you're both free to go."

I began twisting Sam's ring around my finger. Should I take my chances and hand it over? I glanced at my daughter's face then at the man standing before me. Looking into his cold, empty eyes, I knew that handing him the ring would be like handing him a gun loaded and ready to fire at Shelby and me. "The computer chip is in my truck."

"Nice try. We found the chip. I don't think you fully grasp your situation. You're not working with amateurs." The man walked up to me and pierced my eyes with his. "Now I want the real chip and the codes your soon-to-be late husband gave you."

He was so close, I could feel his hot breath against my face. I thought of trying to disarm him, but I was afraid the gun might go off in the struggle. Shelby could get shot, or the bomb might get set off. "I don't have the chip. I've never seen the chip, and I don't have any codes. Why won't you believe me?"

"Your friend, Ben Scolnik, believes you have the chip and the codes. That's why he arranged that little visit near the fountain."

"He's not my friend."

"Of course he's not."

"What've you done with him?"

"I'll ask the questions. You'll provide the answers."

"I don't have the answers," I insisted.

"Then you have your work cut out for you, don't you?" His eyes moved to the lap top computer next to Shelby and he smiled thinly. "There's something exhilarating about not knowing when, don't you think?"

"What do you mean?"

"You're an intelligent woman. You're a doctor after all. I'm sure you can see what's happening here. Ah, the beauty of technology. It does elevate the rather primitive game of Russian Roulette into a whole new dimension, don't you think?"

I looked again at the computer screen and then at the phone taped to my daughter. My God, it was searching for her phone number.

"As soon as it finds the correct sequence, you'll have thirty minutes. Then . . . I'll leave the rest to your imagination."

I countered his piercing gaze with one of my own. "You sick bastard!"

"I suggest you quit wasting your time with childish tantrums and start looking for the answers."

"But—"

"There are no but's. The chip I am looking for, when installed, will send out a signal through the phone lines. That signal will shut down the detonating device," He nodded toward Shelby. "and your daughter will be spared."

"What else will the chip do?"

Another malevolent smile darkened his face. "You needn't bother your pretty little head with details that don't concern you. You should focus on that which is most important to you." Again his eyes fell upon my daughter. I wanted to gouge them out. "Oh, and don't bother trying to find this place and tamper with the wiring. It's tamper proof. Disconnecting the phone lines, too, will kill the dial tone . . . and your daughter." He started backing toward the doorway.

"Where are you going?" I demanded.

His only response was an evil grin, and I was suddenly engulfed by a mixture of rage and panic. I rushed after him blinded by my fury, he managed to shut the door, leaving me to slam into the cold, hard steel. Though I was dazed by the impact, it did little to mollify the raging river of emotion. I pounded my fists and slammed my shoulder against the door until the fight inside of me faded leaving me empty and broken.

I turned my back to the door, but the guilt and shame I felt over my own inadequacy prevented me from raising my eyes toward Shelby. I had failed. Shelby was going to die. We were going to die, and I powerless to stop it. I missed Sam. He would know what to do, but Sam wasn't there. I was, and I hadn't a clue how to get us out of this. Malcom wanted what I didn't have, and he would never believe that I didn't have it. Besides, Shelby and I were doomed either way. Feeling the weight of the world pressing heavily against my shoulders, I slid to the floor, buried my head in my hands, and sobbed.

"Mom, Mom. It's OK, Mom. We'll be all right."

That sweet innocent child was trying to console me. Me. I raised my head and found Shelby smiling at me through tear filled eyes. I don't know if it made me feel better or worse. I had been blubbering like a little baby, while my daughter was housed in an electronic Chinese torture machine. If my daughter could find it in herself to smile in the face of death, then I could at least respond in kind.

Inspired by Shelby's courage, I fought back what few tears I had left inside, forced myself to get up and return her smile. I walked toward her slowly, sluggishly. It felt like I was dragging my feet through tar.

When I came as close to Shelby as I dare, I sank to the floor and my eyes locked onto the computer screen. Malcom had all of the special effects in place. The volume was turned all of the way up, so every shrill beep of the dialing process would pierce my eardrums, and my heart would stop in that eternal moment when the dialing had stopped, and I waited for a phone to ring. Shelby was suffering and would soon die, but it became crystal clear that the torture was intended for me. It was working.

"Am I following the tenets?" Shelby asked.

"Huh?"

"Am I following the tenets?" she asked again. She was referring to the Tenets or principles of training in Taekwondo, and I wondered why she cared.

"Would daddy be proud of me?"

I understood immediately. "Yes, baby, daddy would be proud of you."

"I think I'm finally doing that one, indomitable spirit."

I smiled in spite of myself. "Yes, honey, you're doing that one for sure, indomitable spirit."

A satisfied smile spread across Shelby's face. There are five Tenets; courtesy, integrity, self-control, perseverance, and indomitable spirit. Shelby practiced and lived all of them, probably better than I. But more than that, Shelby thrived on her father's approval. Though I eventually joined them in training, Shelby and Sam shared a special bond through martial arts. It was a beautiful way for Sam to cultivate important human qualities in Shelby, qualities that were an integral part of our home as well as in the dojang.

I thought about the first time Shelby put on a Taekwondo uniform. The smallest size Sam could find was a 000, which fits a child around three-and-a-half feet tall, weighing thirty-five pounds.

Shelby swam in it. When she first put it on, all we saw was a shock of auburn curls peeking out through a v-shaped hole in the top of a white tent. I performed a little sewing machine magic—with an emphasis on "little magic"— and we were able to see Shelby's hands and feet.

Sam's students loved having Shelby in class. She smiled at everything. Nothing phased her. Every time she would kick or punch a shield, she would kiyap or yell in a loud voice that seemed surrealistically detached from the tiny body from which it had emerged. That kiyap became Shelby's trademark.

The most fun everyone had was watching Shelby spar. She would fearlessly flail on anyone, yelling and kicking non-stop. Her kicks never connected with anything but air, but that didn't stop her.

Shelby giggled and fell down the first time anyone actually kicked back and made contact. It was at her fifth tournament. Judging little kids in Taekwondo tournaments is one of life's treasured experiences. Two little peanuts, buried inside of a mountain of sparring gear, square off with one another. As soon as the center referee signals the start of the match, the two kids commence kicking and yelling. The kicking never stops until the judge calls time. Scoring presents a particular problem, since scores are based on contact. When judging little kids, you have to score anything the comes within an inch or two. It's funny how those matches always end in a tie.

The day eventually comes, though, when one kid is no longer satisfied with a tied match. He's out for the win. That's the day when contact first occurs. Five-year-old Jacky Shroeder did the honors against four-year-old Shelby. Even at five, Jacky's budding male ego was not about to let some little girl put a whoopin' on him. He hadn't, though, anticipated Shelby's response. With a characteristic giggle, Shelby got up and returned fire. This time she connected with a beautiful roundhouse kick to Jacky's head. It was a two-pointer. Jacky's was a one-pointer. Shelby's foot barely brushed against his sparring headgear, but it was all Jacky needed. He burst into tears. The match was over. Shelby had been stunned at his response. She tried to console him by patting him on his back, but he would have none of it. He had been kicked in the head by a girl, the shame of it all. That was the day Shelby earned her first winning trophy. She would go on to win many more.

That same tenacious spirit, the ability to smile in the face of what seems to be an insurmountable challenge, was with Shelby in that cold, filthy warehouse.

"Is daddy going to die?" she asked quietly.

Under a different set of circumstances, I would have avoided answering the question like a politician before a group of reporters, answering without answering. In other words, I would have lied to stave off her pain and my own for as long as possible. But Shelby and I were hovering on the brink of death. There wasn't any time to play emotional politics. Gazing at my daughter's tear streaked, open, innocent face, and listening to the repeated dialing process, I knew the truth was all I had left to give my only child. "Yes. He may already be dead."

Shelby's smile faded, and tears welled up in her eyes. "I'm going to die, too, aren't I?" She asked.

The answer stuck in my throat, but Shelby saw it on my face. "It's O.K., mom," she said, her voice almost soothing. Her eyes did not convey fear or panic. She had already accepted her fate...and mine. "Will we go to heaven and be with daddy?" she asked. The question seemed to me more for my benefit than her own.

"Yes, we'll go to heaven and be with daddy?" I replied, hoping I was more convincing that I felt inside. It was hard to talk about heaven when I was no longer sure if God existed. If He did exist, why didn't he care about us? I thought about the story of the Crucifixion, remembering that Jesus Christ, Himself, cried out, asking God why he had forsaken him. The anger surged inside of me. What kind of God would let innocent children fall prey to evil people like Malcom?

Renewing my resolve not to let Malcom win, I got up and walked around the electronic perimeter, searching for a way inside. Malcom seemed to have it all covered. I was studying the wiring to and from the computer when the warehouse door opened with a resounding screech.

"I wouldn't suggest you touch anything." Malcom was standing inside the doorway flanked by two neanderthals.

"Have you had enough time to realize what limited choices you have?"

I responded with a glare. But he knew he had me exactly where he wanted me. I would have handed him the head of the President of the United States on a silver platter if it would save my daughter's life.

"Are we ready to do business?"

"Yes," I whispered.

"What? What was that? I didn't hear you?" Malcom said condescendingly as he cupped his fingers around his hear.

"Yes," I spat back at him.

"Good," he announced arrogantly. He handed a slip of paper to one of the neanderthals who walked over and handed it to me. As I took the paper, I imagined breaking bones, but any attempt would have been foolish with Malcom's Uzi pointed at my head. I glanced at the paper. All it had on it was a phone number.

I gave Malcom a quizzical look. "Dial the number when you have what I want. I will give you instructions as to where and when we will make the exchange. Once I have verified that the chip is authentic, I will release your daughter. If you fail to show up. . . well . . . you know the scenario."

The neanderthal who had given me the slip of paper picked up a pillowcase from the floor and held it out toward me. It must have been the one that had been tied over my head earlier.

"You can put that on voluntarily, or we can use the Tazer again," Malcom said.

I turned and my eyes shared a painful "good-bye" with Shelby. Her whole body trembled, and her soiled face was streaked with tears. "Mom," she cried out as I took the pillow case.

"I'll be back. You hold on," I assured her, though I believed it was probably the last time I would see her alive. Then I placed the pillow case over my head. This time, the man left me a little more breathing room when he tied the bag. Then I was led down several flights of stairs and outside where I was guided once again to the trunk.

"I realize the accommodations are less than desirable," Malcom apologized with blatant insincerity, "but it's a necessary evil." He closed the lid to my temporary coffin.

The minute I felt the car move forward I tore the hood from my head and began counting time, stopping when the car stopped. I also tried to guess the speed we were travelling. I was hoping it would give us an idea where the factory was located. I didn't know that it would be useful, but it was worth a try. At the very least, it helped keep me from going insane.

Seventeen interminable minutes and thirty-one seconds later, excluding stops, I was dumped in the Soldier's Field Parking lot. The whole time I imagined that the computer found the correct sequence, and the red numerals on the clock had begun counting down. My transportation had been a black Lincoln Town car. It sped off, kicking bits of gravel and dirt in my face. Before I had a chance to read its license plate, it was gone, leaving me alone, partially clad, and penniless.

I had no idea what time it was except that the sky was light. As I got to my feet, I wondered if the morning sun, hidden by a sea of clouds, had been red. I pulled my shirt closed over my breasts and gathered the tails into a knot at my midriff, then I started walking toward Lake Shore Drive, already alive with commuter traffic.

Hitchhiking was one thing I had never attempted in my entire life, so I was leery of trying it, even under those circumstances. I tried flagging down a cab. I must have looked pretty awful, because the cab driver recoiled at the sight of me and refused to take me when I failed to produce cash in advance.

Desperate, I finally gave in and stuck my thumb into the air, hoping to encounter a generous human being rather than some lecherous asshole. What I encountered was nonstop moving traffic and blaring horns, so I started walking toward Buckingham Fountain where I had left Richard's truck. Since I didn't have the keys with me anymore, I planned to break the window with a rock and hot wire the ignition, a little trick Sam taught me in case of emergencies.

. The truck was parked where I had left it, and I was thankful some street thief hadn't tried my technique before I got there. There was, however, one minor problem. A cop was standing next to the truck writing a citation. I waited for him to leave, then thought better of it. He could call Richard and confirm who I was. Then I might get a ride home.

When I approached the cop, he eyed me suspiciously, but when I explained my situation, he called Richard, broke into the truck without damaging it, and hot-wired it for me.

29

I arrived at Kim's, and I raced to the front door without noticing what cars were parked in the driveway. My finger was still on the doorbell when the door swung wide with a loud swoosh. Kim's arms were around me before I had a chance to react.

"I thought you were dead," she cried. "What happened? How did you escape?" She dragged me inside and shut the door. Pete was sitting at the kitchen table with Richard. Both got up and greeted me enthusiastically. I was left speechless at the unexpected surprise of seeing Kim and Pete alive.

"Tell us," Kim urged as Richard tried to slide a chair under me. I declined his offer, "where did they take you? How did you get away?"

I looked from Kim to Pete and back to Kim. "You didn't respond when they attacked me. I . . . I thought you were dead."

"Sorry about that," Pete said. "They nailed us both with Tazers. I guess we're lucky they didn't kill us."

"Why?" I asked. "Why didn't they kill you?"

"You wanted them to?" Kim asked facetiously.

"No. They've killed everybody else. Why not you?"

"Hell." Kim shrugged. "A couple of dead cops would bring down too much heat." She frowned at me. "The real question here is: Why didn't they kill you?"

I could feel myself beginning to hyperventilate. I didn't have time for any more talk. "They have Shelby," I said breathlessly.

"You saw Shelby?" Kim asked.

"Yes. They have her wired to a bomb."

"Jesus," Kim whispered.

"That silver-haired bastard still thinks I have the chip. I tried to tell him I don't have it, but he wouldn't listen."

"How long do you have?" Kim asked.

"I don't know. They're using the phone lines. They have a computer dialing random numbers. When it finds the right number, it will trigger a thirty-minute countdown timer. It could happen any minute. Only the chip can save her."

"Deb," Kim said looking squarely at me like someone about to deliver a rude awakening, "you can't give him the chip. Once he has his hands on it, he'll kill her anyway."

"No! I yelled. "Once the chip is installed, it will send out a signal to disarm the bomb."

"You can't believe that," Kim insisted.

"I have to. What choice do I have?"

"Find Shelby and disarm the bomb," Pete said.

"You can't disarm it," I argued. "It's tamper proof."

"No bomb is tamper proof," Pete insisted.

"I'm not going to let you prove your theory on my daughter. Besides, I don't know where she is."

"What?" Kim asked.

"They stuck a bag over my head. All I know is she's in a warehouse or old factory of some sort. It's about seventeen minutes from Soldier's Field. That's where they dumped me."

A light of recognition shown behind Pete's eyes. "I think I know where she might be."

"How?" I asked.

"You remember when I followed the guy who picked up Sam's note from the phone booth?"

"Yes."

"I followed him to the old Chris Craft factory next to the Chicago river."

"You think it could be the one?" I asked.

"Why not? They didn't know I was following them. Why would they pick another empty factory building?"

"It makes sense," Kim said.

"I'll take a run over there and check the place out while you two search for the computer chip," Pete said.

"If you find her, don't do anything until I get the chip," I ordered.

"Listen, Deb," Kim said, "Pete's a damn good cop. He's not going to do anything that will jeopardize Shelby's safety. You have to trust his judgement. I'd trust him with my life."

I turned to Pete. "You page me the minute you find her. I have to have your word on that."

"You've got it." Pete took off, leaving Richard, Kim, and me to solve the mystery of the elusive computer chip.

I pulled the envelope Ben had given me from my pocket and dumped the lens onto the table. "What's this?" Richard asked.

"It's a bullet lens. Ben gave it to me. Now all I need is the damn microdot." I took Sam's ring off my finger and began turning it slowly, inspecting its inside wall, but my hands were shaking so badly I couldn't focus on anything.

"Do you think the microdot's on the ring?" Kim asked.

"Yes," I replied. "Ben said the microdot was on something Sam had given me. I thought his buddies had everything, but they didn't get the ring. I'd forgotten about it until I was in the trunk of the car."

I pressed the ring against the table in an attempt to control my shaking, and I continued examining its inner wall. The sight of our names engraved along with our wedding date tugged at my heart. Then something drew my attention. The wedding date, April twenty-nine . . . nine. The center of the nine was blackened out: I frowned and squinted trying to see it more clearly.

"What do you see?" Richard asked, leaning on his elbows, his eyes riveted to the ring.

"I'm not sure. It could be it." I handed the ring to him, and he studied it intently. He picked up the bullet lens and held it over the nine.

"Jesus!" Richard said. "It's a key."

"What?"

"A key, a passcode. I'll be able to decrypt Sam's document with this."

"Do you think it will tell us where he's hidden the computer chip?" I asked with urgency.

Richard kicked his chair away from the table. "Let's go see," he said. We followed him downstairs where he immediately booted up his computer. "Have you ladies heard of PGP?"

"No," Kim and I replied in unison. "And we don't give a shit about it either," Kim added. Richard smiled and continued talking as he typed.

"PGP stands for Pretty Good Privacy. It's a program for encrypting electronic documents written by a guy named Philip Zimmermann in nineteen ninety. One of his colleagues thought his system should be shared with the world, so this colleague gave it away on the Internet. That was in nineteen ninety-three. The government tossed Zimmermann in jail, charging him with exportation of munitions."

Though my anxiety level grew exponentially with every passing second, and I had no interest in what Richard was saying, I chose not to interrupt him. His fingers flew across the keys as he talked, as if talking kept him focused. I didn't want to risk breaking his rhythm.

"The government has placed powerful encryption software in the same category as nuclear bombs or Sidewinder missiles. It's a federal offense to export munitions. Since the Internet knows no borders, giving things away on the Net is considered the same as exporting them."

As I watched Richard's computer screen fill with meaningless strings of letters and numerals, I found myself, in spite of my growing panic, becoming engrossed in what he was saying.

"The government suddenly dropped the case, and now PGP is available to anyone in the US and Canada," Richard continued. He took Sam's ring and the bullet lens and started handing it to me, then handed it to Kim saying, "Her hands are probably steadier at the moment." I didn't argue. All I could do was glance at my watch every two seconds and try to ignore the loud ringing in my ears caused by severe stress.

Richard typed the passcode string as Kim dictated it to him, then with a few more key strokes, a window, filled with file folders, opened onto the desk top.

"We're in," Richard said. He dragged the cursor over to a folder entitled "e-mail" and clicked it opened. The folder contained a list of dates beginning in January.

"Go to the most recent date and open it," I ordered. Richard opened the document marked with the same date that John Doe had died on my trauma table. It was what I was looking for, though I wasn't sure it would end up being of any help. In his last e-mail transmission to Sam, Cal said he would be carrying the chip on him. He wasn't sure how he would hide it, but he would make sure Malcom didn't get it.

"Who's Malcom?" Kim asked.

"I don't give a damn," I barked. "Can I use your car?"

"Where the hell are you going?" Kim asked.

"To the hospital. Cal's personal effects are in a storage closet in the ER."

"I'll drive," Kim said. "Richard, you keep at it. Call if you find anything we need to know."

Kim's pager went off as we raced out the front door to her car, causing me to nearly jump out of my skin. She glanced at it and said, "It's Pete." Every muscle in my body tightened up.

Kim answered the page as we squealed out of the driveway. She spoke, or rather, listened for only a few minutes. Then she said, "Thanks, Pete," and hung up without looking at me.

"Well?" I asked impatiently.

"I have some good news and some bad news." It unnerved me that Kim's eyes remained on the road. She wasn't the type to avoid eye contact.

With a sinking feeling in my gut, I propped my elbow on the window ledge and rested my head in my hand. Closing my eyes, steeling myself for what was to come, I said, "Give me the good news. I don't think I can handle the other right now."

"Pete found Shelby."

"Thank you, God," I whispered, heaving a momentary sigh of relief. Then, remembering there was bad news, I retracted my prayer of gratitude. "And the bad news?" I asked Kim.

"The SWAT team has already arrived on the scene, and they're awaiting the arrival of bomb disposal."

"So the bad news is that Shelby's still not free of the bomb?" I asked, anticipating from Kim's face, that I hadn't yet heard the worst."

Kim pressed her lips tightly together, then said, "Pete's pretty knowledgeable when it comes to explosives." Her voice trailed off. There was more, but she was reticent to continue.

"And?" I urged.

"He says it looks like the bomb has several back-up fail-safe devices."

"Which means?"

"Which means they can't disarm it without blowing up Shelby and everybody else."

I was right in withdrawing my thank you from God. He was still sitting on his omnipotent ass ignoring my petitions.

30

The storage room where I had placed the yellow trash bag containing Cal's clothing was located in an auxiliary corridor adjacent to the main treatment areas of the Emergency Department. It was most easily accessible from the ER, but I didn't want to see anybody in my current state, nor did I want to waste any time fielding questions from my co-workers, so I chose a more prudent, though arduous, path. It would take less time in the long run.

Kim and I entered through the loading docks. From there, we cut through the laundry and past the maintenance areas. We took an elevator to central supply. A service corridor led us to the Emergency Department storage areas.

I was surprised to find the bag containing Cal's clothing undisturbed in the storage room where I had left it. "I wonder why they didn't come for the bag?" I said, more to myself than to Kim, but she seemed compelled to answer anyway.

"Maybe they did, but what if no one else knew where it was? You and Tony knew it was here, and Tony's dead."

"Thanks for reminding me," I said as I dragged the bag out into the corridor, and across the hall into an unused room that was slated for future use by the radiology department. A snarl of wires with copper exposed at their tips peeked out through the end of metal conduit dangling from the ceiling, while the walls were finished with shiny, hospital green tiles. Everything was in its place awaiting the purchase of multi-million dollar computerized imaging toys. For now, though, the room served as the local dumping site for discarded pieces of hospital equipment, old suction machines, stretchers, wheel chairs, and incubators that had worn out their welcome, along with boxes of out-dated supplies.

"No one will bother us in here," I said as I dragged the bag inside. Kim followed me in and let the door close behind her. "In fact," I continued, "we could live out our lives and die undiscovered in here if we were so inclined."

"That's comforting," Kim said, watching me dump the contents of the bag onto the floor. Both of us cringed at the stale, rotten, metallic odor of Cal's filthy, blood stained clothing.

"It's true," I said. I once heard a story about an intern who was skinned alive in a room like this, and no one heard his screams."

"O.K. What's the punch line?" Kim picked up Cal's shirt, barely grasping it between her thumb and index finger. Her face twisted with repulsion.

"Oh, c'mon," I said. "You have to have seen worse things that someone who'd been skinned alive."

"It's not that," Kim replied. "There are things growing on this shirt."

"Of course, blood's a great culture medium. I wouldn't touch it unprotected."

Kim immediately dropped the shirt onto the floor. "Thanks for the timely advice."

I searched a stack of boxes for old, outdated surgical gloves and grabbed a pair for each of us. Kim found a couple of chairs and placed them beside the pile of clothing.

My anxiety growing with each passing second, I decided to continue my story, if only to keep me calm enough to function. As we put on the latex gloves, I said. "By-the-way, there's no punch line." Kim, already busy tearing out hems and seams in Cal's ragged slacks, gave me an incredulous cursory glance.

With Cal's shirt in my hands, I continued, "A surgical chief resident I trained under told the story to a group of us and backed it up with old newspaper clippings."

"What, didn't a patient like the way the doc had sewn him up?"

"No, but it was along the same lines. It was a group of Gypsies. The head of the Gypsie clan arrived in severe pulmonary edema. He'd had a massive M.I. There wasn't anything anyone could do. The man died in the E.R. The intern, who had cared for the man, turned up missing the next day. They found him several days later, adhesive taped to the wall minus his skin."

"You're shittin' me."

"It's a true story," I insisted.

"C'mon. We don't have clans of Gypsies roaming the streets."

"It was in Canada." After examining every thread of Cal's shirt, I tossed it onto the floor and started on his one shoe.

"I guess it proves that the U.S. isn't the only country plagued by fucking wackos." Kim said as she tossed the pants on the floor. "Where's his other shoe?" she asked.

"I don't know," I replied as I dropped the shoe I was holding. "It wasn't on him when the paramedics brought him in."

Kim immediately snatched it up and said, "You're a helluva doctor, Doctor, but a detective you're not." She then proceeded to demonstrate her detectively skills by methodically destroying the shoe. She yanked the heel off and tore out the sole. "Sometimes you just have to go further than you thought to find what you're looking for." She ripped out the lining, and using a couple of disposable scalpels, tore the shoe apart at the seams. By the time she finished, there was little left that resembled the original structure. "Nothing here," Kim said as she tossed the last shoe remnant onto the floor. "With the kind of luck you're having, the chip's probably in the other shoe."

Kim's attempt at levity didn't go unnoticed. What if she was right? What if the chip was in the other shoe? Fear proliferated inside me like cancerous cells.

I hung my head low and cried as I dropped the last article of clothing on the floor between my legs. "There's nothing here," I sobbed. "It's too late. Shelby's dead. I know it, and I might as well die too."

"Don't talk that way." Kim rubbed my back and stroked my

hair. "If Shelby were dead, I would have gotten a call from Pete. You can't give up on her now. As long as she's alive, we'll keep looking for the chip, and Pete'll keep trying to figure out how to disarm the bomb. That's just the way it is."

"Where do we look?" I argued. "They have the body, and we've come up empty handed here."

"It's obvious they didn't find the chip on the body, or they sure as hell wouldn't be wasting their time with you. It's got to be here somewhere." Kim kicked at the pile of clothing, moving it around with her foot.

I got up and started pacing aimlessly. "Have you ever watched a trauma resuscitation?" I asked angrily.

"Plenty of times. Why?"

"Have you seen how we cut the clothes away and toss them on the floor? When it's over, an aide has to sift through the piles of wrappers and gauze and tubing and God knows what else to collect what's left of the patient's clothes. It's a wonder we recover anything at all."

"Are you saying you think the chip might have been thrown away?"

"It's a reasonable assumption."

"In that case, we're fucked. Right?"

"Yes."

"So what have we got to lose?"

I frowned angrily at Kim. I hated her upbeat tone. I was feeling sorry for myself, and that's the way I wanted it. "What do you mean, 'we'?" I snapped. "I have everything to lose."

"You're missing my point, Deb. Haven't you ever seen that old cliché: You never fail until you quit trying?"

"Try doing what? We've exhausted everything. There's no place else to look."

"Think, Deb. Think. Close your eyes and picture that resuscitation." Reluctantly, I followed her suggestion. "Now try to picture everything from the moment the paramedics brought John Doe into the E.R."

With my eyes closed, the scene replayed itself in my mind. I watched the stretcher roll in. Cal was covered with blood. The paramedics had started an I.V., and it was running wide open. The nurses and I helped transfer Cal to the trauma table. I took the head, and started to intubate . . . "His teeth. I knocked out his teeth."

"Do you think—?"

"I don't know. Tony had them in a plastic bag. I thought he put them with Cal's clothes, but they're not here."

Kim took out her cell phone and switched it on. "Damn! I can't get a signal."

"The walls are lined with lead," I said. "You have to go out into the hall."

Kim disappeared through the door and returned in a couple of minutes. "Richard said it would be difficult, but it's possible to hide a computer chip inside a tooth. It's certainly small enough. So where do we find the teeth?"

"Tony showed them to me in the staff lounge. I had told him to put them into the bag with John Doe's things. I guess he never got around to it."

"Or they fell out."

I looked at Kim and she at me, then we hurried across the hall to the storage closet which I proceeded to tear apart. My search ended in utter failure.

"How about his locker?" Kim asked. I led the way to the locker room in the staff lounge. Tony's name was still on his locker, and the door was locked.

"Damn!" I complained as I yanked futilely on the locker's handle. "I don't know where to find a pass key."

"These locks are nothing," Kim said. "I've seen you in action. Why don't you just kick it in?"

I wasn't sure whether or not Kim was serious, but I assumed she was, so I did just that. A couple of good side kicks dented the door in the center and bowed the edges. Together, we grabbed the edges and literally tore the locker open.

Our efforts, however, did not go unnoticed. The housekeeping lady, dumpy and grey-haired, stuck her head in the locker room and said, "What the hell're you doin'?"

"I'm sorry, but I have to find something in this locker. It's an emergency."

"What's you lookin' for?" the woman demanded.

"I know it sounds strange, but I'm looking for some teeth inside a plastic bag."

The woman's eyebrows shot up. "I got some teeth in a bag."

"You do?" Kim and I asked simultaneously.

"Yeah. I found them on the floor outside the store room in the back hallway." the woman said.

I couldn't believe what I was hearing.

"Where are the teeth now?" Kim asked.

"On my cleaning cart out in d'hall."

"Jesus, let them be the right teeth, and let the chip be inside," I whispered. There I went, praying again.

We followed the woman into the corridor, where she rummaged through a small plastic bucket filled with collected treasures, and came up with the bag containing Cal's teeth. I knew the minute I saw it that it was the right bag.

"Thanks," I chirped as I snatched the bag from the woman's hand. "You may have saved a life."

The woman frowned skeptically. "Any time," she muttered as she rolled her cart down the hall, shaking her head like she thought she had just had an encounter with a couple of nuts. She was probably right.

Kim and I raced inside the lounge and studied the two teeth under the lamp. One was cracked, and it was obvious that it didn't contain anything that mother nature had not put inside of it. The other tooth, however, had a bluish cast to it. "This doesn't look real," Kim said, and I could feel excitement mounting inside of me. She held the tooth against the bulb. It had no filling, but we could clearly see something inside. "I think we found it," Kim announced, her voice filled with the same excitement I felt.

I dashed out to the seldom used dental emergency suite located just outside of the lounge and grabbed a handful of instruments. Kim and I used the tools to cut the tooth open and retrieve its contents, a computer chip encased in clear plastic.

Leaving the chip undisturbed in its plastic casing, I called the number the silver haired creep had given me and arranged the pick up point. The strange voice, not his familiar raspy tone, directed me to a drop off point at the Adler Planetarium. My ride was to leave me there and disappear.

I felt like I had hit third base, and I was racing for home. But home was still a long way off.

31

Lack of sleep had begun to take its toll as we turned east onto the planetarium drive. "I don't like this, Deb," Kim said as she pulled alongside the curb and stopped. "How can I back you up if you refuse to wear a wire?"

"I think we already tried that. Next time he might use real bullets."

"The least you can do is wear a transmitter, so we can find you."

"You know he'll search me. Hell, he didn't have any trouble finding the wire the first time," I said as I combed my hair away from my face with my fingers.

"You want a hair band? I have one in my purse." Kim dug in her purse and came up with a blue ponytail band and a hairbrush.

"Thanks," I said as I reached for the brush.

Kim pulled the brush away. "At least, let me do this for you. Turn around." She was mothering me, and I needed someone to do just that. I also knew she was stalling, not wanting to let me out of the car. I turned my back to her, and she began dragging the brush through my hair while gathering the strands into a ponytail.

"I want you to think about what you're doing," Kim said. "I don't have to tell you these people are playing for keeps."

"I don't have a choice," I replied. "I know there's only a slim chance Shelby and I will come out of this alive, but it's a chance I have to take. If I don't, we're dead anyway." Kim doubled the band around my hair, and I turned around to face her. We stared at each other for a long moment, friends bidding each other a silent farewell. There was little else to say.

Kim touched my arm as I started to climb out of the car. "I'll try to follow."

"Don't. I can't risk them seeing you." I stepped onto the curb and closed the door. After a brief hesitation, Kim drove off, leaving me standing alone.

I watched Kim's car until I could no longer see it. Though dozens of people filled the sidewalks and grass along the Planetarium drive, I felt completely alone. She may as well have left me on one of those desolate planets people see in the Planetarium's shows.

Not knowing exactly what to expect, I looked up and down the drive, tensing every time I saw a black car coming my way. Occasionally, I would turn and glance at the passersby. Some would return my gaze, and wonder if they could see into my soul and know the trouble I was in. But their eyes would divert to the next random object that happened along the path, and I knew I had been little more than invisible.

The waiting and anticipation were taking their toll. My jaws were clamped together with such force, my ears had begun ringing. A viscous haze hung in the August air and threatened to suffocate me. Sweat droplets stung my eyes, while salty rivulets forged their way down my neck, onto my chest, eventually streaming between my breasts. I pressed the fabric of my shirt against my chest, trying to wick away the wetness.

I was losing my resolve, and panic was taking over. I almost bolted when I caught sight of a black Lincoln Town car. The car slowed, but did not pull over to the curb. Instead, a rear passenger door flung open. The windows were heavily tinted, and I couldn't see the faces of the passenger, only their silhouettes, but I heard the chilling rasp order me inside. There was little doubt who was in the car. I took in a deep breath and uttered a quick prayer to God, with whom I had an ongoing love/hate relationship. I wasn't sure which of the two emotions I felt at that moment, but I knew I needed Him on my side.

I had one foot inside the car when I heard the intermittent

burst of a police siren and saw Kim's cruiser racing toward us, her strobe flashing from the dashboard. Confused, I watched her race toward me, but I failed to react. The Lincoln started rolling forward, and a hand suddenly grabbed hold of my arm and tugged hard, trying to pull me into the car.

Kim screeched to a halt behind us and jumped out. "Deb, you can't give him the chip," she cried out. "Don't give him the chip!"

I twisted my arm free of my captor, but another hand grabbed the front of my shirt, while a third caught hold of my ponytail. The barrel of a semiautomatic was pressed against my forehead, and I was dragged into the car.

Inside the car, I found myself sandwiched between, Boyle and Malcom. Eberhardt and Krandall occupied the front seat. "Do you have the chip?" Malcom asked.

Distracted by Kim's persistent siren and our dangerously accelerating speed, I did not answer. I looked through the rearview window and watched Kim giving chase. Why was she following us, and why did she suddenly change her mind about the chip? Had something happened? Was it too late? Was Shelby already dead?

"Get rid of the bitch," the nameless man ordered, and Boyle reached down between his legs and brought up a pump action shotgun. He lowered his window and positioned himself so he could fire on Kim's car. I grabbed his legs and had nearly dumped him out of the window when something hard slammed into my head. Balls of fire flashed before my eyes, and white hot pain shot through my skull.

When my vision cleared, I found myself looking down the barrel of yet another handgun held by Krandall. "Give me a reason," he said, smiling.

Boyle aimed his shot gun and squeezed off a couple of rounds. I heard Kim's brakes squeal, and I turned in time to see her cruiser spin out of control and land against a tree. I held my breath until I saw her climb out of the car and knew she had survived the crash.

"Turn around, bitch!" Krandall demanded, "and give the man what he wants."

I glared at him as I turned and dug into my pocket. Krandall stiffened and his finger inched closer to the trigger, while Boyle took hold of my hand and eased it out of my pocket. Both men relaxed when I produced the chip.

"Let's do her now, Malcom," Krandall said.

"Shut up, you stupid sonuvabitch!" Malcom barked.

"My daughter," I said, "I want my daughter released immediately."

"Not so fast," Malcom replied. "We have to make sure you have delivered the right goods this time."

"There's no time," I argued. "The computer has to be nearing the end of the numbers."

Malcom laughed condescendingly. "It will be dialing away at those numbers forever."

"What do you mean?"

"Did you really think I would let your daughter blow up before I got the right chip? What leverage would I have then?"

"But the computer, the timer?"

"They served their purpose now, didn't they. You were highly motivated and didn't waste anytime finding the chip."

"The police are there," I blurted out, "they'll disarm the bomb."

Again, Malcom laughed. "No they won't, my dear. They'll just go boom along with your daughter. "Ah," he sighed wistfully, "It should give you comfort, knowing Shelby won't be dying alone. Oh, and don't fret. You'll be joining her soon."

A moment later, we pulled into the underground parking garage just west of Garfield park. Eberhardt parked the Lincoln, and we transferred to a dark green Expedition. Before he climbed in with us, Eberhardt changed the license plates on the Lincoln. Soon we were on our way and headed toward O'Hare airport.

32

"Where are we going?" I asked as we headed toward a hangar, its doors wide open revealing a Citation jet that looked large enough to seat about twenty passengers. Malcom and the others ignored my question. The Expedition stopped next to the stairs that led to the jet's fuselage. Eberhardt and Krandall climbed out of the car, as did Boyle, but Malcom stayed behind with me. He showed me a small device that looked a little like the remote control to Shelby's stereo system.

"I know what you're capable of, Dr. Hunter, so I thought I would let you know, before you tried anything, that this little device has the correct number to the bomb. All I need do is press this button, and. . ." A thin smile of self satisfaction spread across his lips. "I guess your daughter's number will be up."

I thought of punching him in the throat and grabbing the device, but his thumb hovered so close to the button I feared his reflex reaction would set it off. I couldn't be sure he was telling the truth this time, but I had no intention of testing him. He owned me, and we both knew it.

"Now climb out of the car slowly and walk to the stairs." I obediently followed his instructions.

The passenger cabin was finished like a high tech office complete with a computer system that would make Richard, the "geek", drool. Malcom directed me to one of the generous white leather seats and reminded me that any unauthorized movement on my part would result in Shelby's immediate demise.

Malcom handed the computer chip encased in plastic to Eberhardt. "Get to work." Eberhardt dutifully took the chip to the rear of the cabin and set it inside a chamber that looked a bit like a neonatal incubator. Eberhardt then locked the hood into place and flipped a switch that started what sounded like a fan motor.

"The chips," Malcom explained casually, as if I were the student and he the professor, "cannot be exposed to the environment at any time. A single particle of dust, you see, can destroy the circuitry or at least make it malfunction. We can't have any of that. What you hear is the electronic filtering system purifying the chamber. Once that is complete, Mr. Eberhardt will melt the plastic casing and install the chip in its carrier. Then I will plug it into the logic board, and we'll be ready."

"Ready? For what?" I asked.

Malcom sat facing me from a leather seat across the aisle. He rubbed his chin thoughtfully. "Hm." He nodded. "Now that's a good question. Do you want to know what the world will think is happening, or would you rather know the underlying plan?"

I knew by his seeming willingness to tell me what he was up to that he had no intention of letting me go. I had visions of my body being jettisoned over Lake Michigan. I hoped that I would be dead before they tossed me out. Since I knew that my life was over, and with it all chance of salvaging Sam's honor, I developed the single-minded purpose of saving Shelby. I would do anything necessary to give her a chance at life.

"Will you let my daughter go?" I asked quietly. "She can do no more than describe you to the police." I gazed around the cabin. "From the looks of things, you'll be long gone before that happens, so killing her has no value."

The sociopathic sonuvabitch leaned forward, and with a syrupy voice—syrup over sandpaper that is—he said, "You love her deeply, don't you?"

I nodded my affirmation toward ice cold, empty eyes that bore no hint of human feeling. I was sitting in front of Satan, himself, begging for mercy. The ridiculous notion fueled my anger and filled me with visions of ripping those ice cubes from his eye sockets and spitting into the vacuum that was behind them.

"It's ready," Eberhardt called out to Malcom, who got up and placed his hands over mine, pinning them to the arms of the chair. He leaned in close to my face. "Since you love your daughter so much, you'll be happy to know that she'll be a participant in a historical event. Too bad neither of you will be around to read about it, but such is life."

My skin burned with rage. I didn't know how, but I was going to see to it that he did not live long enough to take his place in the history books.

"You wanted to know what I am about to do. Malcom walked toward the place where Eberhardt was working. "Well, I'll tell you. As soon as this final chip is in place, it will set off a chain reaction that will knock the United States government on its proverbial ass. Anything transmitted over telecommunications wiring will suddenly malfunction, and in some cases shut down completely. The malfunctions will be random and widespread, with no hope of tracing the problems to their source."

Before I could ask any questions, Malcom depressed a button on the wall, and another section of wall slid out from inside a pocket and closed him off to me. While Malcom was hidden from my sight, I studied every detail on the jet, searching for a usable weapon and an escape route.

One truth I learned in my martial arts training is: Unlike what people see Chuck Norris and Steven Segal do in the movies, you can not fight multiple attackers. Gangs of bad guys who want a piece of someone don't stand around politely waiting their turns to fight with their target. They tend to all pounce at once. Your only choice is to try to take down the biggest or toughest guy in the group and hope the others will leave you alone. At the very least, you'll take a few down with you.

All bets are off, however, when the attackers are heavily armed as was the case with my four captors. My best hope, a rather pathetic one, would be to wait until the jet was airborne, when Malcom and his friends would surely be unwilling to fire their guns, take Malcom hostage and essentially hijack the jet. I played the scenario over and over in my mind, realizing my future was looking dimmer with each passing minute.

After an eternity, the wall slid open and neatly tucked itself back into its original hiding place. Malcom removed the hood to a white environmental suit, and a malevolent smile spread across his lips. "All is in place," he announced as he sat in front of his computer console facing me.

"Do you know how much we depend upon our telecommunications wiring?" Malcom rattled on as if I gave a damn. "No telephones will work, no cellular, no nine-one-one, and—Oh my— no Internet. Computer nerds all over the world will surely go into shock.

"The stock market will crash, and so will a few jets, I might add, since there will be no communications between air traffic control centers. Even simple things like traffic lights will stop working."

"You can't possibly do all of that," I said.

"Oh, but I can," Malcom insisted, spinning on his chair to face me, "and I will." For the first time, emotion poured from this man, a kind of wild-eyed, fiendish excitement that reminded me of old Frankenstein movies when the moment of truth had arrived, and the insane Dr. Frankenstein was about to bring his monster to life.

"How?" I asked, trying to make sense of his insanity and stalling for precious time.

"We communicate electronically whether we talk on the telephone or chat over the internet. Computers communicate constantly with one another over the telephone lines, keeping the world in working order. Did you ever wonder how all those signals seem to get where they're going? Have you ever wondered why everyone is panicking over the transition to the new millennium? Our world is surviving by computer, a few strategic screw ups, and we're back in the dark ages. . .literally."

Until that moment, I had never thought about it. Telephones had been a constant presence in my life. Like my own heartbeat, I needed them, but I never thought about them unless they stopped working. In the past decade or so, the same had become true of computers.

Malcom continued with his lecture as if we both had all of the time in the world. For whatever reason, he was in no hurry to initiate his act of terrorism. Or had it already begun?

"Millions of digitalized switches sort through the electronic signals and route them to their destinations. Each switch is a tiny computer that performs countless functions in the time it takes you to blink and eye. The switches can be retasked as needed to improve the routing system, if you have the right key."

"And I suppose you have the right key," I said.

"My dear, I and my colleagues designed and programmed the switches. Have you ever heard of the concept of the back door?"

My blood turned to ice. If what he was telling me was true, he had the power to commit a global act of terrorism, and I brought that power to him.

"You asked me before," I said, "if I wanted to know what you were really up to. What did you mean?"

Malcom leaned back in his chair, smiled smugly, and clasped his hands behind his head. "This is the best part. As I said before, I'm going to work on a hit and run basis, kind of like the Unibomber. The government won't be able to figure out how the terrorists—he pointed to himself and said "Moi"— are getting inside the systems, nor will they be able to pin point the exact locations where the disruptions are occurring. One of the higher ups in the FBI will recommend they contact this world renowned computer expert he knows about."

"Let me guess. That expert is you," I said caustically. And then I suddenly remembered. "You've already begun," I said. "The nine-one-one systems. The news mentioned calling in experts."

Malcom smiled smugly. "That was just a primer, a minor test. Isn't it rich, though? None of those so-called experts have been able to solve the problems or locate their sources.

"Eventually, I'll be called upon to swoop in like some kind of super hero and fix each of their problems and assure them it won't happen again. And that particular problem won't. They'll be willing to pay me millions.

"Those pesky terrorists will start with the U.S., but soon they'll tire of it and move on to the rest of the world."

"And are these neanderthals your colleagues?" I asked eyeing the rest of the creeps hanging around the cabin.

Malcom laughed out loud. "Heavens no. You're right. They are neanderthals. No, my colleagues are, or shall I say, were a handful of libertarian, wacko geniuses whose ideologies got in the way of more entrepreneurial pursuits. Those fools actually thought I wanted to use these chips to force the government to give control back to the people. It's amazing how much free work you can get out of people motivated by their political ideologies.

"Was Cal one of your colleagues?"

"You mean Patrick? Yes, poor boy. He was the last to succumb, and the most inconvenient."

"You used these people then killed them off?"

"Of course." Malcom gave a cavalier shrug.

"So now you're working alone, and you don't think you'll get caught?"

"The Uni-bomber did it. Why shouldn't I?"

"The Uni-bomber got caught," I pointed out.

"The Uni-bomber is a schizophrenic loser. Besides, I still have a few associates in high places." Malcom held out his hand, gesturing toward the computer console. "All this equipment," he gazed around the cabin, "and the accommodations are a bit costly on a college professor's salary, even a world renowned college professor."

"So it's all about money." It shook my head disapprovingly.

"Not necessarily the money itself, though that will be quite the kudo. I rather like the power that goes with the money, and the fame that will come from singlehandedly, and repeatedly averting what could become a world wide disaster."

"What if they don't hire you as you've planned?"

"Then I'll step up the terrorism scenario until there's no one else." Malcom raised his eyebrows, pursed his lips, turned his palms upward, and shrugged. "And if all else fails, I'll dip into S.W.I.F.T. and divert a few million to my account in the Caymans, but I'd rather not choose that route. It would be so trite and boring. Where would be the fun in that?"

"S.W.I.F.T.?"

"The Society for Worldwide Interbank Financial Telecommunications."

I didn't need to ask anything more. Malcom was an egomaniacal madman driven by an insatiable greed. I also knew that he couldn't let Shelby, or anyone else who had ever seen him, live.

"Oh by-the-way, in case you're wondering how your daughter figures into this historic event, as soon as the dial tone cuts out, the bomb will explode. It's like the 'Big Bang Theory' only I'll own this universe."

"When are you going to—?"

"It's already begun."

Tears welled up in my eyes blurring my vision. "Then Shelby's—?"

"Already dead." Malcom's disinterested announcement of Shelby's death turned my heart to stone. I jumped up from my chair and lunged at him. Instantly, my hands were around his throat in a vise like grip fueled by the extraordinary power of hate and adrenalin. I was barely aware of the arm that caught me in a half nelson, and pressed heavily against the front of my throat. I tucked my chin to reduce the pressure on my airway, and held fast to Malcom's neck, pressing my thumbs into the cartilage surrounding his larynx. His eyes were wide, terrified, and no sound emanated from his cyanotic lips. He grabbed wildly at my hands, but I only tightened my grip. I would have succeeded in killing the bastard if it hadn't been for the butt of Boyle's shotgun slamming into my spine. The pain pierced through my rage and found its way to my brain. My back arched and I let go of Malcom's throat, then my legs gave way and I fell to the cabin floor where Boyle and Krandall began kicking me.

Somewhere in the distance, I heard Malcom gasping for air and Eberhardt saying, "Wood's here with the pilot."

33

The human body is a fascinating creation. It is at once fragile and miraculously resilient. I was distantly cognizant of their heavy boots burying themselves in my rib cage and spine, but I no longer felt the pain. I knew, though, if I allowed them to continue kicking me, I would eventually die along with my husband and daughter. It would have been so easy. The absence of pain and the knowledge that I would be left behind to face life alone carried me to the precipice where I gazed into the abyss of death. But something inside of me, a basic instinctive need to survive, disagreed with my conscious desires and took hold of me. I lashed out at the next boot that came in contact with my body. I grabbed the boot and yanked with all my might, and Eberhardt toppled backward, hitting his head hard against the corner of the computer desk. His head bounced off the console like a rubber ball, and he fell onto the floor, unconscious.

A split second later, Boyle was on me, but I spun around on my left knee and extended my right leg, hooking him behind his knee. I jumped up as Krandall fell on top of Eberhardt.

Boyle, I'm afraid, was a bit smarter than the other two. Keeping his distance, he levelled his semiautomatic pistol at me. "Move, bitch, and it will be your last!"

"Go ahead and shoot, you bastard. What have I got to lose?"

"Hold on!" Malcom held his palm toward Krandall and called out in a voice that had, to my satisfaction, become raspier than usual, causing me to wonder if I had been the first to have my hands around his throat. "What the hell is that?"

I turned to see Malcom staring at the floor behind me and followed his gaze to a tiny black disk lying on the floor next to the broken elastic band from my hair. It must have come out during the struggle. Malcom picked up the disk and studied it for a moment. Then he looked at me with more hatred than I had ever seen in one human being.

"You fucking bitch!"

He raised his hand and swung it toward my face, but I blocked it and maneuvered myself around behind him, pinning his arm to his back and using him as a shield between Krandall and me.

"You and I are going to back out of here nice and easy." I slipped my open hand between Malcom's twisted arm and his back. I clutched a handful of shirt behind his shoulder blade, to anchor my hand. A slight lift of my forearm rotated his shoulder unnaturally backward and caused him considerable pain. "You said yourself you knew what I was capable of. Let me tell you, you have no idea what I can do. I'll rip your shoulder out of its socket. Just give me a reason. Now move one foot behind the other, slowly."

"Shoot her!" Malcom yelled hoarsely.

"I can't get a clear shot," Krandall said. He moved forward with the gun pointing at us, his steps matching ours. For the first time, I thought I might actually escape. Not inclined to take my eyes off Krandall, I was trying to estimate how far it was to the exit door. Seven feet was my best guess. Only a few seconds and we'd be out the door and down the steps where I would have room to maneuver. I didn't get very far when I heard the click of a gun being cocked behind me.

"Stop right there," the man's voice said. I turned and found myself staring down the barrel of yet another semiautomatic. This one was attached to the arm of the other FBI agent from the hospital, Wood. He was accompanied by a man whom I had never seen.

I let go of Malcom's arm, and he immediately spun around and slapped me hard across the face, sending me flying against one of the leather seats. Malcom turned to me with a final narrow-eyed glare. "Good-bye, Doctor Hunter," he hissed, then he turned and sat in front of his computer console. "Take her out and dispose of her," he ordered. "I have work to do." Krandall stuffed his gun in his belt and grabbed my shoulders.

"No, wait. Now's not a good time," Wood said. The airport is crawling with cops. We should take off and dump her later. Again the visions of the free fall into lake Michigan filled my head. I would have preferred a bullet in the brain there and then.

Malcom spun around, looking disgusted. He held his open palm out toward Wood, showing him the disk. Then he handed the small black disk to Wood. "This is the reason the airport's crawling with cops. It's a transmitter." He nodded toward me. "She had it wrapped inside her hair band."

When he said that, I realized Kim must have slipped the transmitter into my hair when she combed it into a ponytail for me. I would have chided her for doing it, had I known what she was up to, but now I was grateful.

"Take it and toss it somewhere inconvenient," Malcom continued, "another hangar maybe. By the time the moronic police figure it out, we'll be in the air." Wood took the disk from Malcom and disappeared out the exit door.

Malcom's gaze then fell upon the pilot, standing motionless and staring wide-eyed. I presumed, from the look on the man's face, he had been hired to fly the plane but new little or nothing about the activities of its passengers. "What are you staring at?" Malcom snapped.

"Uh. . .Uh. . ."

"Well, I see we've gone and hired ourselves an intelligent one," Malcom said. "Get your ass into the cockpit and do whatever it is you people do to get ready for takeoff."

I could see the wheels of escape turning in the pilot's head as he regarded first the open door, then Krandall's gun, and finally Malcom. Seeing the futility of trying to escape, he returned to the cockpit, and closed the door behind him.

"Leave it open!" Malcom yelled. The cockpit door opened slowly, and the pilot nervously took his seat at the controls.

"What about her?" Krandall asked. He had one hand entwined in my hair, holding my head cocked backward farther than was comfortable, and the other pressing his gun against my temple.

Malcom stared at me with silent contempt. He rubbed his chin, thinking. "We'll hold on to her for now. It can't hurt to have a back up insurance policy."

"Where do you want her?"

"There's a roll of duct tape in the cabinet at the rear of the cabin. Tape her to a seat."

Krandall handed his weapon to Malcom who stepped in close to me and smiled fiendishly. "I do love duct tape, don't you? It is so versatile."

I heard Eberhardt moan as he awakened. Krandall stepped over him as he sat up, rubbing his head and looking confused. The carpet beneath his head was soaked with blood from an ugly scalp wound.

"Looks like he could use a doctor," I said sarcastically. Krandall cocked his hand, ready to backhand me, but Malcom caught it. "We don't have time to waste on that right now. You can have at her later, after we take off. Bind her then help Eberhardt."

My tendency toward claustrophobia reared its ugly head as Krandall bound my legs together and my arms to the chair. My heart was racing, and I found myself hungering for air. Spitting a few choice epithets at my captors would have alleviated much of my anxiety, but it would have also earned me a strip of tape across my mouth. That would surely send me into a panic, so I kept my mouth shut and my eyes closed and rehearsed a variety of verbal and physical attacks against Malcom and his buddies.

After finishing with me, Krandall helped Eberhardt into a chair, then found a handful of gauze sponges in a first aid kit. He placed the sponges against Eberhardt's wound.

"You could use a few stitches," he said. Then he turned to me. "I don't suppose you'd be interested in doing the job."

What an asshole! I thought. Give me a needle smeared with

cow shit and a vial of succinylcholine, and I'll be happy to do the job. Outwardly, I simply stared, stone faced, toward the front of the cabin.

"Didn't think so," Krandall spat. "What about your Hippocratic oath? Aren't you supposed to help anyone in need without bias?"

Maintaining my silence at that moment was probably one of the most difficult things I ever had to do, but I kept picturing a large swatch of duct tape covering my mouth, and I held my tongue.

"Krandall," Malcom said, "stand at the cockpit door and keep an eye on our pilot. Make sure he doesn't try anything." Krandall took up his position in the doorway. He leaned his back against the frame, so he could watch the pilot and me.

Malcom was once again typing furiously, and no longer seemed aware that any world existed outside his computer. Occasionally, he would moan with satisfaction or frustration. It was hard to tell. Then suddenly he would cheer in a loud whisper, saying things like "Yes" or "and the crowd goes wild." I strained to see past him and catch a glimpse of the computer screen, but that's all I got. It was not enough to know what was currently happening.

After awhile, Wood returned. He looked past me as if I had no substance and acknowledged Krandall and Eberhardt with a nod. All remained silent, almost reverent, while Malcom worked. None dared to speak to him. They regularly checked their surroundings through the cockpit windows. Krandall and Wood also took turns leaving the plane, probably to check to see where the cops were.

As Krandall reentered the plane from one of his walks, Malcom turned around and faced us. "Don't be alarmed if you hear sirens. It won't be the cops." He looked at Wood. "By-the-way. Where did you leave the disk?"

"I dropped it off at Fed Ex."

Malcom smiled his approval and glanced at his watch. "In less than five minutes, sirens will be blaring all over O'Hare and emergency vehicles will be placed on alert, because the control tower's communications system will shut down and they'll be anticipating disastrous consequences."

34

I was stunned. Malcom was even crazier than I had thought. He looked at me then twisted his lips and furrowed his brows. "Oh, don't get all bent out of shape. They have emergency back up systems. I haven't messed with those yet. Air traffic will be rerouted to other airports until the crisis ends. They'll probably only lose one or two."

One or two! He was playing games with hundreds of innocent people's lives, and expressed no more emotion than someone playing a game of cards. Malcom had to be stopped.

As he predicted, the alarms and sirens were ringing all over the airport. From where I sat, I could see nothing, but having witnessed a jet crash some years earlier, I had no difficulty vividly imagining a variety of calamities.

Malcom suddenly jumped up. "Keep and eye on her," he said to Krandall. "I don't want to miss this."

"Why don't we just turn on the TV. Won't it be on the news?" Krandall asked.

Malcom gave him a scornful glare. "And how do you suppose the news media will find out when all of the phone lines are down?"

"Oh, I forgot," Krandall replied, looking embarrassed.

"Don't feel bad," Malcom said condescendingly. "When it comes to mother wit, there're those who have feasted from the horn of plenty, and those who have tasted but a few table scraps. You, along with ninety-nine point five eight percent of the world's population, happen to be in the latter category." He turned on his heels and left the plane, leaving Krandall gazing stupidly after him.

After Malcom was out of sight, Krandall's gaze caught mine,

and his became defensive and menacing. He was daring me to comment by word or facial expression. Figuring I'd live longer, I chose the more prudent course of giving him neither.

The distant roar of jet engines held my attention but to my relief, I heard nothing explosive. Then I heard Wood yelling from the hangar, "Krandall, get your ass out here and help us. We've got to book. The cops are on their way."

Krandall moved to the exit door. "What about the pilot and the bitch?"

"Eberhardt can watch them. You get out here!"

Krandall turned to Eberhardt who had an ashen hue to his skin. Banging his head against the corner of the desk did more than cut his scalp. He was bleeding inside his skull. I could see it in his eyes as well as his facial coloration. He soon would be of no use to anyone.

"Can you handle them?" Krandall asked him.

"Sure," Eberhardt responded, a slight slur in his speech confirming my diagnosis. He started to get up but sat down again. With a determined look on his face, he forced himself to a standing position, but he didn't let go of the seat. He removed his Beretta from its holster, and leaning his hip against the chair for support, he popped the clip and checked to see that it was full. Snapping the magazine into place, he drew the action back and chambered the first round. I could see then that the left side of his face had begun to droop subtly, and I knew that I would soon have one less captor to contend with.

Eberhardt stumbled toward Krandall. "Are you sure you're OK?" Krandall asked. "You don't look so good."

"I'm fine," Eberhardt insisted, taking up the position that Krandall had vacated in the cockpit doorway. Krandall studied him skeptically then exited the plane. Eberhardt immediately slid to the floor with his back against the door frame. The pilot glanced back at Eberhardt then at me and started to rise out of his seat, but Eberhardt pointed the gun at him and cocked the hammer. The pilot's body stiffened as he eased himself into his seat.

With Krandall out of the picture, I felt less fearful of opening my mouth and could no longer resist it. "You're dying," I said to Eberhardt. "You know that, don't you?"

"Shut up, bitch," he said, pointing his gun at me, or rather indiscriminately in my direction. I assumed his vision was going.

"The weakness and dizziness are caused by bleeding in your brain from when you hit your head," I pressed on courageously or stupidly depending upon the outcome. "I know these things. I'm a doctor. Remember?"

At this point, Eberhardt's eyelids had dropped to half-mast. He was deteriorating too rapidly for it to be a sub-dural hematoma. Those can take hours to develop. I suspected an epidural which required immediate attention or he would die. Of course, in this case, that would be the preferred outcome.

"You need immediate medical attention. I can save your life. I'm bound by my oath to save your life, even if I don't like you."

Eberhardt pinched his forehead and squeezed his eyes shut. "Oh, God," he cried, and I knew he understood that I was telling the truth. Gradually, he slid up the wall to a standing position, and my heart raced with the anticipation of being released from my bonds. He dug in his pocket and pulled out a Swiss Army knife. Then he tried to walk toward me, but his balance was gone. He fell to his knees and vomited, and I wondered if he'd even make as far as my chair before he slipped into a terminal coma. My whole body was tense as I tried mentally to help him crawl toward me. If only he could get close enough for me to get the knife.

Eberhardt dry heaved a few times, and swayed from side-to-side on all fours. Steadying himself, he crept toward me, stopping and catching his balance every few inches. I'm not sure I breathed the entire time he was struggling to get to me. This was now a desperate man who knew he was at death's door, and I was his angel of mercy. Finally, his arduous journey ended. He climbed up my legs and kneeled before me. His left pupil was fully dilated. I was staring into the face of death.

Eberhardt made a movement with his mouth as if he were

trying to speak, but no words formed on his lips. Instead, a thread of saliva trickled down his chin.

I looked down and saw that the knife was still in his hand. It was millimeters from my finger. I struggled desperately against the duct tape and managed to take hold of the knife with my fingertips. Eberhardt was too weak to resist. He looked at me in confusion. And as I saw the final flicker of light fading from his eyes, I said, "You're the first to pay for killing my husband and daughter. I hope you burn in hell, you bastard!" I spit in his face before it collapsed into my lap. I felt no sense of compassion for this man, nor any remorse for being the one who had killed him. All I wanted was that vile, disgusting pile of garbage off my lap.

"Psst! Psst!" I called to the pilot. I didn't want to yell to him, because I didn't know where the others were. I don't know if he heard me, or turned around to check on his guard, but he turned none-the-less.

"He's dead," I said in a loud whisper. "Come here and cut me loose." The pilot turned and looked out the cockpit windows, then headed toward me, stopping just short of the exit door and backing up. He pointed out the door, his gesture telling me that the others were coming up the steps.

"Dammit!" I whispered. "You're not going to make this easy on me, are you, God?" I palmed the knife and rolled my hand so it looked like I was merely holding onto the arm of the chair when the others entered. Krandall immediately raced over to Eberhardt and started yelling. "What the fuck did you do to him!"

Wood came up from behind him and took hold of his shoulder. "She didn't do anything." He tugged at my duct tape tethers. "She's still taped to the chair."

"What happened?" Krandall asked me.

I shrugged. "Dunno. He just crawled over here, drooled in my lap, and died. I guess he hit his head harder than you thought." I smirked at him. That really pissed him off and bought me a fist across my jaw.

"What the hell's this?" Malcom said as he entered the plane.

"Eberhardt's dead," Krandall replied.

"How?" Malcom asked, not with any emotion other than curiosity.

I spoke up. "An epidural hematoma, I surmise."

Malcom responded with a cold stare. "Dump this out of here," he ordered, pointing at Eberhardt's body. "Then lock us down." Then he called to the pilot. "Prepare for take off."

The pilot's voice crackled over the intercom. "The tower's down. I can't file a flight plan. They won't let us take off."

"How would you like your brains decorating the cockpit windows?" Malcom yelled.

A few seconds later, I felt the jet engines rumble to life. Malcom and the others were busy readying the computer equipment for the flight. They weren't paying any attention to me, so I fumbled with the knife, nearly dropping it twice. I finally managed to open the smallest blade, and started cutting my bonds.

Malcom, instead of yelling over the roar of the engines, depressed the button on the wall intercom and said, "Let's go." The jet lurched forward and we started out of the hangar. I knew that any chance of my being rescued was gone. Stopping Malcom was now the focus of what was left of my life.

We rolled out of the hangar and turned onto an auxiliary runway, heading toward the main runway. I frantically sawed away at the duct tape until, finally, I cut through the tape around my wrist. Taking advantage of a moment when they couldn't see me move, I cut away the tape on my other wrist. All I had left was the tape around my ankles, but that was going to be a bit more difficult. There was no way I could do it surreptitiously, so I had to gain control of one of my captors, keeping the others at bay while I cut my final bonds.

I was planning how to get one of them to come close enough to grab when I think God actually answered one of my prayers. Wood sat in the seat next to me and glanced out the window. "Jesus Christ!" he shouted. The whole goddam Chicago Police Department's out there.

I looked out my window and saw a parade of radio cars racing toward us, lights flashing and, I assumed, sirens blaring. I was sure, however, they would never reach us in time, and I wondered what they would do if they did. I didn't think any of them would be reckless enough to park their squad cars in the path of a jet.

Both Malcom and Krandall joined Wood in watching the police approach. The distraction bought me the time I needed to cut my final bonds. It only took a few seconds to complete the task, but Malcom turned around before I got up, so I held my legs together and pressed my arms against the chair arms, hoping he would be too occupied to notice that the tape had been cut.

The jet slowed. Malcom pointed toward the cockpit and shouted to Wood. "Put a gun to that moron's head and tell him he takes off no matter what."

Wood obediently hurried to the cockpit and pressed the gun against the pilot's temple. The jet accelerated once again.

As we turned onto the main runway, the engines revved, readying for the final race down the runway and then the takeoff. I was surprised to see how much ground the police had covered in such a short time. They were on us as the jet started rolling, and they *did* block our path. Luckily, the pilot was not inclined to drive the jet over the squad card, and Wood wasn't suicidal enough to force him to do it. Suddenly the flaps went vertical, and engines reversed with a deafening roar.

"Fuck!" Malcom cried out. "Get her up!" Krandall bent down to remove the tape from my legs, and his eyes opened wide with surprise. Before he could react, my hand slammed into his throat full force. I heard a sickening crunch and felt the cartilage surrounding his larynx give way beneath my blow. Krandall's eyes opened even wider. He grabbed at his throat and fell on top of me. Before I could roll him off, Malcom grabbed his pistol from the floor and pointed at my face, keeping himself out of my reach. "Get up," he ordered in a seething voice. "Woods, open the door," he yelled.

Woods opened the cabin door, and Malcom directed me to stand in the open doorway. I could see that the jet was already surrounded by patrol cars, and a SWAT van. Cops in regular uniforms and SWAT fatigues were lined up behind the squad cars, their rifles and handguns all pointed at the jet.

I was considering, though not savoring the idea, jumping to the ground when Malcom made a fatal mistake. He moved in close to me and pressed the gun against my temple.

"Clear out of here or she's dead," he yelled, but I was not about to let him use me to get away. Believing I had nothing to lose, I raised my arm and knocked the gun to the side. It went off, but the bullet flew past my head and out the door. I rammed my elbow into his chest and jumped out of the door. My left ankle snapped as my feet hit the tarmac. I started to roll under the jet, when Malcom pointed his gun at me and fired, catching me in the ribs. I curled myself into a ball, protecting myself from the flurry of gunfire that followed. In an eternal few seconds, it was all over. Malcom's bullet riddled body lay on the ground near me. Oddly, his eyes looked no more empty than they had before.

My chest hurt and I struggled to breath. I was fading in and out of consciousness when I saw a welcomed face appear above me. Kim knelt down next to me and cradled my head in her lap. "The paramedics are here. You're going to be all right."

"They killed Shelby. They killed my baby," I said breathlessly, but Kim smiled.

"No they didn't," she said. "Pete got her out before Malcom had a chance to set off the bomb. She's safe at my house with Richard."

Nothing around me felt real anymore, and I wondered if I was dreaming. I no longer trusted myself to recognize the difference between dream and reality. Had Kim really said that Shelby was safe, or had it been conjured up by my subconscious need to have a reason to survive when it would be so easy to let go?

Kim must have seen the confusion in my eyes. "Did you hear me, Deb? Your little girl is alive and well." Kim's insistent tone forced its way through the jumbled mess my thoughts had become and compelled me to believe her.

"Thank you, God," I mouthed, but no sound escaped, and my world faded to black.

35

An insistent thumping called me back from a dream filled with confused images and myriad senseless voices echoing in the distance. Once again, Kim's face loomed over me when I opened my eyes.

"Hi," she said softly.

I anxiously surveyed my surroundings, trying to understand where I was and what was happening to me.

"You're in the Life Flight helicopter," Kim said reassuringly. "I ordered them to take you to the University Hospital. I knew you'd feel safer there."

I felt the oxygen mask pressing against my face and the cool air rushing over my nose and mouth, yet I found myself struggling for air. I wanted to warn Kim that Malcom had sabotaged the telephone lines and people could die, but I couldn't seem to draw enough breath to generate a voice.

"Sh-h-h! Don't try to talk," Kim said. "You have a collapsed lung."

Above my head, an I.V. bag rocked with a deceptively lazy swing as the airborne ambulance carried me home, lulling my oxygen starved brain to sleep.

The next several hours were marked by long confused dreams, moments of pain and chaos, nightmarish images of Sam and Shelby exploding into bits or burning to death, their skin melting from their bones, and Malcom's hideous evil eyes looming in the blackness. After awhile, all I saw and heard melted into a single mass and flew away, leaving me in a sea of emptiness.

The sound of bubbling water tugged me awake, a primitive part of my brain alarmed at the sound. "The water's boiling," I mumbled. "Who's boiling water?"

"It's your chest tube, dear," I heard someone say, and I opened my eyes to find myself in a dimly lit room. At first, I had no idea where I was, but then I saw a woman dressed in blue scrubs. Though her face was familiar, I couldn't remember who she was nor where I had previously seen her. The woman was focused on some task above and behind me. I followed her gaze and watched stupidly as she regulated the drip rate on an IV, but my head was filled with cotton fuzz and I made no connection that the IV was attached to me. It was as if part of my brain were awake, but the thinking part that explained the world in logical terms was still sleeping.

Finished with her task, the woman found my eyes. "Hello, Doctor Hunter," she said, smiling. "Welcome back to the world of the living."

The sound of the woman's voice chased some of the fuzz away. I noticed her name badge, "Joan Martin, R.N.", and more fuzz cleared. I had worked with Joan many times. "Where am I?" I asked hoarsely, knowing the answer yet not knowing it.

"You're in the TCCU."

TCCU. I was near Sam. I gazed at the wall wondering how far I had to reach out to touch him.

Nurses who work in intensive care settings become highly skilled at interpreting body language, almost to the point of appearing to possess psychic abilities. It's not surprising, since many of their patients are intubated, and therefore, are unable to communicate by conventional means. Joan was no exception. "He's next door," she said, answering my silent question.

I didn't ask about his condition, because I knew I wouldn't have had to ask if he had made a miraculous recovery, or if he had died. Why ask the question when I knew the answer? I still had before me, the task of letting Sam go. Would it be, I wondered, with the dignity I had promised him? In the process of saving my own life, had I managed to find enough information to clear him? "How long have I been here?" I asked, trying to redirect my thoughts.

"About twenty-four hours. They admitted you after surgery."

"What time is it?"

"Eleven thirty."

"PM?"

"Uh, huh." Joan wrapped a blood pressure cuff around my arm and pumped it up, then she slipped the cold diaphragm of her stethoscope between the cuff and my skin and twisted the cuff's pressure valve. A low hiss was emitted as the cuff deflated.

"What is it?" I asked.

"One-ten over seventy. Pulse is good, too. I think you'll make it."

My awareness of my pain grew with my consciousness and soon, I found myself struggling amidst a torture contest between the bullet wound in my chest and my fractured ankle. It felt as though an elephant was standing on my chest while gnawing on my ankle. I grimaced and moaned.

"Would you like something for the pain? Your menu choices are morphine and Demerol," Joan said drolly. "Frankly, I'd go for the gold. Remember the old adage; Demerol for your patients— Morphine for your friends. I'll give you an IV push now, then hook you up to a PCA pump," she said. "That way you can sip from the fountain any time you want."

She removed the blood pressure cuff from my arm, rolled it up, and stuffed it into the metal basket on the wall next to the gauge. "Your pretty lucky. The bullet grazed you. It broke a rib and lacerated the pleura, but Doctor Holter patched you up good as new."

I glanced down at the cast on my left leg.

"You'll be settin' off alarms at the airport from now on," Joan teased.

"Oh, joy."

With Joan's help, I shifted to a more comfortable, rather a less miserable, position in bed. "Where's my daughter?" I asked. I hadn't seen or spoken with her, and I wouldn't be convinced she was alive until I had done both.

"She's in the waiting room. She's as tenacious as her mother. She refused to go home until you were awake."

"How did she look? Is she OK?"

Joan smiled warmly. "Why don't I bring her to you and let you see for yourself?"

"Thanks," I said as she left the cubicle. Barely a minute had passed when Shelby appeared in the doorway. Her face was scrubbed clean, and her auburn curls were held away from her face by a pair of gold barrettes. There wasn't a scratch or bruise in sight, not a single outward sign of the hell she had been through.

"Hello, baby," I said with a smile.

"Hi, Mom," Shelby whispered self-consciously, her brows furrowed with worry. She didn't move from the doorway. Instead, her gaze wandered over the cardiac monitor, the I.V., the bubbling chest tube, and my casted leg.

"It's O.K. I won't break. You can come give me a hug."

Shelby hesitated at first, then she burst into tears and dashed over to me. "Mom," she cried as she threw her arms around me. "I was afraid I'd never see you again." She buried her head in my chest. It hurt like hell, but it also felt wonderful. Shelby lay there for a long time, sobbing. I stroked her hair and whispered reassuring words next to her ear while I silently thanked God, who was back on my good list.

After awhile, the pain became intolerable. Joan, as if she possessed ESP, arrived with a syringe full of morphine in hand. She patted Shelby on the shoulder. "Your mom's going to take a nap now. You could also use a little rest, young lady. Why don't you go home and get a good night's sleep. I promise she'll be a whole lot better when you come back in the morning."

Shelby pulled away from me and searched my eyes, wanting me to confirm that Joan was telling her the truth. I smiled and nodded. "I'm going to be fine. I promise."

Satisfied with my answer, she kissed me an got up. On her way out the door, she turned and blew me a kiss. "I love you, mom."

I caught her kiss and planted it on my cheek, then blew one back to her. "I love you, too, baby." She caught my kiss and left.

"It's time for La La Land," Joan said as she slipped the needle into the latex port on my I.V. tubing and depressed the plunger. Within seconds, the elephant that had been standing on my chest gnawing at my ankle dissolved along with the rest of the world.

When I awoke some time later, I found Kim sitting by my side. "Howdy, Star," she said cheerfully, holding a newspaper in front of my eyes.

The anesthesia still lingering in my brain, all I saw was a blur. Kim could have told me that the headlines said Martians had landed in Washington, and I would have had to take her word for it.

"You're right here on the front page," Kim said as she pointed to a rainbow colored blob in the center of the page. "You're a goddam living, breathing hero. I had to plow my way through reporters downstairs in the main lobby, and it's the middle of the night." Kim looked at me and shook her head, then she tossed the paper on a table next to my bed. "You can look at it when they screw your brain back into your skull."

I smiled weakly and asked, "Is Shelby with you?"

"She's at home, sleeping. It's four a.m. Either Richard or Pete will bring her here later this morning."

I was happy to see Kim, but a four a.m. visit? I knew she was concerned for my well-being, but I sensed something more. I felt as though Kim were here as a cop, more than as a friend, so I jumped right into to the topic that was most likely on her mind. "Malcom shut down communications to the tower at O'Hare," I began.

"And a lot of other places," Kim added.

"And the jets?"

"The jets?" Kim asked, not following me.

"Did any jets crash? Did anyone get hurt?"

"No, no jets crashed and no one got hurt besides you and the guys you nailed." Kim quipped.

I remembered Eberhardt dying in my lap, but I wasn't sure whether or not my memory of Malcom lying dead on the tarmac was an accurate image. "What happened to them?"

"Let's see, Malcom's coming back as a colander in his next life, and that Eberhardt fellow, you must have smacked him a good one. He died of a massive brain hemorrhage. His skull was cracked wide open. The other three, Boyle, Wood, and Krandall put on a show of defiance, but gave it up after an hour or so."

"Malcom had backers, other partners."

"Oh, them," Kim said. "They were a group of computer whizzes who worked for high-tech companies." She got up and leaned her back against the wall. "He recruited them back in the late seventies, a bunch of misunderstood, post Viet Nam high school seniors with I.Q.s off the chart, who had lost loved ones in the war or non-war, as it were.

"He started a summer camp for the sole purpose of attracting these types. When he found his marks, he guided them toward some of the top engineering and computer science programs in the country. After each of them graduated from their respective colleges and graduate schools, they landed jobs in various companies involved with the development and designing of these computerized digital switches for telecommunications. They followed him like he was some kind of demigod, a technological Charlie Manson.

"He convinced his followers to commit a type of industrial espionage and share design features. They installed a series of back doors common to all the switches. The back doors were to be used later, promising them they would ultimately bring the U.S. government to its political knees."

"That's what Malcom was doing, but did he have the power to do it on such a broad scale?" That pesky elephant had returned to my chest. I groaned, and found the button to the PCA pump. Within seconds of depressing the pump, my pain was reduced to tolerable.

"Are you sure you want to hear this?" Kim asked.

I found it difficult to concentrate on my discussion with Kim, but I wanted to hear the whole story even if she had to repeat it all later. I wanted to understand how my life got tangled in an obscure conspiracy that had been born more than a decade ago. "Yes, I do," I replied with a thick inarticulate tongue. "He was just after money, you know," I said to redirect Kim to the subject at hand.

Kim nodded her agreement, then shook her head. "According to Richard, Malcom not only had the power to bring the US to its knees, but he could have easily expanded his operation to the entire world, since a lot of foreign countries rely on digital switches purchased from U.S. companies.

"Geniuses. Ha! Idiot Savants is more like it. With all that brain power, those fools couldn't see the con Malcom was pulling."

"Cal finally saw it," I said.

"Yeah, but not until Malcom had killed the others off." Kim stepped away from the wall and paced back and forth.

"Is something wrong?" I asked.

"Not really. I'm just. . .I don't know. . .I just don't like being around all of these sick people with tubes sticking into and out of everywhere."

I smiled at the irony of a tough, street-smart cop getting squeamish around sick people, but then I wasn't exactly enamored with her job. Kim stopped pacing for a moment and looked at me. "Cal's real name was Patrick Finnegan."

"I know. Malcom mentioned it once or twice."

"Yes, but did you also know Finnegan was Sam's neighbor?"

"Scolnik mentioned something about it."

"They grew up next door to each other," Kim continued. "That's why Cal called Sam when he was in trouble. He trusted Sam and thought he could bail him out. Instead, he got them both kill—" Kim suddenly crimsoned and appeared contrite. "I'm sorry. That was callous. Here he is, lying on the other side of that wall," she nodded toward the wall separating me from the shell that had been my husband, "and I'm talking about him as if—"

"He's dead?"

Kim nodded and stared at her shoes.

"Kim, you're right. Sam is dead. All that's left is to make it official."

"When'll they do that?" Kim asked.

"I'll do it when I'm assured that his name is cleared and that he receives recognition for his bravery. The world was told he died a criminal. I want the world to know he died a hero, in the line of duty, not as a low life drug dealer." There was something else I wanted to say to Kim, but my thoughts had become cloudy.

"Maybe I should go," Kim said, seeing me struggling with my thoughts. "I didn't mean to upset you."

"No. Don't go. There's something else, something important. Just give me a moment." Rather than trying to force the memory, I relaxed. I nodded off and awoke when I heard Kim leave. "Kim," I called out, remembering what I had wanted to say. "Malcom had other partners. They supplied him with the jet and the equipment. I think they're kind of high up in the government." But Kim was already out of earshot, and the narcotics had taken control. I drifted off again.

36

I dozed on and off for the next several hours, my fingers remaining firmly clamped around the remote button to the PCA pump, one of the top ten inventions of modern medicine.

Around eight a.m., Tom Holter, Sam's doctor and now mine, stopped in to see me. Pleased with my progress, he informed me that I was to be transferred out of TCCU into a regular hospital room. We talked about Sam and agreed that I would sign the final papers when Sam's name was officially cleared, hopefully before I was discharged from the hospital.

After Tom left me, I lay staring at the ceiling, adjusting to the emptiness in the center of my chest, a void that only Sam could fill. I knew I had to learn to ignore that empty place, because Sam would never be there to fill it again. At the same time, I began questioning Tom's diagnosis. Though I knew on an intellectual and professional level that he was right, I suffered from the same internal emotional strife anyone in my situation must suffer. I had had a difficult enough time putting my dog to sleep when I knew her entire body was being eaten up by cancer. I kept questioning that I had done all there was to do. Could I have done something to make her comfortable enough to live a little longer?

I now began questioning my own resolve. When the time actually arrived, and the pen was in my hand, would I be able to ply ink to a paper that was Sam's death warrant. I once again prayed to God, begging Him to kill Sam for me, knowing He wouldn't listen, and I was stuck with the job. Damn Him anyway!

Not long after Tom had left my cubicle, Paula, my day shift nurse, entered with a cheery "Good morning, Doctor Hunter. It looks like you'll be leaving us today." She checked my I.V. and my Pleuravac chest tube suction, then took the blood pressure cuff from the wall and wrapped it around my arm.

"How soon will I be transferred?" I asked before Paula stuck the thermometer under my tongue.

"They have a room ready for you now. Transportation's waiting for you outside. We'll move you as soon as I record these vitals."

It took time, organizational skills, and patience to transfer me and my various I.V.'s and tubes from my hospital bed to the stretcher. Though I must admit it was more exhausting for me, the passive participant, than for the staff that did the lifting and hauling.

Once the painful transfer was completed and I caught my breath, we started out of the TCCU. I asked the nurse to roll my stretcher in front of Sam's cubicle, so I could look in on him before I left.

The swelling and bruising on his face had all but disappeared, and his head was no longer wrapped in a gauze turban. Though his eyes were taped closed and an endotracheal tube was protruding from his mouth, I saw my Sam sleeping peacefully in his bed, seemingly lulled by the rhythmic popping and hissing of the MA-1. My heart ached for his arms, his smile, the sound of his voice. If only I could lay my head on his chest or call his name or touch his cheek, he might wake up and tell me everything would be all right. If only. . .

"Let's go," I said, and the transportation aid, accompanied by Paula, pushed my stretcher out of the TCCU and away from Sam.

A few minutes later, after a short elevator ride to the third floor, I was rolled into a spacious, tastefully appointed private suite, one of the kudos of being a staff physician. Of course, I hadn't ever planned on cashing in this particular perk. The room was filled with the warmth of sunlight streaming through the large picture window. On the table next to my bed was an exquisite floral arrangement of exotic flowers; orange and yellow protea, burgundy antheriums and ginger, the familiar vivid blue and orange Bird-of-Paradise, and white Tiger and Calla lilies. " W h o are those from?" I asked Paula, assuming she would tell me they came from my partners and the E.R. staff. I needed freshness and beauty in my life, and that bouquet couldn't have come at a better time.

"Let's get you into bed, and we'll see," Paula replied, her voice as excited as mine.

After another painful transfer, this time from stretcher to bed, I depressed the miraculous little PCA button. The transportation aid wished me luck as he left. Paula found the enclosure card amidst the flowers and handed it to me. I pulled the card from its envelope, already rehearsing the thank you's in my mind, and then I gasped.

"What is it?" Paula asked.

So stunned was I that I could not read the note aloud. Instead, with trembling hands, I gave the card to Paula. Her eyes immediately opened wide. "What is this, some kind of sick joke?" She barked.

It was sick, but I knew it was no joke. Bedridden and attached to tubes and I.V.'s, I felt exposed, vulnerable, helpless. I took the card from Paula and stared at it, hoping that if I stared long enough, the words would change. But they did not. The sentence, YOU ARE DEAD!, continued to taunt me from the one-by-two inch card. I shook with fear as if a hand would reach out from behind those words and choke the life out of me.

A phone sat on the night stand next to my bed. To weak and shaky to make the call myself, I gave Paula Kim's number—repeating it four times before I dictated it correctly—and asked her to tell Kim to come to the hospital right away. On her own, Paula called hospital security, and they posted a guard outside my door.

Though it seemed an eternity until Kim arrived, I'm sure her tires never hit pavement between her house and the hospital. I was more than thankful to see her face, when she flew into my room with a rush of air as the door swung wide.

"Where's the goddam note! Let me see it!"

I pointed at my overbed table. Kim snatched up the note and read it. "Sonuvabitch! I don't believe this!" She looked at me with a mixture of compassion and determination. "I'll find out who these muther fuckers are and rip their throats out. They won't get near you," she promised.

"They already did."

"Maybe, but there's a Chicago cop outside your door right now, and there'll be one posted there around the clock until I find the asshole who's responsible for this. Don't worry about Shelby, either. Richard and Pete will be with her around the clock. They won't let her out of their sight."

"How are you going find out who's responsible for the note?"

Kim started her back and forth pacing, though I didn't think it had anything to do with hospital anxiety. "First, I'm going to beat some answers out of Wood, Boyle, and Krandall." Kim stopped her pacing and looked and me with a quizzical frown. "Could it be Ben Scolnik?"

"Ben's dead," I said with confidence. "They wouldn't let him live after the things he said to me."

Kim shrugged. "Maybe, but I'm not ignoring any possibility."

"Kim, where did Malcom get the money for the jet and all that high tech computer equipment?"

"I don't know," Kim answered. "I do know he didn't get it from the computer whiz kids. We've checked their backgrounds. There wasn't enough money there to foot the bill for the computers, much less the decadent transportation. The silent trio doesn't have any money to speak of. In fact, their debts are larger than their collective incomes."

"Malcom said he had friends in high places. People who could put in a good word for him as the telecommunications savior when the switches malfunctioned."

"Christ, there're a lot of high places."

"Maybe Richard can get into Malcom's system on the jet. Maybe there are names or—"

"Forget it," Kim interrupted. "The FBI commandeered the jet as soon as we secured it. The assistant D.A.'s in court as we speak, fighting for access to the jet and fighting the FBI from taking our prisoners. They say the crimes are Federal and therefore, under their jurisdiction, not ours."

"Maybe they know something."

"Oh, they know something all right," Kim said, "but they're not about to share it with us. They've been stonewalling us ever they took over. The only information we've got came from the secured documents Patrick Finnegan sent to Sam. I don't think Finnegan knew about anyone else. If he did, he didn't mention it in his correspondence with Sam."

"Where does that leave me?" I asked with ever mounting trepidation. "Someone has threatened my life. We don't know who it is, and we have no way of finding out?"

"I'll find out, Deb." Kim tried to reassure me with words that sounded confident, but a voice that betrayed her uncertainty.

37

I had assumed I could begin putting recent events behind me when I learned that Malcom's death was a reality. All I had left to do was remove Sam from life support and lay him to rest. I had thought Shelby and I were, at least, safe. Now my world was once again shattered, but by whom? Who would be so bold as to send me a threatening note disguised in an expensive bouquet of exotic flowers? How did they know I would be transferred to this room?

I spoke to Shelby on the phone. She begged to come visit me, but I couldn't risk it. As yet, no direct threat had been made on her life, and I didn't want her caught in the middle if someone tried to make good on the threat made against me.

I saw little of Kim the rest of the day. She took off, carrying the note and flowers, determined to find the "perp". She phrased it with a bit more color. I think she planned to dust every petal for fingerprints. That left me alone, feeling isolated, and wallowing in fear and self-pity. I was feeling like a death row inmate awaiting my execution, only I didn't know the time or the executioner. I felt an adrenalin rush every time the door swooshed open.

I called Shelby frequently, reassuring myself more than her. Occasionally my guard, Nate, would come in to chat. He told me he and Kim were second cousins on his mother's side. I had already figured it out that Kim owned Chicago. That she might also be related to everyone in the city, didn't surprise me. It gave me comfort, knowing she had hand picked each of my guards.

The afternoon was busier than the morning. Tom Holter visited me on afternoon rounds. Shortly after his visit, an x-ray tech arrived to take a portable chest x-ray. Later in the afternoon, Tom returned and pulled my chest tube, an experience I'd rather forget. He told me if my lung remained inflated, I would be discharged the next day. By early evening, I had calmed down and stopped hitting the ceiling every time the door opened. I was even regaining some optimism about my future.

The nurse had left me alone after helping me back into bed from my fifteen minutes seated in a chair. The sky was growing dim. The crimson twilight reflected off nearby windows and filled my room with a warm glow. I was beginning to fall asleep when the door opened, and in walked a pair of stone-faced suits followed by Nate.

"These men are from the FBI. They are relieving me," Nate apologized. "I've paged Kim, and I'll hang around until I hear from her," he said.

One of the men, tall and imposing with ebony hair and coal black eyes, turned to him and said, "You are relieved, officer. Thank you."

Nate looked at me and started to speak, but the man ushered him out the door. I found myself in a staring match with the two well-groomed thugs. It was deja-vu.

"That was uncalled-for," I announced, trying to maintain a calm, in charge facade while inside I felt like I was in one of those nightmares where the monster is closing in and you can't get away because your feet are stuck in glue. "He was there for my protection."

"Not anymore," The dark haired man said as he closed the distance between us. "I'm agent Johnson." He presented me with his I.D. I barely glanced at it. I had walked down that road before and learned it was pointless to examine such things. "This is agent Smith." Johnson nodded toward the second agent who nodded, but didn't speak.

"Smith and Johnson," I said. "This is rich. Couldn't you be a bit more original." My caustic remark elicited not even the slightest facial twitch.

"You are a material witness to an act of terrorism and as such,

you have been placed under the protective custody of the FBI."
He showed me an official looking document, and I gave it no
more attention than I did his I.D.

"I was happy with the protection I had. I don't need you."

"This is a Federal matter, Doctor. The Chicago Police no longer
have jurisdiction."

"Maybe not," I argued, "but I don't want your protection. If
at some future date I change my mind, you'll be the first to know."

Johnson stepped next to my bed and did a macho posturing
thing. I was not amused. "You don't seem to understand, Doctor
Hunter, this is not a matter of your voluntary choice. You are under our protection whether you like it or not. We can confine you
to a jail cell if necessary."

I sighed from nervous tension. I had now gone from death
row inmate to caged rat. I preferred the former. At least then I felt
like I had some control.

I grabbed the phone, but Johnson stopped me. "No phone
calls," he ordered.

"You can't do this. I'm not a prisoner," I complained as a
third man entered the room. I knew this one. At least, I had met
him a few times in the past.

"Hello, Doctor Hunter," the man said with a broad friendly
smile. He was, Howard Gray, the assistant director of the FBI, a
distinguished looking gentleman who reminded me of Colin Powell.
He turned to Smith and Johnson. "Gentlemen." The two men
stepped out of the room.

"So they're legitimate?" I asked feeling somewhat relieved.

"Sorry if they put you off. They're nicer than they look."

"Why is the FBI placing me in protective custody, and why
can't I make any phone calls?"

Gray pulled a chair next to my bed. "May I?" he asked. I
nodded my consent. "We have reason to believe an attempt will
be made on your life. Malcom Worthington, the man you killed,
had mob connections. With your picture plastered over the front
page of every paper in the free world, the mob now knows that

you were the one who screwed them out of their money."

"So that's where he got the money he needed?"

"Yes, and they're not very happy with you. They don't like losing money, and you've lost them billions."

I swallowed hard. "Did you say billions?"

"Billions," Gray repeated.

"Are they the ones who sent me the flowers?"

"We believe so."

"What about Shelby? Will they try to kill her?"

"I don't know, but we're placing her in protective custody just in case."

"When will it end?" I asked, exasperated.

"That's part of the problem. It may never end. You and your daughter might have to disappear."

"Are you talking witness protection?"

"It's a real possibility."

I pressed my head into my pillow and closed my eyes. "And the hits just keep on coming."

"One other thing," Gray said.

I opened my eyes and twisted my lips. "What is this, the good news/bad news scenario, and now you're going to give me the bad news?"

"I think you've got the bad news," Gray replied, sitting forward in his chair. "Ben Scolnik may try to contact you as an ally, but we now know that he has been on the mob payroll for quite some time. It's quite possible he'll try to kill you."

"What am I supposed to do?"

"We'll monitor all incoming phone calls to this room. If Scolnik calls, you must do everything you can to keep him on the line, so we can run a trace."

"Your agent told me I was not allowed to use the phone."

Gray stood up and placed his chair against the wall. "He was mistaken. You may call whomever you like, but we would prefer you not discuss the case with anyone."

"What about Sam?"

Gray took my hand in his and patted it. "Your husband is a hero, Doctor Hunter, and I will see to it that he receives the FBI's highest medal of honor."

In spite of my current predicament, I felt as though the weight of the earth had been lifted from my shoulders. "Thank you," I said tearfully.

38

I thought dawn would never arrive to rescue me from an endless night of insomnia. I had not seen or heard from Kim since she walked out of my room carrying the bouquet of flowers bearing the death threat. It had been hours, too, since I had spoken to Shelby. After more than two dozen attempts to call Kim's house without an answer, I was becoming frantic. Something was very wrong, and I felt helpless to do anything about it.

Unlike the warmth and friendliness I had experienced with the cops Kim had scheduled to guard me, I seldom saw the agent who was standing watch outside my door. I had also been used to a friendlier group of FBI agents whom I had come to know through Sam. These Washington people were a very different breed. I wondered in passing why none of the local agents had been assigned as my guardians, then I figured that, in light of what had happened with Ben Scolnik, Howard Gray probably preferred working with agents he knew and trusted.

My nurses, also, were unhappy with the change. Each time one would enter my room, she would be stopped and questioned in detail. Agent Johnson threatened to frisk one nurse when she refused to answer his questions on the grounds it impinged upon her patient's privacy rights.

As the day grew on, my patience grew thin. I had tried calling out to Agent Johnson, without response, so I depressed the call button and asked the unit secretary to send him into my room. If I didn't get some answers about my daughter, I would go insane. Johnson took his sweet time responding and when he finally entered my room, he held the door ajar with his foot ready for an immediate departure.

"You wanted something, Doctor?" he asked coolly.

"I can't get any answer at the house where Shelby's staying. Can you find out what's happened to her?" I asked ingratiatingly.

"Agents've been dispatched to place her in protective custody. They were going to take your daughter to a safe house. They won't reveal her whereabouts to anyone."

"Not even me, her mother?"

"It's a necessary precaution. People might be listening. We'll be doing the same with you as soon as your doctor releases you to our custody. Is there anything else?" he asked in a "don't bother me anymore" tone.

"Yes. Will I be taken to the same place as Shelby?"

"You'll have to ask Mr. Gray that question." Johnson slipped out the door without giving me the opportunity to ask more questions. I guess my time was up.

I had no choice but to accept Johnson's explanation, but the absence of contact with my daughter and my inability to make a connection with Kim or Richard by phone or pager, nourished my growing suspicion that something bad had happened to them.

Tom Holter breezed through the door as the rays of the dawning red sun spilled in through my window. After a thorough examination, Tom announced that I could be discharged. Though I had expected the news, I was also left wondering what I was going to do. Where would I stay and with whom? I wasn't about to go home until it was cleaned up, and my newly found friend, Kim, was nowhere to be found. I would not ask any of my other friends or coworkers to get involved with a death threat hanging over my head.

"I have the consent form here, "Tom said quietly, a clip board in his hand. "Do you want to sign it now?" I stared at the clip board for a long moment before I opened my hand to receive it. "I know this is hard on you," Tom said, "but there's no way to make it easier."

I thought about Shelby. Should she be here when we remove life support from her dad? I recalled the times I had witnessed the torture families had gone through in the moments immediately before and after life support had been removed from their loved ones, and I decided that Shelby did not need to experience her father's death in that way. This was one burden I would shoulder alone. It would be enough for Shelby to know that her father was dead.

I took the clip board and stared blankly at the document. I didn't have to read it. I knew what it said.

"Can you use any of his organs?" The question sputtered from my throat as I choked back tears.

"No. There was too much damage."

I laid the point of the pen on the signature line, but I couldn't make it budge. One final battle of conscience raged inside my head. Is this really the right thing to do? Are you sure you've exhausted all the possibilities? I sighed heavily and looked up at Tom, his arms folded across his chest and his face solemn.

"I know this is a stupid question, but—?" I started to ask Tom if he was sure there was no hope, that Sam was really dead.

"Sam's already dead, Deb," Tom said in his softest, kindest voice. "You're just taking away the machines."

The muscles in my hand finally relaxed enough for me to scratch my signature in the appropriate place. "I want to do it," I said as I crossed the "T" in the name I had shared with Sam for more than a decade.

Tom frowned. "What?"

"I want to be the one who turns off the machine."

"You don't need to do that, Deb."

"I know, but it's important that I do. If there's the slightest chance that a part of Sam still lives and is aware, I want him to know that I am the one giving him the gift of dying with dignity, and I want it to be a private act between the two of us."

Tom was thoughtful for awhile, then he shrugged his resignation. "I don't know that anyone has ever done it that way, but I can't see why not." Tom tilted his head and frowned deeply. "Are you sure you want to do it?"

"Yes," I replied with conviction.

"I'll stay nearby in case you . . . well . . . have trouble."

"I'd appreciate that."

A few hours later, after I had picked at a tasteless breakfast and bathed then dressed in clothes gathered from my home by a female agent, I was ready to be discharged. The female agent, Elizabeth Geiger, had relieved Johnson from guard duty. When I tried to make light conversation, foolishly assuming a female agent might be a little more social with me, Geiger responded with an icy shoulder and tighter lips than Johnson's.

"I'll bet Eli Lilly would be happy to supply your office with Prozac at wholesale prices," I said to Geiger, but my humor impacted against the surface of an impenetrable stone exterior.

Instead of a transportation aid showing up to roll me out the front door, Tom Holter arrived with a wheelchair and took me to TCCU, with my guard dog, Geiger, tagging along. We made the trip in silence, Tom and I because of the heavy task facing us, and Geiger because she was a major bitch. I was beginning to loathe the Washington Bureau.

When we entered TCCU, I found myself at the center of determined non-attention. Some of the nurses greeted me soberly while others gave me a cursory glance then hurried on their way, pretending they hadn't noticed me. I knew their behavior was a product of not knowing what to say, rather than a lack of caring. I was relieved in a way that they chose that route rather than showering me with compassionate and useless comments. With my thoughts turned inward, I was not in the mood to respond to consoling words.

Tom wheeled me into Sam's cubicle, then helped me into the chair next to Sam's bed. On his way out, he drew the privacy curtain and closed the sliding glass door, leaving me alone to share a final moment with my husband.

I sat slumped in the chair for awhile, watching Sam's chest rise and fall easily, serenaded by the hissing and popping of the M-1 and the metronome like beeping of his heart monitor. An endless stream of evenly spaced QRST complexes, representing the heartbeat, flowed smoothly across the monitor's screen while a small green light beneath the screen strobed in time with the beep. In spite of the tube protruding from his mouth, Sam looked as though he were in a long and peaceful sleep from which he might awake at any moment. I would have given my life just to see him smile at me. Although I knew what the answer would be, I prayed again to my Heavenly Nemesis, and begged Him to make a miracle happen, to make time reverse itself so all of this pain and sadness would go away, but Sam remained motionless. God's shoulder was as cold as those of the agents from the Washington Bureau.

I stood up, using the bed for support, and stared down at Sam who had been carefully propped on his side, pillows placed at his back and between his legs. His smooth skin and neatly combed hair spoke of the conscientious care given him by the nursing staff.

I sat on the bed and stroked Sam's hair and started to ramble. "How do you say good-bye forever, Sam? Are there right words or wrong ones? What matters to you? I don't even know where you are or if you can hear me . . . I . . . They're going to give you a medal, you know, for bravery.

"I wish there were medals for good husbands and fathers. That takes a special kind of courage and decency. Sam, I never once in all the time we were together doubted your love for me or Shelby. You're a good man I just wanted you to know that before I . . . before I let you go. I wish there was a way for me to know that you understand."

With a heavy hearted sigh, I took Sam's hand in mine and kissed his palm, then I inhaled deeply to fill myself with his aroma, but the odor was generic, antiseptic. I couldn't smell Sam anymore. Tears welled up in my eyes and spilled freely down my cheeks. I rubbed his hand against my face, hoping to recall his touch, but all I felt was a clay-like emptiness. His soul, the essence of his being, had already moved on to another place and had taken with it his smell and his touch and all that he was. Sam was gone.

I buried my face in that soulless hand and sobbed. "I love you, Sam," I cried. "I miss you so much. If only things could have been different."

I don't know how long I stayed there, because time had lost all of its value. I cried like never before. It was as if the flood of tears was necessary to wash away the remnants of my old life before I could begin a new one, without Sam.

When, finally, I was spent, and the river of tears had dried up, I turned toward the MA-1 and watched the accordion shaped bellows rise slowly and fall quickly. Small pools of water had settled into the corrugations inside of the milky air tubes leading from the respirator to Sam's endotracheal tube. The tiny pools vibrated with the passage of air from the machine to Sam's lungs and out. The hissing, popping, and beeping seemed to crescendo as I touched the black toggle with the tip of my finger, and all my courage seemed to drain from me. I thought of bailing out, calling for Tom to come and take me away. He would have to kill Sam. I couldn't.

As if he knew I was struggling, Tom opened the door and asked, "Are you all right?"

I turned to Tom and almost begged him to take over, but I simply said, "I'm OK."

"I'm here if you need me." Tom slid the door closed.

I closed my eyes, gathered my strength, and prayed, "God, forgive me." Then I pressed hard against the switch. The bellows rose and sighed one last time then fell silent.

Above me, the I.V. continued dripping fluid into Sam's veins. I shut off the power to the I.V. pump and rolled the wheel of the drip regulator until the tubing was completely choked off and the flow of fluid stopped. Then I took Sam's hand in mine and stroked his skin as I watched his dying heartbeat move slowly across the cardiac monitor and fade to a lifeless flat line.

39

Tom came in shortly after Sam flatlined, and he wrapped a pair of powerful arms around be. "There're a lot of people who care about you, kiddo. We're here for you," he said as he patted my back, then he helped me into my wheelchair.

"Thank you, doctor. We'll take it from here," Geiger announced as she took hold of the wheelchair handles outside of Sam's cubicle and rolled me through the automatic doors into the main hospital corridor where Howard Gray was waiting with Agents Johnson and Smith. Completely drained of physical and emotional energy, and with no reserves to draw from, I slumped in the wheelchair and stared vacantly toward my lap.

"The entire building is surrounded by reporters," Gray said to his three agents. "They've even got the service entrances covered."

He squatted in front of me and lifted my chin with his curled index finger. His eyes were kind and his voice was filled with reassuring warmth. I felt safe with him. "We'll plow through the middle of the crowd. You keep your eyes focused ahead of you and say nothing. We won't let them bother you."

When the elevator doors opened, Gray and his agents formed a barrier between the swarming reporters and me. We proceeded en masse out to the waiting Suburban. As Gray had promised, not a single reporter got close to me.

I departed from the hospital amid a caravan of identical vehicles. At various intersections along our route, a Suburban in our parade would turn the corner and be replaced by an identical one.

"You're going to an awful lot of trouble," I said to Gray. "Are you sure this is necessary?"

"Trust me. The people who're after you are very dangerous. Your testimony can put them away for a long time, and they know it."

"But I don't know anything," I insisted. "I thought Malcom was in charge of the whole operation, and those idiots on the plane were the rest of his gang. "As far as anyone else, you'll have to find someone who knows a helluva lot more than I."

"I believe you know more than you realize, as we'll discover during your debriefing. And if you don't, you don't. We still feel obligated to take care of you because of your involvement to this point. You've saved the government one giant headache, not to mention a load of money."

Finally, ours was the vehicle that turned the corner, leaving the caravan behind. Eventually, I arrived at a nondescript motel west of the city where Gray left me alone in a two room suite with the three stooges. Instead of being allowed to rest, I was grilled relentlessly by Johnson, Smith, and Geiger for the better part of next two days. Allowed to sleep for no more than two or three hours at a time and denied medication for my pain or access to a telephone, I was hanging on the brink of an emotional melt down.

They took turns grilling me. Quite often their questions were provocative and delivered with hostile overtones. They asked me the same questions over and over, rewording them slightly and jumping on anything they perceived as a minuscule change in my answers. When I did not answer a question, because I didn't know the answer, the interrogator of the moment would posture over me and accuse me of withholding. I felt more like a criminal than a witness or like the heroine they had called me earlier. More than once, I came close to demanding my Miranda Rights and requesting an attorney be present.

When the agents questioned me extensively about Kim, Richard, and Pete, and wanted to know everything I had said to them or shown them, the communication traffic light inside my head switched from green to yellow.

Sam hadn't trusted anyone in the Bureau enough to share with them what he knew about Malcom Worthington's plans and Cal's computer chip. That's why he turned to me. In the past few days, I had developed a palpable mistrust of the FBI, and my three jailers had done nothing to inspire confidence in me. I began to question in my own mind why they cared what I told the three Chicago cops. Why didn't they talk to the police themselves? With mistrust of my so-called protectors proliferating inside me, I no longer gave a damn about mobs or acts of terrorism, and I clammed up.

I was surrounded by people who placed no more importance on me than yesterday's breakfast. I felt as though I had returned to the status of caged rat. Beyond exhaustion, denied access to my daughter, and deprived of the time to grieve for my dead husband, I finally lost it. I wanted out of that ratty motel suite so I could bury my dead husband and take Shelby to some quiet, remote place where we would be safe, and I could sleep.

Gray finally returned, and I was hopeful for almost a minute. But as soon as he entered the room, I knew something was wrong. His mood was decidedly different. His warmth and compassion had disappeared, replaced by a dark introspection and what I perceived as worry.

Without acknowledging my presence, he called his three agents into the adjacent room and closed the door. I wheeled myself over to the door and listened, though the cumbersome chair and cast prevented me from getting as close as I wanted. Gray's voice sounded angry. I was unable to hear everything, but I heard him say, "I don't know where the hell they are. Someone must have warned them off."

Geiger said something, but her voice was too low for me to understand what she had said.

"Put her on hold. We'll take care of her after the funeral," Gray said in response to Geiger's question. Then I heard a loud thump and Gray's exasperated words, "God dammit! If we don't get this cleaned up soon, it's going to come crashing down around our ears!"

Who was warned off, and what did Gray mean when he said, "take care of her?" Was he talking about me? I heard footsteps closing in on the door and I rolled myself away as fast as I could. In my haste, I ran the chair into the sofa table and knocked over a half-full can of soda.

"Did you learn anything?" Gray said to me as he stepped through the door. His eyes were cold and hostile.

My reflexive response was to cower from him, but I swallowed my fear and chose a more aggressive approach. "You will bring me to Shelby right now," I demanded, "or you'll have no witness.

Gray laughed disdainfully and threw me a curve ball. "We don't need a witness."

"I don't understand. If you don't need a witness, then why am I here answering all of those questions?"

"We had to find out what you knew and who you shared your information with."

"Why?"

"So we would know how to proceed."

As the picture was becoming clearer, the acid in my stomach began to bubble and churn. "Proceed with what?"

Gray responded with a cryptic smile.

"Where's my daughter?" I asked.

"Now that is a problem," Gray replied. "We don't know where she is, but when we find her and that bitch cop you've been hanging around with—"

My head suddenly filled with the same black rage that had taken hold of me on Malcom's plane. "You sonuvabitch!" I rose from my wheel chair and lunged at him, but he blocked my attack and grabbed my arms. Gray's eyes flashed at me from beneath a canopy of deeply furrowed brows. He shoved me away and backhanded me hard across my face. The blow sent me reeling backward onto the floor. I lay there for a long moment, rubbing my stinging cheek. My ribs hurt like hell, and the bandage felt wet.

When I touched it, my fingers came back red. Jesus, I thought, it's happening again. How do I get myself into these binds? I was struck by another, more comforting thought, Kim has Shelby. I climbed onto the sofa. Gray dropped into a chair opposite me and massaged his forehead. I stared at him and he at me, each of us sizing up the opposition.

Shelby was safe with Kim, Sam was dead and I had, in all likelihood, used up my nine lives. Having burned too many heavenly bridges, I didn't think calling upon God was going to be productive. I did, however, give it a shot just in case. Strangely, I found courage in my hopeless predicament.

"What makes you think you can get away with it?" I asked with bravado.

"Get away with what?"

"Killing me."

Another contemptuous laugh escaped Gray's mouth. "Oh come now. I'm the assistant director of the FBI. Who better to get away with it?"

"You're not above the law."

"I thought doctors were smarter than this." Gray leaned forward. "I am the law," he said arrogantly.

"So this whole story about the mob was contrived?"

"Altered maybe, but not contrived. The "mob", as you call it, wants you, your daughter, and your friends dead."

"How much money does it take to buy off the assistant director of the FBI?"

"Nobody bought me off. I am, shall we say, my own boss. I am the mob," Gray boasted.

"How can you get away with it?"

Grayed laughed out loud. "Because I'm head of the Bureau's team investigating organized crime. I hand picked all of my agents. As far as anyone else; grease a few palms, collect enough dirt on people, hand the powers to be a few scapegoats and the occasional "big bust," and they're singing my praises while my hand's in their back pockets stealing their wallets."

"Why didn't you kill me?"

"Loose ends," Gray said bluntly. "As long as you're alive, the lady cop will stick around to play hero and save you. When she comes for you, we'll take her out. We get her, we get your kid."

I was back in the nightmare with my feet sinking in a sea of glue, but now the monster had me in his jaws, ready to chew me up and spit me out.

"How do you expect her to come for me, when she has no idea where I am?"

"I'm sure she'll be looking for you at Sam's funeral."

"Sam's funeral!"

"Did I forget to tell you. While you are safely hidden away in protective custody, one of our agents has been kind enough to make all of the funeral arrangements. The President himself is planning to deliver the eulogy. It will be an unforgettable media event. I'm sure you'll be pleased with the outcome." Gray took in a sharp breath, feigning sympathy. "We will do the same for you. It's only fitting. After all, you are a hero as well."

"How will you explain my absence?"

"But you'll be in attendance, the grieving widow dressed in black, surrounded by friends and family."

I scrutinized Gray's face, trying to see behind his eyes into his skull. Surely he didn't expect me to passively accept my fate and remain silent amidst all of those people including the President and The Secret Service entourage that would be accompanying him. Was he going to use a stand in, someone who looked enough like me to satisfy the media and draw Kim out? I disregarded that plan. Too many people who knew me would get too close for Gray to pull off such a masquerade.

"You're wondering what's going to stop you from screaming for help at the graveside?" Gray asked, having read the question on my face.

"The thought had crossed my mind."

Gray got up and leaned over me. "It was no secret how much

you loved your husband, was it?"

"So?"

"Honey, the bereaved widow was so despondent that it became necessary to medicate her. She'll have so many drugs on board, she won't be able to hold her head up much less say anything coherent."

Gray was as evil as Malcom. No wonder they had migrated to one another. "You seem to have all of the details worked out," I said, and Gray gave me a smug smile. "So tell me," I continued, "how are you going to explain my death while under your protection?"

"I won't really have to explain it. You see, the FBI's ten most wanted list has just been updated. Your friend, Detective Kim Hawthorne, and her brother are numbers one and two. It seems they were members of Malcom's terrorist organization, and they are out for revenge. When the funeral services are over, the President will be whisked away by his secret service guards, and we'll be escorting you back to the limousine. On the way, you'll be tragically struck down by a sniper's bullet. Dozens of witnesses will identify Detective Hawthorne as the shooter. The FBI will give chase, and Hawthorne will die resisting arrest."

"What if Kim doesn't show?" I asked, hoping to find a loophole, a weak link in his plan.

Gray gave a nonchalant shrug. "The witnesses will still identify her, and we'll hunt her down. She'll have to surface some time."

Gray's plan seemed to be fool proof, but I had come to believe in Kim. She was the most resourceful person I had ever known. While I didn't expect to survive, myself, deep down I knew Kim would beat the odds, and with her, Shelby would also.

40

The morning of the funeral, Geiger brought me the appropriate widow's garb which included a plain black dress and one black pump. She also supplied me with gauze bandages to redress the wound on my rib cage that had been oozing all night. I bathed and dressed under her watchful gaze though I avoided eye contact with her. She made no offers to help me, and I asked for none. It gave me the creeps having her stand guard over me, scrutinizing my every move and depriving me of simple privacy.

As I dried my hair, I gazed at my battered face in the mirror. The angry bruise extending across my cheekbone and ringing my eye reminded me of the abused women who frequented the E.R.. Ashamed of their wounds, they would come in wearing sunglasses and heavy layers of make-up, in the hopes that no one would notice. But everyone did. I on the other hand, intended to boldly display my bruises. I wanted somebody to notice and question me about them.

When I finished drying my hair, Geiger reached over my shoulder and offered me a bottle of liquid foundation make-up. "Cover it up," she ordered when I ignored her, and she tapped the bottle against the side of my head.

"Why? Is your boss afraid someone will notice that he's been beating someone who's supposedly under his protection?"

"Cover it up," Geiger repeated angrily. She popped me again with the bottle, and I grabbed her wrist, twisted it into a most uncomfortable position, and shoved her face against the countertop. Johnson must have heard Geiger scream, because he appeared inside the bathroom in a flash with his pistol drawn.

"Let her up!"

Before I freed her, I held my lips close to Geiger's ear and spoke softly. "I think I'll leave my face the way it is." Then I let her go, and she immediately threatened me with her recoiled fist.

Johnson caught her fist before she let it fly. "Hold up," Geiger. The boss wants us to get a move on. You can have at her later."

Geiger struggled momentarily against his grip, all the while glaring at me with a murderous glint in her eye, then she relaxed her hand.

. "Go on. I'll get her into the wheelchair," Johnson said. With one final spiteful glance, Geiger marched out of the bathroom.

Johnson brought the wheelchair up to the door. It was too wide to fit through, so I hopped over to it and sat down. As I did, I noticed a little smirk on Johnson's face. "You got her a good one," he said.

"Not good enough," I replied as I dropped the foot pedals into place. Johnson chuckled as he wheeled me out into the living room where Gray greeted me with a syringe in one hand and a latex tourniquet in the other. I stared at the syringe silently. I knew what it was for.

"Now, doctor, are you going to behave yourself," Gray asked, "or do we have to pin you down?"

I didn't answer. Gray interpreted it to mean I chose the latter method, so he ordered the gang of three to hold me down. Johnson held onto the arm to be injected, while Smith held my other arm, and Geiger wedged my neck between her forearms, one across the back and the other pressing against my Adams apple. She pressed hard enough to let me know she had the power to crush my throat if she wanted.

Gray clamped my legs together between his and when he was sure I couldn't knee him in the nuts, he tightened the tourniquet around my arm and, in spite of my squirming, he buried the needle into my vein, released the tourniquet, and depressed the plunger. Within seconds, the room started spinning, and my lightheadedness was followed by a sudden surge of nausea.

I fought the effects of the drugs with all my strength. My cortex was turning to jello, but I maintained enough control to fold my arms across my chest and surreptitiously clamp onto one of my nipples. The nipples are uniquely sensitive. Pinching and twisting them can cause excruciating pain which in turn acts as a narcotic antagonist. Although my self-inflicted pain was less intense than it would have been if delivered by an objective second party, it was sufficient to keep me from falling over the edge into a narcotic stupor.

I was transported, this time in a black Mercedes limo, to St. Patrick's Cathedral downtown. Gray had meticulously worked out every detail. He found out that Sam and I are Catholics. A Catholic burial without a proper funeral Mass would be suspect.

When we arrived, the interior of the church was deserted. "We're here early to avoid the fanfare," Gray said.

I did not respond to his comment. The effects of the injection were wearing off, but I continued with the athetoid bobbing of my head and I maintained a vacant stare with my eyelids at half mast.

I was pushed into the center of the first pew. Gray and Johnson sat on either side of me, and Smith and Geiger sat immediately behind. A dozen more agents, who may have been legitimate or working for Gray, took up stations around the Church.

"No one is to come near this pew," Gray ordered.

After a long wait, people started filtering in through the main entrance. When I tried to turn around to see who was coming in, Gray stuck a small caliber, silenced pistol into my ribs. "Turn around again and you'll die right now."

I wondered for a moment if that might not be the best thing, but I wasn't ready to give up yet. Though I didn't hear anyone crying amid the low drone of voices, I imagined my mother-in-law and sister-in-law seated in the pews behind me, and my heart went out to them. I wondered which of Sam's friends were there and what they must be thinking with me inaccessible, enveloped by a sea of suits.

A hush descended over the crowd when a bell clanged at the rear of the Church, signalling the beginning of the funeral Mass. A

Catholic all of my life, I reflexively turned toward the sound, and I felt the tip of the silencer press deeper in my ribs.

"It seems you need a booster shot," Gray whispered. He handed his pistol to Johnson who jabbed it into the wound on my side. Then Gray produced a syringe and medicine vial from his pocket. He was drawing the colorless liquid from the vial into the syringe when one of the other dozen agents walked up and stood near the pew. Gray immediately palmed the vial and slipped the syringe up his sleeve. I knew then that the agent standing near us was not one of Gray's boys. He was one of the good guys. Even so, he might not be inclined to help me if I called out. After all, I was seated next to the assistant director of the FBI, a respected and well thought of individual. I was still trapped.

The agent maintained his post as the funeral procession made its way toward the altar, preventing Gray from giving me an injection. With the drugs wearing off and Gray's temporary restraint in giving me an additional dose, I decided to participate, to the extent that I was able, in Sam's funeral while I hammered out a plan of escape.

Again, I turned to watch the procession, daring Johnson to murder me in front of the legitimate agent. A young man, dressed in long white robes and carrying a Crucifix atop a long pole, lead the procession. The priest walked immediately behind the young man. He was carrying a gold embossed, red leather Bible in front of his face. His Alb was white while his Chasuble and Stole were white laced with silver and gold to celebrate Sam's new eternal life with God. Our faith dictates that death is a release to a much better life, but it's hard to swallow the concept of celebrating when you're the one left behind. Six pallbearers, all strangers dressed in the more conventional blacks and grays, accompanied Sam's flag draped coffin to the altar.

As Sam's coffin passed by, I managed to get a quick glimpse of the rest of the people in the Church. I was immediately struck by several observations: There were far fewer people in attendance than I would have expected, and I didn't recognize anybody. Sam's family was not present.

I was turning toward the altar when one woman caught my eye. She was seated a half dozen rows back and across the aisle. Her hat, large brimmed with heavy black veil that I would have thought went out in the late fifties, was the most striking feature. As I strained to see through the veil to the face behind it, the woman carefully lifted one corner and winked at me. It was Kim! I was immediately elated and fearful. Kim had come to help me, but Gray had anticipated her presence. I knew she was walking into a trap.

Kim gestured for me to look toward the altar, which I did with my heart pulsating in my throat. A man dressed in a black suit stood at the lectern. The priest's back was turned toward the Church. The man at the lectern glanced at the priest who nodded, and the man announced, "All rise."

When the entire congregation came to its feet, the priest turned toward us. Gray, Johnson, and I gasped in unison. The man dressed in white and silver and gold was no priest. He was Ben Scolnik!

Ben's gaze first connected with my stunned look, but unable to hold onto the contact, he looked away almost immediately. In that brief moment, he managed to convey his deep remorse. I understood it, but I was not ready to forgive him for it.

Next, Ben grinned at Gray, communicating a decidedly different message. "Surprised to see me, Howard?" Scolnik said in a provocative voice.

Johnson whipped out the silenced pistol that I thought had taken up permanent residence in my rib cage, and pointed it at Scolnik. An agent leapt over the pew at Johnson, knocked the gun out of his hand before he could fire, then threw him over the front of the pew onto the floor. At the same time, Gray's hand slipped inside his suitcoat and grasped his pistol, but nearly a dozen high powered automatics were immediately levelled on his head. Gray, his face ashen, turned around surveying the congregation. I followed his gaze to find that the entire church was armed, and all of them had their weapons drawn. With a deep breath, Gray held his lapel open, and lifted his pistol out of its holster, holding it by his thumb and index finger only. Smith and Geiger followed suit, laying their guns on the pews and shoving them toward the aisle where an agent picked them up. Clasping their hands behind their heads, Gray, Smith, and Geiger moved into the aisle where they were immediately handcuffed.

Kim had removed that ridiculous hat she had been wearing and was strolling up the aisle toward me. "Howdy, girlfriend," she said with a broad grin.

Forgetting that I was temporarily incapacitated, I started out of the pew only to stumble. Immediately, more hands than I can count on my fingers and toes reached out to me. Mistrustful of men in suits due to my recent experiences, I recoiled from their proffered help.

"It's OK, Deb. These guys are family," Kim said. "They're CPD." I studied her face for a moment. Her eyes sparkled with confidence. Then I eyed the men who's hands were still extended toward me, ready to catch me if I fell. Finally, I accepted their help. Once I was out of the pew, one of the men, a kid of about twenty-five possessing many physical features in common with Arnold Schwarzenegger, swooped me into his arms and carried me to a waiting wheelchair.

Once tucked safely into the chair, I looked toward Sam's coffin sitting alone before the altar, no one giving him a second thought.

"He's not in there," Kim said.

I turned sharply toward her. "What?"

"He's not in there," she repeated. "You don't think we'd be so sacrilegious as to bring his real body into the middle of all of this do you?"

I looked at Kim then at the coffin, and my mouth opened almost involuntarily and out poured a river of questions. "You mean this whole thing was a set up? Where's Sam? How did you do it? Is Shelby safe? Where is she? Where did Scolnik come from?"

Kim's opened palms flew out in front of her. "Whoa! Slow it down." The church was filling with reporters hungry to be the first to break the big story. Kim grabbed the arm of one of her buddies and asked him to keep people away from us for a few minutes then she wheeled me to one of the confessionals lining the side walls of the church. She sat and faced me from the priest's booth. "First of all," she began, "Shelby's fine, couldn't be better." Kim shook her head thoughtfully. "You have one amazing kid there."

"How did you—?"

"Ben warned me about Gray before Gray's people arrived. He showed me enough documentation to convince me he was on the up-and-up."

"I thought sure they had killed him."

"That was their mistake now wasn't it."

I gazed around the Church. "How did you manage all of this without Gray knowing?"

"That was more fun than work," Kim boasted. "Did you ever see the movie 'The Sting' Robert Redford and Paul Newman?"

"Yes. It was one of Sam's and my favorites. We have it on laser disk."

"I knew we had a lot in common," Kim said. "Anyway, this wasn't exactly like 'The Sting', but it was along those same lines. The bad guys set up their own downfall."

"How?"

"Ben and I went to my Captain. He went to the chief of police, and the chief of police contacted the Director of the FBI, himself."

"How did you know he wasn't involved?" I asked.

"Trust me," Kim said, her eyes sparkling with delight. "What Ben Scolnik gave us comes only from a cop's most treasured dreams. We have names and irrefutable evidence that's going to nail a lot of heavy hitters. This is going to make us all famous. We'll do Oprah, Montel, maybe even Twenty-Twenty."

"I don't understand why people who have worked so hard to get where they are would throw it all away."

Kim leaned close to me and set her eyes squarely on mine. "I guess they thought billions of dollars were worth the gamble."

"How did you know Gray was planning all of this?" I asked, gesturing broadly around the church.

"Gray wanted to create the illusion that he and his agents were your saviors, so he assigned the head of FBI public relations the job. She set everything up exactly as he asked, except for a few minor details like, no body and a somewhat altered guest list."

I smiled at Kim from a combination of deep respect and eternal gratitude. She had saved my butt more times than I can count. I could take a lifetime and not come close to repaying her. "Where do we go from here?" I asked.

Kim took my hands, and her expression sobered. "The real funeral is tomorrow."

"Who made the arrangements?"

"Shelby."

Surprised, I repeated, "Shelby?"

"Like I said, you have some kid there. She did everything right down to picking out her dad's coffin."

"That must have been horrible for her," I said, my heart nearly breaking. "How did she—?"

"You know, she never shed a tear the whole time until this morning. When I was leaving her to come here, she hugged me so tight, and she bawled her eyes out." Kim's eyes filled with tears in what to me was an uncharacteristic display of emotion. "She asked me to bring you home safely."

There was a time when I thought my first impressions were the right ones, but seeing the tears in Kim's eyes, I remembered the tough little bimbo detective who had come to see me at the hospital little more than a week ago. I had hated her from the start. She was a smart ass bitch who had accused my husband of drug dealing. How far we had come in a week.

Epilogue
a month later

As I sit here watching the waves break onto the white sands in front of the secluded beach front condominium on Curacao, Chicago seems like a fictional city that exists only in my distant memory. Tomorrow it will once again become a reality. Sam had planned a perfect trip, at least it would have been had he been here with us.

I had assumed that Shelby and I would take this trip alone, but she had suggested that Kim come along. After all, Kim had done so much for us. She deserved it. Besides, I wasn't going to be much fun stuck on the beach.

Sam's funeral was marked by all the pomp and circumstance a hero deserves. It was attended by more friends and family than I ever realized we both had. In addition to those who knew and loved Sam, more than two thousand police officers and FBI from around the country participated, a sea of uniforms showing support for a fallen brother.

Thanks to Howard Gray, though it wasn't exactly what Gray had in mind, the President of the United States honored Special Agent Sam Hunter with a eulogy describing him as courageous, loyal, and a true American Hero. The graveside ceremony culminated with a member of the Marine Honor guard handing me the folded flag from Sam's coffin, followed by a twenty-one gun salute and Taps. God, my friend and foe, wouldn't let us keep Sam here, but He allowed Shelby and me to send him off in style.

***

Out in the distance, a sailboat heaves lazily in the gentle swells of a crystal clear, blue sea. Somewhere beneath it, Shelby and Kim are taking there final dive down to rainbow colored coral reefs. I am jealous. The plaster of Paris on my leg has confined me to the shore, a landlubber. I am glad, though, that Shelby has found a friend in Kim.

Sam and I used to dive together. We used to do a lot of things together. Before Sam, the scope of my life had been medicine. I was happy in my narrow world, but Sam opened a much broader world to me. He taught me to drink from the entire cup and experience the real joy of being alive. Now it is my job to pass on the inheritance to our daughter.

Tomorrow, we will head home and once again face the tragedy of our old life. With renewed energy, we will face it together. Shelby will begin her freshman year in high school, a little late, but that's OK. I will embark on months of depositions and courtroom testimony to put Gray and his associates behind bars forever, I hope. Kim will go back to being a cop.

Eventually, I will return to my job in the emergency department, but I will refuse to bury myself in my work. Instead, I will live my life the way Sam taught me to live, relishing every moment. After all, each moment is more precious than we know.

Oh, by the way, God and I have made up.

THE END

Advocate Of Honor

286

About The Author

Linda Cutcliff is a nurse with a background in major trauma and critical care. She is also a TaeKwonDo instructor. Linda and her four children live in Zionsville, a small, picturesque town in central Indiana.